Our camera crew reached deep inside the alley. The hazy gray of dawn had finally reached inside between the buildings, brushing out the dark shadows and dissolving the shaft of blackness around the body.

Dr. Hektor Stefanopolis's face was splashed with yellow paint, including his glasses. His mouth was open, a couple of silver fillings in his upper teeth reflecting back our crew's lights in dull metallic points of grim finality.

"This makes no sense. No sense at all. Hektor's not homeless. Hektor's not nameless. Hektor's not like the others. He doesn't fit."

"Sorry, Ike, but now he's got the most important thing in common with the other victims."

★

Polly Whitney

UNTIL THE
END
OF TIME

WORLDWIDE.®

TORONTO • NEW YORK • LONDON
AMSTERDAM • PARIS • SYDNEY • HAMBURG
STOCKHOLM • ATHENS • TOKYO • MILAN
MADRID • WARSAW • BUDAPEST • AUCKLAND

This book is for Michael, who gave me fresh air; and
for Mark L. Knapp, who taught me almost everything
I know for sure.

UNTIL THE END OF TIME

A Worldwide Mystery/April 1997

First published by St. Martin's Press, Incorporated.

ISBN 0-373-26233-7

Printed in U.S.A.

My object all sublime
I shall achieve in time—
To let the punishment fit the crime.
    —Gilbert and Sullivan, *The Mikado*

ONE

MOST MUGGINGS ARE perfectly simple events. The victim gets ripped off, period.

I certainly saw this one coming, but I was wrong to think it would be simple. And I was wrong to think it was over when the guy took my money and ran.

I was on foot that Sunday night—actually the early hours of Monday morning. My new Rollerblades had given me a world-class ankle blister over the weekend, so I had abandoned the wheels and returned to the most primitive means of getting around New York. Skates give me a lot of security. On my wheels I can outrun almost anything, and without them I was feeling a little paranoid. I wasn't carrying anything worth stealing, but the muggers didn't know that.

The night was steamy. Dense humidity hung over the city, a sickly orange dome of moisture that reflected back the heat and the neon. The haze had the weird electric depth of an oil slick.

The neighborhood around Lincoln Center was quiet, but restless, like a weary old woman, sweating and asleep in the grip of a puzzling dream. Just a few taxis, cruising. A pair of upscale, tawny, long-legged hookers, stepping out of a gray stretch limo and giving me a get-lost look. The old Korean woman standing under the awning of her all-night grocery across Broadway, idly patting limes in a bin and dragging on a cigarette, watching the taxis and the hookers. The soft, fading, final notes of a siren over by Roosevelt Hospital. A determined jogger, shirtless and glistening in and out of the neon spills on the west side of Broadway. A few civilian pedestrians, paranoid and alert like me.

The muggers, they could be anywhere: in the silence of the alleys, or apparently asleep in doorways, or walking the sidewalks like other pedestrians but even more alert, and armed with a new technique.

Up in this westside neighborhood, roughly between Times Square and Lincoln Center, the latest technical advance in the mugging industry is called the Blast. It's fairly simple, like a good mugging should be: they come at you from behind, usually at night, usually near a subway entrance. The pickpocket screams as loud as he can straight into your ear, and you automatically raise your hands to cover your head against the explosion of sound. Then he stuffs his hands into your front pockets, yanks them inside out, grabs your money, and bolts down into the subway.

There's no way you can catch him, and there's a good reason why you wouldn't even want to try: it takes a large pickpocket to use this innovative twist to a once low-profile profession, because the idea is to get right up in your victim's ears and yell like hell, which is a reliable technique only if the attacker is on the tall side. And most of these new thieves, in addition to being urban giraffes, are also big across the chest. They don't get their muscle definition from picking pockets, so I figure they must have some other hobby I wouldn't like.

Most nights, when I'm on my skates and equipped for speed, I have nothing to worry about from muggers, but lately, since these tall bandits have introduced the Blast onto the sidewalk scene, I haven't been dawdling around subway entrances. Although I'm a tall man myself, and the skates boost me above the herd, most of these giants wouldn't even have to stand on tiptoe to give me a rousing buzz in my inner ears. Of course, without my wheels, I'm a sitting duck. Not exactly asking for it, but in a good position to get it.

That hot August night, I was standing at the corner of Sixty-third and Broadway, next to the tiny triangle of green stuff called Dante Park, waiting to cross the street. I glanced around at real and imaginary shadows. There was nobody nearby except the driver of the hookers' limo, backing up against the curb into the crosswalk. His passengers were strolling languidly, regally, into the Empire Hotel.

I was wondering about their fee scale when the colossal stranger in the baggy red sweater breathed on me from behind as I stood there. I didn't exactly jump out of my skin or beg for mercy, but I did jam my hands into my front pockets to hold them down. I couldn't imagine where he had come from, unless he'd been on his hands and knees admiring the flower beds around the bronze statue of Dante.

The man was standing so close to me on the sidewalk that I couldn't help noticing how much he smelled like my Lord & Taylor bills, as though he had been dipped lightly in a vat of expensive perfume. Your average screaming pickpocket is not usually that thorough with his fragrance-wear.

I stepped around the rear of the limo and crossed sixty-third quickly, going south toward Columbus Circle and the thirty-story junior skyscraper that most New Yorkers call the "Emerald City," not fondly and not because they think it's where the Wizard lives. The official name of that building, which provides headquarters for the NTB Television Network's News and Entertainment Divisions, has an awkward ring: the O. Armitage Broadcast Center. And to the eye it has an awkward blend of greens: an ugly mix of bright spinach-colored marble and dirty gray granite, with the celebrated sea-green glass front doors that rise two stories and act like magnets to camera-happy tourists who can't possibly be getting decent shots of the famous news anchor faces etched delicately into the green glass. Close up and with the naked eye, you can sort of make out who the faces are supposed to be. But on Kodak paper the faces all look like Eleanor Roosevelt, even the male anchors. Beyond those green glass doors are offices and studios where a lot of television programs get made, including *Morning Watch,* where I work and where I was headed.

The tall perfume guy stayed with me on the street, just behind me step for step, but he didn't make a move for my ears or my pockets. This was a new approach, tickling my nose with his bouquet.

The sweet, flowery fumes from the big guy seemed to swell in the heat, blossoming around us as we walked. I could see the Hitachi billboard's temperature clock on the *Newsweek* building, and it was still ninety degrees, at 3:59 a.m. Simmering.

As a native New Yorker, I don't know much about flowers, except that they have some nice ones at J.Y. Produce, but on that sticky summer night, as the sumptuous fragrances clung to the air around me, I imagined that the pavement had suddenly sprouted a garden in the record-breaking heat. When it's that hot in midtown Manhattan, using your nose is usually like standing inside a dumpster under an air conditioner in Hoboken behind a meat packing plant. And somebody's been using the dumpster as a urinal. And he may have had a hard-boiled egg in his pocket for a few days.

But my little corner of the island, with that guy trailing after me as I crossed Sixty-third, was sweet. He was towering over me from behind and broadcasting his aggressive aroma like a walking perfume counter.

When I got to the curb, still breathing in that cloud of flowery essences, I spotted a real treasure on the top rack of the corner newsstand, so I turned suddenly and stopped. And the guy stepped on my toe. Not hard like he meant it, but hard enough to scrape my loafer.

If he was going to mug me, it looked like he was going to do it one body part at a time, from the sidewalk up.

I gave his chest a quick, dirty look and reached to the top rack for the last copy of *Dance Quarterly,* sneaking a five and three singles out of my pocket to pay for the magazine. I fanned it in the air across my face and headed south again, thinking about how luck is sometimes with you when you least expect it. You have to have some major help from the Fates to find *DQ* on the street. They're heavy into ballet, but occasionally I run across fillers and ads about ballroom dancing, which is my thing, and even if the American Ballet Theater wouldn't dream of respecting me, I respect them. I flipped the magazine open and headed south again.

The guy stayed with me. So much for luck.

In front of the Lincoln Deli, I stopped, closing *DQ* and pretending to check out the sandwich menu posted on the window but actually hoping he'd pass me on his way to other prey, maybe somebody with a nice purse.

He stopped, too, looming over me and touching the back of my shoulder with his upper arm. His thick sweater felt soft through my short-sleeved shirt, but his muscles didn't.

We stood in the glow of the flashing blue light coming from the Heineken display in the deli window. In the reflection from the window, I could see big balls of wool on his ratty red sweater and big beads of sweat on his deep, black forehead. Everything about him was big.

I went in and bought a Diet Coke. As I paid at the counter, I saw him looking inside the store at me, his forehead against the glass. His long, lean jaw was covered with extremely uniform gray stubble, as if he had given himself an expert close shave around Bastille Day and was letting it age.

I stood for a moment at the deli counter, opening my soda and taking a long gulp and thinking about Mr. Perfume. If this guy was going to pick my pockets, he was sure setting it up oddly. Why let me memorize his face?

I rolled my copy of *DQ*, pointedly stuffed it into my right pocket and went over to study the salads in the refrigerator case. There was something called "Tuscan Ambrosia," a really bright heap of black olives and yellow corn and dill chips and pimientos. Ouch.

I turned and scanned the deli window. His big face was gone.

Well, I thought, that'll teach him not to mess with me. The Great Abby Abagnarro, master of escape and all-purpose tough guy. Wily as a fox, savvy like a mother wolf. Hiding in a deli.

I finished my soda, tossed the can in the recycling box, stepped back out into the heat, and started walking. I passed the faintly pink windows at the Saint Broadway Bakery, and there he was, walking along with my reflection in the windows. Not a pleasant surprise.

We stopped on the sidewalk, in unison, almost like we had the timing down from practice. The light at the bakery was dim, with only the pink glow of the neon croissants over the door and the fluorescent bulbs over the empty shelves inside. But there was enough light for a big gold tooth in his big face to gleam back at me from the window.

"Nice night," he told my reflection.

"If you don't mind the heat."

"Yeah. The humidity, too, man. Like a stinking river of steam."

"Almost need scuba gear, huh?"

"Just about."

We both fell silent, looking in at the empty shelves at Saint Broadway's. That seemed to be it for the small talk.

"Not to pry, but are you following me?" I asked. My voice sounded funny, and I cleared my throat. Outside the bakery, his aroma cutting like a knife through the fat, yeasty scent of bread coming up from the basement ovens, the giant's spectrum of odors took on nuances. He was not by any means a complete bed of roses. Mixed in with his sweet smell was an insistent undercurrent of something nasty, like ammonia. He smelled like a cross between Halston and Windex.

"Yeah. I'm following you."

I shook my head. "You're doing it all wrong. You've done everything but ask me where I'm going so you can catch a cab and meet me there."

He made a noise, not polite. "I look like someone who rides cabs?"

"You never know. What with the cost of the subway."

"Yeah. Sure." He hunched his enormous shoulders. "Anyway, I already know where you're going, man."

I started walking again, toward Columbus Circle. I didn't believe him, but what difference did it make what he said? He could say anything. He could grab my pockets and claim to be my tailor, just trying to take a measurement. The odd thing wasn't that he said he knew my destination, but that he was apparently interested in conversing with me at all.

Sweat was running down my rib cage; I could feel the wetness spreading under my belt. But he had to be in worse shape than me, with the handicap of the woolly sweater. I was thinking seriously about taking off.

"How do you like those Mets?" I asked. Never say die when it comes to small talk, which just about sums up the recent history of the Mets—just small talk, strike or no strike.

He scratched the stiff beard on his cheek, producing a noise like a young cockroach scrambling down Venetian blinds. "Never paid any attention to them Mets," he said. "Baseball's not my game. If it was, I wouldn't watch those losers."

I didn't need to stare at him to figure out he'd swung more linebackers than baseball bats.

"You're gonna be late," he said, matching steps with me.

"I never heard it work like this before. What are you, some kind of stalker?"

"I'm a bum."

"I can't argue with that," I said, eyeing his wild, greasy hair, his red sweater, his loose dirty chinos, his old Reeboks tied with black string, his filthy fingernails, the jarring detail of the elegantly shaped hands and fingers. Pickpocket or pianist mitts.

He smiled at me without showing his gold tooth. But he did not look happy.

Since he hadn't yelled in my ear and helped himself—or cut my throat out—I yielded to what I hoped was the inevitable and reached very deliberately into the pocket of my slacks to see what change I had, but he held up a hand.

"I'm not trying to boost your coins," he said. "I want to talk to you."

"I'm a lousy talker. You should probably try someone else."

He fixed me now with a cold stare, apparently satisfied that I would do just fine for his purposes. Then he popped out with, "You're that TV guy, aren't you?"

Ah, I thought, *he's going to hit me for an autograph.* Much better than a mugging. But who the hell did he think I was? I don't look like anyone famous, so I couldn't think who he had mistaken me for. My ex-wife had once said I look like a Sicilian Fred Astaire, but she had not said it nicely.

Anyway, it's not my *face* that shows up on TV. It's true that I work in television, as a director. But when the credits roll and the name Abagnarro scrolls across your screen, it's not listed as "that TV guy."

"Half this city works in television. Why me?" I demanded, picking up the pace, thinking more about running. He was big, but maybe he wasn't fast.

He shuffled ahead of me in his barge-sized Reeboks and planted himself on the sidewalk so that I'd either have to run into him, run into a fire hydrant, or stop. I stopped. On skates I'd have been long gone.

He put out his left hand, crossing his body to touch my left shoulder, and grinned. Or rather, he flashed a large overbite, both canines gleaming with gold. His aroma seemed to flop in my face in the few inches of humid air separating us. "The name's Tex," he said.

"Yours or mine?" I backed up a step.

"Mine, asshole. Yours is Abagnarro." His eyes were cold and now a little mean, but he pulled his hand away.

I tried to ignore what his hand was doing and craned my neck to meet his eyes. "How do you know my name?" I had to clear my throat again. "Or where I'm going?"

"I'm around, man. I ask. I watch. I sleep in the neighborhood. I hang here."

"Well, you've been hanging around asking for the wrong guy," I said. "What you need is Social Services or something."

"What for?" He leaned over me, closer, and lowered his voice to a hollow, rasping whisper. "This is about killing, Abagnarro. They don't do that shit at Welfare. The wicked have drawn out the sword, and have bent their bow, to cast down the poor and needy."

That sounded like the Bible to me, but his tone sounded more like he was describing how he was going to rip my liver into shreds.

A drop of sweat slithered right down my spine. I felt the shock of it hitting my waistband. He was standing so close, I wondered if he could hear my sweat fall. And it suddenly occurred to me to wonder if he was carrying a gun.

I backed up a couple more steps and glanced around for a cop. A couple of blue uniforms were just disappearing around the corner down at Sixtieth. Way down at Sixtieth. Only two little blocks.

Tex followed my gaze and sighed. "Look at me, man. I know who you are. I know what you do. I watched that entire documentary—*Vietnam, The Legacy*—watched the whole show in the window of the Radio Shack down on Fifty-seventh, even the credits where it said you were the director. Couldn't hear no sound, but the pictures were smooth." He tilted his head down and seemed to consider my nose. The mean look took on depth along his eyes and in the sweaty wrinkles above his cheekbones. "You gotta be nice to a guy like me watches NTB News. You're not exactly *60 Minutes,* or something good like that."

Tex had that part right. NTB News suffers through periodic identity crises, where we counterprogram even ourselves, but we never thought we were *60 Minutes.* Or anything good like that.

I took a breath. "What do you want with me?"

"I got a story for you."

Everybody thinks they've got a story for us. Most of them are wrong, but not as wrong as Tex. Viewers who have stories for us do not accost NTB personnel on the street and touch us with their elegantly shaped big, dirty hands at four in the morning. And talk about killing. And know our names.

With a silent vow never to let a blister come between me and my skates again, and a wild prayer that he wasn't armed, I reached

into my shirt pocket for a business card, shoved it into his un-
canny hand, and got set to take off running. "Call my office,
okay?"

His hand shot out and closed on my shoulder.

"What's the matter with you?" he said.

"Get your hand off me. What the hell is this?"

"You can't even listen for two minutes, you're such a big shot?
You don't know nothing about me except you don't like me. You
don't even know why you don't like me." He shoved my card
into my shirt pocket with his free hand. "You just don't like me.
Give me that little card and make me go away. Make old Tex go
away by giving him that little card." He patted the card through
my shirt. "That about right, TV director? Step around the bum
and move on." He squeezed my shoulder, hard, and let out a long
breath. "I shouldn't have fucked with you, man."

He gave me a shove, back, without letting go, then yanked me
toward him and stepped aside. My head snapped back and I heard
something protest in my neck. I staggered forward, past him. I
got my balance quickly—all that training on skates and in the
ballroom.

I took a couple of steps. And that's when my head exploded.

I could feel the blast of his hot breath in my left ear as painfully
as I could hear the hoarse, shapeless roar of noise, so hot and
intimate and loud that, involuntarily, I put up my hands to cover
my ears.

Before I even knew he had pulled it on me, his hands were in
my front pockets. The touch was so expert and so rough and so
fast and so brutally certain and so angry that my first fear was
that my rotten love life had just gotten permanently worse.

Tex took off in a blur of perfume and ratty red sweater and
stiff, greasy hair. He flew down Broadway and tore into Columbus Circle. He barely one-handed the railing at the subway station
and leaped like a champion hurdler and dropped lightly down
into the well of the stairs.

My pants weren't even torn. My copy of *DQ* lay open on the
sidewalk, Twyla Tharp's face smiling up at me. I bent over my
knees, shaking, sweat dripping onto the shiny pages of the magazine. I realized with aching relief that I was basically unhurt,
and that my love life wouldn't necessarily be any worse than
usual.

And I surprised myself by what I was thinking: *God, that was beautiful. He must have practiced it a thousand times. Legs like a gazelle, hands like a surgeon.*

TWO

I DON'T KNOW how many people get mugged each night in New York, and I don't believe anyone else knows, either.

The people who actually have any reason for reporting the crime to the cops fall into four categories:

1. Those who end up in hospital emergency rooms.
2. Those who have lost insured property and need to get their hands on the police report to file a claim.
3. The quick learners who get the idea from the mugging that they have lost insured property and plan to turn around and mug Prudential or some outfit like that.
4. Nuts with surplus time on their hands, people who don't mind sitting around a precinct house for hours looking at thousands of photos and drawings of faces that all look like they've been made out of modeling clay and ox hair. Incidentally, that's also what the station house coffee tastes like.

The rest of us are better off avoiding that dead legal bureaucracy embalmed in red tape and hopelessness. It's far wiser to follow the old Sicilian saying I learned from my uncle Julius. He doesn't speak any Italian, and his version is probably a little watered down from the original: "Don't waste your time watching a chamber pot to see if it will grow grape leaves."

So, I thought, my episode with Tex would never show up in any official statistics, unless they were being compiled by some inspired guesser, maybe Jean Dixon.

Anyway, there was another obstacle that kept me from trotting down to Midtown North on Fifty-fourth Street, the police precinct of choice for crimes in the Emerald City neighborhood. That precinct is where Captain Dennis Fillingeri presses the back of his trousers, and he doesn't like me, for some reason. As a homicide captain, he might notice if somebody killed me a few times, say with a howitzer, but the only thing he'd get out of the Tex saga would be a good horse laugh. It wasn't up to me to make his day.

I did not loiter at the scene of the crime, but I didn't scurry away, either. Tex already held the land speed record for that two-block stretch of New York, so what was the point in rushing?

I finished the walk to Columbus Circle with my hands in my empty pockets, thinking about how a Manhattan mugger came to have a name like Tex and how he came to know a name like Abagnarro and what he was thinking about right now. If Tex was frolicking down under Fifty-ninth Street, counting his ill-gotten gains, he'd soon find out that the crop from my pockets wouldn't buy him more than two bus rides and a cup of coffee. *If he'd been smart*, I thought, *he would have mugged me before I shelled out eight bucks for DQ.*

I had an unsettled feeling, hot and thoughtful. My large extended family in Queens has provided me with plenty of meaty philosophy from the old country. Unfortunately, the one that seemed to apply most directly to my situation came from my Uncle Tommy, who speaks Sicilian, but it was no help at all: *"Allestiti quannu parli di rubatini, ma sulo cu lu ladru,"* which is the way I learned it, but in English it's something like, "Of robbery, speak quickly, but only to the thief"—and in either language, you can see where that left me. I couldn't think of anything to say to Tex that would make things better, and I figured I'd never see him again.

I pushed my way in through the stingy revolving door at the Emerald City. The lofty, famous, and generously proportioned two-story green glass doors are never open—in fact, we have a lot of nerve calling them *doors*—and everyone who has business in the building is filtered in through the little four-man merry-go-round that, through some fluke of aerodynamism, actually seems to resist moving objects like me.

Carl Honeyman, the world's skinniest and most freckled security guard, waved a bony, spotted hand at me as I crossed the green marble lobby toward his tall desk.

"How come the big doors are never open?" I asked testily.

He shrugged his sharp shoulders. "Search me, Mr. Abagnarro."

"I can't do everything, Carl. I'm a busy man."

"That's a good one, Mr. Abagnarro." He chuckled dutifully. "You're a funny guy."

"Yeah. I'm a regular Jerry Seinfeld." I hoped Carl had a better answer for my next question, the question I really wanted to ask him. "Has anyone been around here asking about me? You know, someone who doesn't work here?"

Carl looked puzzled. "Like who?"

"Like a really tall black guy—about the size of Larry Bird but with muscles like Popeye and an aroma like Coco Chanel. Has anyone like that been around?"

"Not that I've seen. Is he a movie star or something?"

I shook my head. "I doubt it."

I signed the logbook, reached into my pocket for my network I.D. badge, realized I didn't have it anymore, and cussed. And, dammit, my copy of *DQ* was lying somewhere on Broadway.

I started past Carl, mumbling. He put out his nightstick to stop me.

"You gotta show I.D., Mr. Abagnarro."

"Yeah, well, I just got robbed. I don't have I.D." I waved my hand around in the air, as though, for his solitary benefit, I had conjured up a brand-new me on the spot. "What you see is what you get."

With the nightstick, he scratched the starchy leg of his green trousers. "I can't let you upstairs without you show I.D."

I leaned my elbow on the security desk and considered his freckled face. "How many times have you seen me, Carl? A round figure will do."

"I don't know."

"Well, take a guess."

"About a thousand."

"Do you have any doubt who I am?"

"No." He smiled, just like I was someone he recognized. An acquaintance.

"So, showing you I.D. would be pretty stupid, wouldn't it? You might even call it redundant."

"You have to show it every night, Mr. Abagnarro. It's the rule."

I thumped the logbook with the edge of my hand. "God knows you can't break any rules in this city. New York, New York— the ethics capital of the planet."

"All I know is that's the rule. And, anyway, you just said you were Jerry Seinfeld."

"That was hot air." I rolled my eyes back so far they hurt. "Seinfeld's on NBC. He wouldn't be caught dead in this building."

"I'm sorry. I guess you'll have to get someone from the show to come down and get you."

I tried to count the things that had gone right that night but had to stop at getting out of bed, and I wasn't too sure about that. "Nothing personal, Carl, but if I didn't need the money to save up for muggers, I'd stop coming to work altogether."

He looked at the floor, his thin forehead knit like he was trying to fathom the deep thing I had just said. I pulled the house phone toward the corner of the desk and dialed the extension for Control Room #1. Before I knew it, Carl had gently extracted the instrument from my hand.

"More rules?" I said.

He nodded, put the receiver against his head, and told the phone that "Mr. Abagnarro's down here and needs some assistance. You better send an escort." He replaced the receiver with a frown and lined up the instrument neatly where it had been just before I'd had my psychotic episode and moved it all of three inches.

I gave him a look. "I'm glad you didn't tell them to send a stretcher. You didn't have to make me sound helpless or drunk or anything. By now the news is probably all over the twenty-seventh floor that I'm passed out on the marble down here." I turned my back to him and perched both elbows against the desk, looking at New York through the towering sheets of green glass, through the etched profiles of twenty famous anchor faces. The taxis on Central Park South looked green. The few lighted windows looked green. Even the park looked green.

The green marble lobby was reflected in the green glass, and I saw the elevator doors open, like a graceful pleat in the skirt of Mother Architecture, and Ike stepped out. It seemed to be my night for encounters with reflections.

But it was a good thing that I was catching Ike in reflection because she's drop-dead beautiful, and it was curiously soothing to get the evening's first dose of my ex-wife in this diluted form. She shimmered toward me in my glassy vista on the green city. In that expanse of green glass, and wearing a sheer blue pants outfit, she looked like a mermaid swimming out of the Sea of Manhattan.

"Abby," she said, smiling broadly as she approached. "I was never so glad to see anyone."

I may have gawked at her reflection. "Me? Usually you bite my head off before you even say good morning. *If* you say good morning."

"Not this time, baby. I need you in the worst possible way."

I glanced at her sideways, warily. "Have you finally come to your senses? Shall I go buy champagne?"

She shook her head sadly but benignly, with a kind of elegant pity.

"I didn't mean anything like what you're thinking. That's all over between us, as you know." More pity, but she glanced at her watch, like she only had time for so much compassion. "I meant I need your directing skills. Less than three hours to air and the joint is jumping. I've got five guests crammed into the Green Room, packed together as tight as cocktail olives in a jar, and they're turning into icicles." She pursed her lips and frowned. "I wonder why nobody ever fixes the air-conditioning? The budget we're on, you'd think we wouldn't even *have* air-conditioning. Oh, never mind that now."

She poked a finger at my chest to punctuate her next sentence. "Plus, you'd think Alice in Wonderland was running the control room. I've done the lineup for the news blocks three times already, but nothing will stay put. Every time I turn around, the wires are moving some fresh news flash or the National Desk is wringing its hands or the Foreign Desk is asking me to spend my invisible budget on satellites."

She drew a breath, causing the slinky blue fabric of her shirt to whisper across her breasts. "I wish everyone in the world would go sit on their hands for a few hours and let me get two measly hours of TV on the air without all these interruptions. We've got more deaths and power outages on the East Coast from this infernal heat wave. We've got another serial killing. There's a crummy little subway fire in the Village that we're keeping an eye on. We've got an Amtrak derailment in Florida and a Balkan story breaking at the same time, and—speaking of breaking—all that glass crap in the studio. Not to mention the glassblower."

"Slow down," I said, turning back to her reflection in the green doors.

She took another breath, another whisper of blue silk. "What?"

"Slow down. Save the chaos for upstairs. Let's get back to you and me."

She came around to face me, and I got hit by the undiluted force of her good looks. Since it was pretty much my own fault that our marriage broke up, I can't blame Ike for the way I feel whenever I see her—well, maybe *sometimes* I blame her.

Everything about Ike is merely very pretty—her cloud of blond curls, her dark eyebrows and lashes, her sleek body—until you get to her eyes. One of them is deep, dark green, the color you'd get if you rubbed a green crayon hard across a piece of very white paper, and there is no hint of any gold flecks or any of that hazel nonsense. Her other eye is blue, a Caribbean blue, and that's where the gold flecks ended up.

"Stop staring at me like that," she said. "What's all this about you needing an escort? Have you been drinking?"

"I wish." I sighed, torn between a desire for sympathy and a need to escape interrogation. I did not especially want Ike to know I'd been taken on the street. "I don't have my I.D. badge. And Carl's pretending I represent a menace to security."

"I don't see why you're blaming poor Carl." She flashed him a pretty smile but got right back to me without wasting time. "It's your own behavior that's feckless, Abby. You're always losing your things. I mean, I wish you'd learn to take responsibility."

I could feel the dam breaking. I stood up straighter. "Oh, yeah?" I may have raised my voice a little. "It was really thoughtless and feckless of me to get mugged. I'm gonna have to get better organized."

She cocked her head to one side, her golden hair brushing the shoulder of her icy-blue silk shirt, and she let me have it with the laser beams from her eyes. "You? You got mugged? Tonight? Nobody could..." She looked down at my feet. "Oh."

"'Oh,' indeed."

"You should have skated. Everyone knows you can't be touched on your wheels. You're practically the Great Kahuna of Rollerblades."

"What I should have done was stayed in bed." I reached for her waist. The warm flesh under the cool silky shirt felt too smooth to be covered by something as coarse as silk. "In fact, let's clear out of here and go to my place." I thought a second. "In a cab."

She slapped my hand and pulled away, a little short on pity now. "Isn't that just like you?"

"It's exactly like me. In fact, it *is* me."

"Are you completely bananas? In the first place, we've got a TV show to put on the air. In the second place, the glassblower is upstairs ready to tape that segment, as well as three doctors in full makeup, not to mention your pal from NASA with that quartz contraption—and we need a director, if you don't mind. I wonder what they'd think if we just took off to fornicate. Did you ever think of that?"

"Not when I'm thinking about fornication."

"Really, Abby, you ought to take your mind to a French laundry. Now you've made me forget what I was saying."

"That's what I was trying to do."

"Well, stop it. Where was I?" She rubbed her temple with a finger. "Oh, yes: in the third place, you may remember that you and I are divorced and suggestions like that are inappropriate and childish. Just because we have to work together doesn't mean you can take advantage of me with your inability to face facts." She took a breath. "What number am I at?"

I held up four fingers.

She hurried on. "In the fourth place, it may interest you to know that your little mugging is hardly the top crime story of the day. Our favorite serial killer has struck again. Another body with its face painted yellow has turned up in the park, with one of those notes—if I can interest you in anything so humdrum as news. Fifth, there's a U.N. peacekeeping force pinned down under heavy fire on a road outside Sarajevo and we're trying to move a dish in for a satellite feed. And sixth and finally, I wouldn't go to bed with you if your—"

She spun quickly on her pretty blue flats and glared at Carl, who was gaping at us.

"Don't you have any manners?" she demanded. "Or anything to do except eavesdrop? This is a private conversation. Why don't you go secure something?"

"That would be against the rules, Mrs. Abagnarro."

"Don't call me that." She thumped the logbook the way I had

done. "I've been signing this thing with the name 'Tygart' for months now. Don't you ever bother to read your own Captain Midnight Security Bible?"

"Sorry, Mrs., uh..." His voice trailed off into a private gibberish that I didn't listen to because my manners are far too polished to allow me to eavesdrop.

Ike started briskly for the elevator, suddenly all business. "Mr. Abagnarro is with me, Carl. We're going up to the twenty-seventh floor."

I followed her into the car. When the doors closed, I intercepted her hand before she could touch the button panel.

"That wasn't very nice, Ike. Our marital problems are hardly Carl's fault."

"We don't have any marital problems. That's the part you seem to have amnesia about. You continue to act like you have these hideous expectations, when, in reality, the judge fixed that months ago, and furthermore, it makes me very uncomfortable when you—"

"Oh, yap-yap-yap. What's the use?"

"I wasn't yapping. Don't accuse me of yapping. I don't yap."

I acknowledged defeat by putting up my hands, the second time I had done so that night. "Okay. Okay. You don't yap." I pushed the button for the twenty-seventh floor.

There was a small silence.

"Well, I don't," she said. "Yapping would be if I babbled on and on about something that only I cared about."

More silence.

"People who yap," she explained, "aren't like me at all. They get carried away with their own point of view and just won't let go. Whereas, I'm a good listener. I'm objective. I weigh things. I consider all sides. Take it back."

"Jesus, Ike, I already did." I leaned against the wall of the elevator, crossing my arms over my chest. "Don't you even care if I got hurt tonight?"

"One little mugging." She snorted. "I can see you're not hurt."

"What, have you got X-ray vision? Or maybe you can now do CAT scans with those eyes."

There was another silence.

"Are you hurt, Abby?" she asked, barely parting her lips, like it gave her a toothache to humor me.

"Yes."

"Where?"

I let my arms drop and pointed at the depths of my pockets. "Here."

Her eyes flashed at me—kind of the way I wished I had looked at Tex, but my brown eyes do not contain the arsenal that Ike carries around with her. "What a cheap trick, Abby! I swear you'll try *anything,* to get me to return your absolutely unreasonable and apparently insatiable sexual feelings."

I stepped closer to her. "That's right. I'll try anything." I planted a hand on the wall behind her and gazed down into her eyes with real heroism, freely exposing myself to the full danger of her eerie peepers. "In fact, I'll even try yapping. Listen closely and learn something, Ike. I'm going to tell you a little story about a science convention and an ugly man. The way I heard it—"

The elevator door opened and she practically leaped for it.

"Oh, my God, that's all I need. Not another one of your stupid stories." She was off down the curving, plum-colored hallway like Howard Stern was on her heels.

I followed along, at a more leisurely pace, not completely discouraged. She can't elude me as long as I'm one of the best directors in the TV business and she's trying to turn around *Morning Watch,* the Prince Charles of morning news programs—stodgy, dull, increasingly unpopular with the masses, and not particularly interesting even when caught with our pants down.

THREE

WHEN NTB NEWS gets caught with its pants down, the spin doctors in our PR department like to call it "free publicity." If you looked at things that way, we had lately enjoyed the most cost-effective promotion/expenditure ratio among the big broadcast news outfits. Of course, we did not all look at things that way.

Since Ike had left her Emmy-magnet job as producer in the prestigious investigative unit for *Around the Watch* (the only NTB News program consistently winning its time slot, and in prime time) and took the bigger bucks they pay the broadcast producer for *Morning Watch,* the show had been in various kinds of deep trouble, none of her making. We'd lost two anchors within one week, one of whom was now receiving "treatment" in Ossining, New York. We had been threatened with a defamation lawsuit by American Foods Corporation for (they claimed) fraudulently reporting rat droppings in their "European Grains" line of breakfast cereals. The three-part investigative series in question, called "What's Been Eating Your Bran?" had aired on *Morning Watch* the week Ike took over, so she had not overseen the inner workings of that particular months-long NTB investigation. Faced with litigation, the NTB legal department had valiantly decided that we would back down and issue an on-air, as well as a written, apology and, pardon the expression, eat the damage.

Still, you won't catch any of those NTB lawyers buying AFC cereals.

Not so publically as the cereal wars, but still affecting how well our public trousers stayed up, we had had our budget cut by Othello Armitage, NTB's penny-wise owner, and had suffered some production staff cutbacks. To give you an idea, let me just say that we were down to one makeup artist, having previously enjoyed the services of three, thereby saving the network a grand total of around eighty thousand dollars a year. The effect was about what it would be, in terms of product and finance and morale, if the Intensive Care Unit at a small hospital in L.A. fired two nurses during an earthquake.

Rubin Gorman, our sole surviving makeup person—although, since he weighed almost three hundred pounds, some of the producers had a pool going on how long he could keep up the pace—shuttled back and forth furiously between the anchors in the studio and the guests in the Green Room, who often had to wait so long to get their faces powdered that they were stacked up like United flights over O'Hare.

That kind of behind-the-scenes stuff rarely showed up on the air directly, unlike rat droppings and troubled anchors. But *Morning Watch* tended to sag with the big distractions outside the studio walls, and we were watching our affiliate stations jettison the first hour of the two-hour program at an alarming rate. The affiliate in Macon, Georgia, for example, was gearing up to run *Tom and Jerry* in the seven-to-eight o'clock slot and then pick up the second half of our show from eight to nine. If you lived in Macon, and you could see *Tom and Jerry* while you caught up over breakfast on the commercial bargains available in your hometown, would your heart yearn for NTB's *Morning Watch?*

The show was so unsettled that the only thing keeping me aboard—despite Paramount's big-money attempt to lure me into taking a walk down the street to their building on Broadway, to direct some syndicated entertainment shows—was Ike. Proximity, I thought, was my best hope. That, and the waltz contest coming up at Playtime in Brazil, the dance club on West Seventy-second Street. Ike had divorced me without looking back, but a dance partner can't be shrugged off as lightly as a husband, being by definition much better trained and harder to replace. As a husband, I may have been less than satisfactory, but as a dance partner I am one finely honed piece of equipment.

Besides, I felt a tiny sense of loyalty, not just to Ike, but to the program. Even tepid loyalists like me wanted to see from the inside what success, if any, Ike was going to have with her "Theme Week" approach to morning programming. We'd done a week of shows on AIDS and the contributions artists and entertainers were making in the fight to conquer the disease. We'd done a week from Haiti. We'd done a week from a yacht anchored off Cannes for the film festival. We'd done a week on how to quit smoking. We'd done a week on the Alaskan fishing industry, the longest week of my life.

The latest incarnation of Ike's dogged persistence was starting this day: a week on Time. Not the magazine, but the dimension, or whatever it is.

That's what the guests in the Green Room had in common with each other. The doctors were promoting a book that accused the FDA of abusing their sacred public trust by wasting precious time while they denied approval for experimental drugs. And our man from NASA was prepared to show our audience the "Spinning Quartz Ball," a little gadget that would be the heart of the Gravity-B Probe scheduled to blast into space on a Delta 2 Rocket at the end of the decade/century and attempt to prove Einstein's theory of general relativity and thus his definition of time. And the glassblower was going to give us a studio demonstration, sealing glass vials that would, supposedly, keep the liquids inside them fresh until, well, until forever.

The current week's emphasis on science—applied, pure, and popular—was the first of Ike's themes to merit coverage in *The New York Times*, especially after they got wind of the fact that we'd booked Stephen Hawking for Thursday and Brent Spiner of *Star Trek: The Next Generation* for Friday. And *Newsweek* had carried a paragraph on us. NBC's *Saturday Night Live* had roughed us up with a spoof of our upcoming week, and David Spade had included us in his "What's Hot" column. Plus, in the techno-flak spirit of launching a campaign for the White House, one of our anchors, Hannah Van Stone, had also done the Larry King show on Friday.

Hannah, the most veteran member of the *Morning Watch* team, had so far survived the anchor fiascos at NTB, just as she had survived everything else on the show for more than thirty years. Even after that many moons, she never missed an opportunity for "face time," that is, getting her mug on TV—two hours every weekday morning on our show evidently being inadequate for her broadcasting appetite. Nobody ever called Hannah an air hog to her face, although Ike had once lost her temper twenty seconds before the show and told Hannah to "put out that goddam cigarette and get your snout over to the trough on the double." Hannah had jammed her cigarette into a bucket of sand and dashed for the anchor chair, so the reference had not been too obscure for her. But she had seethed under her makeup and professional delivery, and later that day she had taken Ike's failure to kiss anchor-ass all the way to the network's top man.

In a move that surprised all of us, Othello Armitage had weighed in on Ike's side. The result was the no-smoking policy now in place at the Emerald City, something that Hannah was not likely to forget or forgive. Hannah had been forced to confine her massive consumption of lung drugs to her office, and Ike had become the frequent recipient of heated memos from Hannah regarding such crimes as "treachery," "bitchiness," "envy," "unprofessional language," and "small breasts."

Ike had never, as far as I knew, responded to those memos.

Balked of her prey, Hannah had turned on her new co-anchor-of-the-month, J.D. Waters. He had made her mad by accepting an invitation to go on CBS's Letterman show to talk about our week on Time. Hannah had never been on Letterman, an omission that had never seemed to bother her until J.D. got a shot at it. On the previous Friday's *Morning Watch,* she had hissed at J.D. during a commercial break, threatening to tell the world what his real name was.

"Be my guest," J.D. had hissed back, his smile unimpaired by any fear or resentment but marred by his crooked lower teeth. "That'll give *Dave* and me something to chat about. Perhaps he'll call it Stupid Anchor Tricks."

Everyone on the staff of *Morning Watch* already knew the astonishing fact that J.D.'s real name was John Dahlia Pinkwater, but the hissing contest was the first hint we had that Hannah had acquired a foe worthy of her steel in the otherwise perfectly well behaved J.D. Waters. He was already an ideal physical foil for Hannah's dyed-blond warhorse image. A young black man, he was good-looking, articulate, bright, and reasonably competent. As the director of *Morning Watch,* I could suggest only two areas of improvement for J.D.'s appearance on our show: those bottom teeth needed work, and he spoke with the received BBC accent, having been éducated at Oxford. I have nothing against the English, but I never understood why, when the word went out to hire minorities, the only black that NTB News could find happened to come from London. We got a lot of calls from viewers who "can't understand a word that man says. Is that some kind of Creole?"

As I strolled along the hall, my reverie on NTB anchors was interrupted when I almost tripped over Fred Loring, one of our graphic artists, who was alternately frisking and slapping the coin slot in the soda machine in the hall. It was probably his plaid shirt, rather than the noise he was making, that woke me up.

"Allow me," I said. I bent and pulled the electric cord out of the wall and then plugged it back in. "Now try it."

He punched the button for Mountain Dew and a can came rattling out.

"Thanks," he said. "I never knew you could do that."

"Television directors know the oddest things, Fred. For example, I also know how to get a soda for free."

"You do? Show me."

"Don't be crass. I only know how. I didn't say I'd ever do it."

He looked skeptical. "Yeah. I'm sure." He wiped the top of his soda can on the front of his shirt, probably with some germ theory in mind. "You hear we've got another Yellow-Man?"

"Yeah. Ike told me."

"Oh, well, she's acting like everybody ought to get frantic over it, Abby, but you know what's wrong with this Yellow-Man serial killer story? I mean, from a ratings standpoint?"

"Let me venture a wild guess. The fact that the victims are all homeless men and nobody gives a rat's ass if they're dead?"

"Well, exactly." He popped his soda open with one hand, displaying the only skill he has that can't be performed on a computer. "Serial killers always seem to go for prostitutes or other people who don't have, you know, what you might call community standing. So nobody cares. I mean, the story's great for us graphic artists, don't get me wrong, with the painted yellow faces and the grubby notes left on the corpses and all that, and I know it sounds hard, but I bet the nation is yawning."

"Probably. But as long as Ike Tygart isn't yawning, Yellow-Man is here to stay." I glanced at my watch. "Are you going back to your home planet over in Graphic Arts? If so, I'll send you a note after I've seen what we've got on the latest corpse."

"I'll be there. I'm already working on some stuff."

"Drawing some *feelthy* pictures, amigo? A little network T and A?"

He gave me a sour look. "You have such a coarse mind, Abby.

I expect you've got some heavy karma to work off in this lifetime.''

"Nonsense. With all the skating and dancing I do, I'm in great shape. That's all aerobic stuff, you know.''

He narrowed his eyes and gave me the kind of frown you might get from a serious-minded rat. "You deliberately misunderstand me. You do it all the time.''

"Not all the time. I rarely see you.'' Suddenly it occurred to me that here was Fred, standing before me with his ears hanging open, and I was missing a golden opportunity. "Listen, Fred. I heard this great story. It's about a science-convention and an ugly man—''

Although I hadn't meant anything personal, Fred gave me a wounded look and took off down the hall, his scraggly ponytail appearing to be stuck to the back of his plaid shirt. The women who work on *Morning Watch* tend to stay away from Fred, a computer graphics whiz who can't get a date and who spends a lot of time constructing images of naked women on his computer screen. But he's a very valuable computer whiz, despite his hobby. I've never been able to figure out why he spends so much time at his terminal with artificially created nude women. I'd have gone insane by now if I were Fred.

But, since I wasn't getting any more dates than Fred, I was not strutting after I got a Diet Coke from the machine and continued along the hall to my office.

Well, well, I thought, as I stood and faced my door for a full minute, *I guess Tex has the little piece of metal I usually stick in the hole in this doorknob to make it open.* I was wishing I knew an easy trick, like unplugging the door from a socket, to get its lock to work. Since staring at the door wouldn't make it open, I finally trotted down the hall and found a green-shirted security guard, whose ring of keys included a pass that worked my door. He didn't even make me show I.D. Maybe he'd read the abridged version of the rule book.

He opened the door to my office, a cramped irregular space that opens off the outer perimeter of the plum-colored circular hallway that we call the "Tube." The layout of the twenty-seventh floor, where all of our news programs originate, is like a wagon wheel, with spokes that lead from the outer tube into the main control room in the center. Studios and small control rooms,

and the Green Room and large offices for on-air talent, lie between the control room and the outer ring of small outer offices
like mine. The Tube itself is worth a tour, because it's graced
with the long line of portraits in oil by Samantha Harris: every
anchor who has ever worked on *Morning Watch,* including even
Hippie the Sheepdog who had his own chair on the set during the
late sixties, is represented in the gallery. The two ends of the
curving portrait display in the Tube do not yet meet, which is a
good thing, given the way we've been going through anchors
lately. Nice to know we've got room in the hall to screw up a
few more careers.

With my office on the outer part of the building, I actually
have a window—more of a slit, really, just the right size and
shape to launch an arrow from if this was, say, 1500 A.D. and
this was a castle and my enemy was massing down on Fifty-
eighth Street. From my slit, if I stand close to the wall and press
my face against the opening, I can see the traffic blurring down
Broadway. I've learned that's an uncomfortable vantage point, so
I'd probably miss the approach of the troops and, thus, the chance
to fire my arrow.

Since I didn't have an arrow or pressing personal chores—like
counting my change or reading *DQ*—I went right to work, boot-
ing my computer and calling up the show's lineup to see what
Ike had been yapping about in the lobby. None of the guests
presented any special difficulties, except maybe for the glassblower, who, of course, would need to use some respectable fire
in the studio. We had rehearsed that segment on Friday, but without the fire. The NASA specialist would merely be a matter of
good camera work, because the scientific doodad he had brought
along was only the size of a golf ball, if you can imagine a
million-dollar golf ball. The doctors promoting their book—well,
we could do that kind of segment in our sleep, possibly not unlike
our audience.

But the latest of the "Yellow-Man Murders" (so christened by
the *Daily News* a month earlier when the whole thing had started)
looked like it was going to be the story leading the news blocks,
and I couldn't tell from the lineup what videotaped pictures we
had or if Fred and the New Age Graphics Department would need
to be called on to supply art.

I sent a quick electronic note to Fred, who'd done most of the

Yellow-Man drawings for us over the past month, and I mailed him the AP wire story that Ike had sent to my queue. The body of another apparently homeless man had been found overnight, this time in Central Park, and, just like eight other bodies before, this one had been decorated on the face, with yellow tempera paint, and on the shirt with a torn piece of paper on which the letters "U.S.S.R." had been scrawled. The dead man's chest had been decorated with a knife wound.

One of the few things Ike and I always agree on concerns the use of Fred Loring and his graphics department: if we've got actual photography, no matter how grisly and gory and nauseating, we pass on Fred's productions. Nothing against Fred, but we are supposed to be a news program, not an animation factory. If you want to see what a good animator can do, maybe you should move to Macon, Georgia.

I sent Ike a note saying I would preview the tape we were getting on the latest Yellow-Man. The lineup listed Arden Boyer as the reporter on the story, and I hoped he wasn't up on the roof of the Emerald City with his camera crew again, taping his standup for the piece. The puny two-million-viewer slice of the national morning audience that watches NTB might be pretty sick of that shot.

Especially with the recent, but jarring, addition of the spectacular Worldwide Plaza to The Most Familiar Skyline on the Earth, that twinkling backdrop says "glamor-after-dark," and Arden uses it for every kind of story, from riots to ABA conventions to yacht races. I wanted Arden to sign off on his Yellow-Man report from some place that said "murder."

I looked at my watch: 4:42, plenty of time to get Arden off the roof and send him to the park to tape his standup, if need be. Or, even more diabolically professional, make him hang around to do the standup live, after the sun came up. Better light, better picture, makes a good impression on the audience that likes to see we're up and about, teaches Arden a lesson not to be so lazy. I sent a note to Arden's producer, suggesting they do a live shot from Central Park for the seven o'clock news block that opens *Morning Watch.*

I couldn't be as direct with our personnel overseas, but I have more faith than Ike does in technology, so I wasn't worried about our satellite dish making it into Sarajevo. We'd have those pictures, as well as narration from Claudia Bowles (who is not lazy), off the bird and in the house in plenty of time for the first news block.

I scanned the rest of the lineup. While editorial content is not my bailiwick, I know how that side works.

Rule number one: if nobody dies, it's not a story (and today's derailed Amtrak train was carrying freight).

Rule number two: after the first day, even if people die, a heat wave on the East Coast is a local story, not fit to lead a network broadcast, mainly because we're all aware that the rest of the country has decided that all the networks except CNN have a New York bias. They're correct, but we're fighting the bias.

Rule number three: the saddest but truest fact of the TV ratings poker game is that on any given day, one fresh corpse in a serial murderer's career will beat hundreds of people dying in a war, assuming that all the dead are nobodies, either in New York or in Sarajevo.

Even so, Fred was right. Or maybe it was me. Dead homeless men do not provide the same kind of human interest that the story would have had if the victims had been rich and prominent and employed and had died in decent clothing. With a different set of victims, we might even have done two pieces on this ninth Yellow-Man killing, if we could figure out a collateral angle. And with a better reporter than Arden Boyer. Or at least one who wasn't so lazy that he does all his standups on the roof so he doesn't have to leave the building to cover a story.

I sat back in my swivel chair and looked at the blue characters on my terminal screen. It occurred to me that what we had at the top of the first news block was two stories about homeless people. The Serbs were over there shelling the shit out of the Muslims, telling them to get out of the mountain neighborhood where they'd lived for hundreds and hundreds of years. And somebody was telling homeless men in New York City that they couldn't live even on the mean streets anymore.

I scowled at the screen and thought about Tex, wondering if he had a home. If he did have one, he couldn't even buy himself a new philodendron to brighten up the place, not with the pittance he had extracted from my pockets. I dismissed the thought as soon as it occurred and left my office, headed for Control Room #1.

I would have given a little more thought to Tex's philodendron problem if I had known that in the next half hour I would see him again, this time on a Yellow-Man videotape. In a short while, I would be the only journalist in Manhattan who had a real clue about the serial killings.

FOUR

WHEN I PULLED my office door shut, making sure it didn't lock behind me, the twenty-seventh floor Tube was quiet. But opposite my door, the wall of portraits gave off visual echoes.

I never get so accustomed to the paintings on the curving, graceful plum-colored walls of the Tube that I can pass them by without noticing them. It's not just that the portraits are in themselves beautiful—Samantha Harris originals, every one—it's also that the anchormen and -women who sat for them were all professional eye-contact specialists (excepting, of course, the sheepdog). The eyes in the paintings seem alive, and, by the combined force of Harris's genius and the talent of the television stars who were paid to use their faces at maximum wattage, I always get the feeling I'm not alone in that corridor.

The latest addition, jolly-good old John Dahlia Pinkwater himself, marked the temporary end of the NTB gallery. As the only black represented on that august wall of broadcasting history, J.D.'s face was especially arresting, coming as it did as a kind of punctuation mark at the conclusion of a long row of white faces (even including the dog's). J.D.'s smile was rueful and close-mouthed, unlike most of the other anchors whose expensive teeth were prominent features of their portraits.

As I stopped to consider J.D.'s features, the door to the bathroom across the hall opened. Hilda Murray, the glassblower, stepped out, drying her hands on a bunch of paper towels. She walked to my side and helped me look at J.D.'s portrait for a few moments. I'd met her on Friday during the director's rehearsal and had almost asked her to lunch, just to see if it would make Ike mad. But I'd refrained, mainly because I was afraid Ike wouldn't even notice. Not that Hilda Murray wasn't perfectly worthy of being taken to lunch for her own sake, but that wasn't the point.

"He sure stands out in this collection," she said, nodding at

J.D.'s portrait. "Hard to believe how monochromatic the rest of the gallery is."

I sighed, not proudly. "NTB has been the caboose on the train of racial and ethnic equality in hiring. When a memo finally came out from the owner about something called 'minorities,' everyone had to get out a dictionary."

She laughed. She had a nice, deep laugh. "These portraits represent the pigmentocracy in more ways than one, huh?"

I raised an eyebrow. Maybe lunch had been the wrong ambition. Maybe I should have asked her for a lesson in political correctness, or vocabulary.

"You know more words than I do," I said. "The best I could have done would be something like 'hue-premacy,' and that sounds stupid. And the pun doesn't work at all."

She laughed again. "It doesn't matter how many words you know. It's whether you know the ones you need."

"My trouble lately hasn't been words. It's been getting people to stick around to listen to them."

She turned and looked at me like it would be okay for me to tell her more, but I didn't know her well enough to unload a slightly off-color story about a science convention and an ugly man. She might not appreciate it. For all I knew, glassblowers took an oath of purity.

I don't know where I get all of my stereotypes, but, before meeting Hilda Murray on Friday, I had pictured a glassblower as someone with fat cheeks and a powerful chest, which shows how much I don't know about glassblowing. The only physical sign of her craft showing on this petite woman (yes, I had also expected a man) was a set of red fingers, rough, with tiny patches that looked scaly. She had regulation cheeks and, for all I knew, regulation lungs, but her fingers had obviously been in the fire many times. Apparently this glassblower's genius expressed itself in the hand, not the blowing.

Except for her hands and the full makeup already supplied by Rubin Gorman, the rest of Hilda Murray could have been specified by the American Bar Association. She was dressed in a lightweight black suit with a hint of gray pinstripe; her white blouse was open at the throat, enough to show a slim silver chain; her brown hair was sensibly cut just above shoulder length and had been sprayed in place by an expert with a light touch. She could have breezed right in to the Supreme Court on her high heels to argue a complicated tax case and no questions asked.

"This will be my first time on television," she said, crumpling the wet paper towels with her red fingers. She looked down at her hands, displaying the first sign of self-consciousness I had seen in her.

"Are you nervous?" I asked. "You won't even know you're on TV. You'll think you made a wrong turn and wandered into a messy furniture showroom. The biggest difference between Studio 57 and a Levitz warehouse outlet is that you won't have salesmen popping out at you offering to discount the lamps. Most people find their first time on TV to be disappointing."

"I'm more excited than anything else." Her eyes twinkled. "Which is a good thing. The last thing you want from a glassblower is trembling hands." She held out a hand and stared at it like she was giving it a test. "Steady as a rock, for now. I've been soaking my hands in cold water—that helps with the burns, not with the nerves."

We started walking down the hall together, without me having to make any sort of signal or grab her elbow or anything. Maybe I should have taken her to lunch.

"Before we tape your segment, would you like to see the control room?" I asked. "That's the place to be if you want any TV razzmatazz."

"Sure. Razzmatazz is my middle name."

She gave me a sideways glance, and I noticed she had a dimple.

Ike called to us from the Green Room as we passed it on our way to Control Room #1.

We backtracked and stopped in the doorway. I took a gander at what is actually, by industry standards, our fairly pleasant hospitality suite. It's bigger than the Green Room in the CBS Broadcast Center on West Fifty-seventh, and, while our mirrors and chairs are not as nice as theirs, our food is better.

The room was, I admit, on the chilly side. But it was only what I would call respectably uncomfortable, hardly the frozen den of shivering lost souls Ike had prepared me for down in the lobby while I was being held prisoner by Emerald City security.

Four of the five dainty swivel chairs were occupied. Those chairs are lined up in front of the makeup tables along the mirrored wall opposite to the door, but our guests almost always make a point of facing into the room after they've been made up, rather than staring at themselves in the mirrors. I usually figure that, if you've already got stage fright, the last thing you want to see is the very uncertain self at the center of all that anxiety.

Purses, and a couple of briefcases, one of which was propped open, and a steel box lay in a jumble on the big coffee table in the center of the room. Small but bright yellow letters on the steel box indicated it was the property of NASA. I wanted to lift the lid and take a peek, but that didn't seem tactful, given that all the guests in the Green Room probably thought their projects were just as interesting as anything NASA had to show.

There was also, for example, a small stack of books, copies of *Running Out of Time*. The cover art was a cartoon human face with—where the eyes should be—a couple of hourglasses, the sands ominously thin in the upper chambers. It was an interesting cover and I like books, although my skating and dancing schedules don't leave me much time to read, but, let's face it, we receive about two hundred publicity copies of books every week at *Morning Watch* and we only get NASA toys once in a blue moon. So to speak.

I sneaked a peek into the open briefcase, but there was nothing inside to compete with outer space hardware. The briefcase was messy, a jumble of files, with ballpoint pens stuck in the upper pockets, and a few little bottles, full of pills or liquids, lined up against the side of the folders. Doctor messiness, I deduced. Sherlock Abagnarro.

All but one of the guests were in full makeup. Rubin Gorman, our one and only and overworked and obese makeup artist, was pinning a white towel around the neck of the last guest still wearing his street face and looking like a normal human being. Later, under studio lights, the heavy look of the makeup would vanish magically, but for now along the far wall of the Green Room there were three camera-ready gargoyles and the guy wearing the towel. Ike (who will never look normal, in or out of makeup, not with those eyes) was standing, pouring coffee into a green mug.

The homey smells of freshly baked ham and bread and oranges and coffee did nothing to dispel the Siberian touch of the room's eager air-conditioning. I thought the occupants looked gloomy, but much gloomier than mere physical misery could account for. There was an atmosphere, the kind you get when you invite the wrong couples to an intimate dinner party. Everybody's too polite to spit across the candles, and without even that relief, the gloom was piling up.

Ike had a thoughtful look on her face as she eyed me in the doorway, as though for a minute she was trying to figure out what I was. I spotted it in her eyes the instant she got it worked out.

"Abby," she said, looking at me like I was a stain on the door she'd just noticed and would have to tell maintenance about, "I've had to change the glassblowing segment. We can't do it until six o'clock. Okay?"

I looked at my watch: almost 5:00. Hilda glanced at her watch. I could see she was trying to keep the disappointment from showing up on her face. It's tough for guests when they get their adrenaline pumped to the right level and then you have to let them sit and stew in it for a while.

I felt bad for Hilda. I smiled politely at Ike from the doorway, just as though I were a highly paid television director and not a creeping stain. "Since this is a demonstration of the human triumph over Time, why don't we do it now, the way we planned?"

"Because," Ike said, handing the steaming coffee mug to the long, lanky man seated in the last chair on the left, "the fire marshall's late. That fire in the Fourteenth Street subway station is out now, and he's on his cell phone and says he'll be here no later than six."

Hilda sat down on the coffee table, absorbing the delay like a good sport. She knew the rules because we had gone over them on Friday during rehearsal. Company policy dictates that any time we use an open flame in the studio there must be a New York City fire marshall present. Another rule rearing its ugly head in my face. But the fire marshall rule makes better sense than the keep-the-show's-director-down-in-the-lobby rule, so I smiled again. Professional cool.

"Ms. Murray and I will be in the control room." I said, reaching for Hilda's hand and pulling her to her feet. "The glass and tanks and everything still set up in the studio, Ike?"

"All set. If you see Hannah on your way to the control room, let her know about the delay. I sent a note to her E-mail, but she may not be signed on to her computer yet. The fire marshall can only stay for twenty minutes. We have an extremely narrow window to get this segment done."

Whatever uncharitable things we like to say about Hannah Van Stone behind her back—including the weekly anchor-insult contest run by Rubin Gorman that we call the "Hannah Van Scorna-thon"—I can't think of a time when she ever failed to receive an important message, or missed a deadline, or came up cold during an ad-lib, or fluffed an interview through neglecting to do her homework. *And* she could name every U.S. senator.

So what if she was pushy? And arrogant? And publicity crazy? And she smelled like cigarettes, treated us all like lackeys, hissed during commercial breaks, and never sent Christmas cards? So? She was terrific on the air. Hannah's one of the few people in broadcasting who got where she is and stayed there because she's good at the only part that counts for anchors: authority. She's got it cold. Pleasant manners and people skills don't count for beans on network TV.

"Abby, don't just gallop off," Ike said. "I've told J.D. to stand by in the studio." She cupped her hands and blew on them. "We can pretape the book interview with the doctors and let them get out of here." She turned and bestowed a warm smile on the tall, lanky guy, as though she were about to give him a cookie because he was such a good boy. "I hope you don't feel like it's fourth down and you're being brought in to punt."

What he was probably thinking, from the way he was looking at Ike's anatomy, was, *Well, what I was really hoping was to score.*

This tall, lanky guy was no slouch in the smile department. He lost all his gloom immediately and returned Ike's effort with extra candle-power and a slight twist to his wide mouth, and I thought for a moment he was going to reach out and pat her on some part of her anatomy that maybe as a doctor he'd gotten in the habit of thinking he could touch.

I knew he was a doctor because he made some kind of *humm* noise, like doctors make. There was a chorus of other doctor noises from the two other gargoyles, a man and a woman, whom I took to be the other medical co-authors of *Running Out of Time*, hanging out in the Green Room with their tall, lanky pal until show time.

The guy with the towel at the far right didn't make any noise. I knew he wasn't a medical doctor, and I knew he was a veteran in the makeup chair. Tony Jones, NASA's gizmo-guy, had been on the show several times before and was probably saving any noises he was going to make until he got me alone. I was surprised that the gloom had wrapped itself around him, too, because he was usually more prone to private practical jokes than to group wretchedness.

Working for NASA makes for the development of humor, I've learned from their trips to our show. Their work also seems to make for patience, as well as thick hides, quick answers, and a sense of how small the world really is—and if I was marooned on a desert island, I'd trade three doctors and a glassblower for just one Anthony Jones, Ph.D., and a cold case of Beck's. The beer would be for me; Tony limits his recreational intake to high-caliber South American grass, which is in good supply in sunny south Florida where NASA parks its shuttles. The beer wouldn't last long, and neither would the pot, but I didn't think Tony would ever run out of reasons why it was just as well we were cut off from civilization.

I was curious about the blue mood in the Green Room, but Ike did not give me a chance for any snooping. Working for NTB does not breed the kind of patience that working for NASA does, and Ike didn't waste any eye contact on answering my inquisitive glance.

She looked like she was ready to start issuing orders, so I anticipated her. Technically, Ike's in charge of getting the broadcast on the air and is therefore *technically* my boss, but television hierarchy gets weird when it touches directors: nobody tells us what to do, at least not very often, and then they do it nicely. Besides, I make more money than she does.

"Let's go make some TV together, Ms. Tygart," I said, gesturing gallantly toward the Tube, and bowing from the waist. "Whenever you're ready."

She headed for the phone on the wall and grabbed the stack of books from the coffee table. As she stuffed them under her arm, she nodded at the three people who were still strangers to me.

"I'll try to make decent introductions on the fly, doctors, but you'll find that our director only has to be told a name once. Mr. Abagnarro is the one director in the business who never takes or needs notes."

"Yeah," I said, trying to look like a prodigy. "I also do card tricks."

"This is Dr. Olivia Quintinale," Ike said, giving me a look that said I'd better not even *know* any card tricks, as she nodded at the woman seated in the center of the doctor group. "She's an internist."

Dr. Quintinale offered me a slim, icy hand and clutched the steaming mug of coffee in her other hand as she stood. "I don't understand football metaphors about punting and fourth down and such, but getting this interview on track early would be very welcome, Mr. Abagnarro. I've got a tough schedule ahead of me today."

She looked like she could handle a tough schedule. Like Ike, she was dressed in silk, a rose-colored flowing pants suit with a high neck; but unlike Ike, it looked like the flesh underneath was made of steel. Or maybe teak.

I shook her hand, which seemed to make us equally uncomfortable. We both wanted to break contact quickly and did.

I don't know what it is about doctors. When I was growing up in Queens, I had an aunt who told me that the two most important professions in the world are medicine and teaching, because, "Abby," she said, "doctors save lives, and teachers teach doctors." I never had any problem with teachers, because even I could see that my grades weren't their fault, but doctors are difficult for me. Maybe it's because they didn't learn well enough to save my dad's life.

I didn't know what record this medical team could boast in the life-saving business, but in the television business they immediately drew a high score from me. Even compared to our natty glassblower, these doctors were obviously receiving plenty of mail from stores on Fifth Avenue, and maybe Madison. The two men were dressed in blue suits and white shirts and perfect TV ties, not gaudy but just colorful enough to indicate that their surgery professors had not neglected to mention that while a stitch in time may save nine, an ounce of good tailoring is worth a pound of cure.

And I thought that the rose silk mock-pajama thing, on Olivia Quintinale's svelte frame, would play well for a doctor selling a serious book. The equation in the audience's mind might well be, "seriously expensive outfit, this doctor makes serious money, therefore this book must be seriously enlightening." On TV we judge books by the covers their authors wear.

Seriousness also looked to be the key to Quintinale's exercise program. She seemed to be in perfect shape, and I knew from the press sheet that she was forty-seven. I didn't see any reason why she shouldn't promote a book on health. I hadn't read *Running Out of Time*, but if this physician was treating herself, maybe I would read the book. There was no gray in her light brown hair, no crow's feet at the corners of her dark blue eyes, no sag in the deep bosom, and nothing wrong with the clear gaze she leveled at me through the steam rising from her mug of coffee. No sign even of contact lenses.

Ike kept the beat up-tempo and bustled right along to the next doctor.

"Dr. Hektor Stefanopolis," Ike said, skipping the lean specimen she'd been supplying with coffee and nodding in the direction of the man on Quintinale's left. "He's also an internist." It added to my awkward feeling around doctors that Hektor stayed seated. I tried to look like I wasn't looking down at him around Quintinale's silky hip.

I wouldn't have picked Hektor Stefanopolis out of a lineup as someone Quintinale was likely to play raquetball with, or even anything as strenuous as draw poker, not just because he was pudgy, but because he seemed to be permanently busy squirming in his chair. He also looked way too busy to reach out and pat any part of Ike's anatomy, unlike the other male doctor, who was still gazing at my former spouse in what I considered to be poor taste.

Hektor didn't offer me a hand, and I caught myself a split second before offering mine. You have to have a good eye to direct television programs, and I could tell he was going to stiff me. I didn't get the feeling he was being deliberately rude; more like he wasn't certain if a director was the kind of person a doctor shakes hands with, like he hadn't looked that one up in the AMA etiquette book. Just a procedural matter, nothing personal.

Hektor's grumpy expression stood out even in that group, especially grumpy for a man who was about to go on national television for a nice spot of free promotion on a book that was probably going to make him richer. In fact, the distinct lack of cheery fellowship in the Green Room seemed like a pale backdrop to Hektor's mood. Maybe he was distracted by his numb hands and chattering teeth, a medical condition I could have diagnosed for him as being brought on by exposure to the Green Room, that refrigerator that passes for our portal to fleeting fame.

At least one of them, the man I had yet to meet, had a different condition I had no trouble diagnosing: he was suffering from a hormonal surge brought on by exposure to the blond producer I used to be married to. I didn't know why Ike was saving him for last, because at first glance he didn't look like any prize to me.

The three doctors all had various grips on the steaming mugs of coffee, and, from experience, I knew that pouring warm liquids down the guests to keep them from icing over was a bad idea— just about the time you want their bodies in the studio, their bodies get other ideas about where to be. I began to think Ike had an ulterior motive for getting the doctors up and moving toward the studio, aside from their low spirits.

She grabbed the receiver from the wall phone. "I'll let J.D. and the floor crew know we're on our way." Still no indication from Ike that the tall, lanky doctor had a name. His eyes were all over Ike, and I was beginning to wish his mother was present to speak to sonny about his manners.

I glanced down again at Hektor, who was still squirming around in his chair. I gave him a good look, to see if this habit came from stage fright or if he had something more sinister that was going to show up on the air. His short black hair had receded gently from a wide brow, and he looked in every other way to be what you'd expect of a fifty-year-old man, which he was. He was paunchy around the waist and thighs, but nothing alarming. He was wearing a pair of glasses with featherweight, liver-colored plastic rims, the kind of plain glasses everyone's wearing now. But he was using his eyes strangely, I thought. When he turned to look at Ike, he worked himself around in his seat as though he had forgotten that the chair could swivel. When he looked at his watch, he bent his head and turned his face to stare at his wrist. When Rubin dropped a powder brush on the floor, Hektor turned his head to look straight down where the makeup had landed. It was as if the doctor could only see out of the front of his eyes, making no use whatsoever of peripheral vision. And maybe that was why he hadn't offered me his hand. It could be that I wasn't in focus for him.

I gave that some thought, because it was part of my job to

direct the camera angles in the studio, and this was such an unusual quirk that I was glad I had spotted it in the Green Room.

Hektor finally got his odd brown eyes fixed on me and then
turned around in his seat again, leaning behind Quintinale's rose
silk backside to stare at the final member of the medical trio.
"This is my brother Aristotle," he said, maybe to me, although
he was looking at the arm of the chair where Aristotle was parked.

"Oh, I'm sorry, Aristotle," Ike said, gesturing toward the
phone in her hand and then turning aside to talk into it. "Abby's
with me. Did the dish make it into Sarajevo? Yeah? Is the crew
okay?" She listened. "And Yellow-Man? How are those pictures?" More listening. "We'll use the living room set. See you
in a flash." She hung up. She turned to Dr. Stefanopolis Number
Two, or simply "Aristotle" to women on the receiving end of
his passionate glances. Ike smiled at him with such furious non-
chalance that my radar screen started swarming with blips.

"I didn't mean to leave you out, Aristotle," she said.

"The last shall be first, right, Ike?" this new Dr. Stefanopolis
said, with that crooked grin and a deep, quiet, reassuringly steady
voice that women probably thought was sexy. He had to be a
gynecologist.

I didn't tell him that it was too late to be first with Ike since
I'd gotten there long before he laid eyes on her anatomy. If I had
my way, the first would also be last, as well as everything in
between.

The Stefanopolis family resemblance apparently stopped at the
name and the choice of profession. The second Stefanopolis wore
no glasses, and knew how to sit still, and his eyes seemed to work
just fine. Aristotle was forty-five and looked, well, about forty.
He did have short dark hair like older brother Hektor, but Aristotle's was thick and slightly wavy and hadn't receded even a
centimeter since he was eighteen, and there was no sign on him
of any excess weight. His face was long and lean, the cheeks
pitted with what I took to be the shallow scars of acne, scars
visible even under the makeup. But, now that I was looking at
him as someone Ike called by his first name, the odd thing was
that the scars gave him a kind of definition, an edge, a rugged
and appealing humanity. It wasn't exactly a handsome face, not
in the way TV portrays handsome men, but his face was unfor-

gettable and, somehow, *better* than the faces I usually see made perfect by makeup in the studio.

"Aristotle's a neuro-ophthalmologist," Ike said. "And he's the one who races cars," she added with a smirk. "You know, we've got that ESPN footage from one of his races." The look on her face said that racing cars explained everything.

And maybe it did explain something. Maybe those scars were not the erosive signature of acne, but had instead been acquired in the daredevil pursuit of whatever it is that racers are after when they try to kill themselves by driving in circles around a track at the speed of insanity.

A brief vision of Tex crossed my mind, and his world-class sprint to Columbus Circle. Now, *there* was a man who could tell us all something about speed. I gave the doctors a professional glance, assessing them for the cameras. Hektor would never win any prizes for athletic feats, but he was passable; the other two were more than passable, appearing to be in excellent shape. *But still*, I thought...*Tex may have had greasy gray hair and gold teeth and probably stolen Reeboks, but, in a horse race between him and the doctors, my money would have been on the mugger.*

FIVE

IKE GRABBED her coffee cup off the cluttered table, quickly drained the contents—which by now must have been just the right temperature for lemonade—and said, "We're on our way, Doctors. Will you come with me? I promise you'll be much warmer in the studio."

The doctors put down their mugs on the coffee table and left the room with Ike, Hektor grabbing the open briefcase and shoving it closed. They headed around the Tube for Studio 57. Aristotle showed that he was a well-mannered doctor after all by taking the stack of books from Ike and carrying them in his own hands.

Since I had already established the fact that I didn't take orders from Ike, I was in no hurry, so I winked at Hilda and stepped around the coffee table. I peered over Rubin's shoulder at the face he was working on.

"Pygmalion was a slob compared to you, Rubin," I said. "What a miracle. This guy looks almost apelike. A little more pancake across the brow and you could bring him right into the Neanderthal Era."

The face above the towel grinned. "I wondered when you'd get around to me, Abby." He studied my face in return, wriggling a little under Rubin's ministrations. "I see you're already in makeup."

"The director doesn't wear makeup, you horse ball."

"Oh. I'm sorry. That's your regular skin?" He stuck his hand under Rubin's arm and we shook. "Good to see you, Abby." He rolled his eyes in the direction of the Green Room door. "That repellent medicine man seems very taken with Ike. I got the feeling he thinks she might be as much fun to drive as a stock car." His eyebrows wagged. "Probably thinks the world of his stick shift."

Tony craned his neck and glanced over at Hilda Murray. "Sorry. I didn't mean to gossip in front of you."

She flashed him a smile, a smile so perfect that, had she used it, she would have won that tax case in the Supreme Court.

"Please," she said, "don't mind me. Gossip's my middle name."

"I thought your middle name was Razzmatazz," I said.

"I use several middle-aliases. For now, just call me Hilda-the-Mouth Murray. In fact, I was just waiting for the doctors to leave so I could get in a little slander. But I was thinking more of the female barracuda in the rose silk underwear." She made a face at Tony. "Did you catch it earlier when I asked that woman if she had any advice about glassblower's hands"—here Hilda held out her red mitts—"and she told me to call her office to make an appointment? I suppose she thought my middle name was 'discount medicine.'"

"Yeah, well," I said, "you have to expect doctors to get all twisted about stuff like that. It's in the Hippocratic Manual that they don't give away advice for free. But where does it say they have to ogle gorgeous broadcast producers?"

"He's a *guy*, not just a doctor," Hilda said. "The Guy Manual was printed ages before Hippocrates wrote an admiring treatise on his first hiccup. But that female knew I was only gabbing. She still behaved as if I were trying to rip off her medical training. If she'd asked me about glass, I'd have been happy to give her all the hot info, and I do mean hot. Free." Hilda smiled that Supreme Court smile again. "I love talking about glass, which is why I jumped at the chance to do this show. My department chair was going to do it himself, but I actually blow more balls than he does, so I got the job."

"Balls?" I said.

"Pretty bubbles in the air. Sound better?"

"Lots better," I said. "We don't use the word 'balls' on network TV. Your pretty bubbles will probably be the best part of today's *Morning Watch*. The only competition you have is this bore from NASA, the government agency we all love to hate."

"Wrong, Abagnarro," Tony said. "America *hates to love* us. In their secret hearts, everybody adores space exploration; but nobody likes to pay for the real thing. Most Americans figure they can get to space by paying seven-fifty at the box office and taking their popcorn to their seats. Painless, you know?"

"Not always," Hilda said. "Did you see *Star Trek: The Final Frontier?*"

"Ouch," Tony said, probably from memories of the film rather than from anything Rubin was doing to his face.

Rubin stepped back and ran his eye over Tony's round face and red hair, then lifted the towel carefully away and shook the loose powder into the canvas hamper under the table. "You're all done, Tony. Nobody'll know you from Adam. I gotta say Abby's right: I am a miracle worker. You came in ugly and you'll go out presentable."

"I love doing this show. It keeps me humble," Tony said, standing and stretching, showing off a beige suit that had probably cost about a fourth of what either of the Doctors Stefanopolis had spent on his TV attire. "Abagnarro, on the other hand, doesn't need any humility lessons. He's got doctors slobbering over Ike right under his nose and he can't do a thing about it."

I held up a hand. "Don't be so sure, Space Boy. I can make Aristotle look like a toad on national TV—which there won't be any of if I don't split soon." I spotted a copy of *Running Out of Time* that had been left on the makeup table beside Tony's chair. I picked it up and looked at the photo on the back of the jacket. There was the smiling trio of two Stefanopolises and one Quintinale. "What's the deal on the orgy of bad humor I interrupted in here? Did somebody say the wrong thing? I got the impression you all rolled out of bed on the wrong side—I assume not the same bed, however."

Tony propped his hip against the makeup table and frowned.

"For one thing," he said, "Ike should never have scheduled a NASA Jetson like me on the same program with Aristotle Stefanopolis. He's the turncoat who testified to Congress during our budget hearings a couple of years and a few billion dollars ago. The House Committee on Science, Space, and Technology lapped it up."

"Tony, everybody testified against NASA's budget two years ago. I think even E.T. stood up to be counted."

"Yeah. But. Aristotle was the only one on the NASA payroll who spooked on us."

"He was working for NASA?"

"Consultant."

I whistled. "Still, you're both civilized. Or, at least *you* are. Was there something else I missed?"

Tony shrugged, but Rubin's the hottest lip at the network, and he said, "It ain't in the press kit from the publisher, but Olivia Quintinale used to be married to the dumpy brother with the glasses."

"So?" I said. "They must get along pretty well to produce a book together. Divorce doesn't mean you can't work as a team. You just don't screw anymore. Look at Ike and me."

Rubin's fat face wrinkled into a cherubic smirk. "You wouldn't sound so philosophical, Abby, if Ike Tygart had taken up with your brother."

"Aristotle and Olivia? His own brother's wife? Aristotle was doing Hektor's wife? Before or after the divorce?"

"I'm not sure," Rubin said. "My information's from Zelda Markowitz in Publicity. You could ask her." Rubin took a clean towel from the stack on the table and wiped his hands. "From the way Aristotle was looking at Ike, I'd say he gets ideas pretty quickly. Probably didn't wait for the divorce."

The last thing I wanted to discuss with Rubin Gorman was any idea concerning Ike. Like I said, he's got the broadcast lip.

I touched the sleeve of Hilda's jacket. "Let's get out of here. Even a gossip like you must've had your fill, and I promised you a tour of the control room. You can watch me work, which is better than a cold tour."

Tony immediately objected. "What about me? How come you get all the pretty women?"

I produced my best leer. "What can I tell you, Tony? Some people got it and make it pay; some people can't even give it away."

"Last I heard, Abby, you couldn't even find it."

"Tut, tut, Alien Life-Form. We've had enough NASA cracks out of you. Besides, you've been listening to radio signals from the wrong planet. You just sit back down and think about outer space until somebody remembers you're in here. If you're not called by Thursday, try *Good Morning, America.*"

Hilda and I made a quick exit. It wasn't the gossip about the doctors' past that had lit a fire under me. It was speculation about the future. I was bent on keeping track of the promising new flirtation apparently under way between Ike Tygart and Aristotle Stefanopolis, Race Car Doctor and Domestic Raider.

We hung a right down the corridor where most of the editing rooms are located. The flickering screens inside the darkened rooms cast some nice special-effects lighting onto the green linoleum floor where we were walking. At the end of the hall, I opened the door into Control Room #1 and saw that most of the wall of monitors was dark. Only the line monitor, the one that shows what the control room is sending out over the network, was on, and I could see that *Early Watch* was doing the East Coast weather story. A quick glance at the picture showed me that it hadn't started snowing since I left the street.

Ike was at her station, which is perched back and about three feet up from the well of electronic boards, consoles, switchers, computers, phones, headsets, and monitor screens where we turn videotape and live human activity into television. Control Room #1 is the network's most costly single workspace. It's twenty-three feet long, ten feet deep, and looks like the cockpit of the new-model intergalactic starship that Captain Picard would like to have when he gets promoted off that scow the U.S.S. *Enterprise* and gets a real command.

Everyone who works in the control room faces the long wall banked with monitors—until you get used to it, it can be difficult to concentrate with sixty-six screens, sometimes with that many different pictures, in front of you.

Ike's probably the best concentrator I know, and she gets the premier position in the center of the video fireworks, right in front of the line monitor. That's our stethoscope on the heart of the network, the monitor that will tell us we're all fired if we ever go off the air by accident, leaving the affiliates with black screens. Of course, we would also all be fired if we put something out over the air worse than blackness, something that isn't the perfectly acceptable little war or disaster footage full of bloodied and shredded dead bodies that we thought was in the video output—but rather something really nasty like live naked human bodies having a good time.

Ike was wearing her headset, and her fingers were blurring over the keyboard of her computer. She makes a lot more noise than most keyboardists because she types too hard. She didn't even glance up as we stepped past her and down into the well of the control room. I swiveled an empty chair for Hilda and took the director's chair.

I said good morning to Ginger Peloshian, the technical director, who sits to my right. I checked the line clock against my watch, and asked for a camera check. Ginger started flipping keys on her console, and three monitors on the lowest tier lit up one by one.

Crystal clear in their designer clothing and looking as pricey as the hookers I'd seen across from Lincoln Center, the doctors sprang into being on the three monitors, in three different camera angles. They were ensconced on the peach brocade couches of our living room set, getting miked by the floor crew. J.D. Waters was being civil to them and arranging his notes on his lap.

That set is only one of the four independent venues we use on *Morning Watch*. The different sets are spread out at intervals across the vast spaces of Studio 57 and divided from each other by cycs (shortspeak for cycloramas) and various sound breaks: sometimes a curtain, sometimes a Plexiglas wall, sometimes just an air pocket, depending on what we're doing on a given set. Studio 57 isn't big enough to play baseball in, or big enough to host a papal mass, but the Mormon Tabernacle Choir could hold its annual family picnic there with room left over for the New York Islanders to run potato sack races.

I picked up the script from my console and fanned through its pages quickly, with an eye to reminding myself about what was being done where in the studio for this show. I looked up and ran my eyes over the studio monitors: I knew the glassblowing equipment was set up in the kitchen on our fake breakfast counter, but I had that from the script and from memory, not from the monitors. We only have four studio cameras and no robot technology in Studio 57. A two-hour news-talk show is far too complicated for robocams, because we move among our four sets frequently. So, if I wanted to check out the studio without actually going there, I'd have to deal with real people who earn salaries.

The camera operators had already set themselves and the big Hitachi cameras. The control room monitors showed only the living room set where J.D. was schmoozing the doctors. Sitting in the control room is even trickier to the mind than sitting in front of your tube at home and sorting out the question of reality. Studio 57 is halfway across the building from Control Room #1, but when we see the people and the sets on the monitors, it's always tempting to think they're on the other side of the wall, like we could reach through the screens and touch the anchor.

I punched the key for the head cameraman's earphones—those big ungainly things that we call "cans"—hoping he had them on his head and not on some prop table.

"Wally, if you're on cans, can you turn on camera four and give me a studio sweep?"

A monitor just at my eye level sprang to life, showing Hannah sitting in her anchor chair on the news set, with a copy of *TV Guide* in one hand and her telex in the other. She hooked the coil of the telex to the back of her jacket collar and plugged the piece into her left ear, the whole operation one-handed. Years of practice paying off.

Then she took the whole apparatus off and put it back on the desk. Must be a new jacket, I thought, and she was making sure the telex was a good fit. Since she couldn't smoke in there, I knew it couldn't be *TV Guide* that had interrupted her drug pipeline to her lungs.

The camera view swung around, and I saw that the den set was empty of people but ready for Tony Jones and his million-dollar golf ball space doodad, and, as the view swept through another sixty degrees or so, I saw the glassblowing setup in the kitchen. At my left, Hilda smiled when she saw her gear.

At the end of the camera's swing, I saw the doctors sitting in the living room with J.D.

"J.D.," I said to the intercom mike on my console, "are you ready? Wanna do your Princess Margaret impression?"

He tapped the telex into his ear and grinned. "I forgot to bring my mane and tail, Abby. Terribly sorry, but some other time, perhaps?"

"You got it, J.D. Ready?"

"Quite ready."

"Then let's roll tape." I counted into the intercom. "Four, three, two, one—cue J.D." On my signal, we were making television.

Right away I could see that Hektor Stefanopolis was up to his trick of turning around to look at things.

Time to talk like the intercom god. "Cut," I said.

J.D. looked up and waited. The doctors glanced around, trying to locate my voice.

I opened the private line to Wally's cans. "The doctor wearing glasses. I want camera two to roll with his face when he's talking so we keep him full in the eye. Okay? And keep a tight grip on the focus handle—we've got a live one." I leaned over the intercom microphone. "On my signal again, everyone. Four, three, two, one—cue J.D."

Behind me, Ike's keyboard noise abruptly stopped, her headset was plunked down on her console, and she left the control room.

The interview went so smoothly after that first glitch that I knew these doctors had done television before. I listened to the interview, which is how I get away with reading as few books as I do. Five minutes of directing, and I had the gist of *Running Out of Time.* The authors had taken on the Food and Drug Administration in their book, arguing that experimental drugs should get much quicker approval from the government, especially for patients like those suffering from AIDS and therefore *running out of time.*

Aristotle was a natural on camera, and, with his memorable face, he would probably sell more than a few copies of the book to women. Olivia Quintinale spoke only briefly, but her command of statistics was pretty impressive. Without notes, she reeled off numbers about studies showing that participation in experimental drug programs gave patients a lift in emotional well-being, took the edge off feelings of powerlessness, and dramatically decreased the incidence of despair. I thought J.D. should have asked Quintinale what the statistics showed about the physical condition of people using risky new drugs, but the network doesn't pay me to sit in front of a camera and act like I know anything.

But, I thought, Hannah would have asked.

The real surprise of the interview, however, was Hektor.

The man was a poet. His eloquence on the plight of AIDS patients, his masterful handling of the touchy subject of thalidomide, and his simple denunciation of the FDA's refusal to approve a painkiller called Coratrol for the long-term treatment of pain—all these changed Hektor before my eyes from an awkward and difficult human, much less television, personality, into a fascinating rhetorician with a good story to tell. And Hektor's soft-spoken tirade against the U.S. Department of Agriculture for what he called "their slow, slow, torturous paperwork rain dance in search of a clue" on the question of allowing the distribution of medicated bait in the wild to halt the recent spread of raccoon-transmitted rabies in the Northeast—that showed me that Hektor Stefanopolis had cast his net of accusations among federal departments, without having a favorite target. Hektor was versatile in his wrath. Angry people who can control their vocabularies usually make good TV. Once we had the camera position figured out, he was a pleasure to watch.

The subject of stock car racing came up at the end, and Ginger was ready beside me, with the tape of Aristotle's latest experiment in getting as close to death as he could without actually crossing that line you can't ever get back across. I had a feeling that this side of Aristotle would sell books to men.

"Dr. Stefanopolis," J.D. said, in his BBC syllables, "how do you reconcile a dangerous sport like auto racing with your career as a doctor, a doctor who is trying to save lives?"

"I don't reconcile it," Aristotle said, and his wide mouth twisted in that slight, intimate grin that would convince many women in our audience that he wished he was in their homes with them, helping make the coffee or the beds. "I'm a very good physician. I'm a very good auto racer. I can't reconcile the two, so I just make sure I don't do them at the same time." Now the smile was self-mocking.

J.D. laughed. "It certainly seems wise to keep the two practices separate. We have footage of your spectacular crash at Long Pond, Pennsylvania, last month. If you don't mind a replay?"

"I've replayed it a thousand times in my mind," Aristotle said. "It has a happy ending, you know."

I cued Ginger, and the videotape played on the studio living room's huge monitor, as well as on four of our preview monitors in the control room. Aristotle sat forward on the couch to watch, but I could tell he was just working for the cameras. He'd probably memorized the tape. His brother Hektor slewed around to gaze at the screen. Dr. Quintinale looked slightly miffed, like watching car crashes was not what she had come on national television to do with her ex-husband and whatever-Aristotle-was-to-her.

"Your car flipped over completely an incredible seven times," J.D. said, as the black and red Chevy Lumina on the tape crashed into a wall of the Pocono Raceway and flipped so fast it was impossible to count how many times. Anyway, not with the tape playing at normal speed. "Can you tell us, Dr. Stefanopolis, what you were thinking when you stepped out of what was left of that car?"

Aristotle sat back against the cushions of the couch. "I remember thinking I'd never felt so alive."

In my peripheral vision, I could see Hilda's jaw drop when she heard that. And Ginger snorted. Maybe Aristotle wasn't as big a hit with women as I thought.

On one of the monitors I could see Ike standing at the edge of the living room set, where she was cueing J.D. to wind it up. She was evidently satisfied with what they'd gotten.

"We'll keep the tape rolling in the living room in case Ike wants to retake any of that," I told Ginger. "But now I want the Yellow-Man and the Sarajevo pieces in the preview unit, if they're ready."

"Ready when you are."

Above the studio monitors that still showed the doctors, the bank of preview monitors came up with color bars. Then Ginger started the tapes rolling.

The dish had made it into Sarajevo all right, and the crew, under heavy sniper fire, had spooned the pictures out without a wasted frame. You don't overshoot or get fancy angles in a situation like that. Even so, those pictures off the satellite were so clear and disturbing that I knew Ike would tell Hannah to warn the viewers about the graphic nature of the images. They were gory, but I had no complaints about the quality of the tape.

On another set of monitors, New York's latest serial killer's ninth looked just like the eight men who had come before: a scruffy citizen sprawled on the ground, his face painted yellow. I moved over to get my eyes closer to one of the screens. It was more like the paint was smeared on the man's face than painted on. Hard to imagine what the killer was trying to accomplish or say.

I sat back in my chair and watched the tape thoughtfully. The camera had panned down the length of the body, away from the yellow face, down along the center of the chest where there was a small bloody hole, and had paused at the by-now-familiar crumpled note that was the other signal that this killer was trying to tell us something. On the dirty scrap of paper were the letters "U.S.S.R" Good camera work, absolutely clear as a new mirror, and, as with each victim before, we'd all be wondering what this homeless person had to do with Russia. Or whatever part of the former Soviet Union the killer had in mind. Maybe it was a Russian killer. Maybe he didn't know the Cold War was over.

I glanced over at Hilda and could tell the Yellow-Man picture had upset her, or maybe it had been Sarajevo. Her lips were clamped together, and her hands were tight around the arms of the chair. It wasn't like the pictures themselves were something millions of people wouldn't see in their homes in a short while, but here in the control room, up close and on four screens and pre-edited and right in your face and lacking a trained narrator's voice to give them distance and perspective, the pictures were so much more potent than they'll ever be on your screen at home. Control room reality had struck again.

The picture zoomed back slowly. The shot widened. We got the victim at full length, from the angle of his feet, which were covered with crumbling tennis shoes. It was great actuality, but I had to admit this angle was gritty and maybe too much for morning TV. That would have to be Ike's call, but, after I thought about it, I decided I'd advise keeping the shot, mainly because of my conversation with Fred Loring. If nobody gave a rat's ass about the serial killings of homeless men, this shot could maybe provide a little jolt to the public conscience, maybe up the price to a dog's ass.

The ambulance was not in the picture, but its rotating arc of light swept at intervals over the faces of the cops and paramedics and bystanders gathered around the body. There, in the center of the group, was Midtown North Homicide Captain Dennis Fillingeri, dressed in a crisp white dress shirt, not a strand of his thick brown hair out of place. Then, in a gesture I'd seen from him many times before, he ran his fingers through that mop and there still wasn't a hair out of place. He sure as hell didn't use anything as un-macho as mousse, so I wondered what his secret was. I was never going to ask him, mainly because I didn't want to give him a chance to say, "Oh, it just grows that way. Great hair runs in my family."

And then I saw it. Just past all that great hair was a head of greasy gray hair, towering behind Fillingeri, who is himself not a dwarf.

I knew that head of greasy hair. And I knew that flash of gold teeth when their owner opened his mouth in a sneer. And I knew the name of the owner of the hair and the teeth: Tex, the Manhattan Mugger. The man who had about four dollars of my money.

The man who had said he had a story for me. Since it now seemed likely that his story had something to do with the report that would be leading our first news block, I was wishing I had listened to him. Especially if he was the killer.

I sat back and frowned at the screens. Tex didn't look Russian to me.

SIX

WHAT TIME DID the crew shoot this Yellow-Man tape?" I asked Ginger. The technical director of *Morning Watch* sits a lot closer than I do to the one monitor that shows the time code on unedited videotape.

She paused the tape and squinted. "We're looking at 2:34:04." She glanced down at the keys on her console, her hand hovering over color and brightness adjusters. "Why? Something wrong with it?"

"No. It's not that. The tape looks fine."

Superb, in fact, if I was in the market for a moving mug shot of the man who had vacuumed my pockets. It was interesting, I thought, that Tex had been in Central Park, hanging out at a murder scene, before he had picked me up outside of Lincoln Center. Nice command of the neighborhood, this mugger. I sighed at the screen. It was surely too much to hope that he had also cleaned the pockets of Captain Dennis Fillingeri.

I pointed a finger at Fillingeri's face on the monitor. "Correct me if I'm wrong, Ginger. Isn't this the first Yellow-Man where we've seen the great captain himself at the scene of the crime? It's always been underlings before."

"Yeah. I guess nine is Fillingeri's magic number. It's nine bodies now, right?"

I nodded. "Nine." I pushed my chair back from the console and stretched my legs. Leg room's always at a premium in the control room. "Nine homeless men. Nine yellow faces. Nine notes from the killer. What the hell do you think that U.S.S.R. stuff is all about?"

"I don't know. The New Russian Mafia?"

"Who knows?"

"Not me. Maybe it stands for something else, not Russia."

I raised an eyebrow. "Like what? Urgent Serial Slayer Rampage?"

Now it was her turn to raise an eyebrow. "How long'd it take you to think of that?"

"I just tossed it off. Directors have to think on their feet."

"You're sitting down."

"By golly, so I am. Just imagine what I could have come up with if I'd been standing."

Ginger looked back at the screen. "Well, Fillingeri's standing. He looks like he could use some help thinking. I don't think he's got a clue about this Yellow-Man stuff."

"I do," I said, not happily. "See that big guy behind Fillingeri?"

"Yeah?"

"He mugged me tonight."

"I heard you got it on the street," Ginger said, hiding a smile.

"What's so funny?" I demanded.

"I don't know," she said, her smile now out in the open. "It's just funny. The way you think you own the city, skating in and out of traffic, skating backwards, doing flips. It's like you think you're invincible. So, you finally found out you're mortal. That's funny."

"I wasn't on my skates tonight, and getting mugged wasn't funny. The guy's a nut. He quoted the Bible to me and said he had a story about killing."

Ginger lost her smile and cast a look full of meaning at the monitor showing the pictures of the Central Park Yellow-Man. "I guess he had a story, all right. All about a guy lying dead with his face painted a horrible yellow. Too bad it's the same story we've already seen eight times before."

Some movement from one of the studio monitors caught my eye. I could see Hektor leaning back against the cushions of the couch. His glasses were in his lap, and he had his hands cupped over his right eye.

"Check out the doctor," I said. "What's he doing?"

Ginger leaned to her left to look, and Hilda leaned toward me, but just as they both leaned, Hektor lowered his hand and we could see him wincing and blinking hard, like he'd rubbed a piece of grit across his right eye.

"Plucking out his eyeball, it looks like," Ginger said. "Jesus, that's gross."

"I wonder what's wrong with his eyes. You ever see anyone

with that habit he's got of moving around like he's sitting on a spindle?"

"No." Ginger sat back in her chair and put her hands behind her head, cracking her knuckles. "He looks kind of like he's made out of wood from the neck up, doesn't he? Like one of those old-fashioned dolls. Whatever ails him, he's got it bad."

I looked at the line clock: 5:24. I looked at the monitors into Studio 57: the other two doctors were still jawing with J.D. and Ike. I looked at Hilda: she looked like she could use a walk, and I decided that the best therapy for her, after the nasty Yellow-Man footage, would be some glassblowing. And I needed to talk to Ike about Tex.

"Let's go get you comfortable with your props in the studio," I suggested. "Ginger, get those cameras rolled for the kitchen set."

Hilda didn't say anything, but she rose from the chair, gave Ginger a wobbly smile, and headed up the stairs toward the door. *Future item to include in my stereotype of glassblowers,* I thought: *weak stomach.*

We retraced our steps along the editing corridor, turned right at the Tube, followed it a quarter of the way around its circumference, and stopped under the flashing red light over the door to Studio 57.

"You okay?" I asked.

"I am now. God, I feel so guilty. I never cared about those awful serial killings until I saw what you had in there, those gruesome shots of that dead man. Even the *New York Post* hasn't had pictures that bad, and you know what they're like."

"Print pictures have a more subtle kind of impact, you know, where the reader has to do a lot of the work, imagine part of the story. It's different when the image moves. The picture *is* the story. That's why we call it 'tell-a-vision.'" I spelled it for her.

I patted her shoulder and pushed open the studio door.

The *Morning Watch* kitchen is the first set you encounter in that vast cavern, with the living room and the den off to either side and the news set farthest from the door. Hilda went straight to her gear and pulled a heavy apron off the counter. She was tying it around her neck as the doctors, escorted by Ike, reached the kitchen.

"Is that asbestos, that apron?" Hektor asked, ogling her attire in his odd way. "You shouldn't be wearing asbestos, you know. It's carcinogenic."

Hilda shook her head and reached for the waist ties of the apron. "This is leather, just to keep the gobs and blobs off my clothes. It's not fire protection. If I couldn't control my fire better than to need an asbestos wardrobe, I'd be looking for another career."

"Where does a glassblower work, I wonder?" Aristotle drawled, giving us a lazy version of his wide, off-center smile. "I picture a rustic studio in Sleepy Hollow or Croton-on-Hudson, some place with ivy and a blacksmith, with rolling hills in the background."

"That sounds nice," Hilda said, reaching for one of the four glass vials she'd be using. They looked like tiny transparent onions, with perfectly rounded bulbs at the bottom, say an inch and a half in diameter, and long, narrow, hollow stems open at the top and rising about six inches out of the little bulbs. "But I have to make do with a stuffy lab at Columbia University. I work in the Physics Department there."

She got busy arranging the four identical vials in a rack on the counter.

"What's your title?" Olivia Quintinale asked, suddenly alert, as though the university part had rung a chime in her head. Are you a Ph.D.? Should we have been calling you Dr. Murray?"

"My title's Glassblower, Dr. Quintinale. Plain and simple. If you ever need any advice about glass, just call the switchboard and ask for a glassblower. They'll connect you."

"I'm sorry if I offended you earlier," Quintinale said. "I'd be happy to take a look at your hands now. I really just answered you out of nerves, you know. Stage fright."

"Don't worry about it," Hilda said, a preoccupied frown on her face as she reached for a beaker filled with clear liquid. "There's nothing wrong with my hands."

She started pouring the liquid into the first vial, and a sudden pungent aroma filled the air.

Hektor leaned over the counter and waved his nose over Hilda's operations.

"Vinegar," he said.

"Yep," she said. "I've got four different liquids that we're going to seal up in borosilicate glass—most people call it Pyrex.

The idea is that, once the vials are sealed, they're sealed. And I mean *sealed.* Forever. Or at least a few thousand years.'' She lifted one of the stemmed onions and held it up to the glare of the studio lights. ''Unless you toss these little glass suckers on the floor or something, they're as good as sealed for all time— that is, if you measure time by any way that makes sense for people.'' She lowered the vial slightly and, through it, looked Hektor in the eye. ''Not a bad little trick, huh? Considering that the container''—here she flicked a red finger against the glass bulb, producing a *ping*—''is itself a liquid.''

''Glass is a liquid?'' I shook my head in disbelief. ''No way. It's a solid. Just look at it. And listen to it.'' We'd all heard the noise she'd made when she thumped it.

Hilda gave me a superior smile, but her eyes twinkled. ''That's what everybody thinks. However, chemically, glass is a liquid. It shows net movement over time. Did you ever look closely at a stained-glass window that was really old?''

''I guess not.''

''Well, next time you get a chance, take a good look. You'll notice that the bottom of the window is thicker than the top. That's because the glass is *flowing* downward.''

''I'll be damned.''

''Probably,'' Ike murmured at my side. Nobody caught it but me.

As long as I had her attention, I decided to take her aside rather than hold a whispering contest. I touched her elbow and we stepped back from the counter.

''I have to talk to you about the Yellow-Man tape,'' I said.

''Not now.''

''You'll be sorry. My mugger's on that tape.''

''What?''

''You heard me.''

''Jesus, Abby. You mean dead?''

''No. I mean he's standing there in the park—bystanding, I should say. Right there with the cops and the EMTs.''

She thought a minute. ''Let me unload these guests and we'll go talk.''

But it wasn't going to be that easy to ditch the doctors because Hilda had them in the palm of her hand, talking about the miracle of glass.

She was just finishing some philosophic speech about a flowing liquid that is, for all practical purposes, rigid. Hilda glanced around at the countertop, looked up at our faces, glanced over at the vacant news desk, and then fastened on the living room. She replaced the little glass onion carefully in the rack and hurried over to the living room, stooping beside the coffee table to peer at the bud vase with its graceful neck and its single red rose. She hesitated a moment, drawing the rose from the vase, laying it on the table uncertainly. She picked up the flower again. She looked over her shoulder at us, undecided. She bent again and put the rose back in the vase.

We all watched as she returned with the vase and flower, and set the arrangement gently on the counter.

"Can you spare this?" she asked Ike, like a little girl asking to borrow her mother's pearls for the prom. "I hate to waste the flower."

"No problem," Ike said. She reached over hastily and extracted the single red rose from the vase. Some things are not as expendable as others.

Hilda donned a pair of protective goggles, fired up her torch, and took aim at the narrow neck of the vase.

"Now watch," she said. "I'll make what appears to be a rigid object flow for you."

She trained the blue flame on the neck of the vase and held it steady. Soon the neck sagged. Then it leaned. Then it did a U-turn and started running down the side of the little vase.

"The glass is flowing, all right," Hektor said.

"It was flowing before I touched it with the flame. It's merely flowing faster now."

Just as it occurred to me that we were violating company policy with an open flame, Ginger Peloshian's voice came over the intercom.

"Ike, the City of New York is happy to announce that it has a bona fide fire marshall at your disposal. Right now. Shall I tell security to escort him to the studio?"

"Now?" Ike squeaked. "Quick. Turn off that torch, Hilda." She looked at her watch. "He's half an hour early. He said six o'clock."

"No, my dear," I said, "he's half an hour late. He was supposed to be here at five. It's all in how you measure time."

"Don't start on me, Abby." She gave me a harassed look. "Are you ready to do this segment?"

"I'm *always* ready, Ike." I smiled at her with what I hoped was intimacy and tender wickedness. "You used to like that about me. In fact, remember that time on Martha's Vineyard, in the Harbor View Hotel when room service—"

She blushed a fiery red. "I'll get you for this," she whispered. "In public and all, you fiend."

"Keep your hair on, Ike. I was just making a deposit in the memory bank."

I was aware that everyone in the studio was focusing on us, but it seemed that Aristotle's focusing apparatus was most highly attuned to Ike, and he looked like a race car driver who had just roared into the pit with his gas gauge on empty, only to discover that his pit crew was out on a coffee break. Nasty little surprise.

Ike flashed her eyes at me. "I'll be right back."

She hustled out. The doctors lingered a while around Hilda Murray, examining the now fused bud vase and sniffing the beakers on the counter. In addition to the vinegar, the beakers held, as I knew from Friday's rehearsal, ordinary household bleach, ordinary egg whites, and ordinary water. Olivia Quintinale picked up the egg whites and swirled the mess around in the beaker.

"Egg whites," she said. "Why egg whites?"

"Columbia's Physics Department and Nuclear Medicine Department are doing some cooperative studies on DNA aging, and they suggested the eggs," Hilda said. "It doesn't really matter what substances I use for this demonstration, but I thought the egg whites could be interesting because they're from living animals and because they're so sticky and gooey, and the consistency is fun. But it's not just for show. I think it makes the point about glass being so impervious to breakdown if you use something from an animal."

"What about germs?" Aristotle asked.

"That's what I mean. When I seal these vials, the heat from the torch will draw out the air and create an almost perfect vacuum around the liquid. Germs won't stand a chance. You open that vial a thousand years from now and it'll still smell as fresh as it does today."

I thought about that. The egg whites might smell okay a thousand years from now, but what about Aristotle?

Ike returned with the fire marshall in tow. Since he would not appear on camera, it made no difference that he had not been cleaned up by makeup and looked like an honest-to-God fireman, with a nice, sooty smudge on his face and a red hard-hat in his hand. He was in shirtsleeves and, unlike the well-dressed doctors, did not appear to have stepped out of the dressing room at Paul Stuart, Madison Avenue clothier to the self-consciously rich.

Ike, still carrying the red rose, led the fire marshall over to the kitchen counter, introduced him to Hilda, and indicated to the doctors that if they wanted to watch the taping, they'd have to step out of the kitchen set. Hektor swiveled his head in that odd way and made for the living room. He grabbed his briefcase from beside the couch and hurried back to the kitchen.

But Aristotle's opinion of staying to watch the demonstration from the sidelines got put into words. "Thanks, but we've taken enough of your time," he said, and gave Ike a really sickening smile. No limelight, no thanks.

As Ike walked the doctors to the door of Studio 57, I saw Aristotle sneak her a small piece of paper, slipping it into the hand where she carried the red rose. If it wasn't his phone number, I'd join his pit crew and take a vow against coffee breaks.

And I saw Dr. Olivia Quintinale watching the exchange and directing an acid look at Aristotle. The muscles in her cheeks got tight like she was thinking what I was thinking and not liking it any better. And like she knew a little something from experience about gifts brought by this Greek.

As they were all passing out through the big studio doorway, our anchorwoman, reeking of a recently extinguished Virginia Slim complete with the full and deep fragrance of an ashtray dip on her fingers—waded regally in through the little crowd, leering at Aristotle Stefanopolis on her way. She stopped and turned back to face him.

"Don't I know you?" Hannah said.

"I don't think so. But I certainly recognize you, Miss Van Stone."

She didn't even acknowledge the flattery. In her book, Aristotle had probably passed the minimum test for a civilized human being: he was *supposed* to recognize her.

"No," she said. "I do know you from somewhere." She put

a hand on her substantial hip and pushed up the sleeve of her gray jacket with the other hand.

Ike intervened. She didn't have time for one of Hannah's sudden whims regarding boy toys. Besides, Aristotle was too old for a boy toy, and it looked like Ike had her own plans for Aristotle, Stock Car Doctor.

"Hannah, this is Dr. Aristotle Stefanopolis. You may be thinking of his prominence as a race car driver."

"The Winston Cup Tour?" Hannah asked, displaying some of her depth as a storehouse for factoids.

"No," Aristotle replied. "I drive in the second tier. To do the Winston Cup, you really have to dedicate yourself to the sport full time."

"Well, why don't you?"

"I have a demanding medical practice here in Manhattan."

Hannah lowered her professional eyelashes at him. "The doctor who races cars." She emitted a throaty laugh, one of those that I'm sure she rehearses while she's sucking nicotine sticks in her office. "Well, you certainly deserve credit for something, maybe raw irony. If you'd like to stick around and watch the show, I'll take you to lunch."

Those of us who work on the show did not even blink, because we're used to Hannah, but Hektor looked like something out of *The Exorcist* and Olivia Quintinale's eyes widened.

Aristotle, however, met the challenge as smoothly as it had been issued. "I'm afraid I'm scheduled to assist in surgery this morning, Miss Van Stone," he said, managing to look like he was always being asked to lunch by famous old TV queens. "But I'm honored that you asked."

Hannah waved a hand imperiously at Ike. "Just leave your phone number with *her,* and we'll do it some other time." With that, she swept over to the kitchen set. Ike stood there at the door, shaking her head gently.

I watched Ike turn after a moment and shake hands with the doctors, but it was hard to concentrate on anyone else when Hannah had her mind made up to be the center of attention. She picked up the beaker of egg whites and gave it a swirl.

"My, my. Interesting consistency. How did you convince Pinkwater to donate?"

That was Hannah in a nutshell.

She had not participated in the director's rehearsal on Friday, but even so, Hannah knew exactly what Hilda's beakers contained. For every segment of the show, Hannah receives a full "segment packet" that runs down the details of the projected shoot, and I know she reads the packets because she never makes a mistake on the air.

Leaving the floor manager to hold Hannah's reins, I beat a retreat back to the control room, and I did not waste time, because it was the fire marshall's time, not mine. I passed the doctors as they headed for the Green Room to retrieve their belongings from Rubin, who was standing in the doorway waiting for them. As I passed, Hektor's head swung around at me. His briefcase came around, too, and I had to dodge.

"Mr. Abagnarro, thanks," he said.

"You're welcome, of course, but for what?"

"Oh, you know." He fumbled self-consciously with his glasses. "For making sure I looked okay in there."

"No problem. Some people just need a little help. That's my job."

"Well, thanks just the same."

By the time I took my seat in the control room, I had finished revising my first impression of Hektor. Whatever was wrong with his eyes, there was nothing wrong with his manners.

I cued Hannah and sat back to enjoy directing this portion of the pretaping of *Morning Watch*. It went like a well-rehearsed spot should. Hilda, wearing the protective goggles and leather apron, applied the blue flame of her torch, which was rigged to an oxygen cylinder and a propane tank, to the slender stem of the first vial, the one she had poured the vinegar in. As the stem began to droop—at a temperature of 821 degrees Celsius, Hilda explained in a pleasant, matter-of-fact tone—I directed close camera shots. When the stem sagged and flopped over—at 1,552 Celsius, or 2,826 Fahrenheit (a number I had told Hilda to add for our nonscientific audience)—I told our camera operator to widen the shot because this was the best part. We hadn't used fire during Friday's rehearsal, but I knew what Hilda was about to do.

"Watch this," I told Ginger.

Hilda reached her hand out and, with a deft twist of her red fingers on the hot glass, sealed the vial. Bare-handed. That's right, bare-handed.

Hannah gasped like a pro.

From our monitors I could not see the fire marshall's reaction, but he must have had one. It's not every day you get to see someone as pretty as Hilda Murray stick her hand into the inferno and withdraw that same hand with a satisfied smile on her attractive face. Pretty woman, pretty smile, but the payload for the audience was the next close shot: the sealed vial sparkled in the intense light and glowed with the serene, cold beauty that Hilda had given it with a simple manipulation. There was no doubt that she'd ruined her fingers in the cause of art. The little glass onion was now a sculpture, a bauble that looked like it should go on a Christmas tree. In a paneled library high over Park Avenue. And only the butler would be allowed to dust it.

When Hilda was finished, she had a row of four splendidly original pieces of glass, each containing a liquid—maybe forever.

From start to finish, the whole thing took nine minutes, which we shot in real time and would probably run, without editing, in real time, even though it was a longish segment for us. The process was so neat and so absorbing that I wasn't aware that Ike was breathing over my shoulder until she brushed my sleeve with hers.

I looked up and her face was close to mine. I was inhaling the soft, hidden delicacy of her perfume.

"Beautiful," I said.

"Yeah. A lot more dramatic than the rehearsal. This is so cool. I gotta say, Abby, with you, Hilda, and Hannah—well, we almost couldn't miss. What awesome stuff."

She stepped jauntily up to her console, lay the red rose against the old gooseneck microphone in front of her, and put on her headset. She booted her computer, and yellow characters flashed across the screen as she pounded the keyboard.

I reached up and touched her silky sleeve. She pushed her headset off her right ear.

"Ike, I want you to look at this Yellow-Man tape. And I want to tell you what the guy said to me before he pulled my pockets out of my pants."

"He talked to you? You mean, like, *talking* talking, or robbing talking?"

"I mean like weird talking."

Ginger played the Yellow-Man tape, and Ike watched as the camera showed the onlookers at the scene. I pointed at Tex.

"That's Tex."

"Tex? He introduced himself?"

"That's nothing. He also introduced me, because he knew my name before I told him."

She shivered. "That's really yucky. God, you can't even get mugged in New York anymore without someone invading your privacy."

"Yeah. Makes you think, huh? What next?"

"As soon as we go over the lineup together, you can give me chapter and verse. I don't know what we can do with this Tex business, but maybe we should give it to Sally. Although God knows she's got enough on her hands producing Arden's piece, without adding to her burdens. He's trying to bigfoot her plan to tape him in the park and he's insisting on doing his standup on the roof again. She said she's ready to pull his tongue out of his head."

"I wonder why his tongue?"

"Because that's all he's got in his head."

We discussed the lineup for the seven o'clock news block, and talked about the length of the *Running Out of Time* interview.

"It's pretty long," I said. "I'm not sure how germane the raceway tape is, but it's the best part."

"Yeah, I like the idea of using the racing footage," Ike said, "because it puts some sting into the talkiness. But we have to be careful not to detract from the purpose of the piece, which is to focus on Time. Maybe we can cut some of Quintinale's statistics and let Hektor carry the interview? I was a little disappointed that the female doctor was the one with the least charisma. Even though it wasn't our fault, I bet we get viewer calls about sexism."

"I think Quintinale's statistics take some sting out of the medical speculation. It's up to you, but I'd say keep it."

At that moment, the "bulletin alert" signal sounded simultaneously on every computer in the control room. I swung my chair around and punched the function key that calls advisories onto my screen, and, at the same time, a news clerk yanked open the door and skidded into the control room with a police scanner in his hands.

"Another Yellow-Man," he gasped, apparently having run all the way around the Tube from the newsroom.

Ike was typing furiously, switching screens, and talking to herself.

I read the AP wire story. It was short. After the dateline, it read:

The dead body of another apparent "Yellow-Man" victim has been found in an alley off Columbus Circle in midtown Manhattan. Early police reports indicate that the dead man's body bears the characteristic marks of the nine previous "Yellow-Man" serial killer's victims: yellow paint smeared over the face, and, thrust into the man's shirtfront, a tattered, dirty piece of paper bearing the letters "U.S.S.R." If the early reports are confirmed, the dead man will be the tenth victim in the series of bizarre killings that have stymied New York police for the past month. About five hours earlier on this torrid New York night, a ninth Yellow-Man victim was found in Central Park.

Ike yanked off her headset and grabbed the phone. She punched numbers and drummed her fingers on her console while she waited for an answer.

"This is Ike. Get a microwave truck, a goddam camera crew, and sound technicians downstairs on the double and I want them on cell phones. And find Arden Boyer."

SEVEN

THE AP ALERT had come at 6:13. By 6:17, our microwave truck had backed out of the garage, driven into the alley, and was sending pictures to the control room. That was probably the closest we'd ever had a remote crew on assignment.

On the monitors feeding from the truck, we could see a collection of three cops standing at the entrance to the alley that runs the length of the Emerald City, but there's only so much cops can do about journalists. Short of pulling their 9mm. semiautomatics and smacking serious head, which is a violation of the Constitution of the United States of America, they were pretty much stuck with having us make their jobs harder.

From our camera shot just at the entrance to the alley, all we could tell in the control room was that there was a body on the ground. Or, at least, a pile of clothes attached to a pair of nice, shiny shoes.

Nice clothes. Even from the camera's point of view at the end of the alley, they were nice clothes. Clothes that could have come from Paul Stuart—now, perhaps, Madison Avenue clothier to the dead.

And there was a black briefcase beside the clothes.

Ike and I looked at each other.

She was on her cell phone. "What are they saying about identification?" she asked.

Apparently, from the look on Ike's face, they weren't saying.

I shoved my headset on over one ear, grabbed my cell phone, and patched it into Ike's connection.

Sally Goldberg-Petit, the woman who was producing Arden Boyer's piece on the night's earlier Yellow-Man, was on the line from the street. "They're not saying yet. These are just beat cops." As she spoke, I could hear the sirens from her phone. "This'll be Fillingeri, I'll betcha."

The monitors showed the captain emerging from an unmarked

black Ford Crown Vic, looking disgusted. He had not yet taken the time to arrange his handsome face for the TV cameras.

Ike picked up the receiver of her desk phone and shoved it against her other ear. She punched four buttons on the phone's keypad with her thumb. We were certainly cranking up more than our usual share of the 20.5 million business phone calls made in Manhattan on an average weekday.

"This is Ike. We're going to have to cut the earlier Yellow-Man tape around this new stuff coming in. Stand by in that edit room and don't move. Sally will talk you through it from the ground on her cell. We'll have to do the piece live at seven, but be ready with the stuff shot in Central Park. Sally will help Arden with the narration from down there on the street, so we won't need the track he already recorded on tape—just the natural sound. Everything from Arden, straight through the piece, will be live. He'll have the truck's monitor so he can see the pictures. When you're ready, run the tape down there to Sally, and she can feed the whole thing to us in one piece. When we hang up, call her cell. Ready?"

Ike hung up the desk phone.

Into the cell phone, she said, "Did you get that, Sally? Great. Let's clear the line, but keep the pictures coming up here as long as you can."

It was now up to Sally to command the troops on the ground, and I could see Ike was clenching her teeth. She wanted to dash from the control room and beat it to the alley. Having a desk job is tough on Ike. She's a hands-on journalist, never happier than when she's crawling under barbed wire, dodging bullets, or ambushing a reluctant politician.

"Abby, Ginger, let's look at that earlier Yellow-Man again."

While Ginger rewound the tape, Ike made calls to editing about the glassblowing segment and J.D.'s interview with the doctors, mostly telling them to have the openings cued up tight.

Ginger rewound the Yellow-Man tape and up it came on the preview monitor. "Ready, Ike?"

"Just a second." Ike made another call, this time to the Green Room. "Tony? I hate to hang you up like this, but we need you and your quartz ball to stand by. We may not get to you until the second hour of the show, or we may need you on the run sooner.

Okay?'' A brief smile lit Ike's face. ''Thanks. You're a prince, Tony, no matter what Abby says.''

Ginger swiveled her chair and spread her palms apart, looking a question at Ike.

''Go,'' Ike said.

Ginger spun back and ran the tape from Central Park. When she got to Tex's cameo role, I had her pause the tape.

''Ike, that's our man. Tex in all his glory.''

''What'd he say to you?''

Rapidly, I told her what little there was to tell.

''He wanted to talk to you about a killing?''

''That's what he said.''

''Do you think he was talking about tonight's killing in the Park?'' She pointed at the yellow face on the monitor. ''This guy?''

''I have no idea. At the time, I thought he might have meant *my* killing.''

She blinked rapidly and leaned forward over her console. ''Holy shit, Abby. Look at monitor eight.''

That was the remote monitor from the microwave truck, feeding us the live camera pictures. Our crew was deep inside the alley. The hazy gray of dawn had finally reached inside between the buildings, brushing out the dark shadows and dissolving the shaft of blackness around the body.

''Aw, Jesus, Ike,'' I swallowed. ''Look at his face. It's Hektor.''

Dr. Hektor Stefanopolis's face was splashed with yellow paint, including his glasses. His mouth was open, a couple of silver fillings in his upper teeth reflecting back our crew's lights in dull metallic points of grim finality.

Ike rose from her chair and stepped down into the well, next to my chair, staring at the monitor screen. ''This makes no sense. No sense at all. Hektor's not homeless. Hektor's not nameless. Hektor's not like the others. He doesn't fit.''

''Sorry, Ike, but now he's got the most important thing in common with the other victims.''

''It's gotta be a copycat,'' she said, touching the doctor's painted face on the monitor with the antenna of her cell phone. ''I refuse to believe this is the real thing, a part of the Yellow-Man series.''

Her cell phone rang.

"Ike here." She listened, still standing, still staring at the screen. "Tell the cops *we* can I.D. the body. Tell them he's Dr. Hektor Stefanopolis. I'll send a clerk down with the doctor's office address and telephone number." She pulled several business cards out of her pocket and sorted through them quickly. She jerked the one she was looking for out of the little stack and shoved it at a news clerk and told him to get going. Before he was out the door of the control room, Ike was back at the phone giving orders. "Tell the cops we won't I.D. him on the air until they give us the go-ahead. But you better sure as hell tell them we get the go-ahead before anybody else gets it. The *minute* they've notified next-of-kin, they notify us. If any other reporter gets it first, I'll go down there and kill Dennis Fillingeri myself. Oh? Put him on."

I spoke softly to Ginger and she flipped keys. The displays for the other major networks and CNN came on above us, across the top tier of monitors. We'd know who was the first to report this victim's name.

I kept an ear on Ike's conversation while Ginger and I started moving the live feed into the auxiliary editing unit. Down in the microwave truck, they were certainly already cutting the tape on their editing machine, but it never hurts to have backup.

During pressure situations in the control room, you learn to separate your senses, letting them operate independently of each other, and while my eyes and hands were working with Ginger on the incoming tape, my ears were working on Ike, not just to eavesdrop, but because she was the center of this web of remote communications and any shifts or insights would come from her, especially now that she had collected the homicide boss himself in her web, for the moment.

Since our divorce, Ike has made an off-again, on-again project of the Midtown North homicide captain. She's flaunted him at a couple of Broadway openings and media parties, and sometimes he calls her at work. I'm pretty sure they never got to the crucial part of homicide captain/broadcast producer relations, mainly because Ike has rigid sexual scruples, based on her midwestern upbringing (as opposed to the new practical scruples), but it's the "pretty sure" aspect of my knowledge that gnaws at me.

"Dennis?" She said, all business. "That dead man? That's Dr.

Hektor Stefanopolis. He is—was—a Manhatten internist. I've sent his address and all downstairs via a clerk. The doctor just finished taping an interview up here with us. He left the studio about twenty minutes to six. Wait a minute. Abby's shaking his head.''

"It was twenty-five to six when he left the studio," I said.

"Dennis? Abby says twenty-five to six. You know he's always right about stuff like that."

I waved a hand at her.

"Hold on a minute, Dennis," she said, directing her gaze at me. "What?"

"Tell him that Carl Honeyman will know what time the doctors left the building."

She returned to the phone. "Abby says...oh, you heard him. No, I'm sure he knows you can do your job without his help." She covered the mouthpiece with her hand, looked at me, and mouthed, *What an ingrate*. She removed her hand from the piece. "Okay, but remember, we get it first when you release the name. And, listen, when you're done down there, can you come up here for a live interview?"

I heard some squawking over her line.

"No, I don't think that's a nervy request." She banged the phone down on its cradle and sorted rapidly through her little stack of business cards again.

"What are you doing?" I asked.

She summoned a news clerk and handed him two cards. "Call these numbers every two minutes until you get one of these doctors. If you get Dr. Aristotle Stefanopolis or Dr. Olivia Quintinale on the phone, give it to me." She pointed to the console down and to her left. "Sit there and don't take any shit from their answering services."

"Ike, Aristotle may not be next-of-kin," I said.

"I know. But if I can get any comment, we'll have more of a story than anyone else. And with any luck he can speak for the family. Dennis Fillingeri may not think it's as much of a priority as we do to release the I.D." She grabbed the desk phone and punched numbers. "This is Ike. Are you guys awake over there on the National Desk? I want that expert from Boston University on serial killers—oh, hell, what's his name?"

"Henry Amos Jankowski," I supplied.

"Henry Amos Jankowski," Ike told the phone. "You know

which one I mean; all the shows have used him. I don't care if he's in his pajamas. Let me know when you have him." She hung up.

"What did Fillingeri say?" I asked. "Is he coming up?"

She screwed her pretty face up like she'd gagged on a lemon and went into what she thought was her Fillingeri impression. "'Ike, I've got work to do down here. You don't think a television show is more important than solving a murder, do you? That's a nervy request.'" She waved her arms around over her head and wiggled her fingers. "'Oh, God, I'm such a conscientious cop. I love my job.'"

"I thought you liked Fillingeri."

"That snake." She was back to her own voice.

"What'd he, try something on you?"

"None of your business. None of your merry little business, ex-husband." She reached over and tweaked my nose. "What you don't know will probably drive you crazy. Ha. Ha. Put that in your cereal bowl and see if it crackles."

"Ha, ha, yourself. It's way too late for me to go crazy."

"Ain't it the truth? Ain't it just the sad truth? Oh, well, I've got two million viewers biting their nails, waiting to see what I'll do next. Stop distracting me."

The next half hour was a blur of phone calls and traffic through the control room.

At 6:55, Arden Boyer stepped into the picture I had on the live monitor. He was wearing a dark jacket and tie with a perfect Windsor knot.

"Goddam it," I said under my breath, smacking my console. I waited for him to twist his telex into his ear and then let him have it through the mouthpiece of my headset, as gently as I could, considering he had other things cluttering up his mind. "Arden, I hate to break this to you, but New York's in the middle of a heat wave, and we're planning to mention it at the top of the show. Kindly ditch your jacket and tie. It's gonna look like we're reporting from two different planets—Earth and the one you're on. And roll up your sleeves."

He started dragging his arms out of the jacket's sleeves and on the monitor I could see some helping hands yanking at his tie— Sally Goldberg-Petit, no doubt wishing she could give it a nice twist rather than yank it off.

Just then, across the central tier of monitors, Hannah slid into the anchor chair at the news desk and, with a smooth motion, had her telex in place. "Arden, can you hear me?" she said.

Arden's face stayed blank.

"Arden, say something," Hannah said, stacking her script into a neat pile

His face was still blank.

Ike spoke into her mouthpiece. "Arden. It's Ike. Can you hear me?"

"As loud as a fart from Capitol Hill. Who's going to throw it to me, J.D. or Hannah?"

"Haven't you heard Hannah talking to you?"

"I can hear you, Ike. But I can't hear Hannah"

I punched the intercom. "Hannah. Arden can hear Ike, but not you."

Unruffled as ever, she pursed her lips at the hand mirror Rubin Gorman was holding by her side. "Well, just tell Arden I'll say something like 'You've been at two murder scenes tonight, one apparently the ninth in the Yellow-Man serial killings, the other sufficiently different to suggest that someone is copying the Yellow-Man slayer's trademarks.' I'll ask Arden to describe the differences he can discern so far. Tell him we won't be able to do a second question."

Ike put her hand on my shoulder. "I've got that, Abby." She spoke into her mouthpiece and told Arden what Hannah would say at the top of the news block.

But, Arden being Arden, he had to ask. "What's the matter with this thing? Why can't I hear Hannah?"

I looked at my watch. Three minutes till showtime. "We don't know, Arden. My preliminary guess is it's broken."

"What bad timing."

"Just act like you can hear the question from Hannah and we'll cue you when to begin."

"It's probably the patch up there, Abby," he said, nodding his head wisely, like he had a clue. "Everything seems okay down here.

I looked at the line clock. 6:58.

Behind me, Ike said, "Hannah, after the news block, we'll go straight to commercials and come back to you in the kitchen to introduce the glassblowing piece. You'll have to hop over there, because it's only a two-minute commercial break. You and Hilda do a little patter and then we'll go to the tape of the demonstration. The tape opens with a close-up on the torch, with the blue flame, so refer to that—it's a real pretty shot. I'll be making up the rest of the show as we go along because we'll have to hold the doctor interview until we can figure out how or if to use it. We may send Tony Jones and his NASA toy to fill where we need." Ike looked at the line clock. "Ready, Hannah?"

"On Abby's signal, Ike."

I looked at the line clock. 6:59.

The news clerk started waving his phone's receiver over his head. "I've got Dr. Aristotle Stefan-stefano-you-know," he shouted.

Ike glanced at the clerk's phone, saw which light was on, and touched the corresponding number on her phone's pad. "Aristotle. It's Ike Tygart. I'm sorry about Hektor. Are you okay with us using Hektor's name on the air? The family knows? Yes, I know, I'm sorry. Please stay on this line a minute; I'd like a number where I can call you after eight. Okay?" She pushed the hold button and spoke into her mouthpiece. "Arden, Sally, name the victim on the air." She pronounced it for them.

I looked at the line clock. 6:59:54.

"Five seconds," I said. "Four, three, two, one. Cue Hannah."

Ginger thumbed up the first key on her board, and Hannah said, "This is Hannah Van Stone in New York, reporting for *Morning Watch*, where overnight the blistering heat wave has killed three more people and where two more men have been found murdered, bearing the signature marks of the Yellow-Man serial killer. We go live now to NTB's Arden Boyer, who is standing by at the scene of the latest murder, which was discovered within the last hour. Arden, you've been present at two murder scenes tonight, one apparently the ninth in the Yellow-Man serial killings, the other sufficiently different to suggest that someone is copying the Yellow-Man slayer's trademarks. What can you tell us about these latest episodes in the bizarre story of Yellow-Man?"

"Hannah," Arden said, just as though he had heard her question, "NTB News has learned exclusively that the latest victim— apparently the tenth man to die in the Yellow-Man series—is a prominent Manhattan physician named Dr. Hektor Stefanopolis, a man who has almost nothing in common with the previous nine victims, all of whom have been homeless men.''

''Whoa, dissolve,'' I said to Ginger, as I heard Sally's voice in my headset, telling me to go to tape.

And there was our seamless transition: pictures of Hektor on the monitor, his yellow face, his yellow glasses, the dirty smudges on his expensive shirt, the crumpled scrap of paper stuffed into the part of the shirt where Napoleon would have put his hand if he'd been sitting for this portrait.

The only letters showing on the scrap of paper were ''U.S.S.,'' but I was one of at least two million viewers that morning who knew to a certainty that there was one more letter, hidden just inside the shirt.

EIGHT

As IT TURNED OUT, the Boston University criminologist, the guy who specialized in wracking his brains over serial killers, had already changed out of his pajamas when our Beantown affiliate's crew reached his home at 7:20 with a K-U truck. In no time, the crew had popped open their rooftop dish and we had the satellite uplink. After the break for the affiliate stations to run their local news and weather, J.D. conducted a live two-way with Dr. Henry Amos Jankowski at 7:35.

J.D. was sitting deep in the embrace of a red leather armchair in the *Morning Watch* den, conversing with the expert's face on the big-screen monitor across from the chair. And the expert was in his Brookline home next to a potted plant, conversing with a red dot on one of our remote cameras. If you wrote for a transcript of that day's program, which an unusually large number of viewers did, what you'd get of the Jankowski interview, after the polite acknowledgments, is this:

J.D.: Can you tell us if you think the so-called Yellow-Man killer has simply broken his pattern with the death this morning of Dr. Hektor Stefanopolis and is widening the field of his endeavors, or do you think this latest killing is the work of what they call a copycat?

JANKOWSKI: My understanding is that the cause of Dr Stefanopolis's death has not been determined yet, so anything I say is a very preliminary guess. That said, however, I would at least be inclined toward a copier because of the doctor's obvious social and economic separateness from the other victims, differences so apparent from the way he was dressed that the killer could not have mistaken him for a member of that sad brethren, the homeless of New York. It's quite usual for serial killers to choose friendless people as their victims, because that choice itself tends to allow the string of killings to lengthen—the more a serial killer kills, the more he wants to kill. It's like an addiction. And that's the strongest reason for thinking that the death of Dr. Stefanopolis is not the work of the serial murderer. Dr. Stefanopolis, I'm sure, had many friends, and that would make him a dangerous choice for this killer.

J.D.: Are you saying that police investigators do not work as hard to apprehend those who prey on society's more powerless members—those you call "friendless"?

JANKOWSKI: I think that's fair to say, but only because they can't work as hard. You have to remember that it's tough on the police when victims leave no friends behind. It's difficult to learn anything about such victims, and the police have less to work with in terms of data that provides perceptions of motive and opportunity and the kinds of things that traditionally lead to the solution of murders.

J.D.: Until the death of Dr. Stefanopolis early this morning, it seems that the best data the police have had to work with are the yellow paint and the cryptic "U.S.S.R." notes.

JANKOWSKI: It's not unusual for a serial killer to have a signature. The killer wants the credit—or the blame, if you will—for his work. You will perhaps remember William Hierens, who came to be called "The Lipstick Killer" because he would use his victims' lipstick to write "Please catch me. I cannot control myself." Always he left that same message at the scene of his murders, scrawled on a wall or a mirror. And there was Emil DeLancey, the self-styled "Snowbird of Miami." He stuffed cocaine up the noses of his victims before he killed them. DeLancey later said that he heard voices telling him to leave a sign about the power of what he called "God's Medicine." But the Yellow-Man killer is intriguing, to say the least, in that he makes a point of two trademarks, two overt additions to his victims—what I call "artifactual evidence." And that's very unusual—many serial signatures have, unfortunately, involved taking something away from the victim—I hope I put that delicately enough.

J.D.: Well, murder is not a delicate matter, is it? I assume you mean Jack-the-Ripper style mutilation.

JANKOWSKI: Well, yes. You'll remember that Jeffrey Dahmer claimed to have eaten the heart of one of his victims. That's tantamount to a cannibalistic trophy, nothing like these Yellow-Man trademarks.

J.D.: Do these two very striking signatures suggest to you a particular psychological disturbance, or pattern, that the police should be looking for?

JANKOWSKI: He's got us all guessing, which is probably precisely what he intended. He wants us to think about him; that's part of the power he has given himself by embarking on murder. Those "U.S.S.R." notes are as impenetrable as the yellow paint. The only surmise so far that has made any sense to me is that there is a political motif in the signature. Those who have suggested that the yellow paint indicates a racial motif are puzzling over their own hypotheses, because some of the Yellow-Man victims have been white, some black. If you're interested in what I might call the realm of venturesome conjecture, I can offer you one thought: if the Yellow-Man victims were not already, because of their homelessness, an almost invisible society, I'd say the yellow paint was meant to obscure identity. Of course, that applies much more nicely to Dr. Hektor Stefanopolis, who had a visible standing in society. In fact, everything about his death seems to suggest that he is not part of the pattern.

J.D.: A final question: if Dr. Stefanopolis's death is not the work of a copycat, but is actually part of the series that has taken nine other lives, can you suggest any approach that might lead to the discovery of the killer? In other words, does this victim's prominence give the police, perhaps, some help in gaining entrance to the mind of the killer?

JANKOWSKI: I expect Dr. Stefanopolis's death will give the New York police more problems than help.

While J.D. was on the air playing Satellite TV Sleuth, I sent Fred Loring an electronic request for graphics on both Central Park and the alley where Hektor had been found. Fred obliged quickly with topographical maps so good they looked 3-D, and the news block that opened our second hour was more lavishly produced than our first one and better illustrated, but no fatter in terms of information. Nobody was saying yet what had killed Hektor, and certainly nobody was saying who.

Just after the eight o'clock news block, we scored our second coup of the morning, after scooping everyone on the identity of the body in the alley. Ike called Aristotle back, and Hannah conducted a short, intimate, breathily sympathetic on-air condolence visit with him over the phone link. Aristotle said that he had no objections to our running the interview we had taped before Hektor had died in the alley.

"I don't think there's any harm in it," he said, "and if it helps in any way to shed light on this morning's tragedy, then I'll be very grateful to NTB News. Although it's difficult to see what can be learned from that interview."

I didn't think there was anything in the interview that would lead to Hektor's killer—unless the FDA had offed Hektor for badmouthing their drug approval policies—but it was good TV for us to have practically the last words from the victim, especially when nobody but *Morning Watch* had those words. And, if Aristotle's mind worked that way, running the interview would certainly sell more books for the surviving authors than not running it—which is not to say that I suspected Aristotle of murder. Getting major free publicity by killing and then painting your brother/fellow author seemed outlandish as a motive even to me.

We played the interview in its unedited entirety, including the spate of statistics from Olivia Quintinale, and that cold data took on an eerie significance because, while she had been spouting the numbers during the pre-show taping, she was sitting right next to the man who would soon be entering an alley to become the hottest news story in New York.

Under the circumstances, the footage of Aristotle's miraculous escape from death in the Pocono Raceway crash was packed with hideous irony. The long *Running Out of Time* interview ended with Aristotle's answer to J.D.'s question, "Can you tell us, Dr Stefanopolis, what you were thinking when you stepped out of what was left of that car?"

It was extremely quiet in the control room in the pause before Aristotle replied, like we were all holding our breath as we watched the tape, even though we knew the answer.

"I remember thinking I'd never felt so alive."

With practiced, silent signals, Ginger and I dissolved from those words into a bumper slide and from there into a commercial block. The unnatural quiet in the control room evaporated, and we went through the motions of show production. We got through our film critic whinnying about the fact that Disney was changing certain lyrics for the home video release of *Aladdin* because of protests about anti-Arab bias. We weathered our meteorologist's excited report that heavy rain was on the way to the Eastern Seaboard and we'd soon see the end of the heat wave, maybe by midafternoon. We did an update from the alley—now barred with futile police barriers that wouldn't keep out a single single-minded tourist—in which Arden Boyer, drenched in sweat, reported that "sources" had told him that police detectives were convinced that Hektor's death was not connected to the serial killings except in the copycat aspects of the paint and the "U.S.S.R." note. We called the Green Room to alert makeup to freshen up Tony Jones's face for his trip to the den as our closing segment, to tell America about NASA's Spinning Quartz Ball.

But Tony did not make it on the show, after all, that day, because Midtown North Homicide Captain Dennis Fillingeri suddenly, and with suspicious philanthropy, decided to grant us the eleventh-hour courtesy of a visit, which was sort of a coup for *Morning Watch* except that we all knew Fillingeri had his own reasons for doing things. Since all he had to do was step out of the alley, push his way through the revolving door of the Emerald City, and maybe gun down our security guard, I did not stand up and applaud out of gratitude when he phoned the control room to say he'd "take time out of my rough schedule to give NTB a rundown."

Hannah drew the short straw and faced Fillingeri across the

news desk for the interview. He was about to drop a bomb, but I don't think any of us smelled the fuse burning.

Hannah started by covering the definitely lurid but now-familiar Yellow-Man code, without getting anything new. Despite her skilled questioning, Fillingeri did not let slip any little fact about Hektor's yellow face that would send chills down the spine of America. He wouldn't even speculate about the "U.S.S.R." notes.

"We don't know anything about those," he said, raking back his thick brown hair with his fingers. "Whoever is responsible for these killings is not trying to be clear, that's for sure."

"Well, what is he trying to do?" Hannah asked, leaning toward him across the desk.

"We simply don't know."

"Perhaps the killer is trying to distract you, throw you off the scent?"

"What scent? We don't have a scent."

"You still have no suspects, no course to set for the investigation?"

"No. Except we're going to treat the death of Dr. Hektor Stefanopolis like any homicide—meaning, we'll look into it, period. The crime scene itself doesn't look like it's going to be any help." He shook his head. "That paint, that note—maybe. But there's nothing for us in the alley but a bad smell, like any alley in New York." He looked down at his hands on the desk. "The autopsy may tell us something, though, especially since we have a medical history on Dr. Stefanopolis, and we'll release those results to the media as soon as we can."

I could see Hannah's blue eyes narrow a little as she heard that.

"A medical history. You have no such histories for the other victims?"

"No."

"That fact is another big difference between Dr. Stefanopolis and the earlier victims. Are you prepared to say that this latest murder was the work of a copycat?"

"It's way too early to leap to such a conclusion."

"Is it too early for the medical examiner to have *any* conclusions about Dr. Stefanopolis's death?"

"Way too early. We don't know what killed Stefanopolis."

"But I thought all the Yellow-Man victims were knifed."

"Oh, they were knifed, all right, we know that. But, as to that, we're not sure about cause of death."

"Certainly your office has led us to believe that the Yellow-Man killer stabbed the victims to death. They all had knife wounds in their chests, right?"

"We didn't lead anyone to believe anything. We said they were stabbed, and they were. But that wasn't what killed them. These people were all dead when they were stabbed. And I might add that the New York Police Department does not generally release the sum total of its information when it comes to a serial killer."

Hannah showed genuine surprise and opened her mouth, but Fillingeri went on, holding up a hand to keep her from interrupting. "The reason we haven't made this matter public is that we've had nothing to say until now. This serial killer is working more rapidly than most, and it takes time for us to coordinate with the medical examiner's office. All we can say for sure now is that in each case the heart stopped before the knife entered the victim. I'm talking about the first eight, now. Tonight's two victims may show something else."

"The police have certainly done nothing to dispel the common belief that at least eight people have died in this city from knife wounds inflicted by a serial killer who paints their faces. Are you telling us now, Captain Fillingeri, that someone is stabbing dead people?"

"I'm telling you what the autopsies showed."

"Your autopsies turned up nothing but a negative fact? That the Yellow-Man victims did not die from knife wounds? How long have you known this?"

"Since the first victim."

"And you're now telling us that you don't have any idea what killed these people?"

"That's exactly what I'm telling you. The medical examiner is only as good as the information we give him, and we haven't had much to give him. We're required by law to run an autopsy if any death occurs under suspicious, unusual, or unexpected circumstances. Well, the Yellow-Man crimes met all those criteria. The medical examiner ran standard drug scans—cocaine, opiates, and so on—and he conducted standard studies of the organs. The result is nothing. Except that four of the victims had alcohol damage to their livers, and, in one case, the pancreas. But not enough to cause death."

"Then you don't even know that the men were murdered?"

Fillingeri hesitated, studying his hands again. "We think it's a fair inference that they were murdered. The circumstances. Common sense. The repeated pattern. The knifing. I don't think that even in New York we've got somebody going around painting corpses and knifing them as a prank. But right now, meaning as of today, the files are not classified as murder. We're calling them 'unclassified' deaths.''

"What does that mean?"

"It means we can't label as natural deaths these, er, events. It means we can't call them murder. Not yet, anyway."

"But you're handling the investigation," Hannah said. "And your department is homicide."

"I'm handling it now."

Hannah sat back in her chair and swiveled an inch or two, side to side, while she picked up a pen from the desk and gazed at it thoughtfully. "When did you take over the investigation of the Yellow-Man, er, events?"

"Tonight."

"Why tonight?"

Fillingeri kept his face arranged in a carefully bland mask of officialdom, but he stopped looking at his hands and faced the camera.

"Because the ninth victim, the man who died in Central Park tonight sometime around midnight or maybe a little later—he was in a Midtown North holding cell most of last week and got the regulation physical. He was in robust health. A man like that doesn't just keel over. This was the first victim we actually have a modest medical history on—the little scrap of history he picked up in jail.''

"Can you tell us anything about him? His name? Why he was being detained in jail?"

"I can tell you he was arraigned on petty theft charges and released on a P.R. bond—that's personal recognizance—on Friday. About his name, we've got to try to find family first. It's only been a few hours. But at least we know this guy's name and record.''

"I see," Hannah said, putting her pen quietly down on the desk. "May I ask what exactly is the status of the earlier victims from the medical examiner's point of view? They have no histories. Do they at least have names? And what's the bureaucracy surrounding nameless dead people with yellow faces? Where are they?"

Fillingeri didn't do anything obvious to show that he was uncomfortable, but his brown eyes suddenly weren't quite so wide open and his handsome face didn't look quite so much like he was the poster boy for the Policeman's Benevolent Association. He was usually close to perfect when presenting the police point of view on information he wanted to manage before the media got hold of it and put their own spin on it. From where I was sitting in the control room, it looked like his perfection had slipped a little. But help was on the way. A commercial.

"When a homeless person dies on the street," he said, shifting uncomfortably, "we, er, keep the body in the morgue, for two to four weeks, depending on how full the refrigerator is."

I cued Hannah to cut out, and she led gracefully into the commercial. Fillingeri breathed.

"Hannah, you're getting into an area not fit for TV," he said, frowning. "The city buries these unclaimed people in Potter's Field. We sometimes can't wait any longer than two weeks to get them under ground. We're sending bodies out there at the rate of fifty per week. Jesus, Hannah, this is all at taxpayer expense. It costs money to store these men. Here's the kind of grisly detail you don't want on your show: if we don't maintain the refrigerator at a precise temperature, between thirty-eight and forty-two degrees Fahrenheit, the limbs can freeze and snap off, or decomposition sets in. Storage is a costly business. And it costs money to bury these men. I can give you nasty statistics on pine boxes and rotting flesh. You want to put that on the air? A thousand homeless drop on the street every year."

"Don't play gross-out with me, Dennis," she said. "Snapping limbs won't make me faint. My eyelids won't even flutter." I cued her that we were coming out of commercial. "Captain," she said smoothly, picking up where she had left off before the break, "with a serial *painter* at work, wouldn't your department work outside the ordinary parameters concerning the homeless? Don't these victims have a special status because of the unique spectacle surrounding their deaths? You yourself have said that it's a fair inference that they were murdered."

"They're homeless. We follow policy."

"Surely that policy, as hard-hearted as it seems, was designed for the homeless who die *because* they are homeless—from exposure, or hunger, or something related specifically to the fact of their homelessness."

"Miss Van Stone, you make it sound like the police are responsible for social planning. What my men have with the homeless is more like social improvising. At least it's not chaos yet."

"But surely the hasty burial policy was not designed for home-less people who die at the hands of a human madman?"

Fillingeri abruptly held up a hand. "Wait a minute. If you look at the history of this particular brand of homicide, juries have not generally bought into that madman defense when it comes to se-rial killers. Look at Ted Bundy. Arthur Shawcross. And Albert DeSalvo. He claimed he was the Boston Strangler. When he was sentenced to life in prison on charges unrelated to the stranglings, his cellmates—his peers—took care of him. He was stabbed to death in a prison. They certainly didn't cut him any slack because he might be out of his mind. And look at the violent death of Jeffrey Dahmer in that Wisconsin prison. Serial killers are un-popular even among other murderers. Serial killers are evil, not crazy. Most juries, even self-constituted, ad hoc prison gangs who don't agree on anything else, still believe in old-fashioned things like the existence of evil. I'm working on these Yellow-Man deaths, and I believe in evil, too."

Hannah's posture was suddenly very correct. She was done with retracting her claws like a well-bred housecat. "Are you saying that a killer poses a moral question for the police?"

Behind me, Ike said, "Get him, Hannah." I don't know if she said it into Hannah's telex, or if she said it to herself.

Whichever it was, Hannah went for Fillingeri's throat. "You can't have it both ways, Captain Fillingeri. You say you're work-ing on these mysterious deaths. But you're transferring the corpses into the grave before you know what killed them. How would you answer criticism about such quick disposition of bod-ies when the cause of death is still unknown? Some community standards might say that these unclaimed corpses hold crucial information regarding that very 'evil' you mentioned."

"I think I've already tried to answer that question." Fillingeri's voice was soft. "It's a tough solution, but the reality of home-lessness in New York City is a tough problem."

"Captain Fillingeri, questions of evil are necessarily abstract." Hannah leaned her elbow on the arm of her chair. Changing di-rection. "What concrete information can you give us about the first eight victims you've already buried? You said that tonight's victim—the ninth—was known to you. Do you have names for any of the other victims?"

Fillingeri nodded. "Some of them. Of the first eight, we've got positive I.D. on five."

"How did you make those identifications?"

"Fingerprints were the fastest way. They were on national file, either because of criminal records or military service." Here Fillingeri treated the camera to a sad, sad smile. "Or both."

"Were any of the bodies claimed, by family or friends?"

"A couple were identified by a relative or an acquaintance. Not a single one was 'claimed,' meaning for burial. You see, these victims are what we call 'strays,' people who don't get reported missing in the first place and whose deaths rarely touch people who might have known them before they became strays."

"Don't these people have any family?"

"Some are people who strayed from their families on purpose: crackheads, can collectors, street people, winos, baggers, hitchhiker-types, crazies, drifters, prostitutes, junkies. When a serial killer gets started, these are the kinds of targets he chooses, and most times he sticks with that choice. They have no advocates, nobody to watch over them. It's like they're invisible to everyone but him."

"I can't help noticing that you say 'he,' when you speak of a serial killer."

"That's right. They're almost always men. As a matter of fact, they're usually white men between the ages of twenty-five and forty-five."

"Usually?"

"About ninety-nine percent of the time."

Hannah frowned. "You seem to have better statistics on this elusive killer than you have on the men he murdered."

At this point, as disgusted and fascinated as I was by what Fillingeri was saying, I had my own company's tough policy to deal with, like the ironclad rule of getting off the air on time. I nudged Ginger and glanced at the line clock. At the same moment, Ike spoke into her mouthpiece, to Hannah.

"Twenty seconds, Hannah. Wind it up and do the formula."

Two million viewers could not have had a clue that Hannah had a voice inside her ear telling her to get the hell off the air. She looked, as always, as though TV was just a thing that happened to her naturally—the way some people get freckles from the sun, Hannah gets TV from the cameras.

Without any outward sign of pressure whatsoever, she ended the interview, and incidentally got the last word, by telling Fillingeri that NTB News would look forward in the coming days to any information the police cared to release, especially if they were to release it in a timely fashion, and dismissed him with a nod. A natural conclusion to a slice of life.

As we closed the camera up tight on her at the desk at 8:58: 10, she said, "This is Hannah Van Stone, for *Morning Watch* and until next time, I'll be watching for you."

And *Morning Watch* went to black.

Headsets in the control room came off, pictures up on the monitor screens flickered into oblivion, and chairs got pushed away from consoles. The news clerks cleared out to get breakfast. Ginger collected an armload of videotapes and left to call her babysitter. The rest of the crew picked up copies of the script and coffee cups and two hard hours worth of news production trash, and beat it to their offices.

Ike sat at her console, fixed in a stare at the blank screens, her arms crossed under her breasts, not moving.

"Rough morning," I said. "But it was a good show. Hannah had Fillingeri holding on to the cliff with his fingernails. There will be some public howling about this 'unclassified' nonsense. For once we got caught with our pants *up*."

"What?"

"Never mind."

"Abby, let's look at that tape again."

"Which one? The live doctors or the dead one?"

"The live doctors."

"I think Ginger took it with her." I searched Ginger's console, but she had cleaned it as thoroughly as always. "Sorry. All gone. I'll track it down from Ginger or Sally or the National Desk."

She was still, sitting there like she was in a trance. "It's just that it's so strange, Abby, you know?"

"Death?"

"Well, life *and* death." She gave herself a little shake and stretched a hand out for the red rose still draped against the old gooseneck microphone. She held the flower briefly under her nose and then looked up at me. "Life and death. In Hektor's case, we have the two extremes on videotape. We've made him immortal both ways. Isn't that a thought?"

NINE

FILLINGERI DIDN'T even knock before he barged into the control room. He acknowledged Ike with a grim nod, but he gave me a sneer, the spontaneous kind, not the kind he learned at the Police Academy on East Twentieth Street. I bring out the real thing in Fillingeri.

"Abagnarro. What a treat." He eyed my face, which was as innocent as I could make it. "Where's your rubber nose and seltzer bottle?"

"I'm glad you asked, Captain. I messengered 'em to your office as soon as I heard how you're calling the Yellow-Man victims 'unclassified.' Thought you might be looking to add to your prop room over there at Midtown North."

"Don't start on me about that unclassified stuff. Your show got a break when I told Hannah as much as I did. I *chose* to open the bag on the air, with the full backing of the commissioner. But I don't have to defend policy or budget to you personally, Abagnarro, and God knows nobody could ever explain a medical technicality to somebody with his brains in his skates."

To my surprise, Ike piped up on my behalf. "You started it, Dennis. Is that what 'unclassified' amounts to? A medical technicality?"

"That's what I said on your goddam show."

"Not exactly in those words, you didn't. And, Dennis, the fact of the matter is, you *do* have to defend department policy. You help set that policy, and we're not just journalists—we're taxpayers. It's not like you hold this little private duchy down on Fifty-fourth Street and it's all yours to play with as you like. You hold your dukedom at our sufferance."

"That's a nice speech, Ike," the Duke said, "but you and I both know this city is not run on ideals. It's run on personal clout, from the highest levels down to the scum on the street."

"I happen to have plenty of clout, as well as ideals," she said, a dangerous gleam in her luminous, mismatched eyes. "And I'm going to pursue this autopsy hoo-hah on national television until we get an answer concerning your department's clear failure to take responsible steps against a serial killer. If the medical examiner can't figure out what killed these people—*people,* not scum, Dennis—then maybe you're not giving them your full effort. You said it yourself—the medical examiner is only as good as the information you give him.''

"We gave him what we had. We can't give him what we don't have.''

"Yeah, *but.*" Ike moved restlessly in her chair. "But, what does it mean? That the victims' hearts stopped before they were knifed? Stopped how? You mean like a heart attack?''

"As far as I know, that's just an expression of the timing of the events. The M.E. doesn't know what made the hearts stop.''

Fillingeri paused, like he was unsure about whether to give Ike more.

She saw the hesitation. "Well? What'd you leave out?''

"It's nothing. Certainly nothing for quotation. Just something the M.E. said. He was only kidding.''

"What?''

"He said it looked like the victims had just stopped living. That's what the hearts looked like—just shut down.'' He ran a hand through his thick hair. "Like they were scared to death.''

"People don't die of fright, Dennis. If they did, this city would be a ghost town by now.''

"The M.E. said it, Ike, not me. New Yorkers don't scare that easy.''

I put my hands together in the praying position, nodded wisely, and tried to look like the Buddha. "Be careful how you dismiss the power of fear,'' I said. "You could have killed Sigmund Freud with greenery. He was terrified of ferns.''

Both Ike and Fillingeri stared at me, almost like they were Freud and I was a particularly lush fern.

Ike broke the silence by saying, "Jesus, Abby, where'd you learn that?''

"Airport TV, baby.''

She shook her head, tossing her curls, really serious about it like she was trying to clear her sinuses. She turned away from me and seemed to be sharing a moment of unexpected connection with the Duke of Fifty-fourth Street, united briefly by their Freud complex.

Finally she said to him, "What you were saying. Some New Yorkers scare plenty. But their hearts don't just stop for nothing."

"I didn't come in here to argue matters of the heart with you, Ike." He tried an ironic smile on her and turned to me. "Or to throw pies with this clown."

I nodded understandingly. "You probably want to get in some practice on the range first. I'll be ready when you are."

He made a noise. "The day you do anything as heroic as throw a pie." He tucked his chin down toward his perfect blue silk tie and closed his eyes to slits, probably making up his mind to tell us why he had invaded the control room in the first place. He opened his eyes wide and looked up. "It'd be really something if I had to flash my shield at you two. I'm investigating a murder and you both have information I need."

Ike slapped her palm down on her console. "Oh, now it's a murder. Now it's not unclassified."

"I'm talking about Dr. Stefanopolis."

"His death was definitely a murder? Don't you have to wait for the autopsy?"

"You're twisting it all around, Ike. I'm not letting any technicality interfere with how I look into these cases. I just can't officially call them murders without the M.E.'s say-so. There's mandated and sufficient communication between our departments, I'll have you know. I'm not a solo act."

Ike rocked back in her chair and looked at the ceiling, waving the red rose gently at her side. "Tell me something, Dennis. How many tons of paper do you use at the precinct to get to the point where you don't know what you're doing?"

I laughed. But Fillingeri didn't.

"That's not fair and you know it," he said. "And if you're so goddam keen on the police doing their job, stop grilling me. It's supposed to be the other way around."

"You want to grill me?"

"I want to *talk* to you. Cop to citizen. Not cop to journalist. I'm simply going to ask a few questions, and you're just a couple of witnesses with no special status, and we don't need to waste your time or mine on any cracks about my department or on any high-flown bleeding liberal speeches about the homeless or about First Amendment crapola.''

"The only information we have," Ike said, "has already been made available to millions of viewers. In fact, we had more First Amendment crapola than any other network this morning. We're doing our job.''

Fillingeri grabbed the back of a chair, pulled it out from under the sound technician's board, and spun it halfway around, parking himself on the edge of the gray cushion. "Doing your job." He drummed his fingers on the edge of the board and narrowed his brown eyes at me. "Abagnarro, I'd like to know how much you get paid for living off the First Amendment."

"A lot more than you get for enforcing the law, of which the First Amendment is a part," I said. "I'd show you my pay stub, only I don't know CPR."

Keeping his level gaze on me, Fillingeri opened and closed his right fist a few times, tapping it on the sound board, squeezing some substance visible only to him, maybe an imaginary pay stub—his or mine, I didn't know.

"Freud," he said, the squeezing operation apparently concluded to his satisfaction. "Listen, all I want is what happened before the show with those doctors, and I want the tape of the interview you carried. I'm not even going to ask why you identified the dead man as Hektor Stefanopolis on the air without my permission."

Ike smiled at him. "We had the next-of-kin's permission. Really, Dennis, all we did was ask nicely and the family was very gracious about it. You could learn something from that."

"You on terms with the family?"

"No. But I have lovely manners, and I know the rules."

"Yeah." He tapped his fist again on the sound board. "Use some of those manners and tell me about the doctors before, during, and after the taping of that interview. You know, like when they arrived, what they ate and drank, did they have an argument—you know the kind of thing I'm after."

"They arrived before Abby did, so I'd say it was about three-thirty. Did you check with security downstairs?"

He nodded. "Go on."

"Then I took them to the Green Room and talked them through the questions we'd be asking them during the interview—they wrote a book about medical research. And Rubin Gorman did their faces. You know Rubin?''

"Yeah. The fat guy.''

"Rubin has other qualities, Dennis. Anyway, they talked a little bit with our other guests—Hilda Murray, a glassblower from Columbia University, and Anthony Jones, from NASA—and they ate and drank the usual stuff in the Green Room.'' She touched the red rose to her lips and seemed to be contemplating the fragrance. "But, Grandmother, what odd questions you have. What's this about what the doctors ate and drank?''

"Off the record?''

"Until I get it from a different source.''

Fillingeri seemed to go into conference with himself. Then he nodded, apparently to his inner conferee, and said, "Dr. Stefanopolis did not have a mark on his body. No knife wound like the others. No nothing. No bruises, no gunshot wound, no scratches, no nothing. Nada. Zilch. A great big blank. Bupkiss.''

"So,'' Ike said, still breathing the rose, "you're looking for poison.''

"We're looking for anything,'' he said gruffly. "The doctor didn't get killed by the stink down there in the alley.''

Since I had not been in the Green Room for the pretaping food fest, I had nothing to contribute but a growing conviction that Fillingeri was not only at a complete loss regarding Hektor's death but was also personally embarrassed about it, like maybe he was wishing he hadn't waited to step into the picture until the ninth victim got it.

"Captain,'' I said, "you haven't even got a place to start, have you?''

"With the other Yellow-Men, no. With Hektor Stefanopolis, yes. Rule number one about murder, Abagnarro, is that to kill somebody, you have to get close enough to do it. Make sense so far?''

I nodded, a good pupil in the Dennis Fillingeri School for Cretins.

"With Hektor Stefanopolis, unlike the other men with painted faces, we can start with people who were close to him,'' he explained, making sure I was sound on the fundamentals before we went on to advanced material.

"You mean like family, co-workers, maybe even co-authors?" I said.

"Very good. I'll bet you can read without moving your lips, too. But also people who could get physically close enough to him to kill him. Like the people who saw him last. Like the people you had on your show today. Like the people who worked on your show today. Maybe even like you, Abagnarro."

I made a noise.

"I'm not going to ask you to translate that into human," Fillingeri said. "What I can ask you is did you know Hektor Stefanopolis before he came on *Morning Watch?* How'd he get on the show?"

"I didn't know him from Adam," I said. "And I still don't. How he got on the show is he wrote a book. I hardly ever kill people who write books."

"Somebody killed him—between your studio and that alley. That's not much distance, and that's not very many people. At least we've narrowed it down to a small group. With the previous Yellow-Men, we've had the whole city of New York, and maybe commuters. Now we want to narrow it further."

"And you're looking for poison on the twenty-seventh floor of this building?"

"I'm looking for motive on the twenty-seventh floor of this building."

"I don't know of any motive to kill Hektor. In fact, if someone had to get it, I'd have picked the other brother. You know what he does? He races—"

"Dennis," Ike said, interrupting me with a fierce frown, "your best bet on food and drink will be Rubin. He was in the Green Room most of the time with them."

"I've got an officer taking his statement now. And I know about the race cars."

Ike was waving her rose around in the air. "It's no crime to race cars. I wish you'd stop it, Abby." One of the petals dropped off the rose and fell on the carpet. She bent to pick up the little red slice of petal. "I have a question, Dennis. How did the cops find Hektor's body so fast?"

"Nine-one-one from a dog walker." Fillingeri rolled his eyes. "I couldn't believe it when I saw the dog—a white poodle with golden bows on his ears and a rhinestone necklace. I thought those little French fright wigs just dumped on the carpet and never needed walking.''

I swiveled my chair so I could stretch my legs into the aisle. ''I have a friend who owns a blue iguana. That thing crawled up the leg of the table one night at dinner and pissed all over my salad.''

Fillingeri sighed. ''Abagnarro, although I'd like to meet the animal that pissed in your food, I hope you're not leading up to one of your stories.''

''I'm not. Unless you want to hear the one about the science convention and the ugly man?''

He brushed his hand across the console like he was clearing off a gnat. ''That chestnut. It's not very funny.''

''You probably just didn't understand it.''

''You know, I hope you're right. It almost makes me glad to think I didn't understand that story. That would mean that you and I don't think alike. I like that.''

''I could explain the joke to you.''

''No, thanks. What I want you to explain, either of you, is everything that happened next, outside the Green Room, including a copy of that interview. I don't mean a transcript; I mean a videotape.''

Now Ike heaved a sigh, dropped the rose on the console, and gave Fillingeri a verbal guided tour of her morning with the doctors, up to and including the point where Aristotle had given her his phone number. That made Fillingeri's face get a little darker under his tan, but he let the fact pass without comment.

My only contribution was that I thought there was something wrong with Hektor's eyes, and that I thought he was a nice guy. ''Guests seldom thank the director, or even understand what the director is doing for them,'' I said. ''Hektor understood.''

''Congratulations, Abagnarro, you should have been a doctor yourself,'' Fillingeri said. ''There sure as hell was something wrong with Hektor Stefanopolis's eyes. They call it glaucoma.'' He shifted in the chair. ''By the way, about Hektor understanding what a director does—I've never seen you do anything. Don't you just sit there and look at the pretty monitors and tell people to do things they already know they should do?''

''That about describes it, Captain.'' I pulled my legs back out of the aisle and put them up on the gray cushion of the chair across from me. I smiled contentedly. "What a life, huh? The only difficult part is making sure I don't crease my trousers."

Ike stood up and started for the door.

"Are we finished, Ike?" Fillingeri said, barring her way with his arm.

"I am. You and Abby can't resist playing cowboys and Indians. I don't know what your problem is with each other, but it's counterproductive and..." She gave us each a salvo from her mistily beautiful eyes. "If it has anything to do with me, you should keep it to yourselves. It's not fair to make me watch the games you play."

She looked down at Fillingeri's arm, which he moved, and she left, closing the door behind her.

Fillingeri and I sat in silence for a moment.

"I wasn't playing games," he said.

"I was. She's right."

He stood up.

I stood up.

"Abagnarro, you're fond of old Sicilian sayings, right?"

"So?"

"Nun perdere tempo cu li Siciliani; ce tutto di perdiri e nente di quadagrani."

"I didn't know you were Sicilian, Captain."

"I'm not. My family's from the part of the boot that looks like it's about to kick Sicily out of the Mediterranean."

"Ah. Well, here's a little geography update for you, Captain. Sicily's still there." I smiled, one of those tight papal smiles that could mean anything. "You think I'm trying to get in your way. Maybe I am." I lost the smile. "But consider this: you have a lousy way of asking for what you want; it's that nasty habit of sticking your hand out to grab."

I went to the door of the control room. It occurred to me that giving him what he was grabbing for would give me what I wanted: less of his company.

"You chose the wrong Italian proverb," I said. "There is something to be gained from Sicilians. If you'll please follow me, Duke, I'll be happy to get you that little videotape you requested."

It was nice, because he really had no choice but to be killed by my kindness. It was like having a highly intelligent doberman on my leash: he could bite my head off, sure, but then who'd bring him the nice pot roast he had his eye on down the hall behind the locked door that I had the key to?

We walked along the Tube, Fillingeri making a point of not walking behind me, and stopped at Sally Goldberg-Petit's office door, which was open. She wasn't there, but Fillingeri gave the brass nameplate on her door a good look.

"How do you pronounce that?" Fillingeri asked, looking at the name like it was Chinese.

"Like in the story of the world's laziest man."

A pained look descended over Fillingeri's handsome features. "I hate your stories, Abagnarro."

"Just listen. There was this really lazy guy who brought home a ferociously nasty pit bull—worse than most of them, a real bastard. So his wife starts crying and says, 'Ernie, what're we gonna do with a dog like that?'" I looked at Fillingeri and leaned against the door, pretending I was Ernie. "'Do with it? What do you mean do with it? That's the beauty of this dog, Alice. We don't have to do anything. Jeez, the guy who sold it to me said we shouldn't even *pet it.*"

"That supposed to be funny, Abagnarro?"

"It's supposed to be educational. Sally Goldberg-*pet it.*"

"Thanks. Now I know."

"And I bet you'll never forget." I entered Sally's office and glanced around at the newsjunk and piles of videotapes. "Sally should have all the stuff from last night's killing in the park, as well as what we shot in the alley this morning. She should also have a copy of the long interview with the doctors, because she's working on a piece for tomorrow."

Sally arrived at her door, with a can of Diet Coke that she was rolling back and forth across her forehead. Her short dark hair was frizzy from being outside in the steam bath of the alley, and her hands and chin were dirty. "Abby, if you're looking for my can of yellow paint, I threw it out. What do you think, I'm stupid?"

"No, we're looking for clues about your sex life, Sally. Captain Fillingeri's interested in getting close to people on this floor."

Fillingeri forced his face not to react, but his broad shoulders tensed under the starched white brilliance of his shirt. Despite the starch, his shirt couldn't disguise the fact that Fillingeri pumps as much iron in the police gym on Twentieth Street as any other member of the force in Manhattan.

"Forget the clues," Sally said, openly eyeing the effect of the iron. "I don't have a sex life, Abby. How could I? With my hours, the only guys I ever see are Arden Boyer, who almost certainly goes to bed with his mirror, and Fred Loring, who's certainly getting it on with his computer, and you."

"Me? What's the matter with me?"

"You're still in the Honeymoon Suite with Ike, if only in your heart. You are a U.A.S."

"What's that?" I asked suspiciously, hyper-aware that Fillingeri was listening to this catalog of NTB male losers.

"Un Available Stud."

I smiled sweetly first at Sally, then turned it on Fillingeri.

"Let's get this over with, Abagnarro," the captain said, or maybe snarled. "I've got better things to do than listen to kindergarten sex."

I asked Sally for the interview tape and turned her over to Fillingeri.

"I'll take you down to editing," she told him, "and we'll dub the tape you want. I can't let you have the original." She gave Fillingeri a good, hard, assessing look. "I wonder if you're an A.S."

As I left her office, I said, "You left off one 'S'."

I walked a few paces down the Tube and stopped at Ike's door. She was seated at her desk, watching the video playback machine beside her computer. There they all were again, Hektor and Aristotle and Olivia and J.D.

I stepped inside and planted myself on her couch, shoving aside some of her newstoys, including a piece of charred wood from the Waco Apocalypse of David Koresh.

"You found the tape," I said.

"Bo Peep could've found this tape. There must be eighty copies by now, all over the building. With the cops and the other NTB broadcasts breathing down our necks, we'll be dubbing videotape until the end of time."

"Why are you so interested in this interview?" I asked. "Or am I just being obtuse about Aristotle the Great? Is he Fillingeri's replacement?"

She gave me a look like I was a blue iguana crawling toward her salad.

"Abby, it would be impossible to replace Captain Fillingeri because Captain Fillingeri never got a place, not that it's any of your business. And, for your information, I'm looking at this tape because it's all I've got to look at until my meager staff of producers brings me something else to look at."

"Like Fillingeri's head on a platter, for that autopsy baloney? Unclassified deaths?"

"That would do for a start. Or some hard information on burying a person who's homeless and lacking the formality of a death certificate. I've asked Sally to put together a piece on New York City's Potter's Field for this Friday. It's out on some scrubby island in the East River, or Long Island Sound. We'll send off the week on Time with a visit to the eternal resting place of the address-impaired."

"Kind of a bummer farewell to *Morning Watch*'s week on Time."

"Yeah, well, death's a bummer," she said, her tone sharp. "And burial's a bummer, especially if you happen to be homeless. You die homeless, you get buried homeless. You get to be homeless for eternity. St. Peter won't even have to ask any questions when you arrive at the Pearly Gates. He'll take one look and say, 'Ah, a homeless person. Go to Hell.'" She ran both hands through her blond curls, pulling a little as she went. "This whole Yellow-Man thing stinks of corroded bureaucracy."

"A policy is a policy is a policy in the Naked City—the Bare Apple. How many homeless people do you think there are here?"

She stopped pulling at her hair and grabbed a sheet of paper off her desk, tugging it out from under her keyboard, and read from it. "The homeless population of New York City is greater than the population of Greenland. That's a whole country, Abby."

"Well, yeah, but it's not much of a country. I mean, it's too cold."

"Try this one, then. The homeless population of New York is bigger than the population of Bermuda—another whole country. You can't say that one's too cold to count. The same with the Virgin Islands, the same with French Guiana, the same with goddam Monaco. Now there's a nifty comparison: New York's homeless population amounts numerically to the princes, nabobs, and playboys of Monaco. Ha! The March of Progress.''

"Ike, give me a number.''

"I'll give you an American number. You ever heard of a little community called Galveston?''

"As in Galveston, Texas?''

"Bingo. That's the size of our homeless population. On our streets—the population, the entire population, man, woman, and child, of Galveston Fucking Texas. Sixty thousand humans. My hat's off to the Big Apple. We've absorbed a decent-sized city into our midst without most of us feeling anything but a slight inconvenience. And you know what? If all sixty thousand vanished tomorrow, nobody'd stand up and cheer about how the view had changed. We might not even notice. Betcha people would notice if the population of Galveston disappeared.''

The videotape reached the end of the interview, ran past the junk studio footage, and then the high-pitched screech came out of the machine as it automatically rewound the tape. Like punctuation for Ike's lecture.

Here, I thought, is a woman who needs cheering up.

"I don't suppose you'd like to hear the story about the science convention and the ugly man now, would you?''

"Don't be repulsive.''

"Then let's look at that tape together. Maybe the car crash will give me a laugh.''

"You've started to get a thing about Aristotle. What's your problem with him?''

"The part where he plays around with death machines. The part where he puts himself inside the death machines and drives them around in a circle trying to give himself a thrill, so he can feel alive. I stopped thinking of him as a doctor as soon as I saw that tape.''

"Abby, you of all people should understand the lure of speed. You skate like, well, like lightning.''

I was stunned. "How can you compare that to auto racing?''

"The way I just did—the thrill of speed.''

"They're not the same. I, for example, am extremely unlikely to plow into a wall, flip over several times, and burst into flames.'' I put my feet up on her coffee table. "In fact, it's extremely unlikely that anything bad will happen to me on skates. I'm too good to take a fall.''

Her hand shot out and she pointed a finger at me. "That's it. That's what you have in common. It's that arrogance. You think you're so hot you can't lose. It's the same with Aristotle.''

"Play that tape again, Ike, and see if you think my speed skating can compare to that idiot's pastime. We're not even the same animal.''

"Oh, yes you are. It's that animal thing that's left over from when you were swinging through trees and the ape who swung the fastest and farthest got to plant his seed in the choicest female.''

"And just where were you choice females while all this tree swinging was going on?''

"Inventing a way to walk upright so we could get out of the jungle.''

"Are you saying that females were the first to walk upright?''

"Archaeology says it—the skeleton is called 'Lucy,' not 'Luciano.'" She pushed the play button, fast-forwarded through the book talk, and resumed normal speed at the point where J.D introduced the crash tape. We watched Aristotle's car flip again into the infield at the Pocono Raceway and we watched him step out unhurt.

"What a crock," I said. "He was thinking he'd never felt so alive. I'll just bet. What a two-ton crock.''

"If you're such an expert on Dr. Aristotle Stefanopolis—or apes—why don't you tell me what he was really thinking?''

I stood and took the remote from her hand. I rewound a bit and then paused the tape.

"Okay. Remember he's a doctor, Ms. Tygart. I'll tell you what Doctor Death and Demise was thinking.'' I played the monumental series of flips in slow motion and ad-libbed some narration, calling upon the deepest reserves of my medical vocabulary as the car somersaulted in slow, bumpy circles: "There he goes, and he's thinking: 'Oh, my God, my shoulder.' And again: 'Holy cow, that was my pancreatic artery.' Again: 'Oh, no, my right femur.' Watch this: 'Christ, my gluteus maximus.' And now, as the fender goes flying: 'Shit, my lymph nodes hurt.' This one's great, Ike: 'Oh, my God, my rectal thermometer.' Finally, look at all that smoke: 'Jesus, somebody bring me a bed pan.'''

As Aristotle stepped, still in slow motion, out of the Plexiglas-and-metal trash heap that had once been a car, I tossed the remote onto Ike's lap and said, "It's a little hard to believe he was thinking, 'Wow, I feel so alive.'"

Ike put her head down on her desk. "God. Why'd we leave the jungle?"

TEN

FILLINGERI WAS around the Emerald City most of the morning, talking to the staff and poking and prying in Studio 57, the Green Room, the control room, and the editing rooms. The ripest fruit hanging from the grapevine was that he had double-teamed Tony Jones in the Green Room with a couple of homicide lieutenants, and that both Aristotle Stefanopolis and Olivia Quintinale had been issued invitations to join a little get-together at Midtown North. And Hilda Murray was receiving guests in blue uniforms in her lab at Columbia. The only member of our staff who seemed to be having any special difficulty shaking off official attention was Rubin Gorman, our already overworked makeup artist, but according to the rumors, that was only because he was the closest thing we had to a guardian for the Green Room. But he'd been in and out of our guest suite tending to the anchors, and, rumor said, the doctors and the man from NASA and the glassblower had been relatively free to play tag in the hall, if that's how they'd spent their time before the show.

But Fillingeri and his crew weren't as much of a pest as NTB's own *Evening Watch*. Since that program has about six times our audience, they all think that those of us who work on the morning show are untalented, unwanted, untrained, probably unwashed, and certainly unprincipled. That morning I showed them our un-cooperative side, but not until they asked for it, in the person of Tom Hitt, their Broadcast Producer and Executive Shark.

A few associate producers from *Evening Watch* had already come around, wanting to borrow our videotapes and our memo-ries and so on. They were asking who we liked for the murder: The brother, the one who drove race cars and obviously enjoyed dangerous pursuits? The ex-wife, wasn't it always the wife? That glassblower with the red fingers, and wasn't that suspicious, those red fingers, could she have been overdoing it with turpentine to get the yellow paint off? Wouldn't that make her fingers red? Or did we think Tony Jones had gone after Hektor because...and that's where the speculation stopped, because nobody had even a smell of a motive for Hektor's murder.

Some of the *Evening Watch* sleuths, the ones who prided themselves on not belonging to the Geraldo Rivera Lurid School of Broadcasting, wanted to know if there was anything from the director's point of view that would give them a lead on the story of Hektor Stefanopolis's having joined the Yellow-Man Club, and when I told them no, they went off and read the *Times* or called their brokers.

I know *Evening Watch* also talked to other people from our show, but the head shark came straight for me. And he had an entirely different approach to the doctor's death. At first I thought the shark was merely engaging in our usual heckling contest, but I should have known that he smelled blood.

I was on the phone, ordering a maintenance check on the remote link that had failed before the show and forced us to dummy the Q and A between Hannah and Arden, when the shark entered my office.

Tom Hitt—Ike's opposite number on the evening program and a media giant at age twenty-eight—had a reputation for a mean spirit and a notched belt that included manipulating the *Evening Watch* White House reporter into sleeping with him so he wouldn't send her to the Asia Bureau to do stories on the Chinese bicycle industry. He began my torture session by saying, "If your I.Q. were any lower, Abagnarro, we could use your brain to clean blackboards."

Since he started it, he was fair game.

I stood up. What was fair about that is that Tom's ten inches shorter than I am. "If you were an inch shorter, Tom, you couldn't even reach the blackboard."

"I can't reach it now." Tom's too important to be bothered by the fact that he's five-three and has to buy his pants in the boys' department. "But since the only menial task I ever do is wash my hands in the men's room, and I can reach my own hands just fine, who cares?"

"That's 'manual,' not menial."

"Oh, yeah. I still do that myself, too."

"What do you want, Tom? You think I'm having a sale in here on ladders?"

He snorted. "That's not a bad idea, even for you. You could probably use the cash. I hear you got mugged."

I looked down my nose at the top of his head. "Your ears can pick up gossip from all the way down there?"

"People will often get down on their knees for a chance to hobnob with me."

"Then it wasn't Ike who told you about the mugging. She wouldn't get on her knees for you if she thought you had the answer to the riddle of the universe."

A kind of far-away gleam entered his gray eyes, usually steely and dead like an old crocodile's. "The Untouchable Ike Tygart. There may come a day for even that, Abby."

"Does the phrase 'Get out of my office' have any meaning for you, Tom?"

"Oh, I wouldn't dream of staying here." He glanced around at my stuff, sighing ever so minutely at the meagerness of my one and only Emmy, which, when I followed his gaze, I noticed really needed dusting. Tom has four Emmys in his statuary collection, all nice and shiny, lined up in a tidy row on a ruthlessly dusted cherry credenza with a mirrored surface that multiplies the images. He also has a Peabody, a knickknack I'll never get a chance to hold my breath over when they bend close to the microphone and say, "And the winner is..."

"I only came down this way, Abby, to see what you could tell me about the mugging. I don't want you to think I'm interested in the thugs you choose to carouse with on your way to work. I'm interested because *Evening Watch* got the grapevine flash that your personal thief was at the scene of last night's first Yellow-Man, the one in the park."

"Then it must have been Ginger who told you."

"That's what I mean about your I.Q., Abby. You jump to fatuous conclusions. The spy in your camp happens to be one of your ambitious news clerks, thinking that he could buddy up to me and get a real job on my show. Ginger Peloshian wouldn't give me the time of day."

I looked at my wrist. "It's ten thirty-one. Time for you to leave."

"But what about the mugging? *Evening Watch* is going after that guy."

"The mugger?"

"Yes. The word is that you actually had a conversation with the guy before he bounced you on the sidewalk and walked away with your family jewels."

A shadow fell across the doorway. Ike stood there, flashing me an urgent message from her green and blue eyes.

"The jewels are just where the family left them," I said, although I would have added something choice I once heard in a New York Giants locker room if Ike hadn't been standing there. "And there's nothing else to tell. He took my money and ran, that's all. There's eight million stories like mine in the Naked City."

"Can't you describe him or anything, I mean, beyond what your crew got on tape in the park? What did he say to you?"

"Gee, you know, my mind's a blank, Tom. It must be post-mugging trauma syndrome or something. Or maybe it's like you said about my I.Q. Suddenly I just can't think."

Tom turned and walked out the door, brushing against the blue silk thing Ike was wearing. I could hear the touch from where I stood, five or six feet away.

In the Tube, he turned back and looked at me.

"Abby, I may talk to the owner about your unwillingness to cooperate with his network's flagship news broadcast. Othello Armitage likes team players."

"You're scaring me, Tom. I don't think that's going to help my amnesia any."

He squeezed his eyes almost closed, like he could buzz my hair with the bolt of heat he was sending out through the narrowed slits. "We're committing our resources to this story. I give Hannah and Ike great credit for getting that interview with Captain Fillingeri. But *Evening Watch* is going to own the Yellow-Man story."

"Well, good," I said. "Then you won't have any time to think up the answer to the riddle of the universe." I sat back down in my chair. "Happy hunting. Stay busy. What are you gonna do? Start at the Battery and work your way north, block by block, looking at hands for traces of yellow paint?"

"No, that would be a waste of my I.Q." He switched to a cryptic smile, the kind intended to show that the interior designer who had worked on the furnishing of Tom's skull was the kind specializing in trick mirrors, hidden staircases, false-bottomed chairs, and slick hardware. "I've got several ideas."

"I wouldn't know anything about ideas, what with my I.Q. and my memory loss." I glanced significantly at Ike's figure, backlit for me from the fluorescent lighting in the Tube, and tapped my forehead. "But up here, Tom, is a videotape you'll never get to see—some guys don't have to know the answer to the riddle of the universe."

I had the satisfaction of seeing the smug look on his face disappear for a fraction of a moment. Then he walked out of sight down the Tube.

Ike stepped into my office and flopped onto my couch.

"What's this stuff about the universe?"

"Tom's thinking of submitting his coverage of Yellow-Man for a Nobel Prize in astronomy."

She made a noise, not a dainty one. "He's trying to steal my idea."

"About astronomy?"

"About your mugger."

"Tex?"

"How many muggers do you have, Abby? Of course I mean Tex."

I got up and closed my door. "Not so loud, Ike. I don't think Tom has the name yet. His gossip, not unlike himself, is a little short."

She smiled. "I used to think Tom couldn't help being the size of one of the smaller Vienna Choirboys. But lately I've decided that he stunted his growth when he took all those ego pills."

I smiled back at her. It was a rare moment for us, when the timing on smiles worked this well. "So all the producers at NTB News are now volunteer detectives? How come?"

"With *Evening Watch* I think it's that they finally have a victim they approve of. Worthy, you know? A doctor—moreover, a white doctor, a rich white doctor, a rich and prominent white specialist who wrote a book. Lots of cultural goodies."

"Some of the other victims were white."

"Yeah, but no homeless white man gets as high a news score as a white man with a pricey address. Not from *Evening Watch*."

"Maybe so, Ike. But I suspect the real reason for Tom's interest is that Yellow-Man has turned into one of those what-the-fuck stories. You know, are these serial killings or something else? Are the police hiding something? Is the medical examiner practicing voodoo? It reminds me of the flap over Nancy Reagan and astrology in the White House. Remember how *Evening Watch* milked that story? They loved it because they got to flex their eyebrows and skirt the edges of editorializing, show America how much smarter television is than government.''

"But Nancy Reagan was before Tom's time, before what I think of as the Napoleonic Complex Era.''

"I know. But Tom's on board the train of tradition and Yellow-Man is now an *Evening Watch* kind of story, the kind they've always secretly loved while outwardly clicking their tongues. They hide the *National Enquirer* inside their copies of *The Washington Post.* You, on the other hand, don't usually go ga-ga just because some aspect of American public life looks like Halloween. What gives?''

"With me, it's two things. Number one, I feel a little responsible, because I got Hektor on the show and therefore in a position to be killed in that alley.''

"That's Fillingeri's 'you gotta get close to a person' theory warping your brain. You can't blame yourself because Hektor was on the spot when somebody decided to kill him.''

"I don't, exactly. But somewhere I feel a responsibility. That's not the same as guilt. You know what I'm talking about—you're the one who explained to me the difference between guilt and responsibility, after the divorce.''

I looked down at the surface of my desk, not seeing the clutter. I was seeing the sad look on her face when she had found out about my "responsibility" with another woman.

"Let's not go over that again, Abby. I only brought it up to explain how I feel about Hektor. The other thing is the bomb Fillingeri dropped about the autopsies and the burials—cut 'em up and pop 'em in the ground as fast as the city can. 'Unclassified' is what we Missourians call 'warm road apples.' I don't mean to go ballistic or anything, but I think we should make a decent effort to find Tex. He said he wanted to talk to you about killing, and that was right after he'd been in the park with Yellow-Man number nine. If it turns out that Tex is a red herring, well, I've got a couple of other things to try.''

"Like what?''

"Come with me." She stood, and I could hear the swish of her silk again, but this time it sounded pretty. "Let's go see Fred Loring."

"Is he conducting free seances?" I smiled at her again, but this time a little guardedly. "Why are you being so nice to me?"

"Because you're the man who was mugged by the man who may know what we want to know. In fact, he may *be* the man we want to know." She winked at me, with the blue eye open. "But be careful what you say around Fred. He gossips with Tom."

"Fred doesn't gossip with anyone, unless it's the spirit world. You can't call the stuff that comes out of Fred's mouth gossip. He'll probably just end up telling Tom that the killer is a Gemini, with his moon in Virgo, and that the *Kama Sutra* is out to get him."

She laughed.

We strolled companionably along the Tube together until we reached the Green Room, where we stopped. Fillingeri was seated on one of the makeup chairs, facing Anthony Jones, Ph.D., NASA's one-man travelling quartz ball show.

"Tony," I said, surprised to see he was still there. "Are you renting space here?"

The look on his face was not happy.

"Abby, tell this policeman that I'm not the Boston Strangler."

I laughed. I took a seat on the coffee table, next to the steel NASA box. "Captain Fillingeri's not looking for the Boston Strangler. He's looking for the New York Unclassified." I looked at Fillingeri. "What are you, the NYPD's Bad Will Ambassador?"

Fillingeri's face was not as unhappy as Tony's. "Nobody said you were a killer, Dr. Jones. But the guard down there in the lobby says you left the building just before the Stefanopolis brothers and Olivia Quintinale, around five-thirty. And you came back inside around five forty-five, before Ike sent her commando camera crew to the alley. That doesn't make you a killer, but it could make you a valuable witness."

"I went out to smoke a cigarette," Tony said. "There's a no-smoking policy in this building. All I did was stand outside the big green doors and light up. I was in sight of the guard the whole time. Ask him. I didn't go anywhere near the alley."

"How'd you get back upstairs to the twenty-seventh floor?" I said. "Carl Honeyman wouldn't allow even me up without I.D."

Tony shrugged, like it was no big deal. "Since I was already signed in on the logbook before I left the building, Carl issued me a temporary badge to get back in. He's done it before when I've been on the show."

I swore. I shook my head. "God, a congressional subcommittee must be writing the security manual for this building."

Fillingeri gave me a look. "The security in this building stacks up fine, Abagnarro. But what about your own? The word is you got mugged. Which is what I hear but which is what I don't believe."

"You don't believe I was mugged?"

"Nope. Not you."

"Why not?"

"I don't know what you know about making television, but I know what you know about New York: you navigate the streets of this town as well as anyone. If you got mugged, it was on purpose. Which I don't believe. So you weren't mugged."

"Well, that's good to know. What a relief. Now all I have to worry about is the magician who made my money and keys disappear."

"Did you report this alleged crime to the proper authorities?"

I gave him a look. "I don't know any proper authorities."

"I'm sure that's supposed to mean something, Mr. Television Director, but right now I'm too busy to work out the frantic convolutions of your mind. Get out of here and let me work."

"People are so interested in my mind today. I wonder why that is?" I crossed my legs at the ankles, getting comfortable. "If Tony had a ringside seat to this murder, I see no reason why we shouldn't hear what he has to say. He's our guest, not yours. NASA has nothing to gain by sucking up to the NYPD."

Tony flipped a hand impatiently. "I didn't see anything, no matter who's asking. Aristotle and the woman caught a cab going uptown, and, if you want me to tattle, it looked like they were having an argument. I don't know what about. Hektor started walking south. I went back inside. I went up in the elevator. I went to the Green Room. That's it."

Fillingeri ran his hand through his hair. "You didn't happen to follow Hektor into the alley did you, Jones?"

"No. I already said that."

"You didn't see anyone else around?"

"No."

"Didn't hear anything?"

"No. I mean, nothing but what you'd expect to hear. You know, traffic."

"The security guard says he wasn't watching the green doors while you were outside."

Tony slumped in the chair. "That's just great."

"Today was the first time you met Hektor Stefanopolis?" Fillingeri said.

Tony sat up straighter in his chair. "No."

Fillingeri pounced on it immediately. "You knew Stefanopolis?"

"Only slightly. Hardly at all. His brother Aristotle worked on the medical debriefing team for astronauts up until about two years ago. You know, checking the effect of weightlessness on the neurological system and so on. Aristotle was one of the chief advisers on the ground, and I saw him around KSC. We played golf with Hektor once when he was down in Florida for a vacation. Once. We played golf once."

"KSC?"

"Kennedy Space Center."

"Did you and Aristotle reminisce about old times this morning, talk about the project, anything like that?"

"I'd really rather not bring all this up during a murder investigation, Captain, because it's all ancient history and completely irrelevant, but Aristotle Stefanopolis and I don't talk to each other. He testified at congressional hearings on the NASA budget, with disastrous results for some of our programs. He is no longer on the NASA payroll." Tony shifted in the dainty makeup chair. "I guess he did what his conscience told him to, about the greater need for medical research here on earth, but he's not exactly my favorite doctor." Tony grimaced. "The long-range effects of his testimony will never be measured. Congress is even now getting ready to cancel the High Resolution Microwave Survey."

"What's that?" Fillingeri said.

"A project to scan space for radio waves emitted by alien civilizations.?"

"No, I mean what's that in dollars?"

Tony moved in his chair, suddenly uncomfortable. "A million a month."

"And Aristotle Stefanopolis thought that was a little steep, just to phone some Klingons? Imagine that."

Tony shrugged. "We're talking to industrialists, looking into getting private funding for the project."

"It's about time you guys at NASA realized that *taxes* are private funding." Fillingeri shoved a hand through his hair before he shook his head at Tony. "Phoning Klingons on my money."

"It looks like you share Aristotle's view of the hunt for extra-terrestrials."

Fillingeri gave Tony a hard look. "Aristotle. That's the brother who's alive. His brother Hektor—the dead one—did he ever do anything nasty to NASA?"

"Not that I ever heard."

"Did you talk to Hektor today?"

"I don't think he even recognized me, Captain."

"You could have reminded him."

"I didn't feel like it."

"There something wrong between the two of you?"

"Not at all. It was early, I was thinking about doing the spot on the show, we were all busy. My previous acquaintance with Hektor Stefanopolis was so slight as to be meaningless. One round of golf."

Fillingeri rose from his chair and went to stand at the table of cold food. He couldn't even help himself to some ham and bread because all the food was under wraps supplied by evidence technicians from his own department. He looked hungry.

He turned the hungry look on Tony. "So if it was Aristotle that was found dead in the alley, you wouldn't be heartbroken, is that right, Dr. Jones?"

Tony hesitated. "As much as I'd be if anyone were murdered. I didn't hate the guy."

"How much money did he cost NASA at those hearings?"

"Nobody can say for sure about the direct effect of his testimony, but we lost more than three billion in the last two years."

Fillingeri took his time chewing on that sum. "Three billion. That's a lot of money *not* to hate a guy for."

"It's not my personal money." Tony glanced at the steel box on the table beside me, almost like he wanted to be sure nobody was going to take it away from him. Like it was his personal steel box. "But Aristotle Stefanopolis is still alive, Captain. What difference does it make if I hate him or not?"

"I don't know. Maybe none. I'd like you to come down to the precinct and dictate what you saw this morning outside the building. You're the closest thing we've got to an eyewitness, and I'd like your statement on video, as well as on paper. There's nothing about what I'm saying other than a request for help in our investigation of the death of Hektor Stefanopolis. You don't need to be thinking about a lawyer or anything."

Tony looked at Ike. "Would you be thinking of a lawyer, Ike, if you were me?"

I wondered if this was one more comment on my I.Q., the fact that Tony turned to Ike, not to me.

"NASA's got a legal arm, Tony," Ike said. "Why don't you put the question to them? I'd hate to give you bad advice."

"Oh, great," Fillingeri said. "Government lawyers, First Amendment protections, friends in the media. Maybe even the Justice Department, with NASA involved. And you have the nerve to talk to me about policy. Policy! You guys make the NYPD look as simple as Old MacDonald's Farm."

Before I could open my mouth to give that crack the response it called for, Fillingeri snapped his fingers in my face. "Don't say it, Abagnarro."

I didn't flinch. "You have fast reflexes, Captain." I stood up so I could look Fillingeri in the eye. "You know what the odd thing is? You and I are on the same side. Cops and journalists. I want you to catch Hektor's killer. *You* want to catch Hektor's killer." I looked around the room. "I can't speak for Ike and Tony, but I'll bet most of America wants you to catch Hektor's killer. We like law and order. Even when it comes to us personally. *Especially* when it comes to us personally. Why you go apeshit whenever anybody but you knows some law, that's beyond me. What do you expect from us? The working press understood Miranda and had it memorized before the cops got the word that the Supreme Court still liked the Constitution. As a matter of fact, I'll bet you five bucks that you first heard about Miranda on a television set at the precinct house."

Ike's cheeks were glowing. "Bravo, Abby."

Fillingeri's cheeks were touched with pink, too, but his weren't pretty. "I never heard you say so many sentences in a row, Abagnarro."

"Forget it." I wasn't about to touch my cheeks to take my temperature. "It's the amnesia talking."

Fillingeri didn't try to fathom that one. He just stood there stiffly for a minute. He made an abrupt gesture at Tony.

"You can phone a lawyer if you want," Fillingeri said. "But you're not being charged with anything. So, technically speaking, I wasn't going anywhere near your rights."

We left them in the Green Room, not precisely in a staring contest, but close to it.

"Hey, Abby," I heard, when Ike and I'd gone a few paces down the Tube. I turned back to see Tony leaning out the door of the Green Room. "Can I leave this here?" He had NASA's steel box in his hand.

I retraced my steps and took the box from him. "I'll lock it up in Ike's office."

"Take care of it, Abby."

"I will."

Ike and I headed again for Fred Loring's Magic Improved-Reality Factory over in Graphic Arts. The Tube was crowded, with the usual traffic indicating that *Evening Watch* had set its preliminary lineup in motion and that show production was on its legs.

The uncharacteristic amity between my ex-wife and me drew a few raised eyebrows, and probably spurred some gambling among the currently-out-of-favor producers who had time on their hands to gossip because Tom Hitt wasn't letting them work on pieces for the show, but we sailed serenely through the crowd, speaking of neutral topics like hot weather and glassblowing.

But, when we reached the hushed regions surrounding Graphic Arts, a neighborhood largely avoided by normal people because of the nerds who work there, Ike stopped me by touching my wrist.

"I wish I knew the real reason Tony went outside the building this morning," she said, searching my eyes with her eerie gaze.

"Yeah. Me, too." Caught in the glow of her eyes and nearly overwhelmed by the cathedral silence of the Graphic Arts Zone, it was hard for me to think about Tony Jones, or Dennis Fillingeri, or anything but how close Ike was standing to me.

Floating at the back of my mind, like the remnants of a dream from which I was awakening to the greater reality of Ike's nearness, Tony's account of his stroll outside the building was receding, so much seaweed on the shore of my consciousness.

"You know what Tony's like," she whispered. "Are you thinking what I'm thinking?"

"Probably not," I said softly, thinking how I'd like to slide my fingers through the soft blond curls at her temples, to rest my thumb along her cheekbone, to feel the weight of her head as she leaned back against my hand, to...

"Many people who suffer from glaucoma," she said, "regularly use marijuana."

The reason Tony had given Fillingeri, and maybe the security guard, for leaving the building had not washed with Ike or me, not even for a second. Tony Jones didn't smoke ordinary cigarettes. Pot, yes. Tobacco, no. Not that he would have done dope before the show.

But there's always later.

Perhaps Tony had wandered down to Columbus Circle to score some herb off of Hektor.

ELEVEN

THE SILENCE in Graphic Arts is underscored by the constant white noise of their clean air machines, placed inconveniently on the floor in the halls and doorways like giant metal hassocks in The - House - Where - the - Interior - Decorator - Has - His - Own - Ideas - About - Reality. Everyone stubs their toes on the air cleaners, except the GA geeks. Maybe the idea is to filter our shoe dirt as well as our germs and filthy auras and whatever else those hungry, low-lying monsters are sucking off all those who dare to enter Cyberspace.

Or maybe it's as simple as it looks, and they're meant to trip invaders—the outer defensive rim against the infidel computer outsiders.

The animation freaks are very touchy about their computers in GA, and I often think that, if they could come up with a machine that would screen out unnecessary humans as efficiently as their Honeywell Enviracaires screen out dust particles and pollen, they'd probably break out into a tea party. I can't imagine a celebration among these seasoned loners running to more excitement than a few breathless remarks appreciating the delicate teacups someone brought from his grandmother's house. You won't encounter anything as festive as champagne corks popping in this region. I can hear the whining now: "Geez, guys, don't hurt the computers with those missiles."

Fred Loring was sitting dreamily in front of his terminal when Ike and I sneaked up and leaned over the half-wall of his cubby. On his display screen was a glowing electric-green skeleton topped with the head of Diane Sawyer, but Fred had given her Sam Donaldson's eyebrows. Fred squeezed his mouse a couple of times and the skeleton executed a little jig from the knee bones down.

"What's that supposed to be?" Ike said.

Fred jumped like a scorpion had nipped his duff. His fingers raced over the fancy keyboard, and the image disappeared into blue storage: some quiet zone, deep in the computer's gut, where Fred hides his life.

"Don't you get it, Ike?" I said. "It's Fred's version of *Prime Time Live.*"

Fred spun around in his chair.

"Abby," he breathed, gazing at me with a mixture of awe and suspicion, obviously half expecting I had the secret decoder book in my back pocket. "You got it."

"Shucks, Fred. Didn't I tell you that TV directors know the oddest things?"

"Yes, but I never thought you'd understand symbolic art."

"Anything that doesn't require an I.Q. over sixteen is perfect for me, Fred. I could live on symbolic art."

Fred's narrow shoulders slumped. He sighed. He bowed his head, apparently studying his lap. He may even have counted to ten, or run through the signs of the zodiac. When he finally looked up, he gave me the kind of look Dan Quayle probably gives his television set whenever he sees a Sprint commercial.

"Abby, I don't know why I keep having this nagging feeling that there is some substance beneath your shallow facade. Coining all these insults about me has to be chipping away at your moral center."

"I'll start taking vitamins."

Ike reached over the wall of the cubby and patted Fred on the shoulder.

"You should just ignore what Abby says. I mean, ignore the parts that don't involve show production. That's what I try to do."

Now that Fred and Ike were linked by a common bond, the shared experience of writing me off, Fred seemed to cheer up. The red letter fact that Ike had even touched his shoulder would probably fire up some spectacular constructions on the video screen where he worked out the details of his fantasy existence. And, more to the point, he was now inclined to grant the favor we had come to ask.

Ike patted him again for good measure.

"Fred," she said, "I need another map, like the ones you did this morning of Central Park and the alley where the doctor died."

Fred looked at his watch, a piece of equipment almost big

enough to microwave a hotdog. "We've got sixteen, seventeen hours before the next show. Ask me later."

Okay, maybe he wasn't inclined to do us a favor.

"Fred," Ike said, her Missouri twanginess sharpened, probably on purpose, "I'm not *asking* you and I don't want it *later*. If I don't see a map up on that screen within five minutes, I'm going to kick your computer through the closest air cleaner. We'll see how all your little green creatures like the trip."

"All right, all right," he whined, turning back to his terminal. "They're all backed up on disk anyway, so you're not half as annoying as you think. You don't know the first thing about computers. What kind of map do you want?"

"I want you to build a map defined by the locations where each of the ten Yellow-Man victims was found."

"Do you have all the locations?"

"Right here," she said. I heard a crackling noise as she stuck her hand in a silk pocket. She unfolded a piece of NTB letterhead and passed it over the wall. The paper was covered with the geometry of her handwriting—the letters made out of triangles and circles and squares. When she was a little girl in school, she must have used math class to write notes to her boyfriends.

Fred scanned the list. I looked over his shoulder. I could see that Ike had constructed the list in her typical well-organized fashion. The sites were arranged like a project for geography class, with the northernmost site coming first on the list. Maybe Ike had paid attention when the teacher got the maps out.

"This will only take a minute," Fred said.

He's even faster on the keyboard than Ike, although much gentler, and he called up and then dumped several stock maps of Manhattan before choosing the one he liked. I don't know how he made that decision, because he did it too fast for my eye to keep up with the maps. The one he settled on was rich in detail, so maybe that was it.

Bobbing his head between Ike's list and his monitor, and squeezing the mouse with rapid flourishes of his thin wrist while windows opened and closed on the screen, Fred started putting up little hollow red stars on the map. He gets a lot of exercise when he uses his mouse; he claims that's why he has resisted the introduction of trackballs into his department. Above his computer, on the wall of his cubby, Fred has a sign that says REAL

MEN HAVE MOUSE-CONTROL. When the sign first went up, I swear I thought Fred had gotten it off an exterminator.

When Fred had ten stars, he moved the cursor to the north edge of the map and pumped the mouse again, and again, and again, squeezing off the unused territory and dumping it out of the picture. The map kept getting smaller. The blue background was soon much larger than the bit of map he had left in the middle of the screen, digitally whittled down to a scrap of the island.

With a final flip of his wrist, he gave some command that caused the remnant of map to explode, to fill the screen. The whole process had taken him less than three minutes.

"You want to give this thing a slug?" he asked.

Ike was blinking at the screen. "Call it 'Plan B.' And print it." She seemed to be chewing the inside of her cheek as she gazed at Fred's artwork. "No. Wait a minute. Can you label the red stars with numbers, like a superscript or something, if I tell you the numbers?"

"Sure." He handed her the list.

"Do you have a pen?"

Fred looked helplessly around his cubby.

Now, there's a television irony, I thought. Graphic Arts is the last department where you'd be likely to find a pen.

I gave Ike a ballpoint I had filched from the control room, and she started marking up her list of addresses. When she was finished, she read numbers off to Fred and he put them up beside the red stars.

Nine of the stars, including the one with the superscript number ten (for Hektor Stefanopolis), were clustered on the West Side, north from Times Square to Lincoln Center, east from the Hudson into Central Park. The lonesome straggling star, representing victim number three, was down on Twenty-eighth Street. The map was top-heavy with red stars.

"Hmm. I wonder if number three is an aberration?" Ike said, leaning over into the cubby to point. "If you overlook that one, Fred, is there a what-do-you-call-it? You know what I mean? An epicenter? A geographic center? The exact middle."

Fred's fingers did a fast waltz over the keyboard. He called up a grid and superimposed it over the map. He hit a rapid series of keys and, plunk, there was a blue circle on Fifty-seventh Street, between Tenth and Eleventh Avenues.

"The south side of Fifty-seventh," Fred said, just being nerdily precise.

I laughed out loud.

"That whole block is the CBS Broadcast Center, you dope," I said. "You did that on purpose."

"No, I didn't. What I did is pure baby mathematics, nothing creative at all. That circle is the middle. All I did was give the program the pattern, which it digitized and then spun out onto the grid as a graphic."

"Well, well," Ike said, "it looks like we've got Dan Rather by the scruff of his neck. Golly, gee. I'll just take this evidence over to CBS World Headquarters and make him confess. Dan'll be singing about Yellow-Man like he was covering the latest hurricane. This map was sure a brilliant idea." She rested her elbow on the half-wall and looked disgusted. "Just for giggles, where would the center be if you included the victim on Twenty-eighth? Maybe that's not an aberration."

Fred performed some tricks with his machine and another blue circle went up on the screen, on Fiftieth between Eighth and Ninth Avenues. That block is full of French restaurants across from Worldwide Plaza, that giant office/apartment complex designed to lure the affluent to the west side of the island. With its three-story glass pyramid lit at night, that building gets high marks from me. I've been its biggest fan since it erupted onto Manhattan's skyline. It's a scene stealer among the veterans. But I couldn't imagine what it had to do with Yellow-Man, any more than the French restaurants.

"Can you print that out for me?" Ike said.

"I'll print it, but I'll also E-mail it to your queue, if you want. You won't be able to manipulate it without my programming, and your keyboard is pathetically Cro-Magnon, but at least you can look at the map on your screen. The color will be better than the hard copy." Fred gave Ike a wise, compassionate look. "A pixel is worth a thousand pages."

"Thanks. I'll write that down when I get to my office."

While Fred got his printer set, I moved closer to Ike and said, "Don't you imagine Fillingeri has done something like this, too?"

"Probably." She smiled. "But I bet we've got better color."

"That's a comfort."

Fred pulled the map off his printer's chute and gave it a critical glance. He handed it to Ike.

She thanked Fred again, rather absently, and we started to walk away. Fred's thin voice reached out to us across the steady hum of the air purifiers.

"Of course," he said, "both of those blue dots for the geographic center are very unstable. If you want me to update them after the next killing, just send me a note in the E-mail and I'll whiz a correction back to you. That way you won't have to come over here."

The next killing. The words seemed to hang in the clean, clean air of Graphic Arts.

Ten had seemed such a complete number, an ordered set, and the death of Hektor Stefanopolis had rounded off the drama of the series of murders with a flourish, so I hadn't given a thought to what was next on the killer's agenda, if anything. Assuming there was anything as coherent as an agenda. Assuming Fillingeri was correct that the Yellow-Man perpetrator was a killer and not some weirdo prankster who expressed himself artistically on accidentally encountered dead bodies lying conveniently in his path. Dead bodies that all seemed to turn up in roughly the same neighborhood of Manhattan.

We came around the Tube far enough that Fred's department had disappeared around the curve of the wall. I turned, stepped back a few paces, and took a peek; Fred had the green skeleton up on the map and was making those bones boogie to some rhythm a different drummer was banging out in his head.

I caught up with Ike.

"Does it ever strike you," I said, "that Fred's a little strange?"

"Lost in space, blasted out of stable orbit before he reached adolescence. But when I need good art in a hurry, I'd rather have a brilliant fruitcake like Fred than twelve sane people who can construct nice pictures. Fred's a genius. Of course, it takes the show's other genius to tell him what to do. Without you, Abby, he'd be sitting in there, breathing clean air and drawing computer riddles all night."

"By God. Ike, you just called me a genius. I wish Captain Fillingeri was here. I wish Tom Hitt was here. I wish the Peabody Committee was here."

"Don't get the idea that I'm trying to flatter you. I just know what's going on. You and Fred are the only ones on the show who know anything about TV. The rest of us are just reporters, of one sort or another. Without you and Fred, *Morning Watch* would be a newspaper.''

"Well, little girl, since you're the only one today who has not taken potshots at my I.Q., I'm going to share a little secret with you."

"Is this going to be one of your stories? Please, Abby, don't do this to me."

"Nope. Not a story. What our Boston criminologist would call 'artifactual evidence.'" I patted my shirt pocket. "Right here next to my heart is a little thing Tom Hitt would get down on his tiny knees and beg for."

Ike stopped walking. I stopped. A couple of people passed us, two aimless, idle *Evening Watch* producers wandering in outer darkness until somebody different pissed Tom off and they got to go back to work.

"What are you talking about?" she said.

"You wanna find Tex?"

"You know I do."

"You wanna beat *Evening Watch* to him?"

"You know I do."

"Are you cynical enough to wish our show a rating point or two for more First Amendment crapola? Wanna show up the so-called competition?"

"Of course. What's in your pocket, Abby? Did Tex give you his address?"

"I doubt he has an address."

She reached for my pocket and I batted her hand gently away.

"Don't touch," I said. "I have something here that's more fragile than an address."

"What is it?"

"Unless I imagined the whole thing—in that heat I could have been hallucinating—Tex gave me a couple of fingerprints."

"What?"

"I've got four of my business cards in my pocket, including the one I tried to give to Tex." I leaned my shoulders against the wall, spread my hands out, palms up, completely innocent, nothing up my sleeve, ladies and gentlemen. "He gave it back, Ike. Tucked it into my pocket with his own hands."

"Oh, my God," she squeaked. "This is awesome."

Her excitement did not last. I watched her thinking it over as she stood there, tapping her foot lightly on the linoleum. I could see the eagerness fade from her face.

"Well, I guess it's awesome," she said. "I mean, it's great. But how the hell can we do anything with a fingerprint? We don't have access to all that crime scene junk and *Dragnet* BS that Fillingeri uses to track down the bad guys. What are we going to do with a fingerprint? What are you looking so smug about?"

"I finally know why God made me taller than Tom Hitt. My brain maybe smaller than Tom's, but mine's higher off the ground. My brain's working off purer ozone."

"What are you talking about?"

"I know where there's a jukebox."

"Come again?"

"A jukebox. A machine that spins platters. The platters are disks, as in computer disks. And on those disks are millions of fingerprints. Digitized, as Fred would say."

"Didn't *The New York Times* have something about this a few months ago?"

"Yes. So did our own documentary unit. We only made a reference in passing to the jukebox, because the show concentrated on overseas efforts to locate American MIAs. But I learned something about the technology we have here in the States. The techno-glitz is not yet generally available to law enforcement nationwide, because it's mega-expensive, but some of the better-endowed corporations are using it to replace employee I.D. cards. I wish we had it down in our lobby."

"We don't."

"Ah. But I know where there is one, and it's loaded with pictures of fingerprints, just like you'd see on the shiny paper if you were arrested and they'd dipped your fingers in ink. Only the jukebox's pictures of fingerprints have been digitized, turned into binary form, a series of zeroes and ones. And the jukebox will play the tune you request when you insert your quarter." I admit I paused for effect and patted my chest again. Too bad I didn't have a wand to wave. "Abracadabra. Your quarter, Ike, is in my pocket on my business card."

"How many songs can this jukebox play?"

"About sixty-two million. And I'm betting Tex is one of those songs, because a lot of these tunes come equipped with criminal records, if you'll pardon the pun.''

"Where is this jukebox?"

"Twenty-six Federal Plaza."

She gave me a funny look. "That's the FBI."

"You've been studying your law enforcement geography."

"You think they'd let us play their jukebox?" A smile was starting to flirt with the corners of her mouth. "Like, a mutual exchange of deep background? Like off-the-record shinola in return for some trust down the road? Like, do you happen to have a source, Abby? Come on, I'm running out of speculation."

"Morris Cainstraight. I met him when I was directing that documentary on America's MIAs. That was before the Vietnam Legacy documentary. A man of many talents, your ex-husband, or at least of many documentaries. Othello Armitage just can't resist spreading me around the network. So, if you think of it, my enormous salary is not all that ludicrous." I paused and gave that some genuine thought. "No, it's still ludicrous. Directors have it made in the shade. The rest of you peons must hate us."

"Don't get me started. Who's Morris Cainstraight?"

"He's one of the pioneers of the jukebox technology. He helped develop the software, and he was instrumental in the planning of the print-lifter scanner. That's the handheld device, a version of a supermarket scanner, really, that picks up fingerprints. Cops won't even have to get anyone's fingers dirty once the technology is widespread, meaning when it gets cheaper. They'll have this Big Brother shit in their patrol cars."

"You mean, if I was driving around and got stopped, the cops could just grab my hand, read my prints, and—whammo—know who I am?"

"If your prints are in the jukebox."

"Wow. I wonder what Thomas Jefferson would think of that."

"My guess is he would not be happy when all computers are created equal and digitizing our inalienable rights."

Ike was rubbing her chin thoughtfully. "Cops driving on the information superhighway. This is a little creepy."

"Ah, but what if the highway is used to catch the guy who was driving around in the car he stole from you?"

"I bet the ACLU has an eagle eye on this. There will simply be no time for the presumption of innocence."

"No doubt. But that doesn't change the fact that you'd give a lot to have a name and address to attach to the dirty smudges on my business cards. Yes?"

"Well, yeah. Tex is numero uno on our wish list. I wouldn't dream of letting my constitutional scruples get in the way of a scoop. I figure every scoop is another brick in the wall anyway when it comes to defending that document."

"I'll call Morris right now, see if he can do lunch with us."

She used her fingers to make a little cup for her chin, and she got that look in her eyes that told me something unpleasant was coming. One of the things I liked about being married to her was that she doesn't cloak the inventory of her emotions. It's all there on her face. In your face. Now it's one of the things I dislike about not being married to her.

"I've already made plans for lunch, Abby."

"So? Change them."

"I can't. This is business. As a matter of fact, it could be another brick in the wall."

"Should I guess? That fascinating healer who's trying to turn himself into the towering inferno? Where're you going, the Texaco station?"

"Aristotle has very kindly consented to let me offer my condolences, that's all. You should have a little more humanity, Abby. He's not only very sad, he's a news source, and I'm just going to do what I can to help, on behalf of the network. Othello has already signed off on this."

"Because he thinks you're pumping Aristotle, if you'll pardon the expression, for information?"

"Yes."

"That means Othello's paying? Condolence on the company?"

"What difference does it make to you?"

"It makes a big difference. I don't see why you should eat anything Aristotle buys. If Othello Armitage is paying, that's not so bad. Where are you going?"

"Gabriel's."

"Gabriel's! The hottest cafe on the West Side, for a condolence visit?"

"What do you expect? You think Aristotle should be on his knees in the family crypt, absolutely dripping with black armbands?"

"Yes."

"Well, I don't." She started walking along the Tube toward her office. "That's Dark Ages stuff."

I pushed myself off the wall and followed her.

"So," I said, "life goes on for Doctor Death, huh?"

"Just as it should. I wish you wouldn't call him that."

"Excuse me. Doctor Do-gooder. Doctor Domesticity. Doctor Do-Unto-Others."

"What's that supposed to mean?"

"Rubin says Aristotle was doing unto Dr. Olivia Quintinale, fellow author and former sister-in-law. Hektor's ex-wife, if I'm being too technical for you. Let me spell this out: Aristotle and his brother's wife were doing it."

She stopped dead in her tracks.

"That's very odd," she said, cocking her head to one side and looking thoughtfully into the middle distance, the last reaction I would have expected. I was expecting something more heated.

"Abby, Rubin mentioned something about that to me, but I don't like to hear unnecessarily about marital hanky-panky, as you of all people should know."

I winced. "Bull's-eye, Ike."

"I wonder. Hektor may have had a motive for killing Aristotle, yes?"

"Maybe. If my brother was screwing you, I'd be ticked off."

"And Tony may have had a motive for killing Aristotle, yes?"

"Maybe three billion motives, but Tony's mind doesn't work that way."

"Say it does for the sake of argument."

"All right."

"So that's two people with motives for killing Aristotle. Plus, Tony said Aristotle was arguing with Quintinale when they got in the cab. And she certainly didn't like it when Aristotle gave me his phone number and was obviously working up to something with me. So maybe she also felt like killing Aristotle."

"This is all if you believe gossip. And we don't know how mad she was at Aristotle."

"For the sake of argument, say she was mad as hell."

"Okay. So?"

"So. Do you believe that Hektor fits the Yellow-Man pattern?

Or do you believe a copycat capitalized on that pattern to get Hektor?''

''I guess I think it was a copycat.''

''According to our own producer and reporter, that's also what the cops think. It's what that Boston criminologist thinks. Why can't I ever remember his name?''

''Henry Amos Jankowski.''

''Yeah. Him. And if they're all correct about a copycat, that means there has to be a motive, like a motive we could understand, not something stratospherically insane like a serial killer. And we know of at least three people with decent motives to kill Aristotle, all of whom were handy this morning.''

''What's your point?''

''Why was Hektor the one who got killed?''

TWELVE

UNLESS SOMEBODY'S BOMBING the World Trade Center or dropping a 747 unexpectedly, Monday's usually the busiest time on the twenty-seventh floor of the Emerald City. The normal flow of news-making events tends to follow the course of the American bureaucratic river—that nine-to-five, Monday-to-Friday schedule that empties into the major networks' evening news programs. Funny how that works. It's one of those chicken-or-the-egg deals.

This particular Monday was a little above par even for a Monday, because the Yellow-Man Whatever was adding his unpredictable workday to the normal headaches supplied by Washington, the judicial system, the medical community, the military/industrial complex, Our Nation's Schools, and drug cartels (the drug dignitaries, that is, work nine-to-five; the entry-level positions are a different matter).

When Ike and I left the silent Graphic Arts region behind, the twenty-seventh floor Tube was bustling in response to the floodgates opening after the weekend, and I did notice an extra kickstep or two among Tom Hitt's workhorses. I can usually tell when he's slapping the reins by the way his cattle giddy-up in the Tube.

Tom likes to keep his office door open so he can monitor the pacesetters in the Tube. But his door was closed when we passed by, an unusual circumstance and a definite clue that he was either in deep conference or upstairs tattling on me to the boss. Tom had never really tried to pry my mouth open before, so I didn't blame him if he was rooting around for the right tool. What I did think was that Othello would tell Tom to go blow his nose. Upper management—and they don't come any more upper than Othello Armitage—does not like to have its directors hassled by the editorial side. The reasoning is very simple: Othello, if he got the steam up and chose to do so, could come downstairs from his marble penthouse office and do Tom's job for the day, but he couldn't step in and do mine.

As we walked along the crowded Tube, weaving through the

stampede, I thought about why Dr. Hektor Stefanopolis, who struck me as a nice guy, had gotten it in that alley, instead of some other New Yorker—instead of, say, his brother Aristotle. Aristotle seemed much more killable, from my point of view, a man with some habits that could lead to the acquisition of personal enemies. I'd only known him something like seven hours, and already I didn't like him.

When we got to Ike's office, she said, "If you can set something up for later with Morris the FBI DJ, leave a message in my E-mail or voice mail or machine at home. Oh, I'll also take my cell phone along, so, if you need me for something urgent, you can reach me that way."

"What if I just want to ask what you're having for dessert?"

"Write me a letter."

"I can't afford a stamp. I'm a mugging victim, you know."

"Well, that may turn out to be far more useful than a stamp. If Morris Cainstraight can really help us, the needle in our haystack might take on some sparkle."

"Ike, about Hektor. Are you suggesting his death was a mistake? That the wrong brother got it?"

"Oh, I was just thinking out loud. But I'm also acting out loud: I've got a producer and a crew standing by at Midtown North for the autopsy report on Hektor. Nothing's going to get by me while I condole with Aristotle. Let me know about the jukebox. Have a nice lunch, Abby."

Have a nice lunch, Abby. Have a nice lunch.

Swell.

She was treating me just the way she treated Fred. Pat me when it suits her; snap at me when I'm in her way. In fact, now that I thought of it, Ike herself had linked me with Fred—the show's two geniuses, the difference being that he had a green skeleton on a computer screen and I had the ghost of a relationship in my heart. Just me, the genius director, and Fred, the genius cybernaut, in the Emerald City: the Lonely Boys grateful for a pat on the head instead of a kick in the teeth. Or, at least, I was grateful. Fred seemed to have gone well past the point where he could feel anything as human as gratitude.

I was actually wondering if I could still feel anything when it hit me that I was hurt. Hurt by the businesslike way Ike had walked away from my prized fingerprint collection so she could go have lunch with Aristotle, Michelin Medico. I didn't by any means care to dazzle Tom Hitt, but *he* probably would have dropped everything for a crack at the business cards I had in my shirt pocket. I could have roped him in instantly, but I hadn't even made a dent in Ike's social calendar, which had been pretty full since the divorce, if you asked me.

I opened the door to my office (now just a piece of unsecured wood until I could get resupplied with a key) and stood for a moment holding the steel NASA box. There was no way I would go crawling back to Ike's office to lock the thing up as I'd promised Tony, absolutely no way I was going to give her a chance to tell me more things about lunch.

Although I was temporarily indisposed through the loss of my office door key, I wasn't helpless. I could even have a private audience with the NASA doodad, a privilege not available to every citizen of the republic that was paying for the doodad. I thought of doing the honorable thing, curbing my curiosity, and locking the box in my desk without first checking out NASA's bauble-du-jour. On the other hand, I thought, curiosity-control among broadcasters is like a space heater at the North Pole—sure, it'd be nice to have one, but where are you going to plug it in? You gotta be wired right to produce the desired effect.

My wiring told me to open the thing and see if Tony had unloaded his treasure on me because that was better than letting Fillingeri get his hands on the kind of contraband that makes cops look at you funny.

I put the box on the corner of my desk. I lifted the lid. And there was another box inside, a clear plastic cube with a little, fat, pink velvet cushion inside. And resting deep in the softness of the cushion was the prettiest golf ball I'd ever seen.

That's all there was in the steel box. Positively no sign of anything you could put in rolling paper or a bowl in order to smoke your way to outer space. If Tony had left the building before *Morning Watch* to arrange a transfer of herbal medicine from Hektor to himself, he had either struck out or had been dumb enough to take the shit with him to Midtown North in the company of Captain Dennis Fillingeri, which would be pretty clueless for a rocket scientist.

I lifted the plastic box out of the steel box and held it up to the dirty gray light struggling in through my slit of a window.

The little ball was the smoothest thing I'd ever seen, shockingly smooth even to someone like me who'd read the glowing scientific particulars in the show packet. The little sphere's outer skin was a pearly gray from the superconducting niobium, the inner sphere pure quartz, the whole gadget the most perfectly round object ever made by man. Or maybe by any being.

The ball was so perfectly round and smooth that if it was blown up to the size of the Earth, the highest pimple on the surface would only be something like a foot high. NASA's Spinning Quartz Ball, as I knew from the show packet, was a gyroscope, or part of one. Four of these little pearly balls were slated to ride the big fire into orbit. And their trip into space had been delayed several times, along with other NASA forays, by congressional budget cutbacks. Even the projected launch date of 1999 was what NASA calls "under review"—a euphemism for "maybe never, but cross your fingers."

What passions these delays stirred in NASA's blood, I didn't know. But I did know that if I'd spent a decade or so of my life trying to send a ball up into space and a colleague had gone and blabbed that my project was "badly prioritized" in the face of Earthside problems, I'd be inclined to hurt that colleague—even if Aristotle Stefanopolis did not need my help getting hurt, what with his high-speed habit of sending himself into orbit around raceway infields.

I was afraid to take the ball out of the plastic box. If this little gizmo was so perfectly round, its structure machined and engineered and precision-polished and dreamed about and pondered over and babied by the best scientific minds in the country, at a total cost of around a million dollars, it might be a serious faux pas to mess it up with my grubby mitts. But I wanted to touch it, to touch something guaranteed to be the smoothest surface ever known to man.

I'm happy to be able to report in all honesty that I put the plastic box back inside the steel box without violating the sanctity of the Spinning Quartz Ball. *When they finally sent it rocketing up for its two-year date with a polar orbit,* I thought, *it would go without having been sullied by a television director in the Big Dirty City.*

And the ball would levitate cleanly in its electrical field, spinning at 170 cycles per second, without once having known the warmth of my hand. And while it spun there in outer space, sci-entists back on this planet would wait to see if that perfect ball drifted by a certain tiny angle of sight: forty-four times the angle of view a person would have of a single human hair placed ten miles away, which is the tiniest angle I can think of, and even multiplied forty-four times, still so tiny as to be almost unmea-surable. Forty-four times almost nothing is still almost nothing.

And if that little ball—which would spin in the utter cold of outer space, never once having known what it was like to lie in the palm of my hand, to roll across my lifeline or heartline—did drift by that certain tiny angle, then part of Einstein's theory of general relativity would be proved.

An answer worth billions of dollars?

Aristotle, apparently, had thought not.

But, as I closed the steel box over the plastic box, a vision of the Spinning Quartz Ball stayed with me for a moment, a vision trailing across the retina, a vision of a plain certainty for once in this fucked-up universe, and I knew how I would answer the question.

I keep the key to my big desk drawer on the shelf under my dusty Emmy, so I didn't have to call security to help me stash the little golf ball that was waiting for the ride of a lifetime into space and scientific history if NASA could manage to hang on to its dwindling funds. As I got the key down, I wondered how badly mugged Tony and the project team on Gravity Probe B had felt by Aristotle's congressional testimony.

I locked the steel box away and gazed at the clutter on my desk, so unlike the virginal territory of Fred Loring's cyberspace playpen, so similar in loneliness to the space he had carved for himself out of NTB News. Unless I wanted to turn into Fred, if it wasn't already too late, I had to break out of the self-pity that had been creeping over me, maybe inspired by envy of the little ball that was going places while I seemed to be going nowhere.

At least I could go downtown with my fingerprint collection. I didn't really expect Ike to cancel her date with the grieving brother of the murdered doctor, but I didn't see any reason to hang around until she was ready to go make astounding discov-eries in the jukebox. I flipped through my Rolodex and came up with the number for Morris Cainstraight.

I had to go through several government flunkies, all of whom were on the alert for criminal tones in my voice, before I was permitted to speak with the man himself. He had just started his shift and said he'd be happy to entertain a couple of network snoops when his shift ended that night, anytime after 8:30. So maybe I wasn't going anywhere, at least not right away.

I called Ike's voice mail and told her about our appointment.

I gave my Rolodex a vicious spin, watching the high-speed version of my social world twirl around on the desk. Here I was, with a torrid clue in my shirt pocket and nobody to share it with. I thought of Tom Hitt's closed door, and it was some consolation that, while I had no method just yet of learning my mugger's identity, Tom was even worse off, having no clue about my clue.

I got out the show packet for the glassblowing segment and looked at the last page for the press contact number, which was listed as the Physics Department at Columbia University. Maybe Hilda Murray would let me give her the third degree about the interpersonal warfare I'd seen brewing in the Green Room before the show. Maybe she had some insights I could add to the single big one I was hiding from Tom Hitt. Maybe she'd go to lunch with the Lonely Boy.

When I reached the Physics Department, I asked for a glass blower.

"We have seven glassblowers," said a tired male voice. "Which one do you want?"

"Hilda Murray."

"Hold on while I connect you."

Seven glassblowers, I thought. At one university. Who'd have thought there'd be such demand for the ancient craft?

"Hello, this is Hilda."

"What's your middle name?"

I could hear a little chuckle at her end of the line.

"Hungry. Are you about to ask me to lunch?"

"How'd you know?"

"You had that lunch look in your eye this morning." There was a pause. "That was before the murder, of course."

"Yeah."

"Yeah. A couple of police officers have been up here at the lab asking what I know. The urge to gossip suddenly dried up on me. I found myself having trouble sorting out what I'd heard this morning from what I'd seen for myself. So I basically told them nothing. But there was nothing. I can't get over it.''

"Eating's always a good thing to do when you've got something to get over. Food doesn't help you get over it, but at least you've got something to do with your hands. You want to come down to my neighborhood, or would you rather do something up there? My schedule's pretty flexible.''

"I'll meet you down there," she said.

"Do you know Gypsy's?"

"Are you kidding? My middle name is *penne alla vodka*."

She made a few noises about the weather turning ugly, which I could tell by the way my window slit had turned to a black hole. We agreed to meet inside Gypsy's at one o'clock.

I toyed briefly with the idea of borrowing the Spinning Quartz Ball to hypnotize Hilda with over lunch, but I didn't know anything about NASA's insurance coverage. Since I was just babysitting, would the network's insurance cover the thing? I certainly didn't want the ball to end up in the pocket of some grabber like Tex. The thought of Tex made me unlock the desk drawer again. I took the four business cards from my shirt pocket and put them inside the NASA box, on top of the plastic cube. Two sets of man-made objects, two different things to prove, two separate scales of inquiry—from the shape of the universe to the name of one guy.

I rode down in the elevator with Diego Gordillo, the only *Evening Watch* producer that Tom Hitt allows to touch his fly-fishing tackle when he vacations out West. I don't think Diego ever produced anything other than a smoother life for Tom, being sort of an all-purpose gofer and handler.

"So, Abby," he said, pushing the button for the lobby, "I hear you had some problems overnight."

"If you mean Ike, I have problems with her every night. Haven't you guys got anything better to talk about? Isn't there some press conference or riot you could discuss among yourselves quietly?"

"Chill, Abby. I wouldn't gossip about your personal life."

"Then what the hell do you and Tom talk about?"

"Nothing personal, man. Tom's just concerned about you getting mugged. Must've been awful. Were you scared? I would have embarrassed myself, that ever happened to me."

The elevator doors whooshed open. Right away, through the giant green glass doors, I could see the epic beginning of the storm our meteorologist had promised. Raindrops were slashing across the glass sideways, the wind was blowing so hard.

"Holy Mother of God," I said. "Look at that."

"S'awesome, man. Mother Nature comes to town. But, just tell me, were you scared last night?"

"Me? Scared? Of what?"

"You know, getting mugged."

"Was I mugged?"

Diego lowered his heavy brows and looked at me like he'd forgotten my name.

"What's the matter with you?" he said. "Everybody knows you got rolled."

I shook my head sadly.

"Last night's one big blur, Diego. I think I must be suffering from heat exhaustion or something. Do you have a subway token on you?"

He fished around in his change and handed over a token.

"Thanks," I said, palming the slug of metal. "The only thing I remember about last night is something about a couple of good-looking hookers. You know the type, the ones that look like royalty? And something about a gray limo." I shrugged my shoulders. "Oh, well, I hope I had a good time. Gotta run now. Heavy date with Meryl Streep. Don't forget to tell Tom the part about Meryl when you report this conversation."

I headed out through the revolving door and took the plunge into The Storm That Ate Manhattan.

THIRTEEN

I'D LIKE TO KNOW at what point rain over New York starts getting so dirty it paints the town instead of washing it.

Is it that dirty when it leaves the clouds, or does it gather filth power on its way down? Exactly where? At the level of the Empire State Building's observation deck? Higher? Lower? Gradually? Maybe on its way past the Rainbow Room—wouldn't that be something?

Wherever the dirt threshold is, by the time the water reached me, it carried enough grime to turn my white shirt not only wet but speckled with soot. What the heat wave had trapped and stacked up over the city was now flowing down the storm drains with the rain, but it filtered through my clothing first.

And the water wasn't flowing fast enough down the drains. There'd be classic and picturesque urban flooding for at least some voiced-over videotape on *Evening Watch,* so Tom could demonstrate that NTB's New York bias was not limited to heat waves.

Columbus Circle was a pool of dirty water, with traffic swirling around and churning up the surface like one of those water rides at Asbury Park. I made myself a quick bet that the New York *Post* would run a full front-page photo along the lines of what I was seeing in the Circle, only with frolicking kids in its picture, and the fat banner headline would be something like H2OOOH!

I dashed for the subway, skidding down the stairs into the station. I was only two stops away from the theater district and Gypsy's, my mother's restaurant. Without Diego's help I would have had to scoot under the turnstile, and it was getting sloppy down there. All in all, I felt that Diego's subway token was a pretty good return on the investment of lies I had fed him.

The downtown local train was packed tight. I had to squeeze between a damp bosom and a pair of soaked shoulder blades, while the sharp point of some umbrella caught me under the rib cage. And I could feel a warm and soggy kneecap poking into my calf. When the doors closed, my left arm was stuck against them so tight that the woman with the bosom (assuming it was a woman) could have taken a blood sample from me without a tourniquet, if that was the sort of thing she liked to do on subways.

At the Forty-second Street, Times Square, Station, the doors opened on the other side of the platform, so I had to wait for a few passengers to peel themselves off each other before I had room to straighten my limbs and shove my way out of the car. I stayed underground, walking north toward the Forty-fourth Street exit, to get as close to Gypsy's as possible before I had to make the dash again through the storm.

Lunchtime in Midtown Manhattan during the work week is probably the worst time and place on Earth, even without rain, full of crowds going nowhere but around each other. Nobody's leaving. In addition to the real New Yorkers, we've got all these people from the warehouse states like New Jersey and Connecticut where we store some of our working population at night. At lunchtime the commuting element empties out of the buildings and infests the eateries with the rest of us. Rain makes it worse, because soaked New Yorkers are much surlier than nice, dry ones.

There was fresh violence in the air. This storm was making the citizens fight back, with arms and elbows and newspapers, and umbrellas turned inside out. It was a fast and passionate storm, and it pummeled the city like an inexperienced boxer in the early rounds, looking to win on points.

By the time I made it to the restaurant, I was soaked and sore, but pleasantly hungry. The one thing rain never washes away from the city is the smell of food—the unquenchable mixed blessing of enough garlic, onions, uttapam, and sesame sauce to keep eight million people from starving.

The 300 block of Forty-sixth is especially fragrant. It's known in the theater district as "Restaurant Row" and is home to Gypsy's, the restaurant my family has owned since 1952 and where all the theater crowd hangs out sooner or later. My parents had befriended just about every struggling actor and actress and producer and playwright and lighting director and choreographer who ever went on to make it in the bigtime, and a lot more who didn't.

When my dad died eight years ago, my mother took over the

business by herself. It's still Broadway's home kitchen, but Carole Abagnarro has her own ideas about kitchens, and she's feeding the crowd with four-star delicacies that won't raise cholesterol or blood pressure levels. She changed more than the menu after dad died, adding a lot of chrome and subdued lighting and chucking the linen tablecloths in favor of drawing paper, but the clientele is roughly the same. People who used to run tabs there when they couldn't find work now happily pay her exorbitant prices.

Gypsy's is the kind of place where tourists come to gawk at stars, but they get one look at my mother's disapproving expression and sit down to eat, minding their manners.

Hilda Murray was sitting primly in the booth under the cat clock, a machine with roving yellow eyes and a black-and-white tail that ticks back and forth. The cast of *Cats* gave the timepiece to my mother. Since it's black and white, it's a Jellicle Cat, the kind T. S. Eliot wrote about and won a Tony for, just as though he'd actually written the libretto for the smash musical. It's quite a trick, writing anything when you've been dead for about thirty years.

I slid into the booth and, before I could even greet the only glassblower I knew, my mother was there with a pile of warm dish towels and a scowl. I knew she wasn't scowling because I was wet. She was not pleased with the company I was about to keep.

Carole Abagnarro has the idea that this divorce thing is a temporary lull in my marriage to Ike, a condition that will go away as soon as I do the right thing—which, of course, is never specified.

"You're lucky I had a table, Abby," she said, handing me a towel and draping another over my head. "Such a crowd and you didn't even call. This person said she thought you had a reservation."

"This person" made a face like *What did I do?*

"Yeah, I'm lucky, Ma. I'd like you to meet Hilda Murray. She's a glassblower from Columbia University and—"

"What, do you think my TV's broken?"

"No, Ma."

"I saw her this morning. And I saw that *Ike* was doing a wonderful job, as usual, by the way *Morning Watch* beat even CNN on that murder story. *Ike* is a very fine producer."

"Yes, Ma."

"*Ike* should win an Emmy for that show."

"She's already got three, Ma."

"Three's an unlucky number." My mother cast a speculative look at Hilda. "You think about that, Abby, while I get you menus."

I toweled my hair and grinned at Hilda. She must have found a taxi right outside her door at Columbia or she owned one powerful umbrella. She didn't need a towel.

"My mother likes you," I said. "I can tell."

Hilda leaned across the table and said, "Am I three of something? When I came in here, there was only one of me."

"That's just the way my mother counts. I used to be married to Ike Tygart, which makes two people, and there you are now in the booth across from me, which is three."

"We could have gone to a different restaurant."

"No way. I have exactly zero money, and I eat free here. So do you."

"We'll see. I'll lay you excellent odds that your mother brings me a check."

"A little something written in scarlet ink?"

"Yeah. That's the spirit. Make fun of me."

I wrapped a dry towel around my neck and reached across the table for her hand. "I'm sorry." I turned her hand over to look at the palm and the tips of her fingers. "I can't get over what you did to that glass on the show. Must hurt like hell. Doesn't it bother you, what you do to your fingers?"

"Sure. But it would bother me more not to do it. I love shaping the glass."

"Some of the producers of the evening show were asking me about a little idea, an idea that your fingers got red because you've been using too much turpentine to get the yellow paint off."

She gasped and tried to jerk her hand away. "That's pretty stupid."

"It's par for the course. Journalists have ugly minds."

"Get your hand away from me; she's coming back."

My mother dumped a couple of small menus on the table and continued past, on her way to the bar.

"The coast is clear," I said. "Let's not bother with the menus. Let's just order your middle name."

She glared at me. "I hope you told those people what they could do with their idea."

"I ignored them. Ignorance is my new policy."

She sat for a moment. I could see her working it out. She smiled, a little reluctantly. "Serves me right, I suppose, to be the butt of gossip. I seem to remember that I did some myself this morning. In fact, I think I started it."

"No, you didn't. That was Tony."

Her eyes twinkled. "You're right. Let's gossip about him."

The waitress bustled up when she saw we were ignoring the menus.

"We'll both have the *penne alla vodka,*" I told her. "And Snapple."

"Weird combination," Hilda said as the waitress headed for the kitchen. "I'd have picked you for a Chianti man."

"Usually you'd be right. But today I'm working on my I.Q., and I don't want to burn off any brain cells with excess alcohol."

"Why are you working on your I.Q.? Is it broken?"

"That's what I'm working on."

"May I ask you a question, a question about those people with ideas and about your work? Not the I.Q. work."

"Make it an easy question. It'll be a test run on my brain."

"Okay. What's your obligation now, now that the show's off the air and the New York police seem to be shaking a leg on Dr. Stefanopolis's murder?"

"My obligation?"

"Yeah. I mean, do you have to initiate your own investigation, or do you just report what the official investigators say?"

"I don't do either. That's Ike's department. Actually, I'm sort of lying. Let me put it this way: I'm not a producer or a reporter. They're the ones who'll be doing any investigation NTB News gets involved in. But I'm part of the show, and I was there this morning, and I think the guy who killed Hektor should be found. When you're in the control room, as you saw this morning, a story has a way of four-dimensionalizing itself off the screen and into your space."

"I thought you didn't know big words."

"I didn't say I didn't know *any.*"

"Why four dimensions?"

"The regular three and time. Working in the control room gives me a thing about time. About being precise, about being first, about being able to work time to my advantage, about using time like a lot of people use, say, depth or distance. Or like the way you use heat. Time's my medium, much more than videotape. So, even though I'm not directly involved with anything the show does to investigate a story, I supply some of the urgency. I hope that answers your question.''

''I forgot my question.''

''Then let me ask you one. This morning in the Green Room. What was that gloom all about? I thought I'd walked into a wake.''

Two huge steaming platters of *Penne Alla Vodka Carole* appeared in front of us. I looked up, expecting to see the waitress, and caught instead the glare from my mother's brown eyes.

''Chita Rivera is waiting at the bar for a table, Abby,'' she said. ''Don't dawdle.''

''Does she look hungry?''

''She looks the way she always looks.''

''Hungry,'' I said. ''We'll eat like a couple of pigs.''

She nodded at Hilda, like *what else would you expect?* She headed toward the bar, probably to order up some free drinks for the standees in the foyer. And maybe some towels.

''Back to the Green Room wake,'' I said. ''Who started it?''

Hilda took a bite of the pasta and rolled her eyes. ''This is so good.'' She swallowed. Even swallowing she had a nice neck. ''I'm feeling gun shy now about gossip, now that I know how minds work at the network level.''

''Remember? I'll just ignore everything you say. I'm safe.''

She gave me a considering look. ''Okay. I guess I'd have to blame Aristotle. He made a remark that I didn't understand at the time, but I understand it now. I heard on CNN that Hektor had glaucoma.''

''What'd Aristotle say?''

''The doctors were talking about the photograph on the back of their book, sort of criticizing each other but nothing too heartfelt, when Aristotle said something like Hektor had no right to an opinion because he couldn't see what was right under his nose.''

''Yow. Not a nice thing to say to a brother with glaucoma.''

''Well, now I think there was more to it than that. I think Aristotle was also referring to what the makeup man said, about

Aristotle doing the wild thing with Hektor's wife. All three are in the photograph, you know, looking ever so together and filled with a common purpose. Ironic, I think. As I said, I didn't get it at the time, but in retrospect I'm fairly appalled. It's one thing to insult your brother about a disease—glaucoma's a tragedy. Just ask Ray Charles. But then Aristotle piled on an additional insult by a sly reference to what an accomplished swordsman he is.''

"Swordsman?''

She blushed. "That's better than 'expert fuck,' isn't it?''

I laughed. "They're both dynamite. You're pretty good with words. And you're cute when you blush.''

She looked down at her plate. "Now I'll really blush. Betrayed by my vulgar vocabulary.'' She raised her eyes, which were full of fun and speculation. "I'll have to memorize more graffiti. It seems to work for me.''

I laughed again and reached over to pat her hand.

I think what I did could have been interpreted as a brotherly gesture, but Carole Abagnarro has her own ideas about gestures and she bore down on us like she was the health inspector and I'd just pulled a rat out of my shoe.

"I hope you enjoyed your meal,'' she said with a grim smile. She whisked our plates off the table and, nodding at acquaintances along the way, carried our half-finished lunches into the kitchen.

"That certainly takes the awkwardness out of the question of whether to linger over coffee and cannelloni, doesn't it?'' Hilda said brightly. "I'm not leaving a tip.''

"Good. And I'll steal a towel.''

"That'll teach her.''

We left and waded out under the awning of Gypsy's. There were acres of taxis in sight, but they were all full.

"I'm headed downtown to NYU,'' Hilda said, raising her voice to be heard over the honking and the thunder. "How about you?''

"Uptown. To bed. I'm a night creature, remember, and I have to turn around and do the show again tonight.''

She offered me a hand. "Let's just separate, then. It would be impossible to be graceful in this mess.''

I held her hand for a moment. She knew I was going to kiss her. She looked at me, giving me the sign-of-the-lowered-lashes, indicating a kiss would be welcome.

I don't know what came over me. Somewhere between the idea

and the execution of it, my lips ended up on her forehead. Very chaste.

She opened her eyes and looked at me.

"Your I.Q. seems pretty healthy," she said, "but there may be something wrong with your aim."

FOURTEEN

FIRST MY I.Q. and now my aim.

I hated to think what would be next.

But there was nothing wrong with my eyesight yet, and, as I started out from under the awning, I caught a glimpse of Diego Gordillo in a doorway across Forty-sixth Street. He turned away to look at himself in the window, but not before I recognized Tom Hitt's favorite slave. Diego was soggy, his clothes stuck to his lean frame, water streaming off his brown hair, and, even turned away from me, he looked like he had cornered the market on misery.

By golly, I thought, Tom Hitt is having me followed. I didn't know how to feel about it. It should have been creepy, but the odd thing was, I got a lift out of it. Being followed. Me. A virgin in the forest—I'd never been followed before. I didn't count my dance with Tex, because, technically, he hadn't been following me. He'd been setting me up. Diego, on the other hand, was a pure tail. I rubbed my wet hands together.

I played with the idea of taking him on a guided tour of someplace he didn't want to go—like Yonkers—but I decided there was no harm in letting him follow me home. Diego wouldn't learn anything but my address, and Tom already had that much in his directory.

Besides, I needed another subway token.

I dodged around taxis and leaped puddles, crossing the street to Diego's side.

"Can you lend me another token?" I asked.

He looked puzzled for a moment, like he wasn't sure if he should pretend he wasn't there, but we were both getting soaked, so he dug a token out of his pants pocket and handed it over.

"I'm taking the IRT to Seventy-second," I said, "and I'll walk two blocks north and one west. Now we're even."

I went home to Seventy-fourth Street and, since I was still keyless, had to rouse the super to let me into my apartment. I

tossed my wet clothes into the hamper, brushed my teeth, lifted
the shade to look out the window at Diego nine stories down on
the street, and went to bed, pleased with the idea that the rain
would probably keep up all afternoon and his clothes weren't
getting any drier. I pulled the fresh, crisp sheet up to my chin
and hoped he was hungry. Being followed was fun, I thought,
yawning and snuggling into the pillows.

The phone woke me up at 6:45. More than four hours of sleep.
I rolled over and punched the speaker button.

"Abby," Ike's voice said, "I heard you pick up. Say something."

"Something."

"I got your message. You want to meet at FBI headquarters,
or do you want to go together?"

"Is it still raining?"

"Let me look."

I could hear some noise from her end of the line, like she was
rooting around in her bed; then I heard what I knew was the blue
silk shade behind our former conjugal bed go whapping up,
sounding, as it always had, like a newspaper caught in the wind.

"Nope," she said. "I can see clear sky."

"I'm getting homesick listening to the noises you're making.
What are you wearing?"

"That green teddy you gave...Abby, mind your own business.
Are you taking extra hormone shots or something?"

I.Q. Aim. Hormones. The list was getting long.

"I'm still using up the hormones I got when I was a teenager,"
I said. "At the rate I'm going, I'll have plenty left when I'm
ninety."

"That's your own fault, Romeo. You should have thought of
that when you took your hormones to the Kremlin and betrayed
our marriage."

I sat up in bed. "Let's skate."

"Excuse me?"

"Let's skate. As in Rollerblade. To Federal Plaza."

"Oh. *Skate.* I thought you said 'mate.' You want to skate all
that way?"

"Now you're talking. I'd love to go all the way with you."

She snorted into the phone. "I'll be at your place in half an
hour."

"No, wait. We'll have to meet somewhere else."

"Why?"

"Because—oh, boy, I can't wait to tell you this one; get ready to laugh—Tom Hitt is having me followed."

"That's outrageous! Who's following you?"

"I think it's kind of funny. Diego Gordillo."

"I'm going to tell on him to Othello. Can you lose Diego? We don't want company on this errand to the FBI."

"Can I lose Diego? Jesus, Ike, I'll be on wheels."

"Ha! I'd like to be there to see Diego's face when you light out."

"Be at the Emerald City instead and I'll show you my face when I get there. That's the last place Tom'll think of looking for me at this hour, just as they get off the air. That's also where I left the business cards."

"Half an hour?"

"Half an hour. Wear the teddy."

She hung up, not gently.

I shaved, showered, and applied a layer of Band-aids to my blistered ankle, the mass of red and bubbled skin that had kept me out of my skates the night before. The Band-aid wad wasn't pretty, but it looked like it would do the job. I pulled on a pair of cutoff jeans, stuck a white T-shirt in my waistband, yanked on a pair of socks, snatched my extra set of keys from the desk, scooped some change and a couple of tens off the bureau, and grabbed my skates at the door.

On the way down in the elevator, I pulled on the T-shirt and crammed the keys and buying power into my pockets. I went to the lobby door and scanned the street. Diego was leaning against the building, wearing dry clothes. And he was on blades.

Tom Hitt must've sent Diego the reinforcements while I slept. Tom's no fool, so I figured he'd picked Diego for a reason, and that reason might be that Diego actually knew how to skate. I wondered if he was any good.

I parked myself on a bench in the lobby and got equipped for speed.

When I pushed open the door, Diego was admiring the clear sky.

"Nice out," I told him, pulling the door shut behind me.

"Very nice. Beats the heat, doesn't it?"

"You ready to go?"

"Ready, man."

"You had anything to eat today?"

"Yeah. A nice slice of pizza across the street."

"They do a fine pepperoni over there."

He nodded. "They do."

"You need to go to the bathroom or anything?"

"I'm fine."

"Then let's get this over with. It's going to be a lonely night for you, Diego."

"Maybe. Maybe not."

"I play rough."

"Tom says you're not as good as you think you are."

"Tom doesn't know how good I think I am."

"Whatever. He says it's all hype."

"You've been had, amigo. You're toast."

I rolled out across the sidewalk and over the curb, studying the traffic. I looked over my shoulder at Diego, just once, then took off for Amsterdam Avenue. More pedestrians (that includes skaters) are killed on Amsterdam by automobiles than on any other street in Manhattan. As the *only* Manhattan street listed on the Department of Transportation's 1992 roster of the city's ten most dangerous streets, Amsterdam seemed like a logical and appropriate place to take Diego to the races.

The rush was behind schedule that evening, very thick for seven o'clock, probably because of the earlier flooding, and the traffic going up Amsterdam was all I could have wished for—cars and taxis and bicyclists and Rollerbladers and buses and trucks and one lunatic on a skateboard and a panhandler in a wheelchair, shaking his Styrofoam cup with one hand and pushing his chair against the traffic with his other hand. I threaded my way out into the middle lane and put my legs into it, gathering speed and timing the lights, which is another terrific advantage to playing tag on Amsterdam—the lights are staggered. I wove in and out of the fire lane until I saw my opening. Near the corner of Seventy-ninth, a cruising ambulance suddenly flashed its lights and the siren let out a pulsating wail. I put on a burst of sprint speed and broke into the lane, swerving across the front of the ambulance as it took off, the siren blasting in my ears. The driver gave me the finger, and I tore down the short block of Seventy-ninth that dumps out at the Museum of Natural History and made a right onto Columbus. I circled through the dusky shadows lining the pavement and stopped. No Diego.

I took a leisurely tour on the sidewalk around the museum, just to make sure Diego had learned that Tom Hitt was not a good judge of what I think, and headed for the park, going east.

It was pleasantly cool in the park, and I was just hitting my stride when I came out on Central Park South and turned right toward Columbus Circle. I could see Ike turning a speed stop in front of the Emerald City. She waited for me at the entrance and we went in together.

She showed her I.D., and we signed in. We skated to the elevator together. She pushed the button for twenty-seven.

"Where's Diego?" she said.

"I think he's on the front bumper of an ambulance."

"Serves him right."

"You look very pretty tonight, my dear, even if I would have preferred the green teddy."

She was wearing cutoffs, too, and one of those workout tops that looks like a bra with wide straps. Her skates were pink, and the tops of her thick white socks were just visible where the pink ended.

"Thank you," she said.

"You're welcome."

I let her go first when the elevator doors opened, and I saw that she had her cell phone stuffed into her tight back pocket.

"Very fetching phone you have there," I said to her backside.

"Thank you."

"You're welcome."

We went straight to my office, which was as unlocked as I had left it. As I reached up for the Emmy and the key to my desk, Ike sat down at my keyboard, booted the computer, typed in her password, and read the index of her mail.

"The autopsy results on Hektor," she said, pounding the keyboard and switching displays. She read a long memo. "The coroner released the results at three this afternoon." I waited. She turned around.

"Heart failure. Pure and simple. No wounds. No punctures, no bruises. No evidence of poison. The only notable thing about Hektor's blood chemistry is the presence of"—she turned back to the monitor to consult the electronic note—"beta adrenergic blockers."

"That doesn't sound good."

"Unless you happen to suffer from glaucoma. They expected to find it in Hektor, and they did. Nothing funny about it."

"Jeez, Ike. I'd hate to be the medical examiner right now. Fillingeri's probably left teeth marks in the guy's scalp."

"Did you happen to see a newscast today?"

"Nope."

She fiddled with the keyboard and called up the lineup for *Evening Watch*. She sat and pouted at the screen, her elbows propped on the corners of the keyboard, her chin in her hands, and I squatted beside the chair to read along with her.

"They led with it, of course," she mumbled, rubbing her chin with her knuckles. "Tom got an exclusive interview with the medical examiner." She pointed at the first item on the display. "Look at that. They slugged it 'Unclassified Paint Job.' Very funny." She punched keys, switched screens, and produced the full script for the lead story. She read a few lines. "The medical examiner said plenty more nothing." She started laughing and scanned the last paragraphs of the story. "See that? They got a sound bite from Fillingeri: 'If it weren't for the yellow paint and the U.S.S.R. note, we'd be ruling this a natural death. As it is, for now, the death of Dr. Hektor Stefanopolis is unclassified.'"

"Why are you laughing?"

"Look at Tom's note at the bottom of the script."

I read it.

His note, obviously a lighthearted, private exchange with the correspondent and not meant for broadcast, said, "Captain F.— New York's Funkiest unclassifies his own click: 'Hey, just because somebody painted it, hung a sign on it, and it doesn't work anymore, doesn't mean a crime's been committed.'—Hitt."

Ike shut off the machine and swiveled toward me in my chair.

"Tom is going to try to make sure you don't shake loose again, Abby. Next thing you know he'll borrow the traffic helicopter from Channel 5 to keep an eye on you."

Still squatting by the chair, I put my hands on her knees, not amorously, just keeping my balance. "I could always go underground. The only thing I've never seen in the subways is a helicopter. Ike, those guys were all murdered. You know it, Tom knows it, Fillingeri knows it, the M.E. knows it. It's probably driving Fillingeri nuts that he can't call it murder. And he can't, not until the medical examiner says it's murder. Fillingeri's being hung on a technicality, a noose his own department made. I hate to defend him, God knows, but he's got to be as strung out as he can be without snapping in two.''

"I guess.''

"It's more important than ever to find Tex,'' I said, pressing her knees with the palms of my hands. "The killer—whether it's Tex or not—looks like he's getting away with it. And I have a feeling Tex has enough of a criminal record to go platinum in Cainstraight's jukebox.''

"Let's put some serious concrete under our wheels.''

I leaned across her knees and unlocked my big desk drawer.

She lifted out the NASA box and raised an eyebrow. "You still have this?''

"I haven't heard from Tony. The business cards are in there, and while you're at it, you might as well feast your eyes on Einstein's true-or-false test.''

She opened the box, and I took the business cards by the corners, slipping them into my T-shirt pocket. She stared down at the plastic cube holding the Spinning Quartz Ball.

"It's rather ordinary, isn't it?'' she said.

"How can you say that? It's blasphemy. That ball thing is pure music. It makes me want to soar to the planets and know the secrets of the ages.''

She gave me a look. "Well, well, aren't you a combination of Buck Rogers and Indiana Jones? What's come over you?''

I closed the box, put it back in my drawer, and turned the key in the lock. I rose and replaced the key under my dusty statue. I held out my hand to her.

"You are cordially invited to accompany me on a journey into the unknown. Let's go see the jukebox.''

She stood, slipping an inch or so on her skates before she got her balance. "You make it sound like a joyride to Jupiter instead of Rollerblading down Broadway.''

"Ditch your disbelief at the door, little girl, and follow me.''

She grinned. "Now you sound like the Big Bad Wolf.''

I leered at her bosom. "Grandmother will love your space suit.''

FIFTEEN

TRAFFIC WAS thinning out when we left the Emerald City and began a gentle glide down the Great White Way. I looked around for signs of Tom Hitt's Junior Spy League, but trying to find one suspicious-looking person among the hundreds of hustlers in that area is like sorting lentils on a fast conveyor belt. I didn't see anyone who worked for *Evening Watch*, not unless he was dressed as a pimp or a Japanese tourist with theater tickets or a Con-Ed worker or Elvis.

As we passed the Ed Sullivan Theater, with its blue-and-yellow marquee featuring David Letterman's name, Ike pulled out her cell phone and dialed a number with her thumb.

"Who are you calling?"

"The Parker Meridien. That's where we put Tony."

She talked to the phone for a minute or so, returned the phone to her back pocket, and glanced up at the Jumbotron in Times Square. There was a flashy commercial on the giant screen for Columbia Home Videos.

"Tony's not in his room," she said.

"We'd have heard if he'd checked out of the Parker Meridien and moved to a suite at Midtown North. He's probably out playing."

"I'm not worried about where he is now. I'm worried about where he'll be at six o'clock tomorrow morning. Tony and his ball thing will probably be our first segment after the news at the top of the show."

"Tony's a pro. He'll be there. Fillingeri can't be serious about him. Tony won't miss the show even if he has to do it in an orange jumpsuit and leg shackles. After all, NASA needs good PR with the American public about as much as I need good PR with you."

She gave me a long, considering look as we glided along. "You don't have as many accidents as NASA does."

I didn't know how to take that, but my attention was grabbed by a bicyclist trying to cut me off, and I let Ike's remark go. I gave myself a mental pat on the back for restraining myself with the biker and gave technology a silent salute when I checked all the temperature clocks visible from Times Square and saw that they all agreed: it was eighty-one degrees everywhere within a three-block radius. New York's a difficult city to get lost in, with signs everywhere, but I call it downright accommodating—user friendly, even—that we have such a commitment to announcing publicly the weather inside our greatest black hole for tourists. You'll always know how warm it was when all your money got sucked away into the great neon maw of the universe.

Once past Times Square and its random obstacles of street vendors and trash and the pre-theater dinner crowds, we were able to pick up our pace. We skated all the way to Fourteenth Street without exchanging a word. We stopped there for a red light, both of us a little winded. The patches of clouds in the sky were pink and orange, and I was nearly blinded when the light changed and the cab beside me peeled out, its side mirror grabbing a piece of the fireball sun riding over the Jersey hills and throwing it back into my face. I stood there blinking rapidly, and Ike was across Fourteenth before I could see again.

I groped my way across the street, and there on the corner sidewalk was a wriggling mass of things crawling around. At first I thought it was rats, and then I thought I was seeing things, but eventually I got it worked out that they were battery-operated toys: a tiny walking camel, a tiny yellow chicken clucking and laying tiny white eggs on the sidewalk, a tiny cow mooing and squirting white strings out of her udder, and a plastic rat baring its teeth and lashing its tail and dropping rat raisins. These were just the demos; the guy selling them was sitting on a couple of cartons, probably piping hot off the truck. $9.95 American, and you can take a crapping plastic rat home to your wife and kids in Tokyo, if you've decided against a replica of the Empire State Building or sunglasses that light up and turn your head into the Statue of Liberty. What the hell—why not buy one of each and get the full experience?

I caught up with Ike and gave her hand a quick squeeze. She let me hang on (which for me was the trip to Jupiter), and we sailed together down the island, enjoying a fast workout for

twenty blocks or so until we fetched up at the Jacob K. Javits
Federal Building.

There's no sign on the building to indicate that the FBI lives
there. I used to think that there ought to be a law that every
building in New York should be labeled with a brief and accurate
list of contents, but now, since terrorists and semiautomatics have
begun to outnumber cabs, I've changed my mind. Maybe we
should paint all the buildings and street signs black and make the
scare-artists guess. We'd keep the temperature clocks and let them
know how hot they were, but not *where* they were.

We entered the federal building and skated across to the security guard/commando/receptionist/body-builder manning the
desk. If he gave me any sass about rules and so on, I planned to
keep my mouth shut and obey. He was light-years above Carl
Honeyman and the Emerald City's idea of security. He was carrying two guns that showed, and I didn't even want to speculate
on what wasn't showing.

I gave him our names and our work titles, and Ike showed her
NTB News I.D. card, all of which seemed to impress him not at
all. He didn't say any words with his mouth, and he didn't say
anything with his face, and he didn't say anything with his posture. The only way I knew for sure that he wasn't a robot was
his dandruff. I asked for Morris Cainstraight.

The guard/dandruff/strong-silent type punched what I took to
be a security clearance code into the telephone on the desk and
picked up the receiver. There was no way I could have made the
call myself. Carl Honeyman would die of envy if he saw the setup
in this building.

"Special Agent Cainstraight will be right down," the security/
gun/code/scary guy said, "and he'll escort you upstairs. In the
meantime, I'll have to ask you to hold out your hands for the
scanner."

"Huh?" I said.

He lifted a slim gray device attached by a curly white cord to
a computer on the desk. "Fingerprints."

I held out my right hand, palm up. The device grunted five
times and a red flash shot out with each grunt.

"Other hand," he said.

I gave him my left, and he repeated the procedure.

It was Ike's turn.

"Hold out your hand, miss."

"I'm not doing that," she said. "Who do you think you are?"

"I think I'm FBI, miss, and if you don't want to be finger-printed, that's fine with me."

She flashed me a startled look of triumph.

"Well," she said, "I guess it pays to stick up for your rights."

"The only thing is," he said, "if you choose not to be scanned, which is your right, you'll have to wait for your friend here in the lobby while he goes up with Mr. Cainstraight. I'll be happy to have some coffee supplied for you, and perhaps some maga-zines to help pass the time."

Ike stuck her hands out toward him.

"Thank you, miss." He operated with the scanner, and the little grunts and red lights passed over Ike's fingertips.

"I promised you a trip to Jupiter," I told her, smiling. "Wel-come aboard."

"Yeah." She looked at her fingertips. "I'll never be the same. My fingers have just lost their virginity."

They're efficient at the Jacob K. Javits Federal Building. Ike had barely gotten started on the inspection of her deflowered fin-gers when an elevator door opened and Morris Cainstraight stepped out. He was wearing the standard FBI uniform: a dark suit, white shirt, dark tie, square jaw, American Conservative Haircut. No visible distinguishing marks.

He shook hands with me, a standard no-nonsense manly snake, and gave Ike the same when I introduced her. He didn't even glance at the parts of her that were on display due to the brevity of her outfit. Aristotle Stefanopolis could benefit, I thought, by a course in FBI manners.

We accompanied Morris Cainstraight up to the second floor. He steered us through a hushed warren of cubbies and offices. The quiet was profound, pristine; it would have turned Fred Lor-ing so green with envy that he would have been a good match for his computer date, the electronic skeleton.

Our course led us to an open area unblemished by any natural light. A few people dressed like our escort in FBI uniforms were working at computers or on telephones, but they didn't look at us. I supposed they didn't need to: if Ike and I tried anything funny, their lobby scanner already had us.

It was a little unnerving to be so casually dressed and on skates in that serious environment without having anyone even bother to glance at us, but maybe the scanner had already told them we weren't worth looking at.

Morris Cainstraight took us into a glass-enclosed, computer-lined room, and I heard the familiar hum of clean-air machines. I didn't see any metal monsters lying around on the floor, but there were several unusual vents in the walls at eye level. The FBI's air suckers were, by golly, *built in.* Unlike the Graphic Arts Department at NTB News, the FBI's Atmospheric Purity Budget was coming out of the taxpayer's pocket, so the feds had a state-of-the-art environment. Of course, in all fairness, they also had a jukebox and could catch criminals, whereas our GA could only draw them.

Cainstraight closed the door and turned into a human.

"How've you been, Abby?"

"Can't you tell from the scanner guy downstairs? I mean, wasn't that a complete physical?"

"Nuts. When the bureau gives a complete physical, we leave bruises. You just had your prints scanned. Don't be such a baby."

"Ah, prints. I'm glad you brought up the subject. I happen to be in the market for the only thing you can buy with prints."

He nodded. "You want a name."

"And anything else you have. I'm not such a baby that I don't know the FBI has more than names to go with prints."

"What've you got?"

"Four business cards. I don't know which one has the prints I'm interested in." I pulled the cards out of my pocket and held the stack out by one corner. "Can you find Waldo in this picture?"

"Do I owe you a favor, Abby?" Cainstraight said, looking like I'd asked to borrow his toothbrush. "FBI files aren't exactly community newspapers."

I tried a persuasive smile. "Maybe you'd like to put the NTB Television Network in a headlock—we'd owe *you* a favor. We're not exactly a community newspaper, either."

He picked up a clear plastic sheet from the worktable in the center of the room and said, "Drop them here."

I dropped them on the plastic, and he stirred them around with a thin wooden tube, separating them so none of the edges touched.

"Let's see if we can make it easy," he said.

"Fine by me. In fact, it would be perfect if it were easy, because I came by the fingerprints easily."

"How'd you get them?"

"Do I have to tell?"

"No, but when I track down their owner on the jukebox, I'll either have a shrewd guess or the right to ask the question again."

"That's why I brought Ike. She's up on rights."

"Attorney?"

"Babe."

Ike shook her head. "I hate being treated like I'm not even here. I'm the senior broadcast producer of *Morning Watch*, with a graduate degree in journalism from the University of Missouri, Columbia. I'm not an attorney, but I know constitutional law. And whether I'm a babe is not a matter for discussion, unless you men want to play absolutely fair and open the talk up for consideration of your physical attributes, too. I'll start with Abby. I'm only looking for a little clarification here on procedure."

"I told you she was up on rights," I said.

"She's also right," Cainstraight said. "Let's get to work."

He bent over the small spread of business cards bearing my name, title, telephone number, and the NTB logo/address.

"Let's go for the obvious," he said, pointing to one of the cards. "This one's dirtier than the others."

"Can you just use the scanner and get the print?" Ike said.

"Probably not. I'll probably have to dust it. We'll see."

There were several scanners on the table, all connected by long white wires to a central jack on the far wall. He picked up and pointed one of the scanners, and a series of the little grunts and red flashes popped over the card he had selected, but he said, "I'm not reading it."

From a drawer under the worktable, he took a small jar of what looked like dirt. He used an eyedropper-type contraption and sprayed a fine mist of the stuff over the card. He brought the scanner back over the card, made it grunt and flash, and smiled. There was a new noise.

"Did you hear that?" he said.

"Yeah," I said.

"Yeah," Ike said.

The scanner had emitted a high-pitched beep.

He aimed the thing again, and I counted four beeps. He turned the card over with the wooden tube and a pair of thin tongs, and aimed again. This time I counted seven beeps. Twelve in all.

"I hope they're not all yours, Abby," he said.

"Well, one of those cards has somebody's prints on it besides mine."

"Let's see what the jukebox will play for us."

I looked around the room, and so did Ike.

"I don't see anything remotely like a jukebox," she said.

"It's in the basement," Cainstraight said. "We don't take civilians down there. You break one of our live-scanners up here, we're only out a few thousand dollars. You break a disk down there, we're out a few million prints."

"I'm glad you're not treating us like we're special or anything," I said.

"But I am," he said. "Most civilians don't get as far as this room."

He took the scanner, sat down at a terminal, and gestured for us to take seats on either side of his.

He booted the computer, typed for a while, and plugged the scanner into a slot in the wall above the display screen. I could hear the computer working.

"Eight of the twelve prints are yours, Abagnarro," he said. "And one is just a smudge."

"That leaves three strangers."

"They could belong to the guy who prints your cards."

"Shit. I never thought of that."

"Hang on. There it is."

On the screen was some text and, down the right side, windows that held pictures of fingerprints. They were so clear they looked like photographs.

We all leaned toward the screen.

"This guy's got a distinguished service record," Cainstraight said. "Vietnam. Two Purple Hearts and the Bronze Star. 181st infantry. Field commission. Jesus, he certainly didn't spend his time washing jeeps in the motor pool at Camp Saigon. He did two tours of Nam. No criminal record. Date of birth, January 17, 1945. Place of birth, New York, New York. Last address Fort Ord, where he was discharged in 1971. Those are the highlights, and some highlights they are."

"What's his name?" Ike said, gripping the seat of her chair like she was having trouble sitting still.

Cainstraight pushed his chair back from the computer and crossed him arms over his chest.

"This is where we make the trade," he said.

"What do you want?" Ike said. "Just for the name?"

"I want to know how you got the print."

"Abby?" Ike said.

I chewed on it for a minute. "A hypothetical question. What if I got the fingerprint while a guy was mugging me? Would you go after him?"

"Is that all? That's what the NYPD is for, or supposedly for." He laughed at his own little joke. "I thought with all the urgency that your man was a terrorist, or maybe that serial killer. It turns out you only want your wallet back."

He scooted back to the computer and hit two keys.

I looked at Ike behind Cainstraight's back. She had her hand over her mouth, obviously hiding a nonpoker face as she read the words coming across the screen.

A window at the top of the screen had opened up. Cainstraight read the text and pushed his chair back, his face expressionless.

I read the text in the display window.

"There's your man," Cainstraight said, lacing his fingers together over his middle. "United States Army Second Lieutenant Ulysses Samuel Sylvester Raintree." He paused, gazing at the screen. "Interesting initials your mugger has—U.S.S.R." Cainstraight swiveled his chair a quarter turn toward me without taking his eyes off the name on the screen. "How the hell did you really get this fingerprint, Abagnarro?"

SIXTEEN

"HOW'D I GET the fingerprint?" I said. My voice sounded hollow to me. "I told you."

"Yes. I remember. This guy Raintree mugged you, Abby, and that's all you know about him." Cainstraight nodded at the vital statistics on his screen beside the pictures of Tex's fingerprints, and his voice took on an edge I'd never heard in it before. "You're too smart to yank my chain for the hell of it. Did you think this would just fly past my nose like a bad smell on a windy day?"

"I didn't think anything," I managed, trying not to look like the jukebox had just unloaded the answer to a huge mystery. Here I was telling a simple truth, and I felt like a liar. I'm sure I looked like a liar. In the stillness of the room, with only the background hum of the clean-air vents making a sound, I was suddenly aware that I had skater's B.O. I even smelled like a liar.

"You didn't think anything," he said, nodding. "You plan to start thinking anytime soon?"

"What I'm thinking now is that the guy really mugged me," I said. "That's the truth. I'm also thinking I'm surprised the guy was an officer. I'm really surprised he has no criminal record. The way he mugged me was highly skilful. He really mugged me, Morris."

"How'd he get close to you?"

"I was on foot."

"What'd he use, the Blast?"

"It felt more like the Crack of Doom. My ears still hurt."

"That's it? End of story?"

The white, glowing characters of Tex's real name on the monitor screen seemed to pulse with a restless energy that separated them from the other elements of the electronic composition. For a moment, my will suspended, I stared at the name. I imagined that name lifting off the glass and actually floating in front of

Cainstraight's nose. I broke out of the stare, shifting my gaze to Ike. She was staring at the screen.

But Cainstraight was looking at me. "Come on, Abby. What's the real story?"

"Maybe you should give me a little hint, Morris, just so I don't get confused about what you're asking."

He shifted in his chair, nothing threatening, but it suddenly occurred to me to wonder if he was armed. I'd never considered Cainstraight before as a regular FBI sort of agent, the sort that carries weapons and thinks sinister thoughts like people are lying to him. He had always struck me as a techno-nerd dressed up in a G-man costume. But then, this was the first time he was asking me questions about criminal activity.

Cainstraight kept his fingers laced over his middle, lifting only one finger out of the weave to point at the computer screen. "A hint. Sure. You want a hint. How's this for a hint? A man who was a guest on your program this morning died in an alley outside your building, and somebody stuck a label on his shirt that said 'U.S.S.R.' That's interesting. And here you come, bringing me a fingerprint that belongs to a man named Ulysses Samuel Sylvester Raintree. You can't think of anything to add to that?"

"Do I have to?"

Ike stood on her skates and made the time-out sign with her hands. "Can Abby and I talk alone, for a minute or two?"

"Of course." He stood promptly, like Ike was his old school-teacher asking him to clean the erasers. "I have a phone call to make anyway." He left the room.

I watched his exit suspiciously. "I'll bet he's got a call to make," I said.

"Do you think this room's bugged?"

"Did J. Edgar Hoover wear evening gowns?" I glanced around, probably looking shifty as hell. "We're in the FBI's New York headquarters. What do you think?"

"Let's go out in the hall."

We skated out the door and huddled together in the hall, whispering.

"Let's get our priorities straight here," Ike said, "and not get carried away by force of habit. The main thing is to catch the killer, agreed? I mean, that's more important than a scoop?"

"Yes."

"Then you have to tell him everything about Tex."

"We could have said all this inside that room. We sound like perfect Americans."

"Yeah, I know, but it's creepy to think someone's listening to us while we dust off our consciences."

"Let's go back inside and be the model citizens we are. Just act natural."

"And no stupid jokes from you, Abby. I don't want to be here all night."

I raised my hand to make the pledge. "No stupid jokes."

We returned to the room and took our seats. We were silent. Cainstraight came back about five minutes later and laughed out loud after he got a look at our angelic faces.

"Much better," he said. "You both look like you're about ready to crack under the strain. This room's not bugged."

"It's not?" I said.

"Why would the bureau bug its own jukebox?"

"Because you can?"

Ike gave me a warning look. *No jokes,* she mouthed.

"If mere ability were the standard for bugging," Cainstraight said, his face suddenly serious, "we'd have wires strung across this city so tight nobody could move." He sat down between us and said, "I just got off the phone with Dennis Fillingeri. He says he knows you both pretty well; apparently you think you're the funny-man, Abby."

I smiled. "That's only what I think I am. Did Fillingeri also tell you what I think he is?"

Ike cocked her head to one side, curiosity rampant in her blue and green eyes. "What did he say about me?"

Cainstraight hesitated. "Oh. Not much."

"What? I deserve to know. You told Abby."

"He, uh, said you tend to be uptight and self-righteous. But I'm sure he meant that in a good way."

Ike made a few gobbling noises, but Cainstraight was smart enough to ignore them and went on. "The point is, what I was going to say, Captain Fillingeri says you're both essentially good citizens."

"Thanks ever so much." Ike was now able to form words. "I'm just delighted for the pat on the back."

"And the bureau," Cainstraight said, plowing over her words, "with Captain Fillingeri's full blessing, would very much like for you to tell us all the particulars on the fingerprint collection. Consider this an official request."

"Can I get a word in here?" Ike said, her face red. "You're working with Fillingeri on the Yellow-Man killings?"

"Certainly. Serial killers are a little specialty of ours, like kidnapping and terrorism."

"Was this Fillingeri's idea or yours?"

"He called us. That's the chain. The local authority invites us onto his turf."

"How long have you been working on this?"

"Three weeks."

"Almost from the beginning?"

"That's right. Fillingeri's a good cop. He uses his resources well."

Ike snorted.

Cainstraight looked like he'd heard worse snorts in his career. "Maybe you don't understand, but the bureau's been keeping a very low profile on this because our experts have been telling us that the 'U.S.S.R.' note business is a political matter. And Fillingeri has been lying low, keeping his face off of newspaper covers. When it comes to serial killers, law enforcement has to play it close because of all the confessors out there."

"Confessors?" Ike said.

"The people who like to get attention by coming forward and saying they did it. If we released everything we had, we'd have no way of checking their stories."

"You've actually had people coming in to say they did these Yellow-Man crimes?"

"We haven't. Fillingeri's had six so far—that's off the record. But none of the six could explain the 'U.S.S.R.' thing or tell us how the victims died."

I raised a hand. "The part about the medical examiner not knowing the cause of death. Is that just something you're holding back to trap confessors?"

"Unfortunately, no. All six confessors said they stabbed the victims to death, which isn't true. But we don't know what is true. The M.E.'s baffled. We're all baffled. We thought we were on the right track about the political nature of the notes left on the corpses. Until now. Now we don't know what to think. Now you bring us a fingerprint belonging to Second Lieutenant Ulysses Samuel Sylvester Raintree. We want to know the story.''

"I'll tell you what happened," I began, "although first I'd like to say that Fillingeri had a chance to ask me. He heard I was mugged and said he didn't believe it.''

Cainstraight raised an eyebrow. "I wonder why not.''

"We have sort of a difficult relationship.''

"So I gathered. And that surprises me, given what I know of Captain Fillingeri and Midtown North. That precinct has an admirable record in every way—four decades in business, only four men killed in the line of duty—not the kind of record you pile up by cultivating difficult relationships.''

"It's partly my fault.''

"Let's see how you do with me.''

I sighed and told him the Tex epic, starting with how the mugger picked me up at Lincoln Center and knew my name. I told Cainstraight everything Tex said, including his opinion of the Mets and the fact that he wanted to talk to me about killing. I told Cainstraight about trying to brush Tex off by giving him a business card, and I finished with a cold rendition of the mugging, leaving out my strictly personal reactions.

"But you didn't report the crime officially?''

I shook my head.

"Why not?''

"Oh, you know. I had to get to work, I've looked at mug shots before, I've sampled the coffee at Midtown North, I have a weird relationship with Fillingeri, and so on, and so on.''

"You also had that fingerprint.''

"I didn't think of that at the time. It was only after we saw the mugger turn up on the videotape of the crime scene in Central Park that I started thinking about what I had in my pocket. Look, the guy only got about four bucks off me, plus my keys and I.D. I thought he was just a better-than-average pocket artist.''

"Fillingeri has a copy of that videotape?''

"Yeah.''

"I see. And you've had no further communication with this man who calls himself Tex?''

"Not a peep.''

"Have you changed the locks on the places those keys open?''

I was struck dumb. It never occurred to me.

Rather abruptly, Cainstraight stood. "I'd advise you to take care of that, Abby. In the meantime, I'm going to share what you've told me with Captain Fillingeri."

Ike piped up. "Speaking of sharing. You're not going to release this mugging story and the fingerprint to the media, are you?"

"I hope not. A lot depends on you. I can't order you not to use it; I can request that you cooperate with us by keeping it to yourselves. Serial killers don't stop killing until they're caught; a fresh kill sometimes just whets the appetite. What you've brought us tonight may mean a great deal to what we can do in the next few days to stop this guy. You can see that having the name of that man—whether he's the killer or not—will give some new energy to this investigation. But if you put it out on the air, we'll probably never get a smell of him. He'll either be gone or change his methods."

"You've probably already thought of this," Ike said, rolling her skates back against the legs of her chair, the impact so loud in that clean, quiet room that she jumped. "Sorry." She looked to see if she'd bruised the chair. "Wouldn't it be good to have some facts a little more current than 1971?"

"You got that right."

"Doesn't the jukebox have other indexes? You only used the military and criminal files, didn't you?"

He clicked his tongue against his teeth. "That's all we can do, I'm afraid, as far as the jukebox goes. From here we have to go the traditional routes."

"But why? Can't the jukebox check Social Services, the Welfare stuff? They fingerprint their clients, don't they?"

"Some counties, some states. Depends on local law."

Ike looked a little smug. "Well, well. You could run the business card prints against their rolls."

"I can't do that."

"Why not?"

"Because we're in New York."

"So?"

"The state of New York has a law prohibiting the cross-referencing of Welfare files with our jukebox."

"Why?"

"Because, the theory goes, such a mingling of information amounts to the criminalization of poverty."

Ike sat back in her chair, thinking it over.

"I'm sure that's the way the ACLU sees it," she said. "I guess that's the way I see it." She looked down at her skates, seemed to be thinking it over, and looked up. "I don't suppose you'd ever consider breaking a law, would you? Just one teeny little exception?"

He smiled, a real smile, warm and understanding and even a little wistful, if you can picture that on the face of an FBI special agent considering a criminal life for himself. "Not in this building."

"I didn't think you would."

"I'd have been surprised if you didn't ask. Believe me, Captain Fillingeri had a fit just now on the phone when he asked and got turned down, just like I'm turning you down."

"God, you sound like Eliot Ness."

"I practice," Cainstraight said, grinning. But, despite the smile, I could tell he really wasn't going to bend the rules, not for us, not for Fillingeri. Although that didn't mean he wouldn't bend them for himself. "It's getting late, and now that you've brought me the name of Second Lieutenant U.S.S.R., I've got work to do. Your story sounds like gold to me, but we'll be back in touch with you to get it in writing. There's no need for that formality now. But I will have to insist that you leave the business cards with me."

I looked around at the glass walls, at the center worktable, at the computers. "You *did* bug this room. You've got it all on a recording."

"You watch too much TV, Abby. I give you my word."

"Then how come I don't have to do all that written statement hogwash?"

"Because I've got a good memory." He offered a hand, dismissing me. We shook, and he gave Ike the same treatment. "We'll be talking again."

He escorted us back down to the lobby and to the street door. I looked longingly at the security guard, half wishing he had a procedure that would unscan our fingerprints. Ike and I were now in the jukebox, with all the millions of men and women who have criminal or military records, and we didn't belong in either club.

When we were alone on the sidewalk, Ike put her hands on

her hips and looked at the sky. "Uptight and self-righteous. That's the stupidest thing I ever heard."

I looked at the sky.

She looked at me. I kept looking at the sky.

"Abby, I'm not uptight and self-righteous."

"I didn't say you were."

"Well, I'm not." She stood there and breathed. "Dennis is uptight and self-righteous."

I kept looking at the sky. She kept up the loud breathing.

"Whatever." She waved her hand impatiently and glided a few feet toward the street. "There's something fishy about Mr. Ness letting us go like this."

The sky was dark, darker than it had been for a week. The sick orange haze was gone, and, while I could see no stars, I found the nice clean blankness a relief after several nights of staring at the oily belly of a hot air mass squatting over Manhattan.

"Fishy or not, there's nothing we can do about it, Ike. If we're going to use this song the jukebox just played, we'd better get moving."

The street was practically deserted around the government buildings, and we were traveling at a leisurely pace, a thoughtful pace. We turned at Worth Street and made for the even quieter emptiness of Lafayette.

"The map Fred made for us," Ike said.

"The CBS Broadcast Center."

"I know it sounds dumb, but it's a place to start.

"As good as anything I can suggest."

"What do we actually know about Tex?"

I considered as I skated, sorting out the little encounter with my personal mugger. "He smelled like perfume."

"Perfume? Don't you mean cologne?"

"No. Perfume. Very flowery."

"What else?"

"He knew my name."

"That doesn't help."

I thought some more. "He served in Vietnam."

"So did a lot of people."

"He wore a red sweater."

"Probably stole it."

"More likely got it out of a dumpster."

"What else, Abby?"

"Gold teeth. Those cost money."

Ike glanced over her shoulder. "That could be the Army's dental plan.

"Gold?"

"Sure." She skated in a circle around me and kept talking, but she was looking down Lafayette. "Twenty years ago dentists were still doing teeth with gold instead of making caps out of porcelain, unless you were a movie star."

"So Tex wasn't a movie star," I said. "I can't think of anything else. He was just a big, big guy that smelled like perfume."

Ike skated closer to me and said, "Don't look now, but we're being followed. And I don't think it's Tom Hitt's rookie *Evening Watch* goons."

So, of course I looked. There were two dark sedans trailing behind us a couple of blocks back, crawling up Lafayette without lights. And two men in suits, walking in the street between the cars. And a woman on a bicycle, pedaling along slowly beside one of the cars.

"This is just fascinating," I said. "I thought we were pals with the FBI. All that off-the-record camaraderie. All that hand shaking. All that 'we'll be in touch' stuff. You know what?"

"What?"

"I think Fillingeri told Morris Cainstraight that I'm a funnyman who tells lies and not to believe that I got the print during a mugging."

"Well, you didn't help by not even having your locks changed."

"I didn't think of it."

"I've told you a million times not to be so careless with your stuff. Now look where we are. We've got FBI agents wiggling up our spines, and all because you don't have any common sense. You're the same way with your credit cards. You'll never understand that—"

I grabbed her wrist. "Stop yapping at me."

"Let go. I wasn't yapping."

I released her wrist. "*Talking,* then. Stop talking. I want to talk. Do we want those guys following us?"

"Two minutes ago I wouldn't have dreamed they'd do anything so rude. Who the hell do they think we are—Mahmud the

Red? We're the good guys, for Christ's sake. We're not a threat to anyone.''

"Is there something on your fingerprints you haven't told me about?"

She gave me a pure and superior and chilly look, the kind she usually saves for Tom Hitt, or egg salad. ''I've never even had a parking ticket, as you very well know. That convoy behind us is what put the F in FBI.''

"Federal?"

"Fuckers. Hah! If I were so uptight, would I say that?"

I looked over my shoulder at the fuckers. ''They do seem a little pushy.''

"Pushy? Pushy?" She punched the air a couple of times with her fist. ''We told them everything we know. We were awesome. We cooperated splendidly. This is some reward for good citizenship.''

"I guess they want Lieutenant U.S.S.R. bad."

"Then they should find him. We're not stopping them. And we have every right to pursue a story without interference or witnesses.''

"Yeah. And what if we wanted to fool around?"

She ignored that. ''They've sure got a snotty way of showing their appreciation for the huge piece of information we just dumped in their laps for free.''

"So we get rid of them."

She skated around me again while we made a slow progress up Lafayette. ''I'm thinking.''

"I can tell. I'll talk while you think. I've never tried to lose two cars, two FBI foot soldiers, and fuzz on a bike before. My only experience is with Diego Gordillo. This will take some doing.''

"Hmm," Ike said, doubt creeping into her voice. ''I don't wish to invoke a double standard here, but, while it was very stupid of Tom, he had every right to sic Diego on you. You know? I would have done the same for the sake of a story. I wish I knew the code better here. Does the FBI have the right to just follow anyone they want, like we do as journalists?''

"I don't know about that. But they certainly don't have to insult us by doing it so openly and with an entire armored division. Maybe we should tell on them.''

"Who will we tell? The CIA?" She slipped her cell phone from her back pocket and started to dial.

"What are you doing?"

She suspended her thumb over the phone's key pad. "I told you I was thinking. I've got a plan. I'm calling Townline Cab. I'll arrange for a limo to pick me up. One of the FBI cars will have to follow me. Then I'll have Townline drop me at work and I'll go out the back door. I'll meet you at, oh, let's say, how about...I'll meet you in the kitchen at Gypsy's."

I thought a moment. "Have the limo pick you up at Fourteenth and Broadway."

"I should send the Townline bill to Cainstraight. Why should *Morning Watch* pay so we can escape his paranoid delusions?"

"Cainstraight and his delusions could be listening to your plan right now, or following us on a computer screen. We should decide how paranoid we ought to be. Maybe he stuck a tracking device in your bra."

She made an inelegant noise. "He wouldn't dare, not with someone who has my kind of access to the nation's outrage glands."

I raised my eyebrows. "He's daring to follow us." I put my arm around her waist. "I could give you a quick feel, just to make sure."

"Don't be sickening." She skated away from me and resumed dialing Townline. "You're worse than the FBI."

"Sickening? You didn't used to think it was sickening."

"That was used to. This is now."

I shrugged. I turned so I could study our pursuers. I skated backward, my hands in my pockets, thinking about Ike's idea that she and Townline would take care of one of the FBI sedans.

"What does your plan call for me to do?" I asked her.

"You'll have to lose the other car, the guys on foot, and the biker."

SEVENTEEN

TOWNLINE IS the limo service *Morning Watch* uses to shuttle guests to and from the airport and to their hotels and to the studio for the show. Townline is also very good at pampering our anchors when they travel on remote shoots or take a notion to go shopping on Fifth Avenue during the rush hour. The drivers are also experienced at ferrying hotheaded producers into riot zones or through streets cordoned off to other motorists because the pope or the president has business in New York. Townline jockeys just whip out their New York Press license plates from under the front seat and muscle through with some intimidator from their big Mercedes fleet. A flexible company, accustomed to hearing from us at odd times of the day or night, and prompt in servicing our needs.

The Townline driver was waiting for Ike in a white stretch limo at the northwest corner of Fourteenth. We skated across the intersection, and the driver held a white cardboard sign up against his closed window, showing the number 501.

"That's my number," Ike said.

I opened the door for her, and she clambered into the backseat and nestled into the blue velour cushions.

"This looks like a hooker's car," I said.

"I'm much too uptight and self-righteous for that."

I gave her fair complexion a quick but thorough study, as much as I could with the car's tinted windows intercepting the surrounding street light. "I think you're right. You'd make a better pimp." I reached in to pat her knee. "I'll see you in a little while. Save me some *tortellini filetto*."

"You can get your own, buddy. I don't pander when I'm a fugitive from justice."

Ike leaned forward and told the driver, "The Emerald City, and don't step on it. Take the scenic route. And can you find a French Canadian talk show on the radio? Turn it up real loud." She experimented with the buttons on the open door until all the limo's windows started sliding down. The nasal whine of a French Canadian meteorologist came rocketing out of the car's many speakers; I could feel the vibrations in the door.

"What's he saying?" she shouted at me.

I shouted, translating the words howling out of the speakers: "There's an arctic air mass moving in on Quebec. Temperatures tomorrow in Quebec City will be in the low fifties."

Ike sat back against the cushions, stretched out her legs, and put her hands behind her head. "Oh, the weather," she yelled. "I need to work on numbers, so this will be good. I'm way behind on my conversational tapes. If only I had some crackers." She leaned forward again toward the Townline driver. "You got any food up there? *Avez-vous de food?*

I closed the door, smiling at Ike's idea of occasionally learning French, and the limo eased away from the curb, its speakers blasting. I guess she was going to teach the FBI a little French while she was at it.

I stood there on the corner and watched as one of the unmarked sedans slowly and ever so casually fell in line behind the Townline stretch, staying a couple of car lengths back of the long white Mercedes. Technique.

I stood and watched, skating in random circles, until the little parade made the turn to go north on Sixth Avenue. My own more complicated entourage was parked, down a block on Fourteenth, waiting for me to make a move.

I retraced my path across Fourteenth, pulling a couple of bills out of my back pocket and selecting a ten as I coasted into the gutter. The swarm of battery-operated plastic toys still covered the sidewalk, still laying eggs and squirting strings of milk on the pavement. Still going, and going, and going. Energizer batteries, I hoped.

I bent and palmed one of the plastic rats as I skated by, tossed the street vendor the ten, and circled back into the street, holding the wiggling toy in my hand, against my shirt. It felt like the annoying jazz you get from those motel beds that take quarters.

Heading west, I took stock. The entourage was moving now. The car would be easy. The FBI infantry would be a laugh. The bicyclist would be the big problem.

What I needed first, I thought, was a narrow place. I held on to the buzzing rat and leaned on my edges, gathering speed on my way to Chelsea. I knew just the place to drop the FBI sedan. Chelsea is high on my list of places, anyway, where the feds should spend some time.

I led everyone over to Eighth Avenue and made a wide, leisurely turn, going north. The poor slobs on foot had to run to keep up.

I started pushing it on Eighth, skating with the traffic and gathering speed, and made a quick, tight right on Sixteenth. I zipped right again at the middle of the block, through the crevice/alley where the residents of 224 West Sixteenth Street (including an NTB editor named Ariel Colinsky) keep their garbage cans in an orderly row of gray plastic. There was plenty of room for me to navigate, and the only trouble for the foot patrol would depend on their physical fitness, and the cyclist would have to use her hands against the brick walls to keep her tires in a line, but the sedan had about as much chance of entering that alley as Charles Manson has of getting into the DAR.

I could hear the men running behind me, and I caught the sound of a garbage can rolling, but bikes don't make a lot of noise (at least, not the expensive kind they issue to FBI riders), so I had to look over my shoulder to make certain I hadn't lost that element of my fan club. The light was dim, but she was there, pushing along the walls with a smile on her face, enjoying things now that things were going. She knew she was the one I was really playing tag with.

The alley takes a jog before it empties out on Fifteenth, which, if you're not up on the local geography, can give you a nasty shock. I simply shifted my weight for the turn, but there must have been a slight mix-up among my pursuers because I heard a little federal four-letter word. Oh, well, I thought, free speech at work for America.

Once out on Fifteenth, I turned right and again took off for Eighth Avenue, completing the circle I had started. I sailed past Sixteenth, got a view of the rear end of the stranded FBI sedan, and continued north, but now I poured on the speed. I wouldn't have chosen that particular avenue, which is maybe the sleaziest in New York, if I were a novice on skates. And even an expert skater should stay off Eighth—one of the quickest ways to rack up when you're Rollerblading is to pass one of your wheels over a used condom, those little rubber signposts to both what you can purchase and what fate hands out for free on Eighth Avenue. If you hit a dead condom just right, it wraps itself around the lead wheel, and the least that can happen is that you'll probably flip a couple of times.

But Eighth Avenue—that wide strip of garish, flashing neon and cheap food and dangerous games of chance like sex for sale—is one hell of a roller coaster for cyclists, because they can't jump potholes, and because of all the drunks and all the folks raddled on bad drugs and all the fourteen-year-old hookers, male and female, who like to reach out and touch someone, especially bikers. The crazies usually leave bladers alone because we've got more swerve power than people riding on only two wheels welded to a solid body. Bladers can bend at the knees, the waist, wherever is required, or we can simply duck and slide on by.

By the time I was crossing Twenty-third, there was no longer a question of the men on foot. But my grinning friend on the bike wasn't even working up a sweat. When I glanced back at her, from time to time, I saw the same happy smile. I could tell she liked her work. She had a twelve-speed and as much confidence as Muhammad Ali when he was still God. That's how I knew she'd never in her life been on Eighth Avenue after dark. Probably just up from D.C.

I wanted to get rid of her while we were still on amateur turf, before we entered territory where she could really get hurt. Eighth Avenue, by the time you get to the forties, is the War Zone. When you give your regards to Broadway on this avenue, the lyrics are "joints or nickel bags, wanta boy, do coke, wanta girl, blow crack, gimme a dollar, come inside." And the melody lingers on as the song issues from human mouths, and from the porno and slasher movie palaces, and from the peep shows on the side of the Deuce, and from the hooker hotels, and from homemade tapes in boom boxes, and from neon marquees that spell out the lullaby in flashing monotony.

I would soon run out of clean turf to work with, and I decided I'd have to lose the FBI's bicyclist way before we reached the Port Authority, where the massive bus traffic could rip her elbows off and where the pros on foot would either have her wheels or she'd have to pull a gun, assuming she was equipped. And then they'd pull a gun. And then somebody else would see the guns and pull their guns, and then someone would see a better gun than he had and try to trade up and then...

At Thirtieth, I tore into a sudden right turn, the kind of turn my biker friend couldn't possibly execute as fast as I did it—it's kind of the difference between what an ice skater can do on a frozen lake compared to what a sled pulled by a team of very healthy dogs can do. The sled may be faster over the long haul, but the skater's got the moves.

Guessing the wide angle she'd have to follow to make the turn, I lay in wait in the dark on Thirtieth, ducked between two parked cars, for maybe five seconds, and put my jazzing rat down on the street. He went for her front tire like it was made out of plastic cheese. That little battery was a marvel.

The impact wasn't enough to throw her over the handlebars, but her wheels skidded out from under her sideways. And I heard the nails-on-blackboard sound of the bike's chain etching itself into the street.

She was good. She somehow stayed on her feet, leaping aside and hopping on one foot as the bike bumped and rotated, screeching on the cement.

I didn't wait to see if she handled her face and her vocabulary as well as she handled her body there in the privacy of the dark street. I was on my way back to the brightness of Eighth Avenue, concentrating now on my own safety as I sped around the islands of human emptiness, or maybe it was fullness, or whatever interior physics it is that makes these people rob or beg or sell parts of themselves or rent out space in their bodies so they can afford the drugs that rearrange their internal chemistry in a desperate attempt to fix what it was that the physics had done.

I was lucky. Even though I skated through a puddle of lumpy vomit, spraying a guy in black tights and a yellow wig who pulled a knife; and a freckled girl in a tight green dress tossed a Styrofoam container full of beer under my wheels and yelled "Hey, taxi!"; and a tall, skinny pimp in purple sequins grabbed one of my belt loops hard enough to pull it off—I managed to stay upright, an outcome I attribute to the fact that I registered all of those ceremonial dances just enough to escape their suction and I studied the pavement before me for signs of sloppy condoms. All the other stuff is just circus trappings for the expert skater passing through the Big Top; the condoms are an invitation to the Rollerblader afterlife.

I slowed up once I reached the relative civilization of Forty-sixth Street and Restaurant Row. That was good, because it gave me time to realize what a dumb move it would be to attempt to enter my mother's restaurant through the front door. I may be Carole Abagnarro's baby boy, but I smelled like some of the human detritus frolicking in the grim wonderland of Eighth Avenue's nightly flesh-and-drugs bazaar, and I would not be a welcome sight coming through the historic portal of Gypsy's, that theater district shrine my mother runs.

Once again, I chose to pilot a raunchy alley, and it was there, as I politely steered for the back door to Gypsy's like a considerate relative, that I got what Eighth Avenue hadn't been able to arrange. A large and loud white cat leaped from the lid of a garbage can and went for my right leg, grabbing at my laces. He scared the daylights out of me and I went down, mostly on my left elbow, but it felt like my ribs had shaken loose. I cussed in the two languages I know best, but not as loud as the cat. As soon as he was finished with his fit, he made off into the shadows, and I was left to cuss alone.

When I was out of words, I returned to the ones I had already used and cussed some more, lying there on my side in the alley, not really hurt, but angry at the irony of successfully shaking the FBI only to be completely screwed by the CAT.

I picked myself up, bent my arm and held my elbow under the globe of light that was suspended over the kitchen door, and inspected the gravel, blood, and yellow slime that might have been cheese.

I opened the kitchen door and skated into my mother's sparkling slice of heaven, with smells so perfect they seemed disconnected from the mundane details of her shiny copper pots and the fresh vegetables on the cutting island and the beautiful blonde with the strangely misharmonized eyes, gorging herself at the end of the counter on a plate of pasta almost certainly made fresh that afternoon.

Ike looked up from her meal. The chefs, in their white hats and full-length aprons, looked up from their cauldrons. My mother pushed open the double doors and stepped into the room.

"Something smells in here," she whispered, as the doors closed behind her. Then she saw me. "Abby, you're hurt!"

"Yeah, and I'm also what smells."

Ike looked a little sick, and I knew it wasn't the pasta. "Is that blood, Abby?"

I glanced down at my T-shirt and saw bright red smears. My side must be an expanded version of my elbow, I thought.

"It ain't a rare and precious Bordeaux," I said.

My mother was beside me, inspecting my wounded elbow. "You're gonna get infected if we don't clean you up fast."

"You got a glass of wine for me, Ma?"

"Not until we go in the mudroom and wash that elbow off with hydrogen peroxide, and see what you've done to your chest. People in this kind of trauma should not drink." She winked at me. "A head wound, maybe I'd give you wine."

She told one of the chefs to take a mop to the tracks I had left on her immaculate linoleum, and took my hand and dragged me into the mudroom, the double-wide closet where my dad had installed a sink big enough to wash the kind of pots Italian cooks use. Big enough for an Irish wolfhound—or a ten-year-old boy, as I knew from experience.

I felt like a ten-year-old all over again. She even dunked my head under the faucet over the huge sink, and she used the little black spray hose on my skates. The stuff that ran off the skates and down the floor's drain almost made me lose my appetite.

She made me leave the skates in the mudroom, and when I joined Ike at the steel counter, I was no longer full of my triumph over the forces of law and order. I was just hungry and humiliated and my elbow hurt like hell. The skin covering the left side of my rib cage stung, the same kind of feeling as when you have a paper cut on your index finger and you splash aftershave into your hand—but multiplied over a large area.

Ike was toying with a glass of wine and looking a little pale. "So," she said, too casually, "they had the nerve to touch you?"

"Who?"

"Who? You sit there and say 'who'? The FBI, that's who."

"No, they didn't even get near me. It only took me about fifteen blocks to ditch them. How about you?"

"No problem. In one door and out the other."

"How's your French?"

"Abby, what the hell happened to you? You came in here looking like they mauled you."

"It was a cat."

"It was not."

"I swear to God."

"You make me so mad. You're always blaming things on cats."

One of the sore spots of our marriage, as it turns out, was a big orange hairy creature she calls "The Donald." I had never actively harrassed the animal, nothing more violent than an occasional well-placed suggestion on his rump to get off the expensive couch where he piled his fur, but Ike likes to insist that I abused him. I maintain that it was the other way around, in terms of abuse between me and The Donald. My reasoning was that when he went out and got a job so he could charge a couch on his Mastercard, he could poke me in the rump. Ike took my cold, logical, reasonable stand as additional evidence that I'm insensitive (or any male-bashing buzzword; pick one), and has never let me off the hook about cats.

My mother brought me a plate of tortellini and took a seat across from us. "It's good to hear you spatting again," she said, gazing at us fondly. "You wouldn't bother to squabble with each other if your feelings were dead."

"My feelings are very much alive," I said, grabbing the fork my mother was holding out to me, "as I have consistently maintained. Everyone knows the divorce was not my brainstorm."

Ike made a point of checking her watch. "It's after ten o'clock. We've only got a couple of hours to find Tex before I have to change and get to work."

"No problem," I said, "let me just finish this tortellini, and I'll go outside and start yelling his name. Which name should I yell? Tex, or U.S.S.R.?"

Ike took a gulp of her wine. "That's interesting. I wonder why Second Lieutenant Ulysses Samuel Sylvester Raintree calls himself Tex? Why not New York? He was born in New York."

"Nobody," I said, "would call himself 'New York.' Can you imagine? 'Howdy, partner, call me New York.' At least Tex is recognizably a name."

"What I mean is, why not use one of his own names? He has a large collection to choose from."

"Aha, Miss, which is short for Missouri—ever notice how many women are named Miss? I happen to have an answer to that question."

"I'll bet."

"Listen. He's a war hero, with two—no, three—citations for heroism. He did two—not one—tours of Vietnam. He got his officer's commission on the field."

"So?"

"So he's a patriot. That's something we know about Tex."

"Are you suggesting we look for him at the Statue of Liberty?"

"No, I'm suggesting a reason why he'd call himself something other than that long name which can only remind him of the Evil Empire—U.S.S.R."

"That's a big help."

"Look, Ike, you started this conversation about his name. As for where to look, I've got no idea."

My mother held up both hands for silence, the boss in her own kitchen. "Why don't you tell me about Tex, Abby? Ike has told me what she knows, and all about that computer map and the fingerprint, but you're the one who got mugged, and I'd like to hear it in your own words."

"That sounds like fun," I said. "I like telling this story over and over again. Especially because it makes me look so big and strong. I love telling stories where I come off as a major jerk."

"Getting mugged doesn't make you a jerk," my mother said in a gentle voice. "It makes you a victim." She gave Ike a long-suffering look. "Men are such children. It was the same with Abby's father: always he had to be strong, always had to be the winner, always had to be the toughest guy on the block." She looked past Ike's shoulder, into some middle distance, some other time, some different reality than the pristine kitchen on Forty-sixth Street. "That's what made his final days so hard for him. He thought he could beat cancer if he were only strong enough, or smart enough, or man enough. So, in a way, for him, the cancer was his own fault, you know what I mean? Joe hated himself at the end."

Ike reached across the counter and held my mother's hand.

I put down my fork. I'd never heard my mother talk about my dad's death like that before.

"Ma, I'm sorry. That must have made it worse for you."

"I wasn't thinking about me, Abby."

There was a long silence.

I stared at my plate of tortellini. This was the argument I never start with my mother, the one where I would tell her that I am not Joe Abagnarro. *I am not like my dad,* I thought, *not all caught up in that Old World, Saint Paul macho-guilt about personal shame, and being all things to all men, and the humiliation of losing the race, and the sinfulness of being weak.*

"Tell your mother about Tex and the mugging," Ike said, in the tone of voice a shrink might use to coax a patient at the breakthrough point. "Maybe it would help to hear it without the wisecracks you always cover up with. I admit I never really thought of you as Tex's victim; I was only thinking of his connection to Yellow-Man."

I looked at Ike, my eyebrows up. "Since when are you a convert to the idea that the Brotherhood of Man includes me? You all of a sudden act like I'm some kind of basket case. I'm not covering up anything with wisecracks. I was mugged. I never made any secret of the fact."

"You didn't report it to the police."

"Big deal. I only lost four bucks. Lots of people get mugged in New York. It's been in all the newspapers. And you can stop trying to analyze me. I don't personally happen to have a thing about being mugged. Everyone else has a thing about it: you thought it was trivial; Tom Hitt thinks the world rotates around it; Fillingeri doesn't believe it and he's got the FBI not believing it. The only reason I'm still thinking about it at all is that Tex opened his big mouth instead of just opening my pockets."

"Then just tell me, Abby," my mother said, "if it's not a thing for you."

I did, and I didn't skimp on the details. I took her through the whole thing, from the statue of Dante across from Lincoln Center to Tex's sweet aroma, to Tex watching the Vietnam documentary I had directed, to the fact that Tex knew my name, to the copy of *D.Q.* lying open on the sidewalk, to Tex's exit down into the Columbus Circle subway station.

My mother got up and poured me a glass of wine. She brought it to the counter and put it in my hand.

"I have one suggestion," she said.

"What?" Ike said.

"That map you had the computer expert draw?"

"Yeah?"

"Look where he told you to, on West Fifty-seventh."

"At CBS?" Ike was using her fork to draw circles in the sauce on her plate.

"If I remember right," my mother said, "there's a perfume company across the street from CBS."

"Holy mackerel," Ike said.

"You might not know, because their sign only has letters, not the company's full name spelled out—it's W.F.R., or W.I.R., something like that. I think it's a research and development facility. The company has been there since the CBS building was a dairy, a long time ago." My mother started to smile, a slight movement of her lips, almost to herself, pleased with her suggestion. She started for the swinging doors and the dining room. "I've got a large crowd for a Monday night. You think about what I said."

"Wait a minute," Ike said. "Wait just a minute. Monday night."

"What's the matter, dear?" my mother said, her hand on the door. "What difference does Monday make?"

Ike turned to me. "Abby, you said you thought Tex had played football, that he liked to swing linebackers or something."

"Yeah?"

My mother stepped back to the counter. "You never liked football, Abby. Always you were outside on the street running or playing hockey on roller skates; you couldn't sit down long enough to watch a football game with your father on Sunday."

Ike was waving her hand to stop the trip down memory/guilt lane.

"Football," she said. "Football. *Monday Night Football.* It's only preseason games, but it's games."

I gave her a look. "If you ask me, Ike, your addiction to football is worse than your addiction to The Donald."

"Don't start on the cat. I know where to look for Tex—at least I think I do."

"Where?"

"Tex told you himself where to start, Abby." She was bouncing on her stool. "At that Radio Shack. That's where Tex watches TV. And that's where he found out about you, Abby. Anyway, that's where he started—watching television."

EIGHTEEN

WE LEFT BY the back door.

It wasn't too hard to figure that once they'd lost us, the FBI would start looking for the hole we'd climbed into, and it wouldn't take them long to look up Abagnarro in the Manhattan White Pages. We're on the first page of the listings.

And there's only two of us: me and Carole, who gives her number at Gypsy's both under her name and under the name of the restaurant. She doesn't list her home phone.

Of course, if the FBI was looking in the other borough directories, they'd be very busy in Queens, the adopted home of the Abagnarros of Sicily. Our listings start on the first page there, too, but we go on over to the next page. Large family.

I vetoed taking Ike up Eighth Avenue, where we could skate with the traffic to Fifty-seventh, on the most direct route to the Radio Shack where Tex might be spending his hours as a, well, *sidewalk* potato. While Ike's not as fast on blades as I am, she's plenty fast. And she knows as many tricks as I do. But the crazies don't always stop to think before they mouth off or make a grab. Since Ike usually lets me lead when we skate or when we dance, we went over to Ninth and skated uptown against the traffic, which is the kind of stupid stunt we don't usually do and that makes a lot of New Yorkers hate bikers, who do it all the time. Rollerbladers, in general, have much better manners. And they're better looking.

If you want to see good city skaters, and lots of them, you should go to Minneapolis. They've got more bladers than any other town in the world, and that's not per capita. It's just *more*. And Sacramento ranks second in number, but those California bladers are into flashy moves rather than efficient transportation. New York, which is way down at number fifteen on the list, hardly rates as a blading capital in terms of sheer numbers of wheels, but you can't beat the Big Burg for a proving ground. Like the song says, if you can make it here, you can make it anywhere. Lots of would-be bladers wash out here because they can't figure out the rules of the road, and that makes learning the moves difficult.

When I first started blading in Manhattan, I couldn't decide if I was a pedestrian or a car, and wasn't sure which set of rules to follow. Then I discovered that the decision wasn't up to me. For beginning skaters, whether you're a pedestrian or a car depends on the buses, and how they muscle around their stops. Bus drivers in New York actively target bladers. They hate our guts. Often, in the early days of learning the sport, I was forced up onto the sidewalk to save my life, which made me a pedestrian.

After I'd done some improving, learning how to anticipate the buses before they came after me, I was definitely a car, using any lane I chose and staying off the sidewalks most of the time. Still, I never had a parking problem, which gave me a touch of the pedestrian.

I have now passed beyond the petty distinctions that separate pedestrians from cars. When I am on blades, and this goes for Ike, too, I am not a car and not a pedestrian. I am an alien presence, a thing from the great beyond, the advance guard of a superior species, and that's why buses hate me. I don't have to abide by any rules now that I can fly—now that I can warp time and space, can leap giant puddles and down whole flights of stairs, can ignore gridlock as though it were a mere gnat on the bow of the *Q E II*, and, as I had recently discovered, can even thumb my nose at the Federal Bureau of Investigation.

But. I am not immune to bullets. Guns scare me. And the one burning question I had not resolved in my mind about Tex, even more burning than the question of whether he was a serial killer, was the sizzling matter of whether he was carrying a gun. So many people are carrying these days that it pays to keep your Kevlar vest out of the cleaners.

Tex hadn't used any heat on me during our one and only encounter, but he hadn't needed to. However, he had certainly needed firearms in Vietnam, and evidently he was good with them, given his dazzling service record, so my decision to take Ninth Avenue was also a delaying tactic to give me time to think over two things:

1. Should I pass on the Tex project and go home to bed?

2.   If I didn't pass, how the hell could I dump Ike? Dumping a blader who is almost as good as you are takes one thing and one thing only: intervention from an outside agency, like a lightning strike. Gimmicks like plastic rats would work with Ike about as well as Tylenol against sniper fire. You see, Ike *likes* danger. She *likes* being scared. Terror turns her on. The thought of Tex with a gun, which had probably occurred to her, too, would give Ike what she would regard as a legitimate journalistic charge, the kind of energy that had made her crawl under barbed wire in the Negev to get the exclusive story on the Sayeret Matkal, Israel's elite and most heavily armed Spy Gala, during the Gulf War.

"Ike," I said.

"Forget it, Abby."

So we skated up Ninth, switching lanes against the traffic as opportunity knocked, getting fingers and remarks from cabbies who didn't like having us in their faces. At the corner of Fifty-seventh, we stopped and peered down the block and across the street at the dark shop windows. There was a lot of foot traffic on Fifty-seventh, because it's always well lit, but there was no mistaking the big guy in the red sweater. I hadn't for one minute believed that Ike and I would find him, so it was a shock to see him, and he looked much bigger than I'd remembered, even half a block away.

He was standing glued up against a window in the middle of the block, his back to the sidewalk strollers, his huge bulk outlined by the flickering bluish gray lights coming from inside the store from more than one television.

"Damn," I said. "That's him."

"I thought you wanted to find him."

"Wrong. I started by wanting to find out who owned the fingerprint on my business card. It was learning the answer that turned a tiny, harmless errand into the Holy Grail. Now that we know that Tex *is* U.S.S.R., I'd much rather lapse into my earlier amnesia and go to your apartment. I'll teach you some French you'll never forget."

"Abby, you don't mean it. We're this close to him, and you can't possibly mean it. I know you. You've been to more global hot spots than I have, and you've never complained about danger,

not even in Saudi Arabia when that Scud missile barely missed
you. Not even in Panama when your Mets cap got shot off your
head.''

"If I'd had the sense to wear a Yankees cap, nobody would
have shot at me.''

She ran both hands through her hair like she was thinking of
pulling it out in clumps. "I'll go see Tex myself. I don't need
you, as though you were my arm, or my leg, or my mind. There's
no way I'd pass up an opportunity like this.''

"Opportunity.''

"That's right, Abby. Opportunity.''

"You mean *threat.*

"Bull.''

"All right, all right. I never knew anybody so pigheaded. But
you follow me.''

"Why? Because you're the man?''

"Just do it.''

"Why?''

"Because otherwise I won't play. Take it or leave it.''

She couldn't stamp her foot at me, not on blades, but I could
tell she wanted to. "Oh, all right. Do you have a plan?''

"I certainly do. I learned it from a master less than twenty-
four hours ago.''

"What?''

"Stay behind me, at least twenty feet, and watch.''

She nodded her head, and I took off.

I crossed Fifty-seventh with the light, coasted up the curb, and
got behind a couple sauntering along on the sidewalk, their arms
around each other. They looked very cozy, walking along and
squeezing each other and laughing quietly. I skated slowly in their
wake, keeping just far enough back so they wouldn't think I was
trying to listen in. As they drew even with Tex, his face up against
the window, I slid behind him and screamed as loud as I could
right into his ear. His hands went up like lightning to cover his
head, and my hands were all over him, rapidly patting every
square inch I could reach to answer my burning question about
the gun. He didn't have one.

Before he could turn around to hit me, I skated off, fast, about
fifteen feet. The cozy couple was way ahead of me, scampering
down the block toward the lights and safety of Coliseum Books

at Fifty-seventh and Broadway, always open late for folks on the lam.

Tex turned, flexed at the knees, his hands in fists. Some instinct or training had kicked in, despite his obvious disorientation. He looked at me and shook his head. He stood up a little straighter.

"Lieutenant Raintree," I said.

When I said his name, he whirled away from me and started to run.

But Ike was there, and anything Tonya Harding can do on ice, Ike can do with blades on pavement. She turned her speeding wheels into a tight spin and flung her leg out straight in his path, right across his lower abdomen, in a smooth flying camel.

The impact threw her off balance, but it threw Tex to the sidewalk, clutching his gut. Ike concentrated on her edges, stumbled out of the spin that had given her the momentum to put Tex on the pavement, and swept into a wide curve that took her bumping across the curb and into the street before she completely recovered control.

As she skated back to the sidewalk, Tex was getting to his knees. I slid up next to him and offered a hand, which he looked at but did not touch.

"What you want with old Tex?" he said. "What that she-devil want to hurt old Tex for? I ain't done nothing to you."

"You did plenty to me," I said. "Remember me? The name's Abagnarro, and you owe me four bucks."

"I don't know you or owe you, man."

"Well, I know you. You're Ulysses Samuel Sylvester Raintree. You used to be an officer in the United States Army. You were decorated three times for bravery in Vietnam. And you were in Central Park last night when that Yellow-Man victim was found. We've got you on videotape."

"How'd you know old Tex's name?"

"The FBI told me."

"Aw, shit."

He sat down on the sidewalk and inched back against the building, pushing his large shoulders into the bricks like he wanted to knock the building over. "The F-fucking-BI. A videotape. Poor old Tex." He put the heels of his filthy, beautiful hands against his forehead, like that would help push the building over. When he finished the pushing and looked up, either he had rearranged his face or there was a different man looking out of those big eyes. "You should have a better videotape, Mr. Abagnarro. You are way behind the times. You have no videotape of the latest Yellow-Man victim, Mr. Abagnarro, because he hasn't been found yet. I painted him about forty-five minutes ago. What do you think of that, TV director? Life's full of surprises, isn't it?"

What I thought of that was that I wished we hadn't lost the FBI.

But Ike skated so close to Tex her toes touched his big Reeboks. "Two different names, and two different ways of speaking English," she said.

He shook his head and leaned it carefully against the bricks, no longer pushing. "Who's this, Abagnarro? Why'd you bring Cinderella to old Tex's ball?"

"Cinderella makes her own decisions, Tex," Ike said. "There's been another killing? Tonight? Did you kill another man?"

"I didn't kill him."

"Did you kill all those other men and paint their faces?"

"I didn't kill 'em."

"But you painted them?"

Tex pushed his open hand up at her face, showing her the wide yellow streaks across his fingers. "If I did, it must have been bright yellow. If there's a note, it must have my name on it."

"Why?"

"Why?" He gave her a look so cold with hatred, or anger, or something that had eaten away his heart, that I wanted to grab Ike and get her away from him. But Cinderella was making her own decisions, and I didn't think any manhandling from me would work on her. She probably couldn't get a skate across my belly, not with me also equipped, but she would be difficult.

Tex kept his eyes on Ike, maybe sensing she had turned herself into an immovable object. "Cinderella, I'm not your fairy godmother. Why should I tell you *why* anything?"

"Because...because if you tell us, nobody can compel us to repeat what you said. If you have something you want to say, we're the safest people you could tell."

"Is this some Constitution bullshit?"

"Well, the First Amendment is important, of course, but I'm talking about a New York statute called the Shield Law."

"What's that?"

"It's a law that protects the privacy of certain kinds of information. Like the right of a rape victim not to have her sexual history introduced into a court of law. And like right now. The Shield Law says courts can't make journalists talk about information they get from protected sources."

"Old Tex is a protected source?"

"All I have to do to make you a protected source is to promise not to reveal anything you tell me. My promise covers Mr. Abagnarro, too. We both promise to protect you from discovery as the source of anything you tell us."

The flash of his gold teeth as his lips split into a cruel grin made me think of movie vampires. "You plan on believing what old Tex says?"

Ike cocked her head to one side and considered him from the elevation her skates gave her. "Maybe. I can see the paint on your fingers."

"But you can't see the bile in my veins, Cinderella, or the pollution in my soul, or the fire burning in my thoughts. You can't see a *why*. I painted my men because I wanted their deaths to look like something instead of looking like nothing. You believe that?"

"I don't understand," Ike said, slowly and carefully squatting over her skates and looking straight into his scary eyes.

"Homeless man dies on the street, it's nothing. So I made it something. A bright yellow something, bright enough so nobody could miss it."

"And you stabbed them, too?"

"With my little knife." He licked his lips. "Wanta see it, Cinderella? Old Tex'll give you a real nice feel."

"Oh, my God," she said, rising quickly.

She looked at me, but I shook my head.

"I'm not sure," I said. "I was looking for a gun."

"Scare you? Supposed to scare you." Tex tapped his big forehead with a dirty fingernail. "Supposed to scare everyone."

"Okay, I'm scared," Ike said. "Really scared."

"Good."

"But Tex," she said, "you know about being scared, right? You were in Vietnam."

"Scared all the time."

"And it didn't stop you from doing your job, did it?"

"No way. Made me good at my job."

"I'm good at my job, which is finding out the truth. So it's good that you're scaring me, you see?"

He nodded.

She kept going. "If you didn't kill those men, how did you know where the bodies were? How did you know where to go with the paint and your knife?"

"I didn't know all of them. There's a couple or so went without paint. Wandered out of the area and died. Homeless man dies and it's nothing. Just wander around and die. But mostly my men stay close around here. Got nowhere else to go, do they? I try to watch over my men can't watch out for themselves, they too drunk or too stoned or too crazy or too sick. I painted my men so they wouldn't disappear into that boat to Potter's Field without no one taking notice."

"But how did you know—I mean, why did you...what made you start...Jesus, I don't know what I'm trying to say."

Tex looked up at me. It was shocking, like he was transferring his intelligence and his will as he transferred the direction of his gaze. For an instant I was transported back to the ragged jungle that for me was only a history lesson, to the landscape of the Vietnam documentary. And, I imagined, farther back, to the ragged jungle when it was too new and bloody for a documentary, when it was seeding the legacy I would direct for television. I would have followed Tex where he chose to lead. His enemy would have been my enemy. What he said, I'd do.

The power and compulsion of that look faded quickly, and he was just a big, dirty man sitting on the street. "That's what I was trying to tell you last night, Mr. Busy Television Man. Old Tex gotta bear witness. But old Tex can't do it all. I didn't have to tell you squat. There wasn't no FBI looking over my shoulder last night. I selected you, but you're just like everybody else in New York. Step around the bum and keep on moving."

"We're not stepping around now," I said.

"How come?"

"Because Cinderella here wants to know the truth about these killings."

Tex turned his attention back to Ike, studying her face, studying her hands, his gaze moving down to study her skates. "What's your real name, honey?"

"Ike."

"That so?"

"Well, that's what everybody calls me."

"Ike, the truth is, those men knew they were going to die and Tex knew they were going to die and it was for Tex to be there when they died to turn their dying into something so it wouldn't be nothing."

"How'd they know they were going to die?"

"The doctor said."

"What doctor?"

"Don't know. The doctor that was paying them."

"Paying them for what?"

"Experimental drug testing. Good money—twenty dollars each time they took the drug. I told 'em not to do it. It's like Russian roulette with a full metal jacket in every chamber, I'd say. Sipping napalm through a straw, I'd tell 'em. Might as well lie down on a grate and fall asleep so some punk can set them on fire. They do it all the time, the punks. Gives 'em a kick." He shook his greasy head back and forth, back and forth, slowly. "Won't find Tex sleeping on the street. Gotta watch out for his men. Don't let nobody set me on fire."

"Your men. What drug were they testing?"

"You think I know?"

"Tex, you know that one of the dead men was a doctor, don't you?"

He nodded. "Saw it on the headline sign in Times Square. Big flashing words, zipping around to tell the world."

"Did you paint him, too?"

For the first time, Tex looked cagey, like he hadn't made up his mind whether he'd painted Hektor Stefanopolis. "What if I did?"

"If you painted him, maybe you know who killed him."

"Maybe I do. Maybe I don't. Don't suppose I do."

"Tex, the doctor wasn't like your friends. He wasn't being paid as a subject in an experimental drug program."

"Maybe I don't know anything about that."

"Tex, did you kill the doctor?"

"The last man I killed, I got a medal for. And I got paid to kill him by the United States of America."

Ike pushed back on her wheels, away from Tex, and bent over her skates, stretching her legs. She squatted back down, but from the new distance, and faced Tex again. "Does the name Stefanopolis mean anything to you?"

"No."

"He was the doctor who died this morning in an alley near the Emerald City. The doctor whose name you saw on the news zipper in Times Square."

Tex shook his head. Back and forth against the wall, he shook his head. I could imagine the greasy stain that would show up in the morning light on the building's facade.

Ike watched him until the head-shaking stopped. "Does the name Quintinale mean anything to you? Have you heard that name before? She's a doctor."

"Ain't my doctor."

"Do you know the name of the doctor who was giving your men the medicine that was killing them?"

He laughed. "Wasn't ever introduced, like."

"Do you know what the doctor looks like?"

"Only saw him at the shanties the once. Didn't catch his face good, it being so dark and him too far away. I see him from a long way off."

"It was a man?"

"Wasn't no woman."

Ike flipped a hand impatiently. "You stopped Mr. Abagnarro last night because you wanted him to help you, right?"

"Something like that."

"I can help you. But you have to tell me what you were going to tell him."

"How can you help? You on TV? I never saw eyes like yours. I'd remember if I'd seen you on TV. And I ain't seen 'Cinderella' in the credits."

"I'm a producer. I work for the same network Mr. Abagnarro works for."

I thought it was time for me to join the huddle on the ground, show a little team spirit. So I squatted, the one thing Ike does better on blades than I do. It was awkward, and I didn't feel so much like an alien being, the advance force of a superior life-form. "Ike's much more important than I am, Tex. She makes the decisions about what gets on the air."

He eyed her steadily. That look was back.

She met his intensity and matched it. Her eyes are not easy to meet, especially when she's excited. But his weren't, either.

The cell phone in her back pocket rang. She ignored it, but Tex looked at her rear suspiciously, the moment broken.

"That a beeper?" he said.

"Just a cell phone. I'm not going to answer it."

"I'm gonna stand up," he said. "Get some air. Keep your skates away from me."

Ike and I got to our feet and gave him room. Her phone kept ringing.

He stood. He was still taller than me, even with me on skates.

"Outside of that doctor," he said, "which I painted when I saw that a rich man would not pass through the eye of the needle as easy as a bum, but over which I got no jurisdiction, so maybe it wasn't right, the Yellow-Men all lived in the shanties over by the Hudson. At the end of Fifty-sixth Street. They were recruited to take drugs and got paid for it. They were warned that the drugs could be dangerous."

"When did this start?" Ike said.

"About two, three months ago. I got no calendar."

"And these men started getting sick?"

"Yeah. Real bad side effect." He gave her a twisted, mean grin. "Death."

Ike bowed her head and looked at her hands. I kept my eyes on *his* hands. That remark about the little knife had been unsettling, even though I was pretty sure I hadn't missed a weapon during my fast exploration of his body.

Ike kept looking at her hands. "And the only reason you painted them was to call attention to their deaths?"

Tex cast another look at Ike's backside, apparently fascinated by her phone. He was jumpy, agitated, his hands twitching at his sides. "Ain't no other reason a sane man would paint his men. I had a Vietnam buddy made the boat ride to Potter's Field. Wind and weeds and cats and convicts ate his dignity before the worms could get it. A man's place in the ground supposed to be sacred— his resting place, not a human dump. A man gets no rest on this earth. Oughta get it below." Tex edged away from the wall. He was ready to take off. He hadn't liked the sound of Ike's cell phone. Nervous energy danced along his body almost as if it were electrified.

"Wait," Ike said. "I have to know if you saw who killed the doctor. And if he was the doctor giving your men drugs."

"The doctor wasn't my man, Miss Cinderella Ike. I got no responsibility on that except the stain on my hands." He side-stepped the entrance to Radio Shack and backed away from us, his limbs trembling, his hands fluttering. "You can follow me on those skates and harass old Tex, but I got nothing more to say. The subject is closed. You got all I got for you. You can tell the FBI about the shanties, but I won't be there. Shield Law gonna protect you, maybe protect a girl gets raped. There ain't no Shield Law for old Tex."

Ike clutched her hair, but she stayed put.

Tex kept back-stepping. He stuck his trembling hand into a deep pocket in his dirty chinos, a cunning look on his big face. Ike reached for my hand and we rolled backward together, afraid to turn away from him, mesmerized by what he was doing with his hand and his pocket. Maybe I'd missed the knife, after all.

"You want your shit, man?" he said.

"What?"

His hand came snaking out of his pocket, and a spray of silver and gold and copper came arcing through the air, landing in a clash of metal at my feet. Keys.

He kept back-stepping. All the way to the corner. He turned around there, and, without bothering to check the traffic, bolted across the street.

"Hey, Tex!" I shouted.

When he reached the curb, he looked back over his shoulder. "What?"

"Where's my I.D. badge?"

He grinned at me, his big gold teeth looking like rocks in his mouth. "In hell, man."

"I want it back."

"Go get it, then."

He turned away, ready to sprint.

"Hey, Tex!"

"What?"

"Where'd you play football?"

He laughed, a big, booming sound that carried over the traffic speeding down Ninth between our positions.

"U.T., Austin, *Mister* Abagnarro." And he ran, due west. Fast. Faster than fast. Like he was back in Texas at Memorial Stadium, running for daylight.

NINETEEN

I STOPPED AND picked up my key ring.

"That explains the nickname," I said.

"The universe is sliding into place, all right. Very swell."

Ike was skating in impatient circles in front of Radio Shack, flipping her hands against her sides like she was trying to shake raindrops off, only the sky was clear. Maybe the sparks from Tex's nerves had leaped across space and danced now in her veins.

She stopped circling and gazed at me, her mismatched eyes radiant in the glow of flickering images from the Radio Shack window, a display of television screens all tuned to *Monday Night Football.* In a wild fantasy, I imagined I could see the green-uniformed Jets stacking up the aqua-jerseyed Dan Marino, all the action taking place in her eyes, another manifestation of that transfer of electric energy from Tex.

"Abby, he created Yellow-Man. Because he couldn't bear the thought that his 'men' would die unnoticed."

"But Tex didn't create what killed them."

The little skating circles started again, around me, but I found myself pivoting on my wheels so I could watch her eyes as she talked and orbited my space.

"For a very scary man, Tex is very scared," she said. "He's scared that painting the faces of his men and leaving those cryptic notes on their dead bodies—scared that his creation hasn't been enough, scared that he's failed them." She looked me straight in the eyes. "Abby, he stabbed those men in his frenzy to make someone pay attention." She made stabbing motions, driving an invisible knife into the palm of her hand, over and over again. "And he's sick with the knowledge that he's let them down. They are in Potter's Field."

I grabbed her hand to stop the stabbing motions, and she coasted around me as I held her, turning her in a smooth circle. "What Tex created was only a sideshow," I said, "and now he knows it. The real circus is the New York City bureaucracy, and he hasn't got the price of admission.''

"And he thinks we do.'' She pulled her hand away from mine, stopped skating, and stood looking at the television display filled with images of *Monday Night Football*. "Abby, do you think he hates us?''

"Yes.''

"You and me, personally?''

"No. Yes. I don't know.'' I thought it over and made up my mind and faced Ike in the television sets in Radio Shack's window. "No.'' I turned her gently to face me, tired of looking at reflections. "Remember? Tex selected me. He thinks I can beat the system. He thought I could beat the system.''

"Correction. He thinks television can beat the system.''

"Ike, we *are* the system. About the best we can do is produce a two-minute spot on that boat ride out to Potter's Field. Put a nice travel feature for paupers on the air. Shit, I don't even know where Potter's Field is. How bad can it be, anyway, given the way those men live?''

"I'm not so sure we're the system.'' She pulled her cell phone from her back pocket. "That's not what we're supposed to be.''

"We are what we are.'' I put my hand over hers before she could open the phone. "Tex is what he is. I can't imagine what it takes to paint a corpse and stick a knife into a buddy's dead body, but I know it doesn't take logic or reason. You can't appoint yourself undertaker to the homeless and expect the system to stand up and cheer.''

Her hand jerked impatiently under mine on the phone. "Whatever it took, Tex was certainly right about making something out of nothing for those dead men. If he hadn't painted them, none of us would ever have questioned their deaths or even have known anything about them. So he's not a failure.''

"Maybe you should have told Tex that.'' I released her hand. "Maybe you should have told him to feel good about the media coverage of Yellow-Man so he wouldn't feel so bad that his men took that boat ride.''

She opened the cell phone and dialed a number. I didn't have to watch her fingers to know she was calling the NTB National Desk. "Rich, it's Ike. Did you try me just now?'' She listened, cocking the phone against her shoulder and stuffing her hands in her back pockets as she started skating toward Broadway. "I'll look at that when I get in later. Rich, has there been another Yellow-Man killing tonight?" She listened. "No. No special radar or anything. I just wondered. Call me first if you hear anything. I'm on my cell." She closed the instrument.

"Nothing?" I asked.

"Nothing." She stuck the phone in her pocket and grabbed my hand again. "Hold my hand."

I looked down at her. "You scared?"

"Bad scared, man. Makes me good at my job."

We skated together and at Broadway made the left for Columbus Circle. The fountain that rings the statue of Christopher Columbus was so full of lights that my eyes smarted. It was like coming out of a bad dream and waking up in Oz. The fountain looked like a moving, flowing Christmas tree, the spray picking up the gold and red lights from the traffic through the circle, as well as the green hazy glow cast by the huge doors of the Emerald City. The central statue of Columbus rose on its tall pedestal through the splashing, constantly re-forming limbs of water like the trunk of the ghostly tree.

But even Oz has its dirty little secrets. A couple of old and hairy aluminum collectors pushed their rickety mail carts along the sidewalk, stopping to poke around in trash cans, sometimes almost disappearing into the cans as they groped along the bottoms for recyclables. A pair of beat cops passed the collectors and exchanged what seemed to be small talk before they moved on to Central Park South. Nobody was bothering anybody.

We were just skating into the circle, a balmy breeze playing with droplets from the fountain, when Ike's back pocket rang. I thought I knew what that meant.

She tugged the instrument out with her right hand and flipped it open, but she raised our linked hands to point at the Emerald City. Standing outside the giant sea-green doors was a lanky and recently bereaved doctor with an interesting face, a doctor who raced cars so he could detect the force of life pulsing through his veins.

Ike squeezed my hand, and we skated behind the fountain, putting the frolicking water between us and Aristotle Stefanopolis.

"Whatcha got, Rich?" Ike asked the phone.

She didn't have to listen long, probably because she also knew what that call was about as soon as she had heard the faint ringing in her pocket. Her part of the brief dialogue was fairly uncomplicated because, with about nine hours to work with before our show aired, she didn't have to worry about live reporting from the latest Yellow-Man scene. The National Desk would send out crews to get whatever pictures were available.

When she closed the instrument, she didn't bother to put it back in her pocket. She was going to have to start making television, and she'd be on the horn all the way as she skated home to change her clothes.

"Guess what?" she said. I couldn't read the look on her face, the mistiness in her eyes. The weird passage of lights through the spray was playing tricks across her face.

"Victim number eleven?"

"You're good at this game, TV Director. Wanta try another category?"

"Sure."

"Where was the body found?"

I thought a moment. At first I was just going to say that the latest victim was found somewhere within the area mapped for us by Fred Loring. In fact, I had my mouth open and the first word formed when the real answer hit me:

"The...wait. Tex took off like a homing pigeon, straight for the river, due west. In front of Radio Shack, it was your cell phone ringing that stirred him up. He thought that meant his man had been found. He knew where victim number eleven was because he painted the corpse, just like he knew where the Central Park victim was last night. He knew precisely which of the eighty-six thousand trees to look under. He seems to like to be there when his men's bodies are discovered. Therefore, this new victim is in the shanties at the end of Fifty-sixth Street, almost due west from Radio Shack."

Ike, shocking the bejesus out of me, put her hands on my shoulders, phone and all, and gave me a soft kiss, full on the lips. The light pressure pushed us toward the fountain on our wheels, and the spray was all over us, a fine mist covering our arms and legs and faces like perspiration. "Very good, Sherlock. One more category?"

I locked my arms around her waist. "Yes."

"Who killed number eleven?"

I was blank. As much as I wanted a repeat of the game prize, I was blank. I couldn't begin to think. I cleared my throat. "It's not a fair question if you don't know the answer yourself, Ike. This is one game we never cheated at."

She pulled away from me. "Tough," she whispered, but she touched my lips lightly with a finger. She immediately transferred the finger to the buttons on her phone, and I could see that her hand was shaking. She put the phone against her ear and started giving marching orders to the National Desk, instructing them to send up a flare for Sally Goldberg-Petit.

When she hung up, I pointed through the fountain's cascading water, around the pedestal of the statue in the center of the water jets, at our place of employment. "Did you play guessing games like that at lunch with Doctor Feel-Alive?"

She gave me that unreadable misty look. "Not like that."

"Does he eat lunch? Or does he just drink Valvoline?"

"Champagne."

"Champagne? With his brother painted yellow and lying in a city morgue?"

"Gabriel's was passing it out free because all the customers were wet and miserable. What'd you want him to drink? Hemlock?"

"That was Socrates, not Aristotle. I want Aristotle to drink cyanide."

"Cyanide." She scratched her chin with the antenna of the phone. "I wish I knew what drug Tex's men were testing."

"The coroner didn't find anything."

"The coroner can't look for every drug on the planet, especially new, experimental ones. He can only look for standard stuff, and whatever else Fillingeri tells him."

I shrugged my shoulders and nodded toward the doors of the Emerald City. "What's Aristotle doing here?"

"How should I know?"

"Well, I'm putting you in a cab and sending you home. I'll go see why he's knocking on our door."

"Pooh. Why don't you get in a cab and go home and take a nap? You really get surly when you're short on sleep."

"I get really surly when I'm short on sex and my former wife almost knocks me into a fountain while she's kissing me across the street from the man she dated at lunch."

"I didn't almost knock you into the fountain. It was just part of that game, a tiny peck."

"You knocked something. I'm still tingling."

"Then take a cold shower."

I pointedly wiped droplets off my arms. "I *am* taking a cold shower."

She took off around the fountain and headed for the doors to the Emerald City. I had a choice: follow her, like a Spanish duenna; or skate the hell out of there and go home to get some sleep. Through the splashing water I saw the smile on the doctor's face.

Which is what decided me. Why should the NASCAR neurologist have a pleasant evening in Columbus Circle? That crooked smile on his interesting face had appeared exactly when he spotted Ike skating toward him. I watched his face and his grin through the falling and rising of the water, and I didn't like the image suggested to me by the surging power of the screen of fluid separating me from the reunion of the doctor and my wife. I pushed away from the fountain and got the wheels rolling.

Aristotle wasn't actually touching Ike when I skated up to the giant green doors, but the way he was standing and the way he was looking at her made it seem that he'd discovered some sort of metaphysical mode of pawing her. It wasn't like he was undressing her in his mind's eye; I've seen plenty of guys do that before. It was more like he didn't need to undress her, that his magic hands and magic eyes had gone beyond the obstacle of clothing (not that she was overabundantly supplied with any) to reach the flesh without effort, without permission, in some warm and exciting private region that existed only because he was there beside her. X-ray Man, feeling the life in someone else's veins.

"...your machine," he was saying, "and left a couple of messages, but I finally thought I'd try to catch you here. The guard inside told me, very politely, that I could wait in the lobby, but it's such a pleasant night. And here you are."

"And here she is," I said. "And so am I."

Ike gave me a look that told me to back off.

"How are you, Aristotle?" she said, offering her hand.

"Not good," he said, grasping her hand in that fervent doctorly way that always looks like they can diagnose your kidneys with a quick feel of your palm. "And I'm afraid that's what you're thinking—that I'm not good. I wanted a chance to salvage my character with you if it isn't too late. The media. The police. Even my patients. They're all asking. The rumors about me and Hektor's wife are growing like...like..."

"Like cancer?" I suggested.

His eyes flickered over me in the merest casual glance. Not wasting any precious medical energy on diagnosing my kidneys. No bedside manner for the pest.

He turned the rheostat of his wide smile up fully for Ike—and tenderly, I thought.

"I'll go away if this is bad timing," he said.

And she smiled back.

Boy, I thought, he liked speed in a lot of ways, including taking the hint.

"That's nice of you," I said brightly. "Your offer to go away, I mean."

Aristotle, who was about my height when I am not on blades, had to look up at me to take proper notice of the pest. "You're in early tonight, Abagnarro."

"Oh. I wasn't aware that you followed my schedule."

"I meant that last night you got here much later."

"I'm like the wind." I fluttered my left arm by way of illustration, forgetting my scrape from the alley. The resulting sizzle of pain lent an extremely realistic element of spastic randomness to the gesture. "The wind. I come and I go, and nobody can do anything about it. Bus drivers and the FBI hate me, but pollinating trees and sailors worship at my shrine."

Ike's phone rang and she flipped it open. She put it to her ear and listened. She handed it to me. "It's Cainstraight. He wants to speak with the wind."

I took the phone. "Abagnarro. How are you, Morris? Getting plenty of rest down there at the Federal Building?"

"Where the hell have you been, Abagnarro?"

"Here and there. I'm like the wind. I come and I go, impossible to grab hold of. I'm thinking of starting a religion to myself."

"Yeah? Well, I've got some blasphemy all set to go when you're geared up."

"Can you do that? I mean, don't I have to apply for tax-exempt status first or something?"

"Let's get to cases. Answer my question. Where have you been?"

"All my life?"

"Since you left my office."

"Oh, I never tattle on myself. Ask me about somebody else."

"I can subpoena you, Abagnarro."

"Bless my soul. Just how big is your subpoena?"

"Did you find that man?"

"What man?"

"Lieutenant Raintree."

"Why don't you ask the losers you had following me?"

"I'm not going to play any more games with you, Abagnarro. I'm sending a car for you right now."

"I think the battery must be going on this phone, Morris. It sounded like you just said you were going to send a car for me. But that can't be right. You already tried that and it didn't work."

The line was silent for a moment. I couldn't even hear Cainstraight breathing, or grinding his teeth. Ike and Aristotle were gazing politely away at the fountain, obviously eavesdropping.

When Cainstraight finally spoke again, I held the phone away from my ear so Ike could listen. His tone sounded like he'd decided I needed some counseling. "Abagnarro, are you under the impression that you've got some sort of First Amendment thing going with regard to Lieutenant Raintree? Because if you do—I mean do have that impression—I'd like to inform you that Lieutenant Raintree is not a source, and, as far as I can find out, you are not a journalist. I checked."

"I'm not?"

"No. You're a TV director."

"I just want to be sure I understand what you think here, Cainstraight. Do you think they blindfold the director and plug his ears when they're putting news on the air? Do you think that when we interview people on camera and scramble their identities with blue dots and computer voices, do you think the director is sent downstairs to the cafeteria so he can't tell what's going on?"

"I don't know what a director does."

"You and everybody else. Well, I'll tell you. On a news program, Cainstraight, the director does journalism."

"This is bullshit."

"My very thought. I'll say good night now. Why don't you go

read the New York State Shield Law covering journalists? If you can't find it in the J. Edgar Hoover Library, call me back and I'll fax you a copy." I hung up and closed the phone, but it rang immediately. I handed it to Ike without opening it. "It's for you."

She made a face. "Ike Tygart here." She made a series of faces and handed me the phone. "It's Fillingeri. For you."

"Why are they all calling me?" I demanded. "What's the National Desk doing up there, patching law enforcement to your cell? Are they all moonlighting for Ma Bell?" I took the phone. "Why are you calling me, Captain Fillingeri? Is this your daily check-in call to see if I've lied about any muggings in your precinct?"

"Calm down, Abagnarro. I wouldn't call to check on you about anything. I'm not your shrink or your mother, for which I thank Almighty God. I want you over at the shantytown on the river at Fifty-sixth. Right now."

"Why?"

"Because your network I.D. badge was found on a corpse. We want to know if you know the corpse."

TWENTY

BEFORE I SCOOTED over to the river, I escorted Ike and Aristotle inside the Emerald City to the security desk. I figured that with the word out for me from Fillingeri, and with that word coming from the scene of another spectacular crime, it wouldn't be long before the Fourth Estate showed up at our door, fanged and looking for hide. As far as I was concerned, they were welcome to Aristotle's hide, but they certainly wouldn't be interested in him when they sniffed raw media meat. Newspeople find each other endlessly fascinating, and the merest hint that NTB was making itself newsworthy with regard to Yellow-Man would make assignment desks around New York stink with adrenaline.

And, with their smaller fangs, the FBI might not be far behind. I didn't know anything much about subpoena power, but Morris Cainstraight presumably did, and he'd know how to do things right. He had a fresh killing and a fresh fingerprint, and he knew we hadn't ditched his troops solely out of a deep love for our own privacy. Ike and I would be on the hot seat if he could get us there.

"The shantytown will be a media carnival," Ike whispered to me. "How are you going to explain your I.D.?"

I shrugged. "No problem." I tapped my temple. "Bad I.Q."

She dragged me aside, out of Aristotle's hearing. "We made a solemn promise to shield Tex."

"Don't insult me, Ike. I have a bad I.Q., not a bad memory." I grinned. "Maybe I'll also develop laryngitis."

She ran her hands through her hair, tugging her curls hard enough to hurt. Aristotle gave her a doctorly glance. But he didn't say anything.

When Ike's upset, she takes it out on other people, usually underlings who are paid to take some shoving, but the only obvious underling available was Carl Honeyman and he was no challenge. And nobody could take one look at Aristotle and call him an underling. So, in a gruff and businesslike way, she started on me. She thought she had a list of things for me to do and to avoid doing or saying at the shantytown. She started to reel them off before we joined Aristotle and crossed the green marble floor of the lobby, but I stopped her with two words:

"Nine feet."

That shut her up. And I wanted her shut up, because I had no wish to discuss the particulars of a Shield Law. It was going to be bad enough to go and hide behind one.

"Nine feet," I repeated unnecessarily, maybe just to hear the sound of my own voice as I practiced saying something unconnected with Yellow-Man or muggers or boat rides. "Nine feet" is shorthand between Ike and me for "I know what I'm doing and I have the credentials to prove it."

This particular bit of shorthand got started because I happen to own the distinction of being the NTB News staffer who came the closest (nine feet) to embracing one of Saddam Hussein's not-so-smart Scud missiles during the Gulf War, when I was stationed in Dhahran, Saudi Arabia, so we could anchor *Morning Watch* from the desert. Nine feet closer, and I would have had a different part in my hair. But we stayed on the air, by God. I lost my Kevlar helmet when I hit the dirt, but my headset stayed on. The only difference the Scud made to me personally, since we were thirty seconds to the end of the show anyway, was that I directed our orderly sign-off with my belly on the sand and my elbows in a huge crack in the ground that hadn't been there when we selected the site for the remote. Oh, yeah. I also had to do the count in my head, because my stopwatch was in the huge crack.

If I didn't know how to behave on the smaller battlefield at the end of West Fifty-sixth, it would only be because I suddenly got real amnesia. When Ike let it sink in that she was trying to preach to the minister, we didn't exchange any more words beyond some strictly workmanlike phrases about the upcoming show. And I held my peace on the subject of the inappropriateness of her attire for the workplace, but only because I knew she kept a spare sweater and slacks in her office and because I didn't want to give Aristotle any ideas about maybe helping her change. He had struck me as perfectly capable of getting his own ideas.

As I skated back to the revolving door, Ike called out. "Hold on a minute."

She coasted over and thrust her cell phone at me.

I returned to the street and made tracks for the river. I took Fifty-seventh over to the graveyard of the West Side Highway and coasted down toward the docks, taking my time over that pockmarked landscape. Anyway, why hurry? There was no chance death would reverse itself and let Fillingeri's latest discovery sit up and make a last request for a word with me. And I had no burning desire to see the dead man who had my network I.D. Tex had said my badge was "in hell," and that's pretty much what I expected of the shantytown. And I was under no illusions about Fillingeri being happy to see me because I was so prompt.

Even before I made the turn toward the docks, I could tell that all the networks and all the local outfits were on the scene in force. Blazing light from their crews' HMIs and Frezzies cast an unnatural white glow against the hulls of the ships and out into the river and bounced off particles in the air, creating a warped zone of light over one of the darkest parts of the city.

The so-called pavement is very uneven in that wasteland, and usually what faint light there is comes from the strings of yellow bulbs that decorate the Navy's *Intrepid* Museum and the multi-colored but minimal carnival glow of the big cruise ships, but I had no trouble navigating with the place lit up by media field lights like the Second Coming.

Tex's shantytown was one of the last left standing in Manhattan, and I had read or heard that it, too, was slated soon for the bulldozer. Everybody called the encampment "Pier 666" or the "Devil's Pier" because its little acre of hell extended right to the shore of the river, where all the big boats dock, and because the devil called Alcohol lived there, along with his lieutenants, Crack and Smack.

The most famous feature of Pier 666's little shantytown skyline was an eighteen-foot-tall tepee, made out of poles covered with muddy rags and cardboard, which, in the white light from the HMIs, I could see were soaked from the day's storm and might dry out in about a year, certainly long before its occupant did. If the bulldozer didn't get them both first.

The rest of the encampment was built around the tepee, in a jumble of plywood, cardboard boxes, rags, pipes, shopping carts, and scavenged sticks of furniture. A couple of small campfires burned close to the river, but nobody was warming his hands over them. The few residents who were home or conscious at that hour were gathered around the ambulance parked in front of a lean-to made out of mop handles, cardboard, and a *Les Miserables* beach towel, all of it soaked and all of it highlighted in the naked blaze of lights.

That famous sad little face of Cossette, the waif on the towel, seemed to gaze back in sodden sorrow at the bright lights shining ruthlessly on her wet terrycloth cheeks. The *Les Miz* towels are the best-selling towels in the city, and I wondered if the current owner of this one was making a statement and how he had acquired it. He certainly hadn't walked into a store in the theater district and handed over some cash, and a towel's not the sort of thing muggers grab. It had probably arrived at Pier 666 via some dumpster behind an upscale hotel, a victim of a wild party or the embarrassing family secret of some child's bed-wetting.

Fillingeri was standing beside the lean-to, immaculately attired as always, and he had his arm up—gold cufflink glittering—shading his eyes against the lights that camera crews from all over the city had brought to the scene. CNN's lights were a double menace, because they were broadcasting live from Pier 666 and had as much candlepower on their correspondent as they had on the lean-to.

Apparently everybody knew I was the man of the hour, because as soon as I hove into the perimeter of the lights, all the cameras turned to me, all except the one on the CNN reporter. I must have looked just about like I belonged there at the Devil's Pier, with my stained T-shirt and that certain disheveled hairstyle that comes to all Rollerbladers too dumb or too good to wear helmets.

Fillingeri signaled to some uniformed cops to hold back the ravening horde of journalists, but most of the crews knew me by sight and there was a lot of yelling from them before Fillingeri was able to get a word in that I could hear.

"All I want you to do is take a look, Abagnarro," he said, close to my ear. "Inside this *Les Miz* palace. Then just nod yes or no. Meaning yes or no if you know the guy. If you want to tell all your pals with the cameras, you can do it on your own time. Got it?"

I nodded. "That means yes I got it. Not yes I know him."

"Abagnarro, I'm not as stupid as you think."

I put my hands up in protest. "I wasn't fooling around."

He gave me a cynical look and lifted the flap of the dripping towel. Inside the dark, smelly structure there was that familiar yellow paint on a face I'd never seen before.

The odor was overpowering. It was like dead wine mixed with mildew and urination.

I looked at Fillingeri. I shook my head.

"What the hell's your I.D. doing in this guy's pocket?"

"No idea."

"No idea? Or you're not saying?"

"No idea. Honest."

"Get the hell out of here."

"Music to my ears, Captain. I'm gone."

I quickly scanned the place as well as I could against the visual obstacle of the lights. No sign of Tex anywhere. I wondered who lived in the tepee.

Despite the eroded, rotted rubble of the terrain, and despite the darkness outside the perimeter, I put a lot of muscle into my escape, knowing that to outrun a pack of TV journalists you've got to have one hell of a head start. It doesn't matter if they're on wheels or on foot; they've got something the FBI doesn't have: ratings pressure.

I beat it up Fifty-sixth for about half a block and then started using alleys. The pursuit was enthusiastic for only about four minutes. Unlike the FBI, they all planned to outthink me. No doubt they figured I was headed for the Emerald City, and they would realign their efforts in that direction as soon as I lost them.

I swung back to the west and headed up West End Avenue toward my apartment on Seventy-fourth. I skated at a vigorous pace and at Sixty-eighth, I opened the cell phone and called Ike's office.

"Ike Tygart here."

"Me. Dead man. The corpse looks like the rest of them."

She sighed into the phone. "Any idea who it is?"

"One of the 'men,' I'd say. Yellow face. I don't know if there was a U.S.S.R. note or a knife wound. I was so—I don't know—*disgusted* isn't the right word. I've seen dead bodies before. But the yellow paint and wino smell add a dimension."

"I can imagine. Are you going home?"

"Yeah. I'll see you at four."

"Abby?"

"What?"

"Come in earlier. There's an earthquake in Pakistan. The first reports are saying ten thousand dead, and you know that will go up. The Tokyo Bureau's in high gear, but they won't be in place until tomorrow. We'll be getting practically amateur photography from All-Asian News, the kind that looks like newsreel footage."

"AAN's better than it used to be. Have you ordered the satellites?"

"Yeah."

"We'll be okay."

"Abby?"

"What?"

"Was Tex there?"

"I didn't see him. Turn on CNN. They're coming live from the scene."

"I've got it on. They've just got talking heads about the earthquake. Nobody's got pictures from Pakistan yet. They stopped reporting from the shantytown about two minutes ago."

"How'd I look at Pier 666?"

"Kind of dumb."

"That was Fillingeri's fault. He told me to clam up."

"It wasn't that. It was your hair."

"Aw, gee. There goes my fifteen minutes of fame. Fate dumps me into the hands of the media, and with what? Skater head."

"Poor Abby."

"Yeah. Poor Abby."

"Good night, poor Abby."

"See you in a few hours."

"Abby?"

"What?"

"Did Fillingeri say anything about Lieutenant U.S.S.R.?"

"Nope. Not in front of all those cameras and mikes."

I closed the phone, pocketed it, and went home. Although I'd taken my extra set of keys with me, it was nice to have my original set back. I wouldn't have to hassle with changing any locks. At the outer door of my building, when I pulled the key ring out to let myself in, I noticed that my original keys had somehow acquired some friends on their travels. There were two keys on the ring that wouldn't open any door belonging to me.

I skated inside to the elevator and pushed the button. I jingled the key ring in my hand and considered the extras. They could

belong to anyone in Manhattan, or in the world, for that matter.
Tex wouldn't discriminate against tourists. He probably liked
tourists. He could have keys to London town houses. Tokyo apart-
ments. Paris flats. Heidelberg houses. But why would he put them
on my key ring?

In the tiny ninth-floor hall, I used the appropriate keys to open
the three locks on my apartment door and skated inside onto the
parquet floor, too tired to remember that the neighbors downstairs
hate it when I do that after eleven at night. I tossed the key ring
onto my desk, but I was more careful with Ike's phone, putting
it gently on a chair beside the desk. I sat down next to the phone
and worked my blades off, wincing as the bandaid wad got caught
in the speed loops, and wincing again as I peeled off my T-shirt,
which had stuck to my scraped ribs. I left the shirt, the skates,
and the Band-aids on the floor and collapsed onto the couch. I
reached behind the couch to punch the button on the alarm clock
I keep on the radiator and was instantly asleep.

But it was the phone that woke me up. I sat up and glanced at
the clock. According to the red numbers, it was 2:48. I picked up
the receiver.

"Hello."

"Hello yourself. This is Kate Dean at CNN. I—"

I cradled the receiver gently, not wanting to give her an ear-
ache. I was feeling generous because it had taken her all of three
hours to get around to my home number, and there's nothing like
a good nap to make me love my fellow man. Woman. Fellow
woman.

After a hot shower—during which the phone rang constantly,
probably waking the downstairs neighbors—and fresh Band-Aids,
and fresh clothes, and a slice of leftover pizza from the refrigerator, I was back in my skates and out the door. I took the same
route I always take, the same route I had taken the night before,
and, except for the hookers and Tex, saw the same people—the
jogger, the Korean woman at her grocery, the clerk in the deli,
the guy at the newsstand—but I was on skates and the world
seemed mighty different. The world *was* different. I wasn't some
mark, his pockets asking for an airing, his ego for a thrashing. I
was that alien presence, that winged figure, Mercury on Rollerblades, the wind that nobody could touch.

There were no Texes, no muggers skulking in doorways, nobody who had business with me. Nobody who knew my name.

I stopped at the newsstand and checked out the front page of the New York *Post*. Just as I had expected, they had run a photo of kids playing in water—slapping beach balls around with plastic bats in Washington Square Park—during the afternoon downpour that had signaled the end of the heat wave. The banner headline was H_2OOOH-BOY! Somebody should really talk to the editors at the *Post* if their work is so feeble that even I can psyche them out. My guess had only been off by the "Boy." No wonder they go out of business, forever, every three weeks.

I skated at a leisurely pace, doing some window shopping and enjoying what is often the best part of living in a city with eight million other people—anonymity.

But Columbus Circle was full of people who knew my name. As soon as I saw the camera crews and correspondents and print journalists with their notebooks out, "No comment" started running through my brain. Ike had made a promise to Tex, and her promise covered both of us.

But "No comment" turned to just plain "No" when I saw who was at the center of all the lights and people and noise. Othello Armitage, owner of NTB, Inc., and one of the city's most reclusive figures, was holding court on the sidewalk. This was only the second time in my life that I'd laid eyes on the man who pays my salary. For a seventy-year-old man who must have dragged himself out of bed in the middle of the night, he looked fit and urbane and expensive as hell. Each piece of the gray three-piece suit tailored for his seven-foot frame must have cost a couple thousand dollars, and, while he clearly hadn't spent a nickel at a barber's because he's completely bald, the diamond in his left earlobe wasn't the kind you buy at Tiffany's. It was the kind you have somebody dig out of a mine near Johannesburg and have cut to your specifications.

But the hard glint in his eye was something he'd been born with, and I'd rather spend time on my belly in Dhahran than time on my feet in a room with Othello Armitage. Or on a sidewalk, facing the media. Especially when I hadn't seen the script for this little show.

I skated through the crowd and used my brake (a polite rarity for me) when I reached Othello's side. I think I may have smiled at him weakly; at least that's what my face muscles felt like they were trying to do.

He raised a hand and quiet descended in Columbus Circle.

"We have a brief statement to make," he said, "and, just so you save your breath, we're not taking questions after it. NTB News respects your right to gather information, but we also respect the right of our staff to protect its sources. Mr. Abagnarro, the director of NTB's *Morning Watch,* was called by Captain Dennis Fillingeri of the Midtown North precinct to the shanty-town on the Hudson at Fifty-sixth Street. Mr. Abagnarro was called because his NTB Network I.D. badge was found on the Yellow-Man victim who died tonight. He was not able to identify the corpse. Captain Fillingeri will tell you himself, but I'm telling you now that Mr. Abagnarro is not a suspect in the killing. Why Mr. Abagnarro's I.D. was on that corpse is a matter of confidentiality with a source and NTB is invoking the New York State Shield Law on behalf of Mr. Abagnarro. I do have one piece of information we can release to you: agents of the Federal Bureau of Investigation are working on the so-called Yellow-Man case, in cooperation with Captain Fillingeri." I thought Othello's lips curled into something almost like a smile. "You can ask them down in the Federal Building what else they know about the events of this evening. That's all."

Behind him, as if on cue, the giant green doors opened inward. I heard a few gasps, although most of the journalists gathered here on the sidewalk tried to be cool, and I saw a few cameras capturing the miracle of the doors with the sorcery of videotape. There was no creaking or pneumatic whoosh or any indication that the famous doors had opened by anything but magic. Othello stalked through into the lobby and I followed, unable to keep from gawking at the doors as they closed behind me. I sent my gaze around the lobby, looking for anything that could operate those doors. I saw nothing but the sleek marble walls and floor, and the freckled security guard at the desk.

Othello passed Carl Honeyman without a word, and so did I, but I wasn't feeling smug about getting past him without my I.D. badge. I was evidently slated for a chat of some sort with the owner of both the security desk and the I.D. badge and the green doors, and I felt far from jaunty making a racket with my Rollerblades on Othello's nice marble floors. I followed him into the elevator and the door closed on us.

He didn't make a move to push a button, and I certainly wasn't going to reach past him or say "Floor, please?"

He didn't bother with any preliminary intimidation beyond what he couldn't help by being who he is. He got right to the point.

"Abagnarro, I have three things to say to you."

I nodded, like I was glad I could count that high.

"Number one. I do not pay you to make yourself news."

"No, sir."

"Don't interrupt. Number two. I do not pay you to make enemies of the FBI. If I want enemies, I'll make them myself."

I nodded.

"Number three. I sure as hell don't pay you to give Tom Hitt and *Evening Watch* a hard time."

I couldn't contain myself. "I hope you're not paying him to give me a hard time."

His lips twitched and his eyes flashed. I thought thunder would come out of his mouth, and lightning out of his ears.

"One more thing, Abagnarro. This has nothing to do with what I pay you for. This has to do with philosophy. Are you listening?"

"Yes. All ears."

"Forget your ears. Let's talk about your mouth. I've heard a great deal about your mouth. Don't flap it when you are under an ethical obligation to keep it closed and I have publicly endorsed that obligation. You won't have any problem with that will you?"

I shook my head.

"Good." He pushed the button to open the doors and stepped out into the lobby. I wanted to stay there and watch, to see how the door trick was worked, but he said, without looking back, "Those pictures from AAN are in the house. Get to work."

I pushed the button for the twenty-seventh floor and the doors moved. The elevator doors.

TWENTY-ONE

I MADE A major beeline for Ike's office.

"You told Othello?" I demanded.

"Where the hell have you been?" she shot back, almost leaping out of her chair. "I've been trying to call you."

"I thought that was CNN."

"CNN's been tying up the lines *here*. And NBC, and CBS, and ABC, and Fox-5, and every two-bit, third-rate Fourth Estate gang in the world. The New York *Post* claims they have a photo of you with the newest Yellow-Man, in the tent he made out of a beach towel, and they want a quote to run with the picture— on their front page. All the owned-and-operateds have called, as well as the independents. Reuters called here, for God's sake. And the CBC. The only one who hasn't called is *Good Housekeeping.*"

"Did you call Othello?"

"No, because I didn't have to. Andrew Lack, the president of NBC News, called him. And I don't know who else. I was sitting in the control room, dodging phone calls and looking at horrible All-Asian TV, minding my own business and Pakistan's, and I turn around and there's this seven-foot-tall owner standing in the doorway with a diamond in his left ear and orange steam pouring out of both. Jesus."

"What'd you tell him?"

"When I could make my mouth work, I told him we'd found a source that had information about Yellow-Man. That I couldn't tell him anything else. That you and I needed the Shield."

"Did you tell Othello about what we did to the FBI?"

"Yes, because he asked about that, too. I had to tell him. God, maybe Janet Reno called him."

"Holy cow. Let's get the next plane to Haiti. I could use some peace and quiet."

"You said it."

She flopped back onto her chair. Her pink sweater and black

slacks made me remember that when I'd last seen her she'd been wearing a race car doctor.

"What happened to Aristotle?"

"He wanted to bend my ear about how he does not have a sordid past," she said. "God. Pakistan's cracking up and threatening to disappear into the bowels of the Earth, while the New York media is trying to crawl in through the air shafts of this building." She flipped her hand over, like she was tossing a Ping-Pong ball. "And here comes Aristotle, whining about 'pernicious' gossip. Like I've got time to do counseling. He wanted what he called 'assurances' that I believe him that he wasn't dallying with Hektor's wife before the divorce."

"Did he have a notary with him, or did he want a blood pact?"

"Blood, I think. He tried to paw me over, and you don't usually need a notary for that."

"Just tried, or actually pawed?"

"You can't try without doing *some* pawing, Abby. For God's sake."

"Why isn't he out organizing his brother's wake or something?"

"No wake. No flowers. Send contributions to the New York Chapter of the American Glaucoma Society. They can't have a wake without a body, and the medical examiner has not released it to the family."

"What are they waiting for?"

She gave me a long look. "Something to write on the death certificate."

"Oh." I realized I'd been huffing and puffing in the doorway like the Big Bad Rollerblader. I skated inside and sat on her couch. "That little formality." I sat back against the cushions and crossed my arms. "You know, Ike, that's something I never thought about."

"What?"

"The death certificate delay will also hold up some other stuff. For example, the distribution of Hektor's earthly goods. Do you know who inherits?"

"That's a good question. I'd keep my eye and my money on Olivia Quintinale, ex-wife and partner in Hektor's medical practice. Aristotle's furious with her. He had the idea that he was going to inherit Hektor's estate, despite a prenuptial agreement that clearly says the loot belongs to Olivia. Hektor wrote a will that attempts to undo the prenups. Apparently *The New York Times* got a look at some of the documents. So Aristotle is looking for a friend in the media.'' She pointed a finger at her chest. "Me.''

"Aristotle told you all this and still had time to paw you? He must be some pawer.''

"You want to know something, Abby? Hold on to your ego. Nobody paws as good as you.''

I didn't know what to say. It was so matter-of-fact, so nonsexual. She was not coming on to me. It was just as well I had nothing to say, because she wasn't finished.

"But I don't want to discuss pawing,'' she said. "When Hektor died, he was sole owner of the Stefanopolis family pile. And he had written a will in Aristotle's favor. My guess is that Hektor hated his wife more for divorcing him than he hated his brother for cuckolding him, if that's what happened.''

I shook my head. "Probate court will fix both Aristotle and Olivia. If Hektor tried to screw Olivia out of her wedding-vow dough, and if Aristotle wants to unscrew it, they'll both have to wait until the lawyers work it out. And when lawyers get their hands in somebody else's purse, they take their time examining the contents. Aristotle's got years to be furious. By the way, what's in the purse?''

"It was a fat purse, apparently. Greek islands and boats and the medical practice and stocks and securities and a Manhattan town house and—who knows—maybe the Parthenon.''

"Yowzer. Those lawyers are going to be wealthy.''

"Yowzer?'' She laughed. "What kind of word is that?''

"It's Greek. An ancient expression, in use since the Trojan War. It means something like 'Anybody know how to build a horse?' Speaking of Greeks, where is Aristotle? Hiding under our desk, listening to this?''

"He left. Without 'assurances,' without a friend in the media, and without the other thing he came for.''

"Meaning what?''

"He wanted to paw around in the Green Room.'' She stretched her fingers wide and started pawing the air. She pawed her hair, and it was already a wreck. Beautiful, but a wreck. She pulled open a desk drawer, pawed through that, and tossed a little pad of paper at me. I barely caught it as the pages fluttered open, causing it to take a wild trajectory.

"That's what he was really pawing around for," she said.

I flipped the pages to close the pad and looked at it. Then I looked at her.

"It's a controlled-substance prescription pad," she said. "Very stupid thing to leave lying around. That pad of paper is probably worth more than ten grand on the street. It's got Aristotle's name and the DEA numbers already filled in and everything, with all the proper little carbons. Rubin found it earlier in the Green Room and brought it to me."

"Why didn't you return it to Doctor Dope?"

"Because I've taken a sudden dislike to doctors who get careless with drugs. Our little talk with Tex was an eye-opener."

I raised an eyebrow at her. "You think Aristotle is mixed up with Pier 666?"

"How? That ten-thousand-dollar pad of paper couldn't possibly have anything to do with Yellow-Man, or Hektor, or the earthquake in Pakistan. The only harm Aristotle could do with that thing is sell it to some deviant or lose it. If you think he's selling prescription forms on the street, you ought to go tell on him to whatever drug cartel is in charge of that specialty department. But he didn't kill his own brother with that pad of paper, or anybody else that I know of. Tex's men weren't getting prescriptions. They were getting drugs."

"Okay, okay."

Her phone rang, and she dropped her fist gently on top of the receiver. She looked at me. The phone kept ringing.

"Were Hektor's Greek islands and things lush enough to tempt a brother to murder him for them?" I said.

She sat down, her fist still on the phone. She looked off into space. "Aristotle has an awfully expensive hobby, doesn't he? But I don't know how big the legal mess is. And I certainly don't know about murdering a brother. I wouldn't murder mine."

"But you're not Aristotle Stefanopolis."

"I'm not a lot of people. You're a big help."

The phone was still ringing.

"Is Tony here yet?" I asked.

"Yes. In the Green Room."

"Are you going to answer that thing?"

When she couldn't bear the noise any longer, she lifted the receiver. I skated out into the Tube and headed for my office.

After reading in, and sitting at my computer to send instructions to Graphic Arts on the channel they like best, and changing into loafers, I went after Tony. He was in a makeup chair, his face ready for air, talking to Martin Dachow, the guy who had created *Time After Time*, the animated math series for kids whose parents have locked up the remote control in the family safe-deposit box. I've tried watching the show, but it gives me a headache worse than Bill Cosby commercials. We had and were planning to use a twenty-five-second trailer from the show that was full of algebraic dancing, and even that much would probably fry my retinas.

Since Rubin had Dachow surrounded with towels and foundation coat, I didn't have to put much of a strain on my manners to be polite to the man I privately thought was turning more kids off to math than people who hit them with rulers. I don't think Dachow even saw me—Rubin is thorough in his approach to makeup and, at three hundred pounds, he's pretty difficult to see around.

I took Tony for a stroll in the Tube toward my office.

"You want Einstein's left testicle back?" I said.

"What makes you think it's his left one?"

"I could tell by the way it's worn. Einstein was left-handed."

"That quartz ball isn't worn. It's the smoothest, roundest object on the planet. Maybe in the universe."

"I never said Einstein wasn't good."

I returned the NASA property to Tony and, as he opened the box and checked the roundest object in the universe, I asked him why he looked like hell, and I didn't mean his brown suit.

"You can tell?" he said, grinning. "Even with the makeup?"

"I've been directing TV for a long time. You look like you spent the evening at *The Rocky Horror Picture Show*. No. You look like you were in *The Rocky Horror Picture Show*."

"I had a date."

"You did not."

"Yes, I did."

"Not a real date. You mean you hooked up."

"No, Abby, as strange as it may seem to a celibate like you, actually had a date. I took the lovely and talented director of

Public Affairs for NASA to the Edwardian Room, where we dined on figs and prosciutto, followed by seared red snapper—''

I interrupted. "You made her eat prosciutto? With the fat and everything?''

"Don't butt in here. I'm telling this story my way. Let me see...followed by cheesecake, followed by a leisurely walk back to the Parker Meridien. Next time I'm in town, I want you guys to put me up at the Plaza so I can skip the leisurely walk part.''

"Nobody stays at the Plaza except people who've always wanted to stay at the Plaza. If you're really hip, the Parker Meridien is the only place in town.''

"I guess I'm not hip. Followed by...well, you yourself said I look like hell.''

"I was hoping that was from the truth serum.''

"What?''

"Truth serum. You need to roll some in paper. Let's talk about that little fib you told Fillingeri about going outside yesterday morning to smoke a cigarette.''

He pursed his lips. "What about it?''

"Why'd you really go down there?''

"Off the record?''

"Let's make it 'between friends.' I'm swearing off of off-the-record chats.''

"It wasn't that big a deal anyway, between friends. I just thought I'd get a chance to unload some choice words on Aristotle. I haven't spoken with him alone since he testified to Congress. But when he came down, that Quintinale woman was all over him, trying to pick a fight. I never try to pick a fight when a woman has beaten me to the punch, so I left him alone.''

"That's a little sexist.''

"It's a little cowardly.''

"Why didn't you just tell Fillingeri the truth?''

"Because I'm here representing NASA. I'm not supposed to be airing my personal feelings. That's why I wanted Aristotle alone.''

"What was she picking the fight about?''

He hesitated.

"Come on, Tony. Between friends.''

"It was about Ike. Olivia didn't like something about the way Aristotle was ogling the blonde with the queer eyes.''

"They're not queer. They're beautiful."

"*Queer* was the word Olivia used."

"What word did Aristotle use?"

"He didn't use any words about Ike. But he had a couple of choice selections for Olivia."

"Give me a hint "

"*Stupid, porous,* and *clutching.* He must have a pricey speech-writer."

"Ouch."

"That's what I said when I read his congressional testimony. He's quite a rhetorician, even with a woman all over him trying to draw blood."

"Tony, did you see anything? You know, in the alley?"

"Nothing. That part wasn't a fib."

I caught sight of the clock on the wall. 4:43. "That's too bad." I picked my key ring up off my desk and poked his arm. "I gotta get going. Pakistanis to grieve for."

"I hear it's grim over there. We're pitching in with some Earth Observation Sensing Data. You know, orbital photography, see if we can locate the worst damage in populated zones."

"Mother Earth tries her hand at serial killing, making us mortals look like amateurs. And then you NASA guys use the big lens in the sky to help out in a jam."

"The least we can do. Anything new on the Yellow-Killer?"

"Watch the broadcast and be ready to talk space jargon at seven-ten—it'll be a rough transition, from the lowly, broken Earth to the lofty skies."

He shook the steel box. "This quartz ball was made out of the lowly, broken Earth."

"And to dust it shall return. Let's move. We're going to do you and your quartz ball right after the first news block."

I let Tony find his way back to the Green Room and made a quick stop over in Graphic Arts. There was no sign of any green skeletons, and no noise but air cleaners and keyboards. GA was busy making maps of Pakistan and Pier 666, and slides with relief numbers from the International Red Cross and the U.N.

I was in Control Room #1 by five o'clock. Ginger and I worked on the pictures from AAN, and we kept Fred Loring busy at his computer, building maps and fault lines, filling in the pictorial gaps inevitable on the first day of earthquake coverage. The first day isn't too bad, if you're not there and you keep score by the pictures, because it isn't until the second day that you get video of grieving people digging relatives and perfect strangers out of the rubble.

The pictures we did have were mostly architectural blight, just a lot of gray, uncertain mess until we enhanced the contrast, and there was a lot of camera shake not caused by temblors, so Ginger and Fred and I had little time for the pictures from Pier 666. Fortunately, those were from our own NTB crews, and we wouldn't have to worry about amateurisms. And Sally Goldberg-Petit was producing the shantytown Yellow-Man piece around Arden Boyer's narration. It was good to have Sally, a veteran, at that helm.

I barely noticed when Ike slipped into her chair behind us. She worked at her keyboard almost nonstop, making electronic shop with the Tokyo, Asia, and Tel Aviv bureaus, getting the last drop of coverage she could on the Pakistan disaster, dragging in free-lancers from all over the Orient and the Middle East.

Ike let out a shout when she finally found a woman with a camcorder in Shikarpur who could drive to Sukkur where there was an earth station to feed the satellite. The control room takes its mood from Ike before the show, and her shouts were echoed by shouts of congratulations. Excited, tense congratulations.

But, when we count down the last minute to the show, the mood switches to me, and I was loose. Hannah and J.D. were in their chairs at the anchor desk; the teleprompter was ready, the satellite was holding the Sukkur signal and Hannah was prepared to narrate the unedited amateur pictures, having spoken over the phone with a translator in Sukkur; our lead piece on Pakistan from All-Asian News was cued up to follow the live satellite feed from Sukkur; Sally's Yellow-Man shantytown piece was in the auxiliary machine. We were ready. Loose.

I cued the anchors. "Five, four, three, two, cue J.D."

J.D. told America good morning and read the lead to the Pakistan story, and just when I signaled Ginger to hot-roll direct from the satellite and cued Hannah to begin her narration, the bulletin alert "pings" on every computer in the control room went nuts. With one eye on the stopwatch in my hand, because I wasn't 100 percent convinced within a couple of seconds about the length of the Shikarpur tape, I hit the function key on my computer to call up the advisory. But I didn't have to read it.

"Shit!" That was Ike behind me. "Shit!" I heard her punch her console. I kept my eye on my stopwatch and on the line monitor. By my watch, we were coming up on the end of the live Sukkur satellite feed.

"The wires are moving another Yellow-Man story," Ike said. "On Fifty-seventh Street. Only this victim has yellow hands instead of a yellow face."

I could see from the studio monitor that both J.D. (open mouth) and Hannah (slightly raised eyebrow) had heard her.

Ike lowered her voice and said, "Hannah. It's gotta be Hannah."

I spoke into my headset and said, "Camera two on Hannah," and watched the monitor as camera two swung in close on her.

Ike kept going, speaking into Hannah's telex. "Hannah. Another Yellow-Man, but with a difference. When we come out of the satellite pictures, we're still going straight to the Pakistan tape. No change there."

Hannah continued her smooth narration of the Sukkur feed while she listened to Ike's voice in her ear.

Ike kept talking into Hannah's telex. "But Abby will cue you as we come out of the Pakistan tape. I will be reading wire copy into your telex, and you will repeat what I say. I'll give you about ten words at a time."

I reached across Ginger and keyed the Pakistan videotape. I reset my stopwatch.

The Pakistan pictures from AAN ran, with prerecorded narration from a clipped Indian voice. It was a short piece, only a minute and ten seconds.

I looked at my stopwatch and opened the intercom to the studio. "Five, four, three, two, cue Hannah."

There was nothing I could do but sit back and watch and listen.

Ike said into the mouthpiece of her headset, "The Associated Press is reporting a breaking development in the Yellow-Man story," and she read the wire report into Hannah's telex, in bursts of about ten words. It was a brief urgent bulletin, and it looked like Hannah was reading professionally scripted copy for America, instead of listening to Ike gasp into her ear electronically. When Ike was finished reading the bulletin, she said into Hannah's telex, "Late last night, NTB News was at the scene of the Manhattan shantytown where victim number eleven was found. Arden Boyer has that story."

Hannah said Ike's words into the camera, and I cued Ginger for the piece Sally and Arden had put together. The tape rolled. Our out-of-date story looked just perfect on the line monitor. Great pictures, great sound bites, nice narration, old story now that we were behind on the victims.

I heard Ike say, "J.D., sneak away from the desk and into the living room. Hannah, you'll read all the rest of the news copy and stay there for updates."

On the studio monitor I saw J.D. scoot and Hannah nod calmly.

When we came out of the shantytown piece, Hannah read the rest of the news segment. I kept the camera in tight on her to cover J.D.'s exit. We went to a commercial at 7:09:14, and rolled the cameras in the living room. I was on the edge of my chair, ready for the close shots we would need once Tony was ready to open the NASA box and candle his toy.

Ike already had a remote crew on its way to Fifty-seventh Street, and Ginger keyed the remote monitor so we'd know when they had the microwave dish up and pictures flowing.

I remember thinking that Tony was good—personable, easy-going, his explanations of the NASA gee-whizzery down to Earth and audio-friendly, his brown suit not as ugly as I'd thought. I remember thinking that J.D. was well prepared. His questions seemed spontaneous but thoughtful; his appreciation of the Spinning Quartz Ball and the work it would do in establishing the truth of the relativity theory was grounded in the realities of Earthly financial and technological and political concerns. I remember thinking how beautiful the quartz ball was on its pink velvet cushion, and how much more beautiful it was when J.D. took it out of the plastic box with his perfectly manicured black fingers and held it in the palm of his hand.

As our remote monitor continued to stay blank, Ike spoke into J.D.'s telex: "Draw him out on the history of this project's funding. Congressional cuts in NASA's budget. We need time in here."

My eyes swept the upper tier of monitors, the ones showing us what the other networks were doing. And there was good old CBS, with the first pictures from the newest Yellow-Man location, right across the street from their broadcast center. There was a man down on the sidewalk, surrounded by cops and a few early morning pedestrians, and gorgeous Giselle Fernandez, the CBS reporter.

Our remote monitor was still blank. We were getting beat bad.

Ike was watching the CBS pictures. I kept my eyes on the clock. We'd have to go to a commercial block again. There was no way to keep stringing out the interview with Tony.

And then I heard Ike say, "Wind it up, J.D. Now! Say we're going back to Hannah for an update on Yellow-Man."

I looked at our remote monitor. Still blank. I slewed around in my chair and frowned up at Ike, wondering what the hell she thought we could do without any pictures or a reporter on the scene. All she had was CBS pictures we couldn't use.

And Ike said, into Hannah's telex, as I directed camera two, "Say this, Hannah: NTB News has learned exclusively that this new victim is Ulysses Samuel Sylvester Raintree, a former second lieutenant in the United States Army." She paused while Hannah got that out. "During the Vietnam War, Raintree was decorated three times for conspicuous bravery. His honors included two Purple Hearts and the Bronze Star."

Our remote monitor suddenly sprang to life, and there he was. Big black face, ratty red sweater, black strings in his huge Reeboks. Gold teeth in a sad, big face. Elegant, big hands streaked with yellow paint, just as they had been when we had seen him outside of Radio Shack.

Ike sat down in her chair and burst into tears.

I told Ginger to roll our live remote pictures from Fifty-seventh Street into Hannah's recessed desk monitor, and told Hannah to watch the pictures there. I'm not as good at producing as Ike. All I could tell Hannah was, "Narrate what you see. Cops and crime techs. We'll keep the live pictures up, no camera on you. You'll have to ad-lib forty-five seconds of that voodoo only you do so well."

TWENTY-TWO

LONG BEFORE Hannah wrapped her ad-lib narration of the live pictures from Fifty-seventh, Ike took control again.

She brushed her tears away and got her hands back on the reins, and we made it through two grueling hours of updating Pakistan and Yellow-Man around our segments on Time. The math guy who was trying to wipe out the minds of America's youth was a complete dud. It wasn't his fault, maybe, but it's difficult to put algebra up against the deaths of tens of thousands of humans and up against the death of one human with a pair of yellow hands and still expect your equations to compute. Or anybody to care. Martin Dachow's premise was that repetition (thus the title of his show *Time After Time*) was the key to removing what he called "unknown variable-aphobia." Duh.

I could have told him to call it "Dachow-itis," and that the key to algebra was explaining to kids what the hell all that "x" stuff was about and why they should bother with it when they could get all that X-*rated* stuff on their home screens, but I didn't. If he would have listened to me, he wouldn't have been animating algebraic formulas in the first place. The screwed up thing, I thought, was his idea that bad TV could replace good teaching, or that bad TV was better than no TV in the classroom. Kids aren't that dumb. They'd probably learn more math by watching Three Stooges festivals or *Hawaii Five-O* reruns or *90210* than by broiling their eyeballs on his program.

Morris Cainstraight, who got paid by the FBI to know all kinds of math and computer language, did not give us his opinion of Mr. Dancing Unknown Quantity when he called the control room at 7:46. Cainstraight's mission was to find out why we had broken our promise to keep the name of Second Lieutenant Raintree to ourselves.

Ike gestured to me to pick up the extension when Cainstraight called, but we all had to hold on until the show reached a commercial break.

"We didn't break a promise," Ike said when a margarine commercial came up on the line monitor. "We made no promise. If we'd made a promise to you, we'd have used the word *promise*."

"The promise was understood," Cainstraight said.

"That kind of promise is never understood. We say practically a whole paragraph when we agree to protect a source. And what difference does it make now about his name?"

"It's the principle of the thing. And there's the practical matter that we reserve certain details when it comes to serial killers."

"Was it practicality or principle that made you follow us last night as though we were a couple of shady characters?"

"I'd still like to know where you shady characters went, and what you're protecting with that Shield, but not as much now that we've got our man." Cainstraight was gloating. "Anyway, we're working on getting under your Shield. It's not going to hold."

"What did you say about having your man?"

"Yellow hands, Ms. Tygart. They speak volumes. We've got the painter. I'd say we've also got the killer."

Ike was ready to explode. "Then who killed Raintree?"

"That's a separate crime, completely different M.O."

"I can't get into this now, Cainstraight. I have to keep a television show on the air that's barely held together with Scotch tape and good intentions. But you're wrong about Raintree."

She hung up her phone. Cainstraight hung up. I looked at the receiver I was holding. Cainstraight thought he had his killer. I blinked at the phone. Yellow hands were speaking volumes to the FBI. I cradled the phone softly.

While we made ourselves crazy in the control room so that what went out over the air would look professionally calm and under control, Sally Goldberg-Petit and a couple of editors put together a video collage of the home planet from film supplied by NASA, and after Hannah gave her sign-off, we ran the show's credits over their collage with the show's theme music. Their collage of pictures of the blue and white Earth dissolved at the end into a shot of the Spinning Quartz Ball in J.D.'s hand, the last image right under the NTB copyright logo.

Everybody in the control room sat and breathed. On the studio monitors I could see that J.D. was perspiring. But Hannah casually extracted the telex from her ear, patted her hair, and took a pack of Virginia Slims out of her pocket. She picked up a copy of *People* magazine from a table, flipped it open, and strolled out of the studio, working a cigarette out of the pack as she read the table of contents.

We debriefed the senior staff in J.D.'s office, around his walnut conference table, because the only other big comfortable office—Hannah's—was not fit to breathe in, what with all the fresh smoke she was puffing into the air and what with all the full ashtrays. She was late to the meeting, and she smelled like three bums in the smoking section of the Port Authority, but when she walked into J.D.'s office we burst out into a spontaneous round of applause.

Ike said, "Great job, Hannah."

Hannah raised her eyebrows. "Applause? You don't clap every day because the Empire State Building remains standing, do you?"

Sally hung her head, mumbling at her lap. "Now she thinks she's a skyscraper." I don't think anyone heard Sally but me.

There was a disgusted silence. J.D. finally broke it by saying, "You're an architectural marvel, Hannah, that much is certain, but the day may come when somebody takes the wrecker's ball to your fat flying buttress."

"I'd watch the personal remarks if I were you, Pinkwater," Hannah said, parking her buttress on a chair. "I'd be very surprised if there isn't some clause in your contract about orthodontics. How much time did Othello give you to get those sharp little things in your mouth fixed? At least I don't draw blood when I sit on my buttress."

"No, Hannah, you draw blood with words. You're a linguistic vampire."

"Is that what you studied at Oxford, Pinkwater? Vampires? Know anything about werewolves?"

"I know one when I see one."

Ike waved her hands around in the air. "Stop it. Or go outside."

Another silence descended, this one very welcome.

Ike ran the meeting, but she looked like she should have been tucked into bed, running her dream machinery: gray circles under her eyes; her eyes themselves bloodshot; her posture droopy; her gestures random and jumpy. I figured she'd had maybe three hours of sleep over the past two days, and she hadn't exactly been loafing.

"Sally," she said, rubbing her eyes, "that was a nice touch, that collage under the credits. You were thinking on your feet. I'd like you to do something similar for Friday, using a compilation of things relating to Time. We've got all those Swiss clocks on tomorrow." She took her hands away from her eyes and looked at Sally. "Okay?"

Sally nodded. "I'd like to ask Tony Jones to let us borrow the Spinning Quartz Ball. Abby can tell me about the technical aspects of what I want to do, but I think the ball on a black velvet background, with a lot of light shining on it, could be the image to end the week. Stark. Telling. Right after those Swiss clocks, it could be a neat juxtaposition. Or maybe I'll put Stephen Hawking between those images. Anyway, we'll need the ball for another day to shoot it."

"Our insurance covers anything NASA brings to the show," Ike said. "But we'll stash the ball in my office until you need it, so it's my responsibility." She squeezed her eyes shut for a moment. She opened them and stretched her jaw muscles, like she was popping her ears. She says she learned that in Tokyo, that it helps to keep her awake. The Japanese chew gum to stay alert, working their jaws rather than dosing themselves with caffeine. She passed a stack of memos to Sally, who distributed them around the table. "You've all heard by now that Othello, has pulled out the Shield Law to cover something Abby and I learned last night. That memo going around the table is the background. You are all bound by the Shield. But I consider us partially released from our promise to shield our source—regarding only the information he gave us as background to the Yellow-Man killings. If I get ahead of you here, don't worry. It's all in the memo, which is for your eyes only. I sound like James Bond." She worked her jaw. "You will all be covered by the Shield Law. But the death overnight of Lieutenant Raintree changes things a little with respect to the shielded information. Raintree painted those faces yellow, and he left the U.S.S.R. notes, and he stabbed the dead bodies. But he did not kill them."

Nobody gasped. But all eyes were on Ike.

She went on, after contemplating each pair of eyes. "Drugs killed those men. Not street drugs. Medicine. The men were being used in what I can only term a grossly cold-blooded and terrible medical experiment, in blatant disregard for the essential humanity of those men. We are still bound not to mention Raintree's involvement in the painting of the corpses, and the U.S.S.R. notes, and the knife wounds,'' she said, ''especially now that the FBI believes Raintree was the Yellow-Man killer. I feel we are obligated to do a 'reliable source' thing about the drug experiment being conducted on those men who died. Note well: that Raintree was our source is part of the Shield Information, and we are not released from any part of the Shield covering Abby or me. The background's there in the memo, but you may not use that. There is no way we can release the fact that Raintree himself told us about painting the corpses. Sally, use only what he told us about the drug experiment, not how we got in touch with him. I want you and any associate producers you choose to comb that shantytown for drugs—anything exotic, not the usual stuff that the coroner would have looked for automatically. Look for applicators, needles, bottles. We have no idea what form the drug took. Interview the residents. Ask about a doctor who solicited them for a pilot drug program. Start now. I mean after you read the memo. And after you reach Tony Jones.''

Sally shook her head. ''Ike, I've got to be on the boat to Hart Island, you know, for the Potter's Field story. That place is not exactly open to the public. I had to twist arms at the Department of Corrections to get this appointment.''

''The Department of Corrections?''

''They use prisoners on the burial details,'' Sally said. ''I got clearance for me and a crew. They're holding the boat for us until ten-thirty. Today is the only day this week they could let us go— you said you wanted the Potter's Field piece for Friday.''

Ike stared at Sally. Then she started blinking. ''I'll go.''

Sally shook her head vigorously. ''Ike, you're not fit to go. You look like you'd fall over the side of the boat at the first chop.''

''I'm going. I'm the one who should go. I should be the one to cover Potter's Field.''

Sally opened her mouth to protest, but she closed it immediately. She knew that look on Ike's face. Sally sat for a moment, considering it. She looked at her watch. ''I've got a Townline car scheduled for ten, out front. You take it, Ike.''

"Townline? We're outrunning our budget with all these satellite feeds from Pakistan. Why don't you go with the crew in one of the trucks?"

"The crew's already in the Bronx, for the Steinbrenner news conference about moving the Yankees to New Jersey. The crew is supposed to meet us at the boat."

Ike nodded. I knew her even better than Sally did, especially the mulish streak, and I didn't think there was a chance a little sleepiness would get between Ike and the story, but I made up my mind to give her some company on the boat. She might or might not fall overboard, but what if a prisoner pushed her over to test a theory that eyes like hers could only belong to a mermaid?

Ike turned to J.D. "You stay put here and be ready to go on the air for Special Reports. Tom Hitt is in, and he wants you because you're already familiar with both breaking stories."

J.D. put his hands together and bowed his head over the table. "It will be my pleasure to serve the Emperor."

Hannah didn't like the sound of that. "Why J.D.? I'm the senior anchor in the morning."

"Just hold on, Hannah. I have a plum for you." Ike gave J.D. a tiny smile. "The best advice I can give you about Tom, who will try with every fiber of his being to get the Shield stuff out of you, is to clam up. Clam. Period. You know nothing."

"Absolutely nothing."

"Don't even say that. Just don't open your mouth at all."

Hannah couldn't resist. "Good advice for you any day, Pinkwater."

"Hannah," Ike said, dropping her wrists on the table loud enough for us all to hear the slim bones hitting the polished wood, "Captain Fillingeri has agreed to an interview, but you'll have to do it at the precinct. He says he hasn't got time to come here. Tom has assigned an *Evening Watch* crew."

Hannah beamed. "They re using me on tonight's show?"

"Fillingeri said he'd give the interview only to you."

"Well, well, well. *Evening Watch.*"

Ike raised her right hand from the table, but only from the wrist. "Cautionary note, Hannah. Dennis Fillingeri always has his own reasons for doing things, and the fact that he requested you may have something to do with the fact that you anchor the program that is protecting a source he'd like to get his hands on. Dennis is going to try to wrap himself around you about who our 'source' is and about Abby's network I.D. badge being found on that corpse in the shantytown. That's one of the details we're reserving. You'll have to invoke the Shield Law if Fillingeri gets persistent. Othello has the Legal Department working to put our position on paper. Read my memo, and know what's under the Shield.''

"I won't need the Shield Law. I'll just knock him on his ass with my charisma.''

J.D. snorted.

Ike put her hand back down on the table. "I don't care how you do it, Hannah. I was only suggesting the legal way. It's your interview.'' She gave Hannah a suddenly hard look, a look with some energy in it. "Unless you let Dennis take it away from you.''

"Cold day in hell,'' Hannah said.

Ike turned her sleepy eyes to me. "You're directing the Special Reports.''

"For Tom?''

"*With* Tom.''

"No, I'm not. He's got a director almost as good as me.''

"But you know the drill on both Pakistan and Yellow-Man.''

"That's the best reason I can think of for someone else to do it. Tom will never leave me alone to direct a Special Report; he'll be too busy pumping me, worse than he'll go after J.D., because he thinks I'm I.Q.-deprived. And the Shield Law will mean nothing to Tom. He'll say he's one of us and will insist on being told. Need-to-know basis.''

"So stiff him.''

"I can do that. With my hands tied behind my back. But I can't direct Special Reports at the same time. Those are two different sets of skills.''

She sat back in her chair. "You're right. I'll tell Tom you broke your leg.'' She smirked at me. "Rollerblading.''

"Make it my ribs. That way I won't have to limp every time I see him.''

She looked at the faces around the table. Nobody had any questions, suggestions, or complaints.

"Then I'll see you all again tonight," Ike said. "I hope there's time for sleep." She stood and walked out of J.D.'s office.

"Abby," Hannah said, "since you've managed to weasel your way out of doing any work, what are your plans? Will you skate around town enjoying your endless childhood?"

"I'm glad you asked, Hannah. I'm like the wind. I come and I go, and nobody can account for my whimsies."

"I have some errands that need running."

"What'd you say?"

"I said I have some errands that need running."

I jiggled my earlobe. "Bless my soul, I've gone deaf," I said, adding yet another ailment to my growing catalog.

J.D. was smiling into his hand.

I stood. "That settles it. I think I'll blow my way to an ear doctor and get fitted for a prosthesis. Can I bring you anything, Hannah?"

She gave me an ugly look. "A horsewhip."

"Just write down your size and leave it on my desk."

I left the room, jerking at my earlobe.

Out in the hall, I looked at my watch. 9:55. I'd have to hustle to catch Ike. *Evening Watch* staffers tried to grab me as I made my way along the Tube, which was swarming with activity: people trying to run with videocassettes held over their heads, people trying to talk on cell phones, people grabbing at their waistbands and trying to read the displays on their beepers, people like me pushing against the grain of the traffic, *Morning Watch* people trying to get out of the flow of news production completely so they could go resume their lives. Those that had lives, anyway.

As I tried to edge myself into the crowded elevator, Diego Gordillo, just arriving for work, pushed me back into the Tube. I had last seen him playing in the traffic on Amsterdam.

"You got me in trouble with Tom, man," he said.

"Oh, grow up, Diego. I don't have time to listen now." I watched the elevator doors close on my escape route.

"Seriously. He says I can't go to Montana with him to go flyfishing."

"He'll change his mind."

"What makes you think so?"

"Because Tom won't tie his own shoelaces, much less his own

flies. Just suck up a little. He'll get over it. It wasn't your fault anyway.''

I kept my eyes on the indicators over the bank of elevators, tapping my foot impatiently.

''Tom says only a sap would've lost you.''

I considered telling Diego about the FBI posse I'd played cat-and-mouse with—or rather, cat-and-plastic-rat—but then I thought, why give away trade secrets? Maybe I'd do my Christmas shopping down at Fourteenth and Broadway, get Tom a nice little plastic cow with a nice little plastic udder shooting nice little white strings. He could put it next to his Peabody.

When the last elevator on the left opened, I bolted.

Over my shoulder I shouted, ''Tell Tom I cheated and used a stunt double.''

TWENTY-THREE

IKE WAS STEPPING into a black limo outside the Emerald City when I caught up with her.

"If you give me a ride in your coach, Cinderella, I'll speak French to you."

"Don't call me that. Tex called me that."

"Okay. I'll call you Grouchy. Move over."

"Why should I?"

"Because I've got as much interest in this boat ride as you do."

She moved across the cushioned seat without putting up an argument. As soon as she got herself curled up in the corner, she was sound asleep. Snoring.

"You still going to the Bronx?" the Townline driver said.

"Yeah, and make it nice and smooth. Grouchy here needs a nap."

"Nice and smooth. In the Bronx?"

"Just do the best you can."

I glanced around at the accoutrements. TV. Bar. Stereo. CD player. Behind one of the sliding paneled cabinet doors was a collection of sample bottles of designer perfumes and colognes. I opened a bottle of Jilsander's "Feeling Man" and splashed it on my cheeks. I looked at the driver as the limo pulled away from the curb.

"Do you drive hookers at night?"

"Hookers?"

"Yeah. Hookers. Working girls. Career lovers."

"No client has ever so identified herself to me, sir."

"But, you know, you can tell."

"No, sir. I can't tell."

"Part of the Townline service?"

He nodded. "Part of the service."

Townline's service is excellent, as I can testify because I didn't wake up until the driver opened the door for me right beside a green plywood shack on the East River. An NTB News truck was parked in front of the limo.

I gave Ike a gentle shake, and she came up swinging. I grabbed her wrists until she had time to clear out whatever monsters had rattled their chains in her dreams.

We got out of the car. The door of the green shack opened, and a fiftyish man, with deep cracks in the thick skin around his eyes, came out into the bright sunshine. He was wearing a blue uniform and a tan flier's vest, and he smelled like bacon and fried eggs and cigarette smoke.

He offered his hand to Ike. "Ms. Goldberg-Petit? I'm Captain McKibben."

"Sally couldn't make it," Ike said. "She had to rush to a different assignment. I'm Ike Tygart, Sally's boss."

They shook hands, and Ike introduced me.

McKibben gave me a hearty shake and said, "A TV director, huh? You're the guy who says 'Lights, camera, action,' huh?"

"That's me."

"Well, your cameraman is already on board, the freight is loaded, and we're paying these prisoners fifty cents an hour, so we'd better be on our way."

McKibben took two surgical masks from the pocket of his flier's vest and handed them to Ike. His own mask dangled from an elastic string around his neck, and he pulled it in place over his face.

He turned and strode down a weathered dock onto the deck of a rusting red boat, a double-ended, miniature version of the Staten Island Ferry, without the seating. The boat's name, *The Michael Cosgrove,* was on a plaque nailed on the side of the wheelhouse, and, in smaller letters, it said BUREAU OF FERRIES AND MARINE AVIATION.

Ike and I followed him with our eyes. The prisoners he had mentioned were lined up along the deck, six men dressed in green fatigues and also wearing surgical masks. Wordlessly, Ike handed me one of the masks. We looked at each other. We put the masks on.

The dock was reassuringly steady under our feet as we crossed onto the *Cosgrove.* I guess it was my stomach that was heaving. There was a funny smell coming from the ferry.

One of the prisoners pulled the chain across the back of the boat and locked it in place as the *Cosgrove* eased out into the river. "Don't want no shake, rattle, and roll," he said through his mask. "Some of these boxes ain't nailed all that good."

Cheap pine boxes were stacked in two groups on the open deck. One stack consisted of ten things that looked like coffins, about six feet long and the correct width. But the other stack was made out of smaller pine boxes, each about the size you'd need to package a couple dozen roses.

"Babies," our convict said.

The whole collection stank. Ike pointed to our masks and at the boxes, raising her eyebrows at the convict.

"They ain't embalmed," he said, in the same tone of voice he might have used to tell her it was going to be a nice, sunny day.

I looked over the side of the boat, hoping I wasn't going to need the facilities provided by the East River.

"How'd you get this job?" Ike asked.

"I'm a minimum security man—turnstile jumper in my previous life. This is good duty, huh? Fresh air and you can smoke if you don't mind taking off the mask." He leered at her through the mask and swept his hand out over the water. "And there's the opportunities for travel."

The passage across the strait into Long Island Sound was short and uneventful, but I got a view of the city I'd never seen before—the chunky towers of the Throgs Neck Bridge; the masts and clapboard houses of City Island, so pretty they almost looked like Nantucket; the tight channel where the sound dumps into the East River.

Ray Kinsey, our cameraman, was getting the same view on videotape, but he wasn't wasting his spool by making a mere travelogue. He got down on his knees to shoot the boxes; he leaned along the rail to shoot the line of prisoners in their surgical masks; he climbed the rusted metal steps of the wheelhouse to shoot the captain hunched over his radar screen.

We docked at little Hart Island. The shore was littered with the same kind of trash you can see on any New York street, but the litter was mixed in with beds of mussels. I didn't think I'd ever eat mussels again.

The island itself was littered with a different brand of cultural garbage for future anthropologists and archaeologists: abandoned buildings that looked like they dated from the Civil War; old bleachers from a baseball field—the prisoner said they'd come from Ebbets Field, but I didn't know if he was pulling my leg; a flaking yellow sign that said PRISON, KEEP OFF; house cats neglected and wild, howling and scurrying in and out of the abandoned buildings; a rosebush growing out of the side of a beached rowboat.

Past the small central plain, where I could see an open mass grave, there was a hill, and on the hill was a white tower, about thirty feet high and inscribed with the word PEACE. And standing near the plain, beside the hill, in a waving mass of yellow flowers, was a granite cross. On the cross it said, HE CALLETH HIS OWN BY NAME.

I closed my eyes and wished I could have told Tex about the cross.

The iron chain on the forward end of the ferry was pulled back. A big green pickup truck was waiting, tailgate down. The prisoners lifted the coffins onto the truck like they were loading crates of grapefruit.

Captain McKibben used the rails along the metal steps to slide and drop to the deck by our side. "You going along with them?"

"Yes," Ike said.

"Keep your masks on."

Ike and Ray and I left the boat and climbed onto the back of the truck with four prisoners and the coffins—no guards. I hadn't seen guards anywhere. We sat on the tailgate as the truck rocked over the stubble and through tall weeds. Ray was shooting tape all the way, sometimes standing on the tailgate to get the panorama.

When the truck stopped at the open grave—about a hundred feet by six feet, and maybe ten feet deep, obviously gouged out of the island by a backhoe—we got off the tailgate and stood aside as the prisoners handed the coffins down off the truck and then down into that massive hole. They stacked them tight, six boxes on top of each other in each stack, like building blocks. At the rate of fifty a week, that hole would fill up fast. The baby coffins came off last, two at a time, the prisoners carrying them gently, one under each arm. Those were stacked at the other end of the vast trench, along with similarly sized building blocks.

"You lookin' for anybody special?" It was our convict, standing beside us and brushing dirt off his hands.

"How would that be possible?" Ike said, frowning. "Aren't these people just, well, unknown?"

"Unclaimed doesn't mean unnamed. Most of 'em's got names. They got that much. The grown-ups, anyway. The babies is sometimes just 'unknown female infant' or 'white boy' or something like that. If they got 'em, they names is on the boxes."

Ike took a deep breath, denting her mask, and gazed down into the yawning wholesale grave, half filled with pine coffins, some of them much more weathered than the fresh white pine boxes that had just been unloaded.

"You're not going down in there, Ike," I said.

She looked at the prisoner. She pointed into the grave. "Is that the only place where there are names?"

"Captain's got the manifest."

The coffins were left there in their stacks in the uncovered great hole, open to the brilliant sunlight, the circling gulls, the scrambling cats, the wind. No words were said, no earth was thrown over the boxes, nobody cried.

The green truck took us back across the plain to the dock. We boarded the boat, on our way to the wheelhouse, but we spun around when a sharp odor suddenly poured into the air around us. Prisoners were spraying down the green truck with hydrochlorine from drums stacked against the pilings. Ray didn't need any prompting to get that shot.

The return crossing to the Bronx was filled with macabre jokes from the prisoners about what they were going to have for lunch, terrible descriptions of macaroni and spaghetti and Chinese food, punctuated behind the surgical masks with lip smacking and sucking sounds and congenial laughter. The prisoners sounded like macho boys from a frat house, enjoying a gross-out party.

When we had docked, and the prisoners were locked inside a truck that would take them back to their minimum-security hoosegow, Ike asked Captain McKibben for the manifest.

He laughed. "Cargo report, you mean. 'Manifest' is what the prison details like to call it. It's this little nautical game they play, pretending they're sailors. They even call themselves 'Potter's Navy.'" He laughed again. "Or 'The Ghost Guard.'"

Ike swallowed, her cheeks red. "Okay, the cargo report."

"Come into the shack and I'll show you the cargo reports for the last year. We got 'em going back into the last century, but I expect a newslady like you is after current events. That right?''

His cargo reports were stiffly bound ledgers, just lists of dates and names—or lack of names. Ike flipped through the pages of the one McKibben had handed her until she had the section starting in June.

"Can I take this out in the sun?" she said to McKibben.

"Don't see why not. Those books don't have any secrets. I guess they're public records."

Ike carried the book outside. McKibben and I stood back, keeping our shadows away from the pages, as Ike put the ledger on the ground and held it open. Ray knelt beside her and panned the camera down the handwritten entries. She turned the pages for him as he finished each one, and they shot videotape until the last entry, the load that had gone over to Hart Island with us.

She picked the ledger up and dusted it off. She handed it to McKibben.

"You want to stay for lunch?" he asked.

"No, thanks," she said, too emphatically.

"Better stick to crackers and soda water for a few hours," he said, laughing. He turned to the green shack, not exactly whistling, but doing something with his mouth that involved blowing air and producing an occasional chirp. I guess he liked his job.

Beside us in the sunshine, the limo was waiting.

Ray opened his camera and handed Ike the tape.

"Where are you headed now?" she asked him.

"Kennedy Airport. I'm on my way to Pakistan."

"Jesus," she said. "Don't you ever get to cover rock stars or anything?"

"I did Steinbrenner this morning. All in all, the boat ride was more interesting."

"When you get back from Pakistan, I'll make a point of seeing you get some cushy assignments."

"Thanks, Ike, but I volunteered for the earthquake."

"You're a good guy, Ray."

"I didn't get into this business to shoot weddings and birthday parties."

He patted her shoulder and hurried to the NTB truck, which took off across the gravel.

The Townline driver opened the limo's door.

Ike hesitated, tapping the videocassette against her thigh and shaking her head at the long black car. "This stinks. It's the most hideous irony of my life, Abby."

"Yeah, I know. Riding away from the paupers' cemetery in a limo." I looked at her sad eyes. "If it makes you feel any better, we can leave these masks on."

TWENTY-FOUR

WHEN WE GOT back to the Emerald City, Ike and I spent about twenty minutes in her office going blind, sitting side by side at her desk, viewing the videotaped list of names from Captain McKibben's cargo list.

Since June first, the city of New York had buried 551 people on Hart Island. About eighty-five percent of them had names, which was a higher rate than I had expected. Still, that list of names wasn't much of a biography of the 551 souls who had died in New York, or arrived here stillborn. It wasn't much of a testament to human worth or human evil or human mediocrity. It was just names and dates, hollow and meaningless. I'm not big on reading, but if I were, I wouldn't spend my time specializing in indexes. That's what this videotape was—an index to all the real stories buried in the mass graves on Hart Island.

At any speed, videotaped text is difficult to look at. Playing or pausing or running slo-mo are all as bad as Martin Dachow's animated algebra. And the list was full of dots that connected names with dates, and those little suckers drag the viewer's focus. My eyes felt like they were wearing spandex contact lenses.

After playing the tape twice and trying various speeds, I got us sodas from the machine in the Tube. When I returned to Ike's office, she was swiveling in her chair back and forth, staring at the open door, holding the steel NASA box on her lap. I looked at her eyes. Bleary. She spun slowly in the chair, a full circle, before facing her desk and the playback machine.

"Do my eyes look as bad as yours?" I asked, inserting my face between her and the display screen.

She pushed her chair back a few inches and opened her eyes wider. She looked at me. "No. Yours match." She rubbed her eyes and stretched her jaw in that Japanese cure for drowsiness. "Can't Fred do something to this tape to make it easier?"

"Nope. His graphic arts software is geared all wrong for something like this. We don't need enlargement or enhancement or even turning it around backwards. We need this list to stop moving. A good editor might be able to help a little, but only if we knew what we were looking for. I could maybe tell editing to take out the dots, but that's at least a twenty-minute job, and I'm sure they're busy doing tape from Pakistan. They won't relish what is essentially secretarial work.''

''Then we'll just have to go back to the beginning, keep pausing the tape, and read it a few names at a time.''

I opened a Diet Coke for her and put it on her desk. She moved the NASA box from her lap and placed it to the left of her computer.

''We better get started,'' I said, ''or at least figure out what we're supposed to be looking for. I think I've only got about thirty minutes of vision left.''

''You and me both.'' She opened the NASA box and took out the plastic box. She opened that and removed the little quartz ball.

''What are you doing?'' I asked. ''You think you should touch that thing?''

She looked at the ball like she was surprised she had it. ''Oh. I don't know. I guess I just like holding it. Have you held it? J.D. held it this morning on the air.''

''Not me. It's so dainty, I was afraid to mess it up.''

She handed it to me. ''Try it. It feels nice.''

I rolled it across my hand, and, outside of sex, it was probably the nicest thing I'd ever touched. *Smooth* doesn't begin to say what it felt like. I was startled when Ike reached into my hand and took the ball back.

''Don't let it hypnotize you,'' she said. ''We've got work to do.''

We ground it out, watching the Hart Island videotape through the middle of July. We were forging ahead when Hannah came sauntering in, a videocassette in her hand.

''I knocked Fillingeri on his ass with my charisma,'' she said. ''If you need any more miracles, go to church. I'll be in editing with Tom Hitt.''

Ike reached for the tape Hannah was clutching in her mitt. ''Is that the interview?''

''A copy. I had it dubbed for you on my way in.''

''Has Tom seen it yet?''

"No. If I let him get his hands on it first, you'd see only his version of what went on. He tends to overedit. Mr. Soundbite has no respect for the flow of conversation."

She swept out of the office. Ike and I looked at each other.

"It would be awfully tempting to interpret this as a generous act on Hannah's part," Ike said.

"I wouldn't," I said. "She probably thinks this interview is so historic that we should archive it. She's just afraid Mr. Soundbite will cannibalize her best stuff."

Ike took the tape of the Hart Island names out of her machine and inserted Hannah's tape. She pushed play.

The whole thing ran almost forty minutes, long enough to tempt even mild-mannered editors to savage it, much less Tom Hitt's tape-eaters. Ike and I took random turns at standing or pacing around the office at several points while we watched the long interview. We handed NASA's ball back and forth. I went for more soda. It's difficult to sit still for videotape when you're accustomed to managing it from a control room. I even have trouble going to most movies.

But Hannah got the job done. And she got it done on Fillingeri's own turf. There, in the setting of a Midtown North conference room and after the obligatory skirmishing, Fillingeri tried to pry our Shield information out of Hannah. She responded consistently by saying "NTB's Legal Department will be happy to answer all your questions after their review of the situation"—which meant "never." By the time they got down to brass tacks, Fillingeri looked weary, but Hannah looked like she still had nine rounds in her.

Hannah gave Fillingeri the few particulars Ike had sanctioned on what Tex had told us in front of Radio Shack—just the outline of a "reliable source," experimental drugs, a doctor, the shantytown. No mention of Tex's involvement in turning the unspectacular homeless victims into Yellow-Men. Hannah did not consult the memo Ike had prepared, probably didn't bother to bring it with her after reading it through once, so Fillingeri couldn't even grab anything away from her.

What Hannah got in trade from Fillingeri was the information that Second Lieutenant Raintree had died from a massive stab wound to his heart, a wound engineered by a large knife, delivered through the chest. A big wound, not anything like the little holes Tex himself had inflicted on the earlier Yellow-Man victims, but which we weren't telling Fillingeri about.

According to Fillingeri, the shantytown Yellow-Man I had seen under the *Les Miz* towel was officially "unclassified," like the others, but there had been no "U.S.S.R." note found on him. Just my I.D. badge, which I knew had to have been supplied by Tex, and Hannah knew it, too, but she did not let that slip out. Fillingeri confirmed that his department was working with the FBI on the serial killings, which now might not be serial killings, but he did not tell her anything about plastic rats, which he probably knew from the FBI. It came across on the videotape that the conversation was full of careful gaps, and they both knew it. That was partly what made the interview so difficult to watch: it was not a natural conversation.

But, in the last two minutes of the interview, Hannah went fishing and caught a fat one for Tom Hitt and *Evening Watch*.

"If they're not serial killings," Hannah said, a deep frown creasing her brow, "what would you call them?"

"We'll have to talk over possible charges with the D.A., now that we have this information from your so-called source. We'll have to reconsider the whole investigation in light of what you've told us, but that doesn't mean we'll stop pursuing our already-established leads. Sources aren't always right, you know. Changing course now would be a lot easier for us if NTB News would stop hiding their source behind the Shield Law." Hannah put up a hand, like she was warding him off, but Fillingeri didn't seem to notice the gesture, or maybe didn't want to.

"We've got two ways we can go," he said. "Way number one makes sense: Raintree had yellow paint on his hands, paint that matches our analysis of the Yellow-Man paint. That looks like Raintree killed homeless men he probably knew. Way number two is that some shadowy doctor was at that pier supplying dangerous drugs. And it opens a door on speculation about that doctor's identity that I can't possibly get into during this interview."

"I understand that. But what I don't understand is why the involvement of a doctor, as our source has told us, changes the way you describe the crimes. Why wouldn't these deaths still be considered serial killings?"

"Experience tells me, Miss Van Stone, that even when a patient dies during a medical procedure, it gets tricky. There are few precedents in criminal law. This could be a matter for the civil courts.''

"Medical procedure?" Now she made a gesture broad enough both for Fillingeri and for *Evening Watch* viewers. "At that shantytown? Giving drugs to homeless men, as part of an experiment?—that's a medical procedure?"

"Miss Van Stone, a properly licensed doctor prescribing and administering drugs is doing a medical procedure. There's only been one case in the history of New York State, that I know of, when a doctor was charged with murder involving the death of a patient during a medical procedure—and that was an abortion. We had witnesses then that said the doctor let the woman bleed to death without offering the slightest help.''

"What if the drug in question for these Yellow-Man victims has not been approved by the FDA? A rogue drug, or an outlaw drug. Is that still what you would call a medical procedure?"

I watched Fillingeri scratch his head on the videotape. "That's another can of worms.''

Tom, I thought, would open the show with the anchor reading a headline about Pakistan over animation and another headline about Yellow-Man, dissolving to the "can of worms" sound bite.

Ike tapped the video screen lightly with a pencil and reached for the pause button. "Medical procedure?"

"Tom Hitt will light on that like a cat on a roach."

"He's welcome to it. I hope every news organization in the country picks it up. I'm disgusted.''

"Hannah manages to draw out the worst bureaucratic bullshit from Fillingeri.''

"That's why she gets paid the big bucks. She pounces when she smells blood. But I have a thought, which is why I get paid the smaller bucks. Abby, let's forget Hannah, and Fillingeri, and Tom Hitt. Let's count. Let's do the math.''

"How do you mean?''

"Twelve murders. Let's call them all murders, including the ones who died because they were being used in a dangerous medical experiment. Forget legal precedent and terminology. Just use math." I grabbed the quartz ball from her, and she tapped her fingers with the tip of the pencil while the image of Fillingeri's face on the screen stayed frozen. "That gives us ten men who died from some still unknown drug, and they were all found with yellow faces and those notes—no, one was found with your network I.D., not a note.''

"That's if we build only on Tex's story.''

"Fillingeri seemed genuinely to be considering it.''

"Yeah. But nothing else confirms it. I haven't heard that the medical examiner has had any flashes of insight yet. The only evidence is our protected 'source.'''

"Right. But we can still be bare-bones about this, and do the math.''

"While you're counting, don't forget that Tex said he thought he'd missed a couple men.'' I stared at the ball in my hand. It *was* hypnotic. "So there are probably more than ten.''

"Right again,'' she said. "But, for the sake of clarity, let's stick with those ten that we're pretty sure about.''

"Go on.''

"Now we add Hektor, also painted by Tex. No cause of death determined yet. Just those beta-blocker things in his blood, from the glaucoma medicine. This looks at first like a copycat crime to the cops, mainly because Hektor was not homeless. Now Fillingeri doesn't seem to know what to do with it.''

"And neither do we.''

She smacked her palm with the pencil. "Keep listening. And then there's Tex, with his dirty yellow hands. Tex, who was really stabbed. An old-fashioned, no-nonsense knife wound. A cause of death the medical examiner had no problem with. Remember what Fillingeri said about murder?''

"I treasure his every syllable. He said the basic fact of murder is that you have to get close enough to somebody to kill them. Can't argue with that unless you're a letter bomber.''

She nodded. "So the question is, who would Tex allow that close to him?''

I sighed. "Nobody.''

"*Somebody* killed him. Tex was a big man. Whoever killed him must have been a person he knew and trusted, somebody who could get close to him.''

"It wasn't me.''

"I know that,'' she said, smacking my knee with the pencil. "He didn't trust you.''

"He trusted me a little.''

"Little doesn't count. It has to be somebody he really trusted.''

"One of his men?"

"I don't think so. I think Tex would have inspired something in his men other than murder. Maybe not feelings as strong as his own fierce protectiveness, but nothing bad."

"I don't know, Ike. There's a lot of bad chemicals over at the Devil's Pier. I mean beyond what the experiment was all about. Start with alcohol and go on from there. Drugs kill."

She gave me the full force of her gaze. "But Tex wasn't killed in the shantytown. He was killed on Fifty-seventh Street, away from his men, out on a street where he would have been alert, paranoid. It would be hard for anyone to take a knife to Tex on the street, and he was wise to the alcohol and drug thing. That's one of the reasons he was looking out for those guys."

I looked down at my hand where it was perspiring around the quartz ball. I wiped my palm on my trousers and gave the NASA trinket a spin on the flat of my hand. Ike plucked it off my palm so fast I almost didn't see her do it

"Are you paying attention?" she said.

"I'm thinking."

"About what?"

"About who Tex would trust. I mean, he was weird even with us, and he was trusting us plenty, giving us the story of his men. I could never have gotten a knife into his chest. Maybe from behind, but not facing him. Not in the chest, not with him conscious."

"That's what makes Tex's death different from the other homeless men, who were stabbed *after* they died. And that's what makes Tex's death similar to Hektor's—we don't know how anyone got close enough to kill either man. All the other victims were taking drugs; they got close to a doctor."

"Hektor was a doctor," I said. "The only doctor we know of with any connection to Yellow-Man."

"I know. After what Tex told us, that stares us in the face. But how do we place Hektor at Pier 666? All we have is Tex's incomplete story. We need proof. Evidence. Or Tex may very well take the blame for all the deaths." Her eyes took on a slight sparkle as she mulled some thought and rolled the ball around between her hands. "Hektor's death. It's a mockery of the others. An imitation. Perhaps a retaliation."

I blew breath out through my mouth. "That's too subjective."

Ike sat and ran a hand through her hair, just primitive combing, not pulling this time. She leaned forward and jabbed the eject button on her player and popped out the tape Hannah had brought us. "Then we keep plodding." She inserted the Hart Island tape and rewound it. We watched the voyage we had taken, the camerawork superb, the video reenactment of the trip to the mass grave supported by our own memories. When we got to the ledger, Ike sighed and pushed the pause button. "You've got a better eye than I do, Abby. Fast-forward to July. That's when the Yellow-Man murders started. Or at least when the yellow paint showed up."

"I wish the medical examiner had labeled the coffins of the guys he shipped with yellow faces. And I wish McKibben had recorded all that in his tidy ledger."

She scowled at the screen. "You'd think there'd be at least that much ceremony."

We were two pages into the July roster when Ike said "Look at that," gesturing at the list with her pencil.

I looked. I saw a bunch of names. A lot of dots. Dates.

"What?" I said.

She touched the screen lightly with the tip of her pencil. "John R. Murray."

I blinked and shook my head. "So?"

"Murray."

"I don't get it, Ike."

"John Murray. We had Hilda Murray on the program yesterday when Hektor was killed."

"You must be more tired than you look, Ike." I pushed my chair away from her desk and swiveled toward her bookshelves. I got out the Manhattan White Pages. I flipped through it until I got to the Murrays. They spanned two pages, and there were twelve Johns. "Nice try, blind lady." I held the book open on her lap to show her the wealth of Murrays in Manhattan. "We also had Tony Jones on the show. Want me to look through all the Joneses? Betcha twelve bucks there's a Jones on the Captain's Hart Island roster. Too bad *Morning Watch* didn't schedule anybody named Smith. You could really go nuts."

"It was just a thought," she said, shrugging her shoulders.

I put the phone book back on the shelf, and we plowed through the tape again, and we actually came up with a Charles Jones, buried on Hart Island on the first of August, and a baby, Karen Ann Jones, buried on the third of August. "It's about what you'd expect," I said, not gloating. "Common names are common; that's all there is to it."

Ike rose from her chair and made a dive for her couch. She lay there on her stomach, her cheek smashed into the cushions. She seemed to be studying the coffee table.

"What'd you say?" she said suddenly, raising her head.

"When?"

"Just now. About Smith."

"Scheduling. Hilda was not the glassblower I scheduled."

"Huh? Something about scheduling a Smith. Why?"

"Big deal. Guests crap out all the time. She told me herself she was second choice." I thought a minute. "Ike, Hilda volunteered. We didn't choose her. She practically told me she talked her chairman into letting her 'blow balls' on the show."

"The glassblower I originally scheduled was a man, her supervisor. Hilda filled in for him when something came up. In fact, he's probably the one listed in the *TV Guide* entry for yesterday. They print the book too far ahead for us to get any changes in, so I never even bother to try phoning in updated copy."

I remembered having seen Hannah with a *TV Guide* in the studio the day before, as I was getting the camera sweep of the facilities before we taped the interview with the doctors. Maybe the guest change had caught her sharp eye, and that's what she had been looking at. Not much gets past Hannah's "show feel."

Ike sat up on the couch. "We were notified of the change on Thursday. It didn't matter to me. One glassblower is as good as another, I thought. The change was very civilized and sensible, and Hilda made the Friday rehearsal. I never gave it another thought."

"Are all the other guests correctly listed in the *TV Guide?* I mean, this theme week on Time got so much publicity that everybody in the world knew who was going to be on yesterday's show. Anybody who wanted to kill Hektor would know where to find him—the Emerald City's not as famous as the Empire State Building, but it's not exactly a tenement."

She glanced disgustedly around her office at the stacks of newspapers and magazines and the towers of free books sent our way by every publicity organization in the free world, and some places beyond it. She even had a little pamphlet produced by Somali Christians and composed of drawings in the three primary colors.

"Boy," she said, "you'd think that the broadcast producer of a major network's morning news program would at least have a *TV Guide*. I'm going to start chaining it to the wall. People steal *TV Guide* and *People*, and they leave me all the highbrow trash like the *Wall Street Journal* and *The Atlantic*. I can't even give away that Somali comic book."

I left and went to my office. I unlocked the door, went in and got the desk key from under my dusty statue, and opened the big drawer. I got my copy of *TV Guide* and beat it back to Ike's office. I tossed her the magazine.

"Wow," she said. "You must keep it under lock and key."

"I'm just organized better than you are." I waved my hand around at the paper chaos in her office. "I'm sure your copy is here somewhere."

She gave me a dirty look. She opened and read the morning listings. "Yep. Hektor and Aristotle and Olivia, and Tony Jones, and Dr. Millard Evans, glassblower."

"Millard?"

She nodded. She tossed the magazine onto her coffee table.

"Tsk, tsk, tsk," I said. I grabbed *TV Guide* and took it back to my office, locking it in the desk.

When I returned to her office she was back at the video player, but she was watching the doctor interview this time, just at the end of Aristotle's car acrobatics, only the car flips were going backward. She was rewinding.

"Aren't you sick of that thing yet?" I asked. "How many times can you look at Aristotle feeling alive by almost killing himself?"

"Look at this. After the car crash. I've been so enthralled by the crash that I never noticed what's on the end of the tape. Did you know this stuff was here?"

She was looking at junk studio footage, the undirected cameras picking up the studio living room after the interview. There was Hektor, doing something to his eye.

"Yeah. Ginger and I watched it from the control room. She said it looked like he was plucking his eye out," I said. "Hilda was there, too, in the control room."

Ike sat forward and watched. I stood behind her and watched. Hektor was doing something, but what?

"It must have something to do with his glaucoma," I said.

"What do you think I am, stupid?"

"Pardon me for opening my mouth."

"As though you knew anything about the disease."

"I know more than you do."

"You do not."

"Yes, I do. Ray Charles went blind that way. Did you know that?"

She glanced over her shoulder at me, her green eye narrowed skeptically. "Oh. Really?"

"It's true."

She snorted. "Where'd you hear that? Airport TV? Like Freud and his fern?"

I stood there, a light going on. "Hilda told me. She knew all about Hektor having glaucoma." I shook my head at the memory. "She said she heard it on CNN."

"When did she tell you this?"

"At lunch yesterday."

"You had lunch together? I'll bet you made your mother pay for it."

"As a matter of fact, I did. If you will be kind enough to use your memory, Tex had helped himself to my lunch money."

Ike booted her computer and started pounding her keyboard. She called up the electronic memo detailing the medical examiner's report on Hektor.

"Abby, this report was not released until three o'clock yesterday. Therefore, CNN did not air it until then. Nobody scoops the medical examiner. Not that tight bureaucracy. And why mention the glaucoma at all, except in connection with that medical gobbledygook in the coroner's report? Nobody had the glaucoma stuff, except us. We got it from Fillingeri."

"Maybe CNN got it from the same place."

"There'd still be no reason to mention it on the air without the coroner's findings." From her playback machine, Ike grabbed the tape of Hektor and his eyeball exercise.

"Can Fred do something with this?" she said, waving the tape at me.

"Probably."

We took the tape and left her office. The Tube was bustling. I looked at my watch. It was just after five o'clock, meaning that *Evening Watch* was in the worst part of its labor pains. Nobody in the Tube was talking or making nice in any way. They were grim, with their eyes focused on making the definitive news statement to America in less than ninety minutes.

Fred had left for the day. The clean-air machines purred. The graphic artists were hunched over their keyboards, making art for *Evening Watch.*

"I'll ask Bill Brady," I said. "He's not as close to a nervous breakdown as the rest of these guys."

Bill nodded when I told him what we wanted. He took a moment to back up the project he'd been working on and went with us to the editing room reserved for the artists. He put the tape into an ADO machine, fiddled with the tracking button, and sat down at the fat, elaborate keyboard that commands the ADO's digital video effects. Since the graphic artists belong to the Writers' Guild, it's spooky how silent most of them are around outsiders, and how few words most of them use. Bill said only a couple of minimal sentences, such as "Here?" and "Like this?"

But he didn't need words to isolate Hektor's face and hands on the videotape or enlarge them without losing contrast, and we could see that Hektor was giving himself eyedrops from a clear little bottle that was full of clear fluid. When Hektor lowered his hand, his eyes were squeezed shut, he looked like he was in pain, and the little eyedropper was stuck at an angle into the bottle. Hektor put the bottle on the coffee table and leaned back against the brocaded cushions, pressing his fingers against the bridge of his nose.

"That's all?" Bill said.

"That's all," I said.

He extracted the tape, handed it to mc, and left the room.

Ike lifted the telephone receiver from the wall and dialed a number. "Dennis Fillingeri, please. Tell him it's Ike Tygart calling."

Apparently Fillingeri was handy, because Ike almost immediately swung into the reason for her call.

"Dennis. Was a bottle of glaucoma medicine found on Hektor Stefanopolis's body? You know, that beta-blocker stuff?"

She listened. I could hear Fillingeri squawking, but I couldn't make out the words.

"In the briefcase? Oh. Well, just tell me if the bottle was full," she said.

More squawking.

"I wondered," she said, "because the bottle was still full yesterday morning after he used the drops in the studio. Abby and I found some junk tape that shows him using the drops. Something happened to that medicine between the time Hektor used it here and the time you guys found the empty bottle in his briefcase in the alley."

More squawking.

"Well, don't ask me," Ike said, a little huffily. "How should I know what happened to his medicine? You ought to be glad I'm such a good citizen that I call and share my every little discovery with you."

More squawking.

"Well, maybe I don't tell you *every* little discovery, but NTB News gave you a copy of the same videotape I've been looking at, and you could have noticed what I noticed about the bottle, so put a cork in your accusations, okay? And keep it in while I ask one more question."

I didn't hear any squawking, so I guessed Fillingeri was either holding his breath or hanging himself.

"Did CNN release the fact of Hektor's glaucoma before the medical examiner did?" Ike said.

Now there was squawking, and a lot of it. Ike held the phone away from her ear. When the squawking kept up and showed no signs of abating, she put her mouth to the speaker.

"You're such an ingrate," she said, over the squawking. "You couldn't get it out of Hannah, and you're not going to get it out of me. Call our lawyers."

More squawking, but this time I could make out some noise about "that goddam Shield Law."

Ike gently replaced the receiver on the wall.

"That's the last time I tell him anything," she said.

"Be fair, Ike. You didn't call to tell Fillingeri anything. You called to pump him."

"So what? I still told him something."

"What did he say about the glaucoma?"

"He said he didn't tell anyone but us. The M.E. released it to the media with the autopsy results. Dennis doesn't think the family released it, because they were tied up all morning by police procedure. And why would they?"

"Ike, do you know what you've unleashed? Fillingeri's going to hotfoot it over here now to look for that medicine—right now."

She grinned. "He won't find it."

"He won't?"

"I don't think so. Because I'm going to find it first."

"Not if it's down some toilet."

"God, I hope not." She blinked at me. "I was thinking of something more sanitary."

TWENTY-FIVE

IKE UNLOCKED the heavy door to Studio 57 and pushed it open. That place is really a mausoleum when the lights are off. And, with all the sound baffles, when the noise is off.

She didn't waste any time picking and choosing among the light switches; she put her arm flat against the wall beside the door and pushed up, turning on a full bank of lights that lit up a quarter of the house. I wish she wouldn't do that. Those switches need repair more often than any single piece of equipment in the studio, and it's because of impatient people like her, not knowing what they're doing, who abuse the privilege. And it doesn't do any good to try to correct her, because her answer is always the same: "I'm keeping some poor lighting tech off the unemployment line."

"What are we looking for?" I said, refraining from setting myself up for a dose of social wisdom.

"A glass bauble. Sealed forever."

"You didn't need all these lights for that. I wish you wouldn't be so careless. Hilda's gear is behind the kitchen cyc." I reached for the banks of switches. "These three little switches—"

"I don't mean the ones she sealed on the show. I mean the bud vase she used before the show for that spontaneous little demonstration. Remember? The vase with the red rose in it. She went over to the coffee table and grabbed the vase. Hektor had left his eyedrops there on the table."

"You think she dumped his eyedrops in the vase? Why would she do that?"

"Maybe so nobody would look at the drops and find the nasty substance in them that killed him."

"Very good, Ike. And maybe somebody else dumped the contents. And maybe nobody did. Maybe, maybe, maybe."

"Nobody but Hilda showed any interest in that vase, and only Hilda could have sealed it up." She stepped away from the light switches. "And maybe I'm just plain wrong."

"Speaking of you being wrong, wouldn't Hektor have noticed that the bottle was empty when he went back for it? He must have picked it up before he left, because the empty bottle was found in his briefcase."

"I don't know. I don't know the limitations of his vision."

We rooted around behind the cyclorama that separates our kitchen set from the blank and ugly concrete wall of the studio. When the stage crew clears off the set, they don't take their time and use white gloves. There was a lot of junk from past shows in that narrow tunnel between the real wall and the fake kitchen wall, and the junk was not neatly filed and labeled. It was just there, our equivalent of a stuffed attic.

I started by taking a stack of books from a cart and dropping them on the floor so I could see what was behind them.

"Be careful, Abby. Don't break anything."

"Oh, glass is breakable? Thanks for telling me. It's nice to have an expert around."

"You don't have to get snitty. You at least got some sleep last night."

"Three hours."

"That's more than I got."

I lifted aside some bowls and wooden spoons that were stacked on a cart. "You should have let me put you in a cab last night, like I suggested. But oh, no, you always know best."

Ike sneezed. "We need some air cleaners back here."

"They'd interfere with the sound."

I spotted propane and oxygen tanks a yard away, half hidden by a plastic philodendron. I pointed at the tanks and we moved.

The four glass vials Hilda had sealed for the show with her bare hands were sitting in their little metal rack on a small table, all lined up and sparkling with originality and craftsmanship, even in the dim light behind the cyc. There was no sign of Hilda's goggles or her apron, and I assumed she had taken those with her or that the Traffic Department had sent them to her lab, having recognized them as personal belongings. But I saw no sign of the bud vase she had ruined/sculpted to give us and the doctors a demonstration of the fact that glass is a liquid.

"Damn," Ike said. "It's gotta be here."

"It may have been thrown out."

"The stage hands throw out only obvious garbage, like bags from McDonald's."

"One man's bud vase is another man's garbage," I said.

Ike returned to the light switches by the studio door and shoved with her arms until every light in Studio 57 was on. She went to the living room set and perched on the very cushion where Hektor had administered his eyedrops. She pursed her lips and pulled her feet off the floor. She leaned over, looking under the couch. She got to her knees and crawled to the end of the couch.

"Abracadabra," she said.

She reached over the arm of the couch and lifted a glass doodad from the end table. She held it up to the lights, and sparks seemed to shoot off the glass in the glare. She gave the bauble a little shake.

"Sure is an odd little thing," she said, smiling to herself. "I wonder what's inside. Rose sediment—or a substance that, by any other name, would smell deadly?"

"We'll need a glassblower or some other expert to open it—unless you're planning to take a hammer to it, possibly destroying evidence—and we'll need a chemist to analyze the liquid."

"Oh, dear. I wonder if I should even be touching this?"

"Some stagehand has already touched it. Somebody put it there. It didn't fly."

She placed the glass vase, with its ugly, twisted, drooping neck, down on the coffee table in front of her, gently, on the flat end. She picked up the telephone from the end table and put it in her lap. She lifted the receiver and looked at me.

"What's Cainstraight's number?" she said.

"I don't have it memorized. Call information. And what good do you think it will do to call him? He'll just squirt subpoenas through the wire."

"Pooh. Trust me." She got the number from information and dialed.

She didn't get put through to Cainstraight directly. Several FBI phone-call-stallers interceded before she got the jukebox man.

"Good evening, Mr. Cainstraight. This is Ike Tygart."

I went to the news desk and picked up on the extension she was using. Cainstraight was talking when I tuned in.

"...when you'd change your mind and see that the interests of justice supersede your privilege."

"Oh, I haven't changed my mind. A promise is a promise. But my interests and your interests do happen to coincide at some points and I wanted to ask you a question."

"You have a question. That's interesting. *You* have a question. What about our questions? Listen, if you think the Shield Law can cause some convenient silence for you, wait until you see all the neat, tricky laws we know at the FBI."

"I can imagine. Are you recording this call?"

"Yes."

Ike held the receiver away from her and blinked at it, like she was worried it had turned into a snake. She shook her head at it and put it back against her face. "You admit it, just like that?"

"That's one of the neat laws I know. I inform you we're recording, you give tacit agreement, the tape is admissible in court."

"We'll see," she said. "It's not always that cut-and-dried. Remember, I'm in the taping business, too."

"If you already knew the answer, why'd you call?"

"Oh. That wasn't my question, about taping the call. My real question is about one particular Yellow-Man victim."

"And you call me. Are you under the impression I'm running a research service down here? Some kind of public library?"

"No. But—be human, Cainstraight—you've got the best resources on Yellow-Man, don't you?"

He grunted. "Which victim are you interested in, just for the sake of argument?"

"Was one of the victims named John Murray?"

There was a silence. When Cainstraight answered after about ten seconds, there was a note in his voice that sounded like he'd thought it over and decided the question was so interesting he was thinking of answering it to see what Ike's reaction would be. But he wasn't going to make it easy, because he was still thinking about it.

"Why do you ask?" he said.

"To make my life easier. Those names are a matter of public record, and I can get them by going down to the Midtown North precinct house. Calling you seemed easier and faster."

"The record is sealed. We can do that in the case of a serial killer. One of those little laws I mentioned."

"Just yes or no, Cainstraight? You can't even tell me that much?"

"I'd be interested in seeing where you're going with this. Okay. Yes. John Murray was one."

"Did you jukebox his fingerprints?"

"What do you think?" Cainstraight's fuse was starting to burn faster. "We juked yours when you came into the Federal Building pretending you were just paying a social call. Of course we juked a Yellow-Man victim."

"And," Ike said, crossing the fingers of her free hand and looking across the studio at me, "what did you find out about John Murray?"

"That's information we're not releasing. Call it *sealed.*"

"Come on, Cainstraight, I've got a good reason for asking."

"I'll bet. I have a good reason for refusing comment."

They went at it, around and around, for about three minutes, neither giving an inch.

I cradled the desk phone and crossed to the living room. I sat beside Ike and made the time-out signal with my hands. She told Cainstraight to hold the line and covered the receiver.

"Cainstraight's not going to give you the connection between John and Hilda Murray, not for free," I whispered to Ike. "Why don't you give it to him? Make him work it out from there."

"Not on your life." She snatched the melted bud vase off the table and hung on to it. "It's our story. Not just in the sense of a news story, but in the sense that you and I have lived part of it. If I have to, I can get the answer myself from Fillingeri. However I have to get it, I'll get it. We owe it to Tex. We owe it to ourselves."

I shook my head. "Fillingeri is going to stonewall as soon as Cainstraight passes the word. They're going to use this to attempt to break our Shield."

"Shit."

I took the receiver from her.

"Morris, this is Abby."

"I thought you were the wind."

"I am. And, like the wind, I'm changeable: the despair of meteorologists and crime stoppers, the delight of old men looking up skirts. I have a deal for you."

"A deal? What kind of deal?"

"I'll give you our Shield information for the answer to Ike's question.

Ike tried to grab the phone from me. "Abby, you can't!"

I tugged at the receiver and got it to my mouth. "Hold on, Morris. High pressure from the Midwest."

Ike crossed her arms over her chest, hugging the bud vase in her armpit, and gave me a look. "What the hell's the matter with you?" she demanded.

I covered the receiver. "Tex is dead. If they knew the truth, the best they could work up against him is obstructing justice, or something like that. What difference will it make to him now? What if we can buy some justice with the information we're shielding?"

"We promised Tex—no—we took a sacred oath."

"I know. But sometimes you have to break a promise."

"Othello has taken a public stand on this."

"What's the worst he can do? Fire us?"

"Yes. But, Abby, I don't care about that. Well, I do, but that's not what's crushing my gut. Our Shield information will just put the finishing touches on their case against Tex. I can see his big face when I made the promise. He trusted us."

"He trusted us. To help his men. It's a question of what we have to do to help."

She placed the bud vase in her lap. Now she really had her hands in her hair. Rubbing and pulling. I didn't know what Cain-straight was doing to pass the time, but he probably wasn't laying waste to his hairdo. He was probably doing a little something electronic and a little something like whatever passes for FBI praying.

"Ike," I said, "Tex's men are in the Potter's Field. Tex couldn't do anything about that. We can't do anything about that. And Tex is probably going to take the same boat ride. And we can't do anything about that, either. And Hektor is probably going to be cremated and strewn over a Greek island. And we can't do anything about that. But there's a killer on *this* island, and maybe we can do something about that. I think Tex would approve, and I'm going to make this deal."

She raised her eyes and looked at me. No matter what she does to mess up her hair, she can't make herself ugly. She could wear a bale of hay on her head and still take my breath away. Her lovely, mismatched eyes were full of trouble, but she nodded at me.

I took my hand off the receiver.

"Cainstraight, here's the deal. You answer Ike's question about John Murray, with all the details you have, holding back nothing, and we'll give you the Shield information. But we need some time."

"I don't like this, Abagnarro. What's this 'time' bullshit?"

"We just need time. Give us, say, twelve hours, until our next broadcast. A mere half day."

"I don't like it."

"Then say no more. I may see you in passing, about the town as I come and go, redistributing the smog and pollinating the trees. You may feel me coming at you around a corner some icy morning. I hope you slip and fall as I blast by."

"Wait a minute. I'll give you one hour."

"No deal. An hour's nothing."

"What do you need the time for?"

"I'm going to blow around a little. Pollinate some trees."

"Two hours. Take it or leave it. My shift ends in two hours. That's all I can give you. We'll call it a personal favor, and it has to come out of my personal shift. That's my deal."

"Hang on." I looked at my watch. 6:27. "My two hours starts now. No stalling. Everything you have on Murray."

"Okay."

"You answer the question. In two hours, we'll meet you out-doors. Outside the Emerald City. I don't like talking on this wire."

"Your word better be good on this, Abagnarro, better than your word to your 'source' of this Shield information."

I winced. "I know. You've got it on tape. Admissible in court."

I nodded at Ike. She clasped the bud vase carefully in her hand before she stood, and, assured the glass was safe, she raced over to the news desk to pick up that phone.

I could hear Cainstraight operating a keyboard.

"John Richard Murray," Cainstraight said, "was born in 1937 in Youngstown, Pennsylvania. Graduated from Trafton High in Youngstown, no further schooling. No military service. Patented a lawn-mower fan belt in 1961 that went into development at R.F.

Tools in Brooklyn in 1963 but was never marketed. Married in 1960 in Brooklyn, New York, to Dorothy S. Williams. Two children. Murray had a long list of arrests, only two convictions, both for theft. Small shit, like the cash box in a filling station where he worked, a car stereo, stuff like that. Did time at Rikers Island. Model prisoner, early release. Violated parole by dropping some dirty urine—alcohol and coke. Did a little more time and some rehab. Wife died in 1978 of breast cancer. Murray died July 12, this year, cause of death unclassified. Coroner says alcohol damage to liver and pancreas, as well as respiratory cancer, neither of which killed him. Homeless. Known to Social Services and the Saint Vincent de Paul Society of Queens, which sheltered him off and on. He didn't like to stay in the Queens shelter because they wouldn't let him drink. Murray is survived by the two children, John, Jr., and Iris Hilda.''

Ike was standing at the anchor desk, her mouth open. She got it closed and worked her jaw. After those contortions, she said, ''He has living relatives. How could he have been homeless?''

''Don't be so naive, Ms. Tygart. The guy was a bum. What do you think, the homeless just sprout from the sidewalk?''

''No. Of course not.''

''They don't. They sprout out of their real lives, just like you and me, only they're bent wrong and they can't make it here.''

''Why didn't the children bury their father?''

''John, Jr., is somewhere in Florida. Some people would call him a beach bum. Some people would call him homeless. Seems the family has a problem with that. It is not known the last time he saw his father. The daughter saw the medical examiner when Murray died and she identified the body, but said she couldn't afford funeral expenses. She'd had some contact with her father, off and on, said they fought because he wouldn't dry out, said he'd chosen his own path. I'm not in the business of providing sympathy for society's ills, but I'm not inclined to argue with her point, either personally or professionally. If you want to look at it that way, these homeless people are victimizing their families by the choices they make.''

''I'm not so convinced homeless people choose homelessness,'' Ike said. ''Murray sounds like he was sick.''

''He was a bum. Some people are just bums. That's a fact.''

I was looking at my watch and didn't want to waste our two

hours listening to the social history of homelessness, so I interrupted the symposium. "We'll see you at eight twenty-seven, Cainstraight."

"Eight twenty-seven it is."

"The deal's off if we see so much as one federal agent during those two hours."

Now I could hear Cainstraight cover his receiver.

Ike looked at me from across the studio, her eyes wide.

Cainstraight unwrapped his mouthpiece. "Make it eight-thirty, Abagnarro. In front of the Emerald City."

Ike and I hung up.

"Iris Hilda Murray," she said. "Maybe the daughter of one of Tex's men could get close enough to kill the big guy."

"We've got less than two hours to find a connection that gets her close enough," I said. "If we don't, I may have just sold out the big guy, big time. The FBI will never believe that Tex only painted those men so people would notice them. They'll believe he was crazy, nuts, and lost—typical homeless pathology. When we remove the Shield and tell Tex's story, the feds won't look for some doctor a crazy homeless man invented. Cainstraight will use our Shield information to 'solve' these homicides, he'll get law enforcement off the hook, and Lieutenant Raintree will go down in history as the Yellow-Man killer."

TWENTY-SIX

"THEN WE NEED to find two connections, and fast," Ike said. "We need to connect the real killer—the doctor experimenting with drugs—to John Murray. And we need to pin down how Hilda found out what was happening to her dad, just exactly how much she knew. Why in God's name did you settle for two hours?"

"Cainstraight wasn't going to give me any more. Period. I hope you're not going to end up hating me for what I just did."

"I did it, too, Abby."

"I know, but it was my idea."

"I never thought we'd break a Shield."

I caught a glimpse of the clock on the wall facing the anchor desk. "If we're going to break it, let's make it worthwhile. What about Hilda?"

"Her homeless father must have told her that Hektor was the Pier 666 house physician." She raised her eyebrows. "*If* Hektor is the doctor we're looking for. Cainstraight said Hilda had come down to the coroner's office to identify her father's body, and that father and daughter had been in some sort of regular contact with each other, usually fighting over his drinking. Hilda killed Hektor because she knew he had used her father to test dangerous drugs and her father died in the experiment. That's a powerful motive. A father's a father, Abby, alcoholic or not. We need to get a look at Hektor's files. If it was some *other* doctor playing God over in that miserable shantytown—or some figment of Tex's imagination—we're up the creek and out of jobs. God, Abby, what if we were right in the beginning, and the killer was really after Aristotle? With only two hours, we *have* to assume that Hektor was the killer's target, don't we? The only incontrovertible fact we have about the brothers is that Hektor is dead and Aristotle is very much alive. And Hektor is the one who took the eyedrops and left the building with an empty bottle that should have been full. Hektor *has* to have been the intended victim. What time is it?''

I didn't have to look at the clock again. The seconds were ticking out loud in my mind. ''Six thirty-two.''

''It's after office hours. But what the heck? Even if they were still in the office, his staff wouldn't let us grope around in Hektor's medical files anyway.''

I took my key ring out of my pants pocket and looked at it.

''You know his address?'' I said, gazing at the extra keys.

''It's in my office.''

''I may have Hektor's keys. I've got somebody's keys.''

''How?''

I jingled the key ring. ''Got them in trade for a network I.D. badge. I think. If these keys belonged to Hektor, Tex must have taken them from the doctor's body in the alley. Picking a dead man's pockets must have been as easy as picking mine. Of course, Tex didn't paint my face, so there's that consolation.'' I saw the skeptical look on her face and shook the keys. ''We can try. Tex put the keys on my ring. He must have had some use in mind for them, something he hoped I would do. Some door he wanted me to open. Why not the doctor who was doping his men? Maybe when Tex saw Hektor dead in the alley, he caught the resemblance to that doctor he'd only seen from a distance.'' I shook the keys. ''So he peeled off Hektor's keys and painted him. The thing about Tex was that overriding purposefulness, you know?''

''Tex said he didn't know the doctor.''

''Correction. He didn't know the doctor's name. But he'd seen the doctor at the shantytown. Once. From a distance.''

''It doesn't matter. If those aren't the keys for Hektor's office, we'll have to break in or seduce the guard or something. Start thinking up some lies we can tell.''

We raced from the studio, leaving the lights on in that empty TV factory that echoed with our footsteps. With *Evening Watch* on the air at the opposite side of the building, the Tube was also quiet and full of the echoes of our swift passage.

''Skates?'' I said.

''Let's pray for a cab. Not enough time to get laced up.''

Ike had left the door to her office open, and she ran inside to grab a stack of business cards, scattering papers all over her desk and sending a storm of wire copy onto the floor. As we ran for the elevator and I pushed the button, she sorted through the cards frantically.

"He's in Worldwide Plaza," she said, yanking a card out of the stack. "Same office as Olivia Quintinale. But I can't believe she was involved with Hektor in anything as dangerous and probably criminal as experimenting with drugs on homeless men. That would have given Hektor a hold over Olivia that would have kept her out of Aristotle's bed, at the very least. A nice little bit of domestic blackmail that would have prevented what seems to have been a fairly public romance."

"So we rule her out," I said. "Which is fine by me since, as long as we're doing so much guessing, that leaves us with one less doctor to crucify. I like keeping this as neat as possible with a two-hour deadline—now less than two hours."

"We're not guessing. We're *reasoning*."

We got lucky in Columbus Circle. Ike frantically waved her hand and a taxi screeched to a halt at our toes. We jumped inside. I couldn't see much of the driver because of his huge, mustard-colored turban. I could tell he was short, because the turban barely rose above the steering wheel, but that's about all I could tell.

"Go down Broadway to Forty-ninth and make a right," Ike screamed at the cabbie.

"Ha, ha, ha," the driver laughed out loud. "You in a bigga hurry?"

"Yes!"

"Ha, ha, ha," he repeated. "Good thing you gotta small fella at the wheel."

The cab squealed into the traffic and howled down Broadway.

I've never been so scared in my life. The driver completely ignored all the lights, and everything else in his way. The first red light he ran was at Fifty-seventh, and we almost got creamed by another cab flying through the intersection. Our driver swerved, nearly flipping our cab into the window at Lechter's.

"Ha, ha, ha," he exulted, shaking his fist at the Lechter's customers, who were standing there among the pots and pasta makers and cutting boards and gaping at us through the big plate-glass windows. "You think I'm a small? Ha, ha, ha. So, I'm a small. Well, I tell you, nuclear bomb, that's a small, too. Look out, buddies, for the smalls. Ha, ha, ha."

The cab screamed away from the curb. Ike clung to the door handle, her eyes closed.

I fought the force of the G's that were gluing me to the vinyl cushions, and got my arm over the front seat. "Hey," I gasped. "The next time you run a light, at least honk your horn."

"Ha, ha, ha. Big Apple for the smalls."

He jammed his foot down harder against the accelerator, and I was thrown back against Ike. But I had gotten a look at his Taxi and Limousine Certificate, posted beside the meter. "Bahad Ahmed, Trainee," it said. I didn't catch his certificate number, not at that speed.

We roared down Broadway, and Bahad showed he was a quick learner. He didn't slow for the next red light, but he leaned on his horn and shot across Fifty-third, scattering both vehicle and pedestrian traffic like it was a bunch of drunken waterbugs and he was a bright light suddenly switched on.

"Ha, ha, ha," he shouted. "They think I'm a big. But I'm a small. A wasp is a small, but look out for your butt!"

When he slammed on the brakes in front of Worldwide Plaza, Ike and I were both thrown to the floor on our knees.

"Two dollars seventy-five, please," Bahad said.

I helped Ike out of the cab and pulled a twenty from my pocket. She pulled the melted bud vase from the pocket of her black slacks. Her knees wobbled when she saw that it was intact, the contents sloshing against the sides.

The driver looked at my twenty.

"Got no change that big bill, ha, ha, ha. I'm a small."

"Keep it," I said. "You're going to need a bail fund."

"Ha, ha, ha. Big tipper. See you next trip." He grabbed the twenty and yanked the steering wheel, laying rubber all the way to Ninth Avenue.

"Holy Christ," Ike gasped. "Did we break the sound barrier? The speed of light? What time is it?"

I looked at my watch. "Six thirty-seven. But I don't know which side of the International Dateline we're on. What are you doing with that vase?"

"I meant to lock it in my office. I didn't know we were taking a rocket to the doctor's office."

I breathed. I thought a moment. "Fillingeri might be on his way now with a search warrant, ready to tear the Emerald City apart looking for a container of glaucoma medicine. He probably looked at his copy of the videotape and saw what you saw.''

"He's not as dumb as you like to pretend, Abby. In fact, he's smart." She slid the vase gently into her pocket. "I'll be in deep doo-doo for tampering with evidence or something. Which wouldn't be so bad if I meant to bring this goddamn vase along. I'm just too tired to think.''

We stood and breathed for a moment, composing ourselves.

"Give me Hektor's business card,'' I said.

She handed it over and we entered the lobby. We walked sedately to the security desk. I smiled at the guard and waved the card vaguely in the air. "Dr. Stefanopolis,'' I said, signing the logbook.

"Good evening, Doctor,'' he said.

"Yes, it is. Hope you're feeling tiptop.''

"Thanks.''

We entered the elevator.

"Tiptop?'' Ike said, a nasty curl to her lips.

"It could have been worse. I was going to say 'ducky.'''

At the eighth floor, we followed the numbered signs to Suite 821. One of the strange keys opened the outer door, which said STEFANOPOLIS AND QUINTINALE, INTERNAL MEDICINE. We stepped inside. Nobody home.

"Answer number one,'' I said, waving the key in Ike's face. "Tex had a key that opens Hektor's door.''

"I guess Olivia's got custody of the practice now,'' Ike said, glancing around the pricey reception area. Lots of pink leather chairs and a couple of telephones on tables for the use of busy, pricey patients.

We could see acres of files through the glass window of the receptionist's desk. Hektor and Olivia must have had a thriving practice, because the files stretched from the desk all the way down a long interior hallway. There were no drawers, just open shelves crammed with color-coded folders, floor to ceiling. More paper than I'd seen in one place outside of a newspaper production plant.

"You take Murray,'' Ike said. "I don't know where I'll start.''

I found the light switches and turned on as many as I could with one sweep of my hand. They weren't my light switches.

We went through the inner door, and I hurried down the length of the files, pausing only for alphabetic reference. Munson, Murdock, Murraidian, Musselman. No Murrays.

"Now what?" I said. "No Murrays."

"Look for anything like experiment, or test...no, if Hektor kept the records of his experiment here with these other files, he must have given the file a name, so it would look like the others. What would he call it?"

"Homeless?"

"Try that. But it's probably going to be a name, like a person's name."

I tried. No "homeless." No "Pier 666." No "Devil's Pier." Out of desperation, I even tried "Tepee" and "Bum."

Ike was sitting on the floor when I turned to look at her.

"Get busy," I said. "We're running out of time." I tossed the key ring at her. "Go look in his desk or something."

"I know, I know." She caught the keys one-handed. "I just can't think. What the hell would Hektor have been experimenting with, or on?"

It hit me. It had to be right. "Glaucoma," I said. "His own disease. The cure for his own disease."

We both pawed through the G's. No file named "Glaucoma." Ike was pulling her hair. I was afraid to look at my watch.

"If Hektor was using those men to look for a treatment for his own disease," Ike said, "what would he name the file?"

"I don't know. Look in the E's for Egomania. He must have thought he was God. You want me to look under 'God'?"

"Egomania. Ego. Himself." She grabbed my trousers leg. "Look under Stefanopolis."

I did. No file on Stefanopolis.

"Maybe there is no file," I said.

"He had to keep records. Otherwise, how would he know about effective dosages, what was safe to try on himself, that sort of thing? There must be a record."

"I'll look under Hektor." I did. No file.

"It's got to be in his office," Ike said. "Something this sensitive wouldn't just be stuffed in with the rest of this fire hazard." She made a sweeping gesture to indicate the wall of files. "We've just wasted ten minutes."

"Nine."

We hurried down the hall, turning on lights and opening doors.

Examining rooms. Bathrooms. A lab. An office, finally, but it had Olivia's framed degrees and certificates on the wall. Next, a supply room. Then another office. This one was Hektor's—his degrees were from Georgetown and the University of Miami.

Hektor's office was Spartan, so there was only one place to look. I twisted the second key in his center desk drawer. Together Ike and I pulled all the drawers open.

And there it was, right side, second drawer. A manila file folder. "Hektor" was typed neatly on the blue tab.

Ike sat in Hektor's big leather swivel chair and opened the thick file. She scrambled through the pages and pulled out three sheets with the name John Richard Murray. She scanned the handwritten entries. I read over her shoulder. There were words and phrases that were completely foreign to me: "intraocular pressure, timolol, betaxolol, tetaxolol, levobunolol, tonometry, ophthalmoscopy, ocular hypertension."

Repeatedly through the file were references to "PH,2AA." And dates, starting June 10. John Murray had been a "patient" of Hektor's, involved in what Fillingeri would call a "medical procedure," if that's how you label the experience of paying a bum twenty bucks to take drugs you're curious about. Hektor had found a way to get away with murder.

"I don't know what most of this stuff is, but PH,2AA is that fad hormone," Ike said thoughtfully. "It occurs naturally in the body, but they've come up with a synthetic PH,2AA—supposedly a new Fountain of Youth. People are taking it for everything from baldness to heart palpitations. *Around the Watch* did a piece on the only two pharmacies in this hemisphere where you can get it, both in Canada. And they only do mail-order business. It looks like Hektor was mixing PH,2AA in his eye potions." Ike flipped hurriedly through the rest of the pages in the Hektor file. "Some of these names look familiar, but I can't be sure," she said. "I can't remember what was on that videotape. There were so many names."

I slipped one of pages with John Murray's name out of the file and looked at it. "Ike, a lot of this medical terminology is pretty much just hieroglyphics to me, but, besides the PH,2AA, the one substance that keeps reappearing is betaxolol. And Hektor had beta blockers in his blood. *Beta* in both. I wonder what betaxolol is? And if you could overdose on it."

"Let's find out." She used Hektor's phone to dial a number.

"Who're you calling?"

"My pharmacist."

"How come you know the number by heart?" I asked, a sudden and hideous worry hitting me somewhere in the stomach. "Are you okay?"

"Fine." She gave me a look. "I rent movies there."

"Oh."

Ike spoke with her pharmacist for a few minutes. I occupied myself by looking at more stuff in the file that I couldn't understand.

Ike hung up, a smug look on her face.

"Betaxolol is the principal ingredient in the eyedrops they give to glaucoma patients. It's meant to reduce the pressure in the eye. Side effects include reducing pressure elsewhere in the body." She leaned back in Hektor's chair. "Usually that's not a problem, but. But. If you increased the concentration of betaxolol in the drops, then you could cause some nasty side effects, like stopping the heart."

"How would you increase the level of betaxolol? Wouldn't that be hard to do, I mean, unless you were a chemist or a pharmacist or something?"

"Not according to my pharmacist." Now she smiled, but it was a grim production. "In these eyedrops, the beta blockers are in suspension. To get a more concentrated solution, if you wanted to stop somebody's heart by spiking his eyedrops, all you'd have to do is take ordinary glaucoma eyedrops and reduce the amount of liquid. What would be left would be high-potency betaxolol. Which you would add to your victim's eyedrops. Bingo. Poison eyedrops."

"How would you reduce the liquid to extract the betaxolol?"

"Simple. You apply the one thing that makes a liquid evaporate. Get it?"

I nodded. "Heat."

"And," she said, "my pharmacist says any medical school would have beta blockers around. Hilda's department works with one of the medical departments at Columbia. Nuclear medicine, I think she said." She closed the file and hugged it to her chest. "And you couldn't ask for better access to heat than a glassblower's lab. Hilda could make deadly drops as a sideline, a little cottage industry while she turns out glass baubles. If I'm on the right track, she literally gave Hektor a dose of his own medicine.''

"What do we do now?''

"What time is it?''

"Just past seven,'' I said.

"Damn. I wish we had a neater package. We know a lot more than we knew sitting in Studio 57 talking to Cainstraight, maybe even enough to clear Tex. But we don't have a clue about *his* death.''

TWENTY-SEVEN

"WE KNOW PLENTY about Hektor," I said. I crossed the room and stood by Hektor's ego wall and looked at his degrees and certificates. If you went by what was on the wall, Hektor Stefanopolis was an okay doctor. He had lots of pedigrees and paper testimonials. Plus all those files out in the hall—he had so many paying customers that he certainly hadn't had to mortgage his Greek Islands to afford the rent in Worldwide Plaza.

I looked back at Ike, still seated in Hektor's big chair. Her hair was a mess, and she looked a little crazy, her weird eyes sparkling with energy and purpose. Despite the setting, nobody would take her for a doctor if they suddenly walked in on us.

"We know the nature of Hektor's research," I said. "And through John Murray, we can connect Hektor to at least one of the Yellow-Man victims—give the medical examiner something to look for. And there's other names in the Hektor file that might also be in Cainstraight's Yellow-Man file, just like poor old John Murray. If Cainstraight can get the bodies exhumed and finds PH,2AA or high levels of betaxolol or any of that other stuff in killing quantities, Hektor's nailed. I'll bet you any sum you care to name that they find high concentrations of betaxolol."

"But Hektor would only be nailed as a doctor treating patients with experimental drugs."

"It still nails him."

"Not good enough," she said, shaking her tousled head vigorously. "The stuff in the Hektor file will never get to a jury, not with Hektor dead. He can't be put on trial for anything, not even a minor thing like screwing around with a medical procedure. The killer of the Yellow-Men will never be put on trial, unless there's a tribunal at the Pearly Gates waiting for Hektor."

"Ah, now that's a different dilemma. We don't have time to debate God."

"I know that." She stomped her foot under the desk. "Don't

tell me about how much time we don't have and how much time we need."

"You're the one who brought up the Pearly Gates."

"Holy mackerel, Abby, will you shut up about the Pearly Gates? What we need is a solid fact that will put somebody else on trial here in New York—for Hektor's death, or Tex's. And if the liquid in the vase I'm carrying around is the solid fact we can give Cainstraight to indict Hilda for Hektor's murder, I still want to know who killed Tex." But despite her huff, Ike smiled victoriously. She smacked the Hektor file with the flat of her hand. "And the Hektor file is a solid fact we can give Cainstraight. All this paperwork is hot stuff—if the substances listed in it match the substances in the dead men."

"I wish Tex had kept a file," I said.

"Wouldn't that be nice?" She replaced the Hektor file in the desk drawer. "Abby, I wonder if Tex did keep anything. He kept those keys. He kept your I.D."

"Those he probably carried in his pockets."

"But where'd he keep his paint? We'd have heard if a supply was found at Pier 666. He had to keep it somewhere. Somewhere handy."

"West Fifty-seventh Street was handy, according to Fred Loring's computer map. We should have used the map when he made it. And we should have listened to my mother. She thinks anything a computer does is automatically correct. She told us to look at that perfume place. On Fifty-seventh Street."

"God, Abby, quit saying 'we should have this,' 'we should have that.' We can't do everything. Hektor only died yesterday."

"We should get going."

She tossed me a look, but she patted Hektor's desk with a smile on her face. She did a little two-step jig. "Nailed, nailed, nailed," she said, giving the desk an extra pat.

We turned out the office lights and returned to the building's lobby, where I nodded in a medical way to the security guard. He nodded in a patiently way to me. Deferential to Doctor Director.

We got a cab on Eighth Avenue. Our new driver lacked Bahad's zest, but he got us to Fifty-seventh, between Tenth and Eleventh Avenues, without breaking any laws or the vase, and in good time.

He used the pauses at red lights to work the crossword in the *Daily News,* but that was better than him honking or opening his door to spit on the street, the two other favorite pastimes of New York cab drivers. I paid him and we got out on the sidewalk.

A stream of CBS employees was exiting the Broadcast Center at 524 West Fifty-seventh. The *Evening News* must have been put to bed. I looked at my watch. 7:14.

We stood on the sidewalk, with our backs to CBS, looking at the blank faces of the buildings. I didn't know what a research facility that specialized in perfumes would look like, and there was no sign saying PERFUME to help me out. But in the middle of the block there was a ten-story building with a small purple-on-white sign that hinted tastefully in graceful, understated initials that something interesting might be inside. WFI, the sign said.

Ike wrinkled her forehead and took in the sign. "Your mother said something about initials, didn't she?"

I nodded. "This must be it. World Fragrance Institute?" I guessed. "Wild Flowers Inside?"

"Could be Wicked Fetishes, Inc.," Ike said. "Or even Wait for Iggy." She sniffed the air, looking a little like a rabbit with messy blond hair. "You'd think we could smell a perfume distillery."

The door to the building was locked and nobody was around.

"I could go across the street and ask somebody at CBS," I suggested.

"We may have to." She stood, hands in pockets, gazing at the building. She turned and looked west, to the Hudson. "We're only, like, two blocks from Pier 666."

"Yeah. Convenient location for Tex."

"Tex wouldn't have gone across the street to ask at CBS about this building. What would he have done?"

I didn't even have to think. "He would have looked for the dumpster."

She nodded. "Then we look for the dumpster."

Through a narrow alley that I thought would hardly have been wide enough for Tex's shoulders, we walked the length of the WFI building. The alley veered into an L-shape and opened into a wider passage, where there was, indeed, a dumpster. It was the sweetest-smelling dumpster the island of Manhattan has ever known, full of bottles and vials and beakers and the scents of enough flowers and spices and herbs and the good things of the Earth to make my head spin. It was intoxicating. It was nothing like the overwhelming and overwrought miasma of odors you'd find at the perfume counter of a department store, where all the smells get mixed together to produce a sort of industrial stench.

This dumpster was filled with discrete, small fragrances, tiny and distinguishable from each other. Pure. Simple. Exotic. Perfect. It must have seemed like paradise to Tex.

That he had been here Sunday night before mugging me, I had no doubt. He had smelled exactly like this dumpster, except for that lingering under-aroma of his days as a homeless man. This dumpster was Tex's boudoir. Lieutenant Raintree's refuge from the stink of poverty.

I momentarily lost my sense of urgency, my adrenaline slowed or absorbed by the subtleties and nuances of the fragrances surrounding me.

Ike pinched my elbow, and I wrenched myself back to ordinary awareness.

"Watch it," I yelped. "That's where I fell when that cat tripped me."

She was looking up. At a fire escape.

"There's no yellow paint around here that I can see," she said. "Maybe Tex took the high road. He said nobody would ever catch him sleeping on the street. Afraid some punk would set him on fire."

I sighed. I hoisted myself up on the side of the dumpster, stood, and reached for the first rung of the ladder. I clung to the metal and took my weight off the dumpster. The ladder slid down noiselessly. It was in regular use, obviously. I put a hand down to Ike.

She waved my hand away. "I'm okay. I'll follow you."

Once past the ladder, it was simply a matter of contemplating a nine-floor walk. Merely stairs. If they had been inside a building, I wouldn't have given them a second thought, except maybe about the nuisance. But outside a building, especially since the steps were the metal see-through kind, nine floors of walking took on an air of—well, air. Sure, there was a brick wall, a solid brick wall, beside the stairs. But walking those stairs, especially as we rose higher and higher, was an entirely different exercise from walking up a flight of stairs nine times indoors. The difference increased exponentially the higher we went, the smaller things below us got.

At the seventh floor, Ike stopped and pointed toward the river.

"There's the pier," she said, a little breathless.

Nestled in the rubble at the end of Fifty-sixth Street, barely having existence in the shadow of the huge luxury liners, was the shantytown, the little community of cardboard and rags built around that rotting tepee.

"Strategic lookout point Lieutenant Raintree chose to watch over his men," I said. "Assuming we have his address right."

"*High* point he chose. This is creepy when we stop. Makes me dizzy. Let's keep moving."

We came out on the roof. It was bounded by a low brick wall that was interrupted at intervals of about ten feet by architectural doodles that looked like miniature turrets. The setting sun practically hit us in the eyes, a giant and painful fireball sinking over the Jersey hills. I looked away from it, blinking from the sting of the light.

Over in the northwest corner of the roof was a pile of rags and cans and something that looked like a plywood-and-rag doghouse, a badly built doghouse for a very big dog, a very poor dog.

We crossed the roof to the debris in the corner.

The pile of rags alternately stank and smelled sweet, and I wondered why Tex had collected them. Perhaps they represented his carpeting, or his porch, or his lawn. Or, it occurred to me in a practical flash, his plumbing.

I went down on one knee beside the pile and started pulling it apart. I didn't have to look far. There were four little plastic jars of yellow tempera paint, mostly empty, among the rags. Those school-kid jars you can buy, or shoplift, at Woolworth's. Tex's paint warehouse. I didn't touch the jars, and I was sorry I had touched the rags. I wiped my hands on my trousers.

"Yucky," Ike said.

"Especially if you touch. Wanta feel?"

She shuddered. "No, thanks."

Ike squatted at the door of the doghouse, looking inside. I knelt beside her, and she moved to make room so I could see. Inside there was a big green sweater, and one of those little Bibles that the Gideons issue to new soldiers. It looked like the Bible had been thumbed and read many times, and there was a faint streak of yellow on the worn black cover. There was a neatly folded white-and-green Holiday Inn towel. That was it in the doghouse.

The Bible almost came apart when I picked it up. The spine was cracked, and the pages were falling out. On the flipside of the picture of the American flag on the flyleaf, in flowing, faded script, it said, "Presented to Private U. S. S. Raintree, 12 May 1967." Very carefully, I turned the pages. Tex had circled some of the Psalms, but his favorite part seemed to be John's Gospel. The margins were full of notations, in tiny, angular handwriting, some of the ink faded, some of it fresher. He had written mostly questions: "Does Jesus love Gooks?" "Why am I hungry, if Jesus is the bread of life?" "How many rooms are in my Father's house?"

I turned to the Psalms. This Bible was organized backward from what I'm used to, with the Psalms coming after the four Gospels. Psalm 35 had a hand-drawn border around it, and one verse was circled: "I behaved myself as though he had been my friend or brother."

In ink, in the margin, was written "Am I Murray's little girl's brother? Tex got to watch over the children that visit the men dying on the battlefield of the devil?"

I passed the Bible to Ike and showed her the circled passage. She read without saying anything, and turned the pages slowly. At Psalm 38, she stopped and stared. I read over her shoulder. Verse 12 was circled: "They also that seek after my life lay snares for me"; and there was a notation in the margin, in the same handwriting that was displayed throughout the book: "Old Tex won't let them burn him asleep. Thou shalt not kill without serving your country."

I stood and looked around Tex's roof home. The fiery sunset gave the place a temporary glamour, a burst of color and freedom from squalor. It was something like the perfume in the dumpster, an illusion of another life.

I felt Ike grabbing my elbow again.

"Will you stop doing that?" I whined. "It hurts."

"Look at this, Abby." She handed me the little Bible, open at Psalm 46. Tex had circled verse four: "There is a river, the streams whereof shall make glad the city of God." In the margin, in fresh-looking ink, he had written, "Ain't the Hudson. Ain't the pier. Murray's little girl say she'll burn down the place to stop the doctor killed her dad. Old Murray had no call to tell his baby the doctor was bringing him unto death. Do I got responsibility on that?''

I closed the book and held it between my hands.

"Hilda knew all about it," I said. "And she knew Tex was talking to me. She was in the control room when I spotted him on that Central Park videotape. She knew Tex was ready to tell his story. Part of which was her story. Ike, I was yapping about it in front of her. Just as Hektor was getting set to take eyedrops she had poisoned. Christ Almighty, I practically told Hilda to kill Tex.''

Ike touched my hand where I held the little Bible. "Abby," she said, "it doesn't work like that. It's not your fault. It's hers.''

I knelt and replaced the Bible, backed out, and stood up.

"And when Hektor died in the alley,'' I said, "Tex knew. Knew it was Hilda that killed him. Knew she was out for revenge. So he painted the doctor's face to hide her crime under the cover of his Yellow-Man creation. And Tex's actions—the Yellow-Man signatures on Hektor's body, who was *not* one of his 'men'—told Hilda that Tex had involved himself in her crime. She knew there was no serial killer at work and she knew there was no copycat; she knew about Hektor's drug project from her own father, according to Tex's Bible. She must have known that Tex *was* U.S.S.R., maybe from her father, maybe from Tex himself. Tex knew her well enough to wonder if he was her 'brother,' if she was his responsibility.''

Ike stood, brushing off the knees of her black slacks.

"I wonder if Tex knew what he had taken upon himself,'' she said.

"It seems he was asking his Bible questions. I hope it gave him some answers.''

"His Bible gave *us* some answers.''

I looked at my watch. 7:40. I looked at Ike. She was staring at the doghouse, her hands in her pockets.

"Let's go meet our deadline,'' I said.

I took Ike's hand, and we walked to the fire escape. At the top landing, before we stepped off the roof onto the airiness of the metal stairs, we turned back to look at Tex's doghouse.

"I wonder if I should go back for the Bible?'' I said.

"Leave it alone, Abby.''

"It seems like such a personal thing."

"You have to let go, Abby. It's over. Cainstraight has a right to see everything up here the way it is. It's all that's left of the story, except for the Hektor file." She hesitated. "And this." She held the melted bud vase up to the rays of the setting sun.

"And that," I said.

She returned the glass thing to her pocket, and turned to the metal stairs. Hilda was standing on the top step.

"I wondered where that vase was," Hilda said. "I tried to look for it in the studio after my segment yesterday, but things were happening so fast. I was hoping somebody threw it out."

"What are you doing up here?" Ike said.

"I like the sunset. And this will be one of the last sunsets when I'll see that pier. The city's tearing it down, you know."

"You didn't have to kill Tex," I said. "He was going to keep your secret." I didn't know if I was telling the truth about that. Tex had been wrestling with his Bible and his pen.

She looked blank. I looked for a sign—a flash, anything—of craziness in her clear eyes, and saw only calm rationality.

"Throw the vase over the wall," she said quietly.

"You're crazy," Ike said. "I'll kick you down the stairs before I do any such thing."

Hilda quickly lifted her hand from her side. I didn't immediately recognize what she was holding.

She moved her foot on the metal stair and flicked a switch on the thing in her hand. A two-foot, blue-and-orange jet of flame shot out, just missing my ear.

"Fire is my business," she said. "I'm extremely precise when I use it."

Hilda moved the hand torch about a centimeter. I could feel the heat of the flame on my cheek as I flinched.

"I don't play games with fire," she said, in that cool voice. "If Ms. Tygart does not take that vase and throw it over the wall, I'll burn your face away to the skull. It'll only take a couple of seconds. If you move, I'll just turn up the flame."

I could smell Ike's pink sweater, burning wool. The flame had touched her, too.

"Do you always carry a flamethrower with you, Hilda?" Ike said. "Or were you planning to work some special arson up here?"

Hilda moved her hand again, again by only about a centimeter, and I could smell the collar of my shirt scorching, like a hot iron had been left on it.

"Toss it over, Ms. Tygart," she said.

"Abby?" Ike said, but her voice trembled.

"It's hot, Ike."

Ike edged away from me to the fire escape's railing and removed her hand from her pocket. She looked back at Hilda and held her hand up, out over the railing, the setting sun catching the object in her hand and seeming to set it on fire. I didn't dare turn my head, but my peripheral vision almost burned when the red and orange sunlight cut around her hand like she was holding a prism.

Ike stared at me. I couldn't see the expression on her face because I was afraid to move, but I could feel her eyes on me.

The flame from Hilda's torch never wavered. In an absurd moment of clarity, I realized that the air was too still for any movement to disturb Hilda's fire, that there was no wind to lick away the heat from my face. The fire held steady in her steady hand. I wasn't the wind after all. I was solid, flammable material.

It was utterly still at the top of the fire escape. There was no sound, except what I could have merely imagined as the slight rushing noise of the fire at my face. Nothing moved.

Ike opened her hand and brightness flashed out broken, red sunlight at us. And fell. I heard it crash in the alley below, a tiny, tinkling sound, ten floors below us.

The torch was withdrawn from my face, but Hilda did not turn off the flame. I could still feel the heat on my neck and my cheek. I put my hand up to touch my cheek, but all I could think was, *There goes Hektor's poisoned medicine. There goes a murderer. She got away with it.*

Hilda was down the next flight of stairs before I could collect myself to lash out at her. I was surprised that I did not hear her footsteps on the fire escape. She was light as a cat.

Ike was at my side, peering at my chin.

"Not even a mark," she said. "Hilda certainly knows her fire. What a pro."

I glanced at her sweater, where there was a long brown streak. "Jesus Christ, Ike. That's all you've got to say? Words of admiration for her skill? I'm going after her."

Ike gently grabbed my singed collar. "I do admire her skill. She used just enough fire to get what she wanted."

"But she was dumb to leave us to tell the cops what she just did."

"Assaulting us with fire?"

"Yes, assaulting us with fire. It's not as bad as murder, but it's got to be a felony."

"Pooh." She opened her hand and offered me the little fused bud vase. "We'll get her for murder."

"But...I saw you drop it."

"No, you didn't."

"I did."

"Nope. I dropped something else."

"What?"

"NASA's golf ball."

TWENTY-EIGHT

I STILL DON'T KNOW what Time is. I can measure it and use it up, but I have no idea what it is. The part about using it up, of course, is the scary part. You can't exhaust length or width or depth, as far as I know. If you had enough Time, you could go on forever, measuring and measuring and measuring as much length or width or depth as you wanted to. But nobody has that kind of Time. That's what makes Time the only dimension that can scare me, and that I need to control. I don't need to control, say, length, because I'm never going to run out of it.

But *timing* is something else, something I do understand. We made it to our appointment with Cainstraight, with zero minutes to spare.

And he didn't spare us. He took us downtown to the Federal Building to unload our information, in the very same glass-enclosed jukebox room where we had earlier been assured there were no hidden microphones or recording devices. A bug-free environment. Sure.

Since Ike and I had decided to spill the beans, and since our original beans had now been augmented by better beans, we only had to be careful how we talked about getting access to Hektor's office. We were perfectly sure that our excursion through his files had not been 100 percent legal, so we simply refrained from mentioning how we knew there was a file in Hektor's desk drawer that spelled out his experiment with homeless men at Pier 666. With that omission, we could tell our story in the presence of their bugs, if any, with nothing specific to fear from electronics. Of course, there's always the general fear that comes from technology you can't see. What if, for example, the FBI had developed some sort of radioactive scan that could monitor our brain waves to determine our voting histories, or our hormonal impulses, or our opinions of Barbra Streisand movies?

When Cainstraight saw and heard our beans, he called in a parade of transcribers, videocam operators, and, finally, a young

FBI attorney named Anne Trensky. After she quickly read our transcribed statements, she went to the table in the middle of the room to make phone calls. In response to one of her calls, apparently, a couple of paralegals showed up. Together, they prepared the paperwork for search warrants, found a judge, and directed the judicially sanctioned federal troop movements to four places. After a call to the New York City medical examiner, Trensky also had the judge working on exhumation orders for the Yellow-Men on Hart Island. I thought it must be nice to have that kind of clout, to have a judge practically on call. Not that I have any need for a judge; it would just be nice if I had one of my very own, standing by to take my calls, a better status symbol than a Ferragamo's charge card.

When we learned the FBI had obtained a search warrant for Hektor's office, I felt good, even smug. I knew exactly what story they'd find in his office. Hektor was nailed, even if he was beyond FBI justice. His story was about a bad guy who'd got his, without the law butting in. I'm not saying I approved; only that I knew the story.

When we learned that the second search warrant was addressed to Columbia University, in care of the Physics Department, I was pleased but not gloating. Hilda's story was written in glass. For all its strength and longevity, it was fragile. A lot would depend on what the chemists found in the bud vase she had fused. In FBI talk, she had motive (her father's death), and means (the contents of the bud vase), but it was on opportunity that the FBI thought their case needed help. How and where had she dosed Hektor's little bottle of eyedrops with fatal beta concentrate? But that would come with the fourth search warrant.

The third warrant was for the doghouse. When we learned the FBI had a search warrant for Tex's rooftop hideaway, addressed to "WFI," I merely felt sad. Tex's story, as written in that little Bible, was not like Hektor's, not as neat from my point of view. And his story was not like Hilda's, which was not fully written yet.

Tex's story was not neat, but it was ended. His was the story of a man who got nailed by forces he was better than. I didn't let myself get carried away in my thoughts by comparisons between Tex and the Man the Bible is Really About. And I also didn't kid myself that Tex's story had any tidy value as a parable

for modern times, or for modern poor people, or for modern soldiers in any army, real or imagined. The way I see it, Tex was
just a guy who lived the way he thought was right, which happened to include mugging as a survival skill as much as it included painting his fallen friends. His death—though it did not
come because he had fallen asleep on a grate and was being fried
for the amusement of some local gang—was, I think, about what
he expected. From the same Psalm where Tex had circled "I
behaved myself as though he had been my friend or brother" also
came the wisdom that "destruction comes unawares." I don't
read much, but for the Abagnarros the Bible isn't reading. It isn't
even religion, or the church. It's family.

When I learned that the fourth search warrant was a compre-
hensive document that would give the FBI access to certain precisely defined areas on the twenty-seventh floor of the Emerald
City, I was not pleased. My heart sank. The areas included the
Green Room, all the bathrooms, Control Room #1, and Studio
57. The FBI was walking carefully when it came to NTB News,
but that wouldn't impress the owner of the broadcasting facilities.
The FBI wanted physical evidence or testimony on when and how
Hilda had made Hektor's glaucoma medication turn into death
drops. What Othello Armitage would want was another question.

I tried to talk Cainstraight and Trensky into limiting the Emerald City warrant to the Green Room. "She must have tampered
with his drops there," I said. "They were in his briefcase, and
everyone else was busy getting into makeup. It had to be there."

"Yeah, maybe. But we'd like to do a certain chemical analysis
of that coffee table in your studio. Maybe Hilda got a little sloppy
when she dumped the drops into that vase." He nodded to himself, smiling. "I like this, you know. We've got a warrant to look
at a coffee table that millions of Americans see every day. Only
we get to look real close. I like this fine."

"Come on, Morris. We gave you the vase."

"Don't tell me about the nice gifts you brought the FBI,"
Cainstraight said. "Agent Hayes showed me that plastic rat.
You've already used all the rope we're going to give you, Abag-
narro. That search warrant reads just fine." He smiled again.
"We're happy with it. We like it when we're happy."

Ike and I were allowed to eat, and walk around freely, and
behave like welcome guests of the federal government. They let

us make phone calls, and, after it became clear just where the search warrants were directed, Ike squared her shoulders and dialed Othello's number. She told him what we had done, said that we had the damaged Spinning Quartz Ball, and reported rather tersely that the FBI was on its way to his broadcast headquarters with chemicals, to do things to the Green Room and Control Room #1 and the bathrooms, but especially to the coffee table in Studio 57.

When she got off the phone, I asked her how it had gone, and she shrugged. Maybe it was more like a twitch.

"He didn't say anything about canning us," she said bleakly. "He's getting replacements to fill in for us tonight, since I said I didn't know when the FBI would be done with us."

"Doesn't sound good," I said.

"You don't know the half of it. His voice was like steel." She closed her eyes. "No. That's not right. It was more like a snake." She sat there, eyes closed, and wrinkled her brow. "No, it was like an iceberg gently brushing against another iceberg." She frowned. "No. Picture a tunnel about a mile long. At the end of the tunnel is a giant THING, only you can't tell what it is. As it gets nearer and nearer, you start to hear this sort of low—"

"Stop it, Ike. I get the message."

She opened her eyes. "It's very rude to interrupt like that. When we get canned, don't say I didn't try to warn you."

"Well, did Othello say anything? Anything in words? Or was it just that iceberg stuff?"

"He said he didn't want to see either of our faces on any network news but our own." She thought a moment. "Don't you think that's a good sign?"

I didn't bother to answer her. I started thinking about giving Paramount a call to see if they still wanted to hire a director. That would mean not working with Ike, which in turn would mean...

By 3:30, they had the Hektor file in the Federal Building. The FBI medical team studied it and concluded that Hektor was giving the homeless men the same kind of drops he himself used, but at an increased potency that would stop their hearts. Nobody seemed to know yet what effect the fad hormone PH_2AA would have had.

"Eyedrops," we were told, by a male doctor who looked about nineteen, "are like tears. They drain into the nose and throat, where they are absorbed into the bloodstream. If the dosages in this file indicate what those men were actually taking, we'll probably find minor damage to the nervous system as well as the cause of the heart failures. The medical examiner did not find the drug the cause of death in Dr. Stefanopolis's death because he was looking for the presence of the drug, not the potency. He'll look closer now."

There didn't seem to be anything I could add to that, so I kept my mouth shut. Cainstraight would soon have a copy of the videotape that showed Hektor pressing the bridge of his nose and leaning back against the couch after he took the fatal drops in Studio 57. I guess Hektor knew how tears work, too.

They finally let us go at 4:13 in the morning. We were both wired on federal coffee. I knew we'd never find a cab at that hour in that neighborhood, and walking seemed like the last straw.

Somewhere around Canal Street, Ike said, "I've been thinking. Tex was terrified of going to Hart Island. He said a man couldn't get any rest there."

"Yeah, I've been thinking the same thing." I cleared my throat. "Listen, Ike, the Abagnarros own a bunch of plots in St. Stephen's Cemetery. My great-uncle Salvatore got them in a deal. What do you think? Would Tex rather be with his men? He might prefer Hart Island to a tight-knit community of dead Sicilians. You know how all the females are in my family, trooping out there once a month in their black sheets—"

"They wear black dresses, Abby."

"Black sheets, and dusting headstones, and sticking artificial daisies in those cement holes, and 'Ave Maria-ing' until the whole thing looks like Italian Halloween."

"I think the custom is very touching," Ike said, a little loftily for someone who hasn't been inside a church since we were married. She squeezed her hands together and sighed, long and loud. "That would be perfect. No, Tex would definitely not prefer Hart Island. He hated the thought of the pauper's burial ground. And the boat ride. And the wind and weeds and cats and convicts."

I nodded, sort of priestlike for a man who hasn't been inside a church since he was married. "I think the family would go along with this. I'll talk to my mom."

She threw her arms around me and kissed me. "I love you, Abby. That's the most heroic thing I ever heard of—telling a bunch of Mafia widows you want to stick a black bum in their sacred ground.''

I held on to her. "It won't be so bad. I'll tell them Tex was a war hero. You can't top an Italian-American when it comes to waving the American flag.''

She pressed closer to me. "You can't top an Italian-American when it comes to a few other things," she whispered.

"I'm surprised you remember.'' I slipped a hand up the back of her pink sweater. "It's been a long time.'' We stood there together, a few yards from the corner of Broome Street and Broadway, in the pale glow of lights from the Roosevelt Building—that perfect Manhattan paradox: a huge building with delicate, lacy architectural detail, like a concrete cake. "Ike, it's been such a long time.''

Now it was my hands in her hair, making a mess. "Let's go somewhere and make love.'' I kissed her the way I'd been doing it in my fantasies, skipping no little nuances or details.

She moaned softly. "Let's do it here.''

I looked around. "Here?'' There was nothing but concrete everywhere I turned.

She looked around. "Maybe not.''

A can collector shuffled by with a big, noisy garbage bag and said, "Good morning. You folks got a quarter?''

Ike wasn't very steady on her feet after that application of Abagnarro passion, but she shelled out some coins. The can collector counted them in his palm, giving her a dirty look before moving on, mumbling to himself.

We resumed our walk, holding hands.

"Abby, you know that story about the science convention and the ugly man that you've been trying to tell lately?''

"What about it?''

"I assume it's a dirty story. Tell me. As long as we have to walk before we find a place suitable for bawdy pleasures, you might as well entertain me. Think of it as foreplay. Make it sexy.''

We passed the can collector, who was still mumbling over his palm and dragging his garbage bag full of jangling aluminum.

"There was this science convention,'' I began, raising my voice a little over the sound of the cans bouncing on the pavement. "At the keynote meeting, in a big auditorium, the speaker is up on the stage. There's this huge white cube, about the size of a room, on the stage with him. On the side of the cube facing the audience, there's what looks like a window, but it's really a one-way piece of glass. You can look in from the outside, but not out from the inside.''

"This doesn't sound like a racy story so far," she said, a mild trace of irritation in her voice.

"Don't interrupt."

I looked back to see the can collector trailing in our wake, his head nodding.

"I heard this one before," he said.

"You keep the punch line to yourself," I said. I turned back to Ike. "Anyway, the speaker says this cube is a simple test of the scientist's most precious skill—keen observation."

"I think I've heard this one, too," Ike said. "Is this the one where they all look in the window, but nobody notices the cube itself?"

"No." I said. "Will you stop interrupting?"

"All right."

"Yeah, lady, stop interrupting," our shadow said. "I wanta see if he tells it right."

"I tell it just fine," I said. I took a deep breath. "So the speaker says he wants three volunteers from the audience."

"Supposed to be four," our friend mumbled.

I gave him a look.

"*Three* volunteers from the audience," I repeated. "Three guys come up on the stage. The speaker tells them he wants each in turn to look in through the window and describe what he sees. They all nod like 'What a cinch,' and the speaker smiles."

"Abby," Ike said, pointing. "There's a cab."

"Off duty," I said. "His light's on." I had to get my bearings for a minute, to remember where I was in the story. "Oh, yeah. Now, what's inside the cube is a room that's been made to look like a garden, with palm trees, and lots of flowers, and a little brook, and grass that looks like velvet. And there on the grass is the ugliest man in the world, making love to an absolutely gorgeous woman. She's got all the right cushions, in all the right places, if you know what I mean." I put my hands out in front of me to sculpt a woman out of thin air.

"Ain't seen any cushions at all in a while," the can collector said, one man of the world to another.

"Will you butt out?" I said.

He shook the coins in his closed fist, holding it close to his ear to listen to the tune. "When are you going to say this story is really about religion?" he asked.

"I thought it was about a science convention," Ike said, exasperated. "Why don't we just drop the whole thing? It was a bad idea to ask. I should have known better. Your jokes are always so stupid."

"Give me a chance," I said, making an impatient gesture at the can collector. "If Siskel and Ebert here would shut up for ten seconds, I'd have the story finished."

"I'll shut up," he said. "You go right ahead."

"Thanks a lot." I looked at Ike, making a point of turning away from the can collector. "Okay, the story's really about the history of religion. I wasn't going to say that until later, because it sort of spoils the joke."

"We're listening," Ike and Siskel and Ebert said in unison. And with weary tones. Like they'd practiced.

I forged ahead. "The speaker has the first volunteer look in the window of the cube. The volunteer stands there for a few minutes, and when he turns around, he has this look on his face like he's seen a vision. The speaker says, 'Tell us what you saw.'"

I slowed my walking pace a little so I could get in the gestures, making the first volunteer wave his arms around like "Hallelujah." "Then the volunteer says, 'I saw heaven. It was a beautiful place, with total happiness and peace.'" I smiled, like I'd seen the vision, too. "Get it, Ike? He's a fundamentalist. A believer. An absolutist."

She pursed her lips and kept walking. The can collector shook his head, in silent, disappointed criticism of my delivery.

I frowned at him and went on. "So the second volunteer goes up and looks. When he turns around, he says, 'I can't honestly say I see anything in there. I have no objective evidence that my eyes aren't playing tricks on me or that you haven't arranged some video display. So my answer is that the cube is empty on the basis of the evidence of my senses.'"

Ike waved her hand abruptly. "He's the atheist, right? This is too obvious."

"Right, he's the atheist," Siskel and Ebert said. "You're quick, lady."

"I ought to pop you one," I told him.

"Sure," Ike said. "Beat up on a poor, homeless man. Hasn't the past couple of days taught you anything, Abby?"

"Yeah, Abby," Siskel and Ebert said. "You should listen to her."

I put my hands up in resignation. "Okay. You win. I won't tell the story."

We walked another block in silence.

"What did the third man do?" Ike finally said. "I can't stand not knowing."

"Well..." Siskel and Ebert began.

I stopped and put a hand on his shoulder. "This is my story. I'll give you five bucks to keep your mouth shut."

He mutely put out his hand, I stuck my hand in my pocket, and I shoved over a five.

We all started walking.

"The third volunteer looks in the window of the cube," I said. "He stands there for a long time. He just stands and stands, and looks and looks. The speaker finally has to pull him away from the window."

"And he's the pervert?" Ike said.

"No," I said, "he's *not* the pervert. Pervert?" I heaved a sigh as heavy as lead. "Jesus, Ike. This third volunteer's the agnostic. He tells the speaker, 'I can't be sure, but it looks like there's a really ugly guy getting laid by the prettiest woman I ever saw. To be really certain, I'll have to go in and try her myself.'"

I caught her smiling, just a little.

"What's the point, Abby?"

"I'm like that third guy, an agnostic. When it comes to you," I said. "Me. Mr. Agnostic. I think you and I should try again. It's that simple. You and me, the scientific method."

"Is this a pathetic attempt at a proposal?" she said.

"No. This was just meant to soften you up so you'd listen to a real proposal."

"No way, Abby. I like being divorced. For one thing—"

The five-dollar bill came smacking back into my open palm.

"I can't stand it," Siskel and Ebert said. "You left out the best part."

"I did not. That's the whole story. I should know—it's my story."

"That ain't the way I heard it. You see, there's a fourth volunteer."

We all stopped under a streetlight and formed a circle. Ike had to give me a tug to make it a circle.

"And this fourth volunteer is a nun," the can collector said. "She goes to take a look in the window and runs away into the audience screaming, 'It's a vision of hell! It's a vision of hell! It's hell, I tell you!'"

Ike looked at the can collector like he had turned himself into a brussels sprout. "What's that supposed to mean?" she said.

"Simple." He waved his fist, jingling the coins. "The fourth volunteer is a female. She looked at it from the woman's point of view." He gave me a look. "You did say the man was ugly, didn't you?"

Ike laughed.

I slapped the five-dollar bill back into the guy's hand and said, "Take a hike. You're killing my evening."

"Spoiled the mood, did I?"

"Scram," I said.

He bowed from the waist, looked offended, and turned abruptly, heading back the way he had come, dragging his noisy plastic bag.

We finally got a cab at Prince Street. We got in, and I looked at Ike. She hesitated and then gave her address on Eighty-second.

We rode in silence for a few minutes, seated on opposite sides of the backseat. Ike moved over and took my hand.

"Abby. Your aunts make a big deal out of those tombstones. They've all got inscriptions in Italian. What in the world will it say on Tex's?"

I looked out the window, not really seeing the lights, and the city starting to wake up, and the trash, and the first hint of dawn.

I swallowed. "I think it should be a question. Tex had questions in his little soldier's Bible. Questions all over the place. You don't expect to see questions in a Bible. Questions, of all things."

"But which name will go on the tombstone?"

"He was Lieutenant Raintree a long time ago. When he died, he was Tex."

We rode a few more blocks in the silence of the gray dawn.

I turned to her. "Remember the words on that granite cross on Hart Island?"

She nodded. "He calleth his own by name," she said softly.

"I think we should use that." I withdrew my hand from hers, so I could work with the empty space between me and the cab's plastic partition, to outline in the air what I had in mind. "The stone should say," I said, sketching the tombstone with my hands,

Does He call His own by name?
Tex.

I held my hands in the air, on the sides of the stone I had carved.

Ike reached up to take one of my hands away from the air sculpture. She put our linked hands between us on the seat and we went home.

Well, to her place.

Dust Devils OF THE Purple Sage

Barbara Burnett Smith

A Jolie Wyatt Mystery

First Time in Paperback

BACK IN THE SADDLE AGAIN

With one solved murder behind her—a worthy credit for any fledgling mystery writer—Jolie Wyatt is now working as a newscaster for a local radio station. And the news is as hot as the blazing Texas sun: an escaped convict, a local boy named James Jorgenson, is believed to be heading straight for Purple Sage.

When a college kid is found dead, everyone thinks Jorgenson did it, even Jolie's teenage son, who vows to catch the killer of his longtime pal. But Jolie is riding a different trail that's leading her straight to a killer. She may even get a new way to experience the murder mystery—as a corpse.

"[Jolie] Wyatt is a charming, strong-minded contemporary character…"
                                        —*Houston Chronicle*

Available in April at your favorite retail stores.

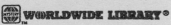 **WORLDWIDE LIBRARY®**   DUST

MEADOWLARK

First Time in Paperback

SHEILA SIMONSON

A Lark Dodge Mystery

When ex-California book dealer Lark Dodge is cajoled into running a seminar at a local writers' conference, she couldn't know where it would lead her.

Then Hugo Groth, the tenant renting the apartment above Lark's store, is found dead at the organic farm where the conference is being held. Curiously, he is found packed in ice meant for the broccoli harvest.

But the conference must go on—and with it a hunt for a killer with another murder in mind.

"There is a light touch of humor combined with taut writing and an enjoyable mystery."   *—Mystery News*

Available in June 1997 at your favorite retail stores.

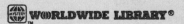

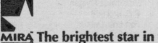

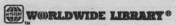